MORE PRAISE FOR
AUNTIE MAME

"Gorgeously funny . . . AUNTIE MAME is enchanting—a very bright light in a dismal world."
—*Boston Herald*

"In the jargon, Auntie Mame might be considered an unmitigated screwball, albeit on a high and intellectual plane. She is utterly without inhibitions, but she's no barroom Girl Scout. Any one of the several escapades in AUNTIE MAME is enough to last the ordinary person a lifetime and provide readable and salable memoirs. Auntie Mame doesn't do anything by halves. The eleven chapters in this hilarious comedy are filled with some of the most titillating original humor imaginable. . . . AUNTIE MAME is most refreshing and stimulating reading."
—*Columbus Citizen*

"A package of wacky humor that will keep the reader chuckling to the end."
—*Chicago Tribune*

"Rollicking, side-splitting."
—*Houston Press*

AUNTIE MAME

PATRICK DENNIS

BALLANTINE BOOKS • NEW YORK

This novel is a work of fiction. No characters, except certain renowned persons who are identified by their true names, are fashioned after actual persons, living or dead, and any resemblance between the characters in this book and actual persons is wholly coincidental.

ISBN 0-345-37650-1

This edition published by arrangement with the Estate of Patrick Dennis.

Manufactured in the United States of America

First Ballantine Books Edition: August 1994

10 9 8 7 6 5 4 3 2

To the worst manuscript typists in New York, V. V. and Mme. A.

CONTENTS

ONE

AUNTIE MAME

AND THE ORPHAN BOY

IT HAS RAINED ALL DAY. NOT THAT I mind rain, but this is the day I promised to put up the screens and take my kid to the beach. I also meant to daub some giddy stencils on the composition walls of the place in the cellar which the realtor called a Rumpus Room and to start finishing what the realtor called an Unfinished Attic, Ideal for Guest Room, Game Room, Studio or Den.

Somehow I got sidetracked right after breakfast.

It all started over an old issue of the *Digest*. This is a magazine I rarely read. I don't have to, because I hear all of its articles discussed every morning on the seven-fifty-one and every evening on the six-oh-three. Everybody in Verdant Greens—a community of two hundred houses in four styles—swears by the *Digest*. In fact, they talk of nothing else.

But I find that the magazine has the same snake-bird fascination for me, too. Almost against my will, I read about the menace in our public schools; the fun of natural childbirth; how a community in Oregon put down a dope ring; and about somebody whom a famous writer—I forget which one—considers to be the Most Unforgettable Character he's ever met.

That stopped me.

Unforgettable Character? Why, that writer hasn't met anybody! He couldn't know what the word *character* meant unless he'd met my Auntie Mame. Nobody could. Yet there were certain parallels between *his* Unforgettable Character and mine. His Unforgettable Character was a sweet little New England spinster who lived in a sweet little white clapboard house and opened her sweet little green door one morning expecting to find the *Hartford Courant*. Instead she found a sweet little wicker basket, with a sweet little baby boy inside. The rest of the article went on to tell how that Unforgettable Character took the baby in and raised it as her own. Well, that's when I put the *Digest* down and got to thinking about the sweet little lady who raised me.

In 1928 my father had a slight heart attack and was confined to his bed for a few days. Along with a pain in his chest, he developed a certain cosmic consciousness and the instinct that he wasn't going to last forever. So, having nothing better to do, he telephoned his secretary, who looked like Bebe Daniels, and dictated his will. The secretary typed an original and four carbons, put on her cloche, and took a Yellow Cab from La Salle Street to the Edgewater Beach Hotel to get my father's signature.

The will was very short and very original. It read:

> "In case of my death, all of my worldly possessions are to be left to my only child, Patrick. If I should die before the boy is eighteen, I appoint my sister, Mame Dennis, of 3 Beekman Place, New York City, as Patrick's legal guardian.
>
> "He is to be reared as a Protestant and to be sent to *conservative* schools. Mame will know what I mean. All cash and securities which I leave are to be handled by the Knickerbocker Trust Company of New York

City. Mame will be among the first to see the wisdom of this. However, I do not expect her to be out of pocket on account of rearing my son. She is to submit monthly bills for my son's food, lodging, clothing, education, medical expenses, etc. But the Trust Company will have every right to question any item that seems unusual or *eccentric* before reimbursing my sister.

"I also bequeath five thousand dollars ($5,000) to our faithful servant, Norah Muldoon, so that she may retire in comfort to that place in Ireland she's always talking about."

Norah called me in from the playground and my father read his will to me in a shaky voice. He said that my Aunt Mame was a very *peculiar* woman and that to be left in her hands was a fate that he wouldn't wish a dog, but that beggars couldn't be choosers and Auntie Mame was my only living relative. The will was witnessed by the secretary and the room service waiter.

The following week my father had forgotten his illness and was out playing golf. A year later he dropped dead in the steam room of the Chicago Athletic Club and I was an orphan.

I don't remember much about my father's funeral except that it was very hot and there were real roses in the vases of the undertaker's Pierce-Arrow limousine. The cortege was made up of some big, hearty men who kept muttering something about getting in at least nine holes when this thing was over, and, of course, Norah and me.

Norah cried a lot. I didn't. In my whole ten years I'd hardly spoken to my father. We met only at breakfast, which for him consisted of black coffee, Bromo-Seltzer and the *Chicago Tribune.* If I ever said anything, he'd hold his head and say, "Pipe down, kid, the old man's hung," which I never understood until some years after his death. Every year on my birthday he'd send Norah and me to a matinee performance of some light entertain-

ment involving Joe Cook or Fred Stone or maybe the
Sells-Floto Circus. Once he took me out to dinner at a
place called Casa de Alex with a pretty woman named
Lucille. She called us both Honey and smelled very
good. I liked her. Otherwise I rarely saw him. My life
was spent at Chicago Boys' Latin School, or at Super-
vised Play with the other children who lived in the hotel,
or messing around the suite with Norah.

After he was Laid to Rest, as Norah called it, the big,
hearty men went off to the golf course and the limousine
carried us back to the Edgewater Beach. Norah took off
her black hat and her veil and told me I could get out of
my serge suit. She said that my father's partner, Mr. Gilbert, and another gentleman were coming and that I
should be around to sign some papers.

I went into my room and practiced signing my name
on hotel stationery, and pretty soon Mr. Gilbert and the
other man showed up. I could hear them talking to
Norah, but I couldn't understand much of what they said.
Norah cried a little and said something about that dear,
blessed man, not cold in his grave and generous to a
fault. The stranger said that his name was Babcock and
he was my trustee, which I thought was very exciting because Norah and I had just seen a movie in which an
honest convict was made a trusty and saved the warden's
little daughter during a big prison break. Mr. Babcock
said something about a very irregular will, but water-
tight.

Norah said she didn't know nothing much about
money matters but that it sounded like a good deal of
money, she was sure.

Mr. Gilbert said The Boy was to endorse this certified
check in the presence of the Trust Company official and
then it was to be notarized and the whole transaction
would be finished and done with. It sounded faintly sinister to me. Mr. Babcock said, Um, yes, that was right.

Norah cried again and said such a big fortune for such
a little boy and the trustee said yes, it was a considerable

amount, but then, he'd handled people like the Wilmer-dings and the Goulds who had *real* money.

It seemed to me that they were making a lot of fuss about nothing if all this didn't involve real money.

Then Norah came into the bedroom and told me to go out and shake hands with Mr. Gilbert and the other gentleman like a Little Man. I did. Mr. Gilbert said I was Taking It like a Regular Soldier and Mr. Babcock, the trustee, said he had a boy back in Scarsdale just my age, and he hoped we'd be Real Pals.

Mr. Gilbert picked up the telephone and asked if a Notary Public could be sent up. I signed two pieces of paper. The Notary Public mumbled some things and then stamped the paper. Mr. Gilbert said that was that and he had to step on it if he wanted to get to Winnetka. Mr. Babcock said that he was staying at the University Club and if Norah wanted anything she could reach him there. They shook hands with me again and Mr. Gilbert repeated that I was a Regular Soldier. Then they picked up their straw hats and went away.

When we were alone, Norah said I'd been a dear and how would I like to go down to the Marine Room and have a good dinner and then maybe see a Vitaphone talking picture.

That was the end of my father.

There wasn't very much to pack. Our suite consisted of a large sitting room and three bedrooms, all furnished by the Edgewater Beach Hotel. The only *bibelots* my father possessed were a pair of silver military brushes and two photographs. "Like an Ay-rab, your father lived," Norah said.

I'd got so used to the two photographs that I never paid any attention to them. One of them was of my mother, who died when I was born. The other photograph depicted a flashing-eyed woman in a Spanish shawl with a big rose over one ear. "A regular Eye-talian she looks," Norah said. That was my Auntie Mame.

Norah and Mr. Babcock went through my father's personal belongings. He took all the papers and my father's gold watch and pearl studs and the jewelry that had been my mother's to keep for me until I was old enough to Appreciate them. The room service waiter got my father's suits. His golf clubs and my old books and toys were sent off to a charity. Then Norah took the pictures of my mother and Auntie Mame out of their frames and cut them down to fit my hip pocket—"So you'll always have the faces of your loved ones near your heart," she explained.

Everything was done. Norah bought me a suit of lightweight mourning at Carson, Pirie, Scott's and an epic hat for herself. Mr. Gilbert and The Firm made all the arrangements for our trip to New York. On June thirtieth we were ready to go.

I remember the day we left Chicago because I'd never been allowed to stay up so late before. The hotel staff took up a collection and presented Norah with a fitted alligator traveling case, a malachite rosary, and a big bouquet of American Beauty roses. They gave me a book called *Bible Heroes Every Child Should Know—Old Testament.* Norah took me around to say good-by to all the children who lived in the hotel and at seven o'clock Room Service brought up our dinner, which featured three different kinds of dessert, with the compliments of the chef. At nine o'clock Norah made me wash my face and hands again, brushed my new mourning suit, pinned a St. Christopher medal onto my B.V.D.s, cried, put on her new hat, cried, gathered up her roses, made a brief last inspection of the suite, cried, and settled into the hotel bus.

It was easy to see that Norah was as unaccustomed to de luxe rail travel as I was. She was nervous in the compartment and gave a little scream when I turned on the water in the basin. She read all the warnings aloud, told me not to go near the electric fan, and not to flush the toilet until the train started. She amended this by telling me not to use the toilet at all—you couldn't tell who'd been there before.

We had a little quarrel about who was going to sleep in the upper berth. I wanted to, but Norah was firm. I was pleased when she nearly fell climbing into the upper, but she said she'd rather perish than ring for a ladder and have that black man see her in her night clothes. At ten the train started to roll and I lay in my berth watching the lights of the South Side glide past my window. Before we got to Englewood Station I was asleep, and that's the last I ever saw of Chicago.

It was thrilling to eat breakfast while the big New York Central train was racing over the countryside. Norah had lost her awe of train travel and struck up quite a conversation with the colored dining steward.

"Yes," Norah was saying, "thirty years I been in this country now. Come over as a girl from the other side, and green as grass I was, too. Went into me—*my*—first service in Boston, Massachusetts; on Commonwealth Avenue it was—oh, the *stairs* in that house—when this boy's mother was just a little girl. Then she married, and took me with them all the way out to Chicago. La, but I was frightened! I full expected the place to be run over with red In-di-uns. Eat all your egg, darling," she said to me.

"First herself died," Norah went on, "and I stayed on to care for the child. Then Mist-her Dennis passed on. Went off like *that* in the Athyletic Club. And now it's me melancholy task to take this poor little boy to his Auntie Mame in New York. Imagine, only ten years old and nayther father nor mother does he have." Norah dabbed at her eyes.

The steward said I was very brave.

"Show him the photygraph of yer Auntie Mame, darling," Norah said. I was embarrassed, but I reached into my hip pocket and brought out the Carmen picture of my aunt.

"Tell me, is this Beekman Place a *decent* neighborhood for bringing up a child? He's only used to the best."

"Oh, yes, ma'am," the steward said, "that's a *very* nice location. I got a cousin works on Beekman Place. Nearly everybody there's a millionaire."

Spurred on by her social success with the New York Central personnel, Norah ordered another pot of tea and regarded the other passengers with an imperious air.

We spent the rest of the morning in our compartment, which had mysteriously changed from a bedroom to a sort of living room. Norah said her rosary, with a special mention of the Seven Cities of Sin, and then began her tatting. After breakfast Norah managed to tell both the porter and the conductor, with mounting hauteur, that I was a fabulously endowed little boy—"jist like that King Whatsisname of Ro-mania"—who was going to live with his Auntie Mame, a woman of means and mystery who dwelt in a marble palace on Beekman Place.

It was six o'clock when we pulled into Grand Central, and Norah, for all her Pullman airs and graces, was scared and flustered in the throng on the platform.

"Take me hand, Paddy," she screamed, "and don't fer the love of the Lord get lost in this . . ." The rest of her warning was muffled by the uproar. Clinging to me with one hand and clutching at the money bag in her corset with the other, Norah fought a losing battle with a red-cap, who, ignoring her protests, tossed all of our luggage onto a hand truck and rolled it away, with Norah and me racing after him.

He hadn't meant to steal our belongings after all. Instead, he hailed a cab and started tossing the baggage into the back seat. We wedged into the cab with the luggage and, before the redcap could express his true appreciation of the ten-cent tip Norah had given him, the taxi lurched out into the street.

"Take us to Number Three Beekman Place, driver," Norah said, "and don't think I'm no greenhorn ye can drive all over town to run up the tab."

It was still light and very, very hot. I don't know what I'd expected New York to look like, but anyhow I was disappointed. It wasn't a bit different from Chicago.

There was a bad traffic jam on Park Avenue and Norah was outraged to see the meter register an extra five cents while the cab was standing still. Third Avenue, despite its many Irish names, distressed her; Second, even more.

"And may I ask where ye think ye're takin' us, my good man?" Norah shrieked at the driver.

"Where you said: Three Beekman Place."

"Glory, it looks no better than a Dublin slum," she wailed. But when the taxi drove into Beekman Place she was somewhat relieved. "Pretty little spot," she said with just a hint of patronage. The cab stopped in front of a big building that looked exactly like all the buildings on Lake Shore Drive or Sheridan Road or Astor Street in Chicago.

"Not half so grand as the Edgewater Beach," Norah sniffed with a certain Midwestern loyalty. "Jump out, darling, and be careful ye don't muss yer hair."

The doorman looked us over with more than casual interest and said coldly that we were to go to the sixth floor.

"Come along, Paddy," Norah said, "and mind yer manners with yer Auntie Mame. She's a very elly-gant lady."

In the elevator I took one last quick look at the picture of my aunt, just so I'd remember her face. I wondered if she'd wear a rose and a Spanish shawl. The elevator door opened. We stepped out. The door slid closed and we were alone.

"Motheragod, the halls of hell!" Norah cried.

We stood in a vestibule which was painted pitch black. The only light came from the yellow eyes of a weird pagan god with two heads and eight arms sitting on a teakwood stand. Straight ahead of us was a scarlet door. It didn't look like the sort of place where a Spanish lady lived. In fact, it didn't look like the sort of place where *anybody* lived.

Even though I was ten years old, I took Norah's hand.

"Oh, but don't it look like the ladies' rest room in the Oriental The-ay-ter," Norah breathed.

Norah pressed the bell gingerly. The door swung open and she let out a faint little scream. "God love us, a Chinese!"

A tiny Japanese houseman, hardly bigger than I was, stood smirking in the doorway. "You want?" he said.

In a faint, humble voice Norah said, "I'm Miss, that is, I'm Norah Muldoon bringin' young Mist-her Dennis to his aunt."

The little Japanese jumped back like a mechanical doll. "Must be mistake. No want little boy today."

"But," Norah said with a pitiable bleat of desperation, "I sent the wire mesel—*myself*—sayin' we'd arrive at six o'clock today, the first of July."

"Not important," the little Japanese said with a shrug of superb Eastern indifference. "Boy here, house here, Madame here. Madame having affair now. No matter. You come in. You wait. I fetch."

"Do you think we ought to?" I whispered to Norah. I took one more look at the black walls and the idol and squeezed her rough old hand. It was trembling worse than my own.

"You come in. You wait," the Japanese said with a sinister smirk. "You come in," he repeated. The effect was hypnotic.

On leaden feet we advanced into the foyer of the apartment. It was, in its dazzling way, even more terrifying than the black entry hall. The walls were painted an intense orange. A huge, bronze Japanese lantern cast a bilious light through its yellow parchment panes. On either side of the foyer was a great archway masked by tall paper screens, and behind them a lot of people were making a lot of noise.

The Japanese gestured toward a long low bench. It was

the only piece of furniture in the room. "You sit," he hissed. "I fetch Madame. Sit."

There was a big parchment tapestry hanging behind the bench. It depicted a Japanese man disemboweling himself with a samurai sword.

"You sit," the houseman repeated with a giggle, and disappeared beyond one of the paper screens.

"Heathenish," Norah whispered. Her joints cracked painfully as she lowered her bulk onto the bench. "What could yer poor father be thinkin' of?" The roar behind the screen grew louder and there was a crash of glass. I gripped Norah.

Our knowledge of Oriental fleshpots had been strictly limited to what we'd seen in the movies—hideous tortures, innocent virgins drugged and sold into a life worse than death along the Yangtze, bloody tong wars—but Hollywood had made pretty clear what happened when East and West met.

"Paddy," Norah cried suddenly, "we've been tricked into a opium den to be killed or worse. We've got to get outta here." She started to rise, pulling me with her, and then sank back to the bench with a defeated moan.

A regular Japanese doll of a woman had strolled into the foyer. Her hair was bobbed very short with straight bangs above her slanting brows; a long robe of embroidered golden silk floated out behind her. Her feet were thrust into tiny gold slippers twinkling with jewels, and jade and ivory bracelets clattered on her arms. She had the longest fingernails I'd ever seen, each lacquered a delicate green. An almost endless bamboo cigarette holder hung languidly from her bright red mouth. Somehow, she looked strangely familiar.

She glanced at Norah and me with an expression of bemused surprise. "Oh," she said, "the man at Private Procurement didn't tell me you were bringing a child as well. No matter. He looks like a nice boy. If he misbehaves we can always toss him out into the river." She laughed, but we didn't. "I suppose you know what's expected of you—just a little light slavery around the place, and of course Thursdays you'll be left to your own devices."

Norah stared at her, wide-eyed. Her mouth hung open.

"You're a little late, you know," the Oriental lady said. "I really wanted you in time to serve this mob," she gestured to where all the noise was coming from. "But it doesn't really matter. If you have no things with you, I suppose I can get you fitted out into something suitable." She moved on toward the noise. "You just wait here, I'll have Ito show you to your quarters. Ito! Ito!" she called, and swept out of the room.

"Motheragod, did you hear what she said—all them *words*! One of them regular Chinese singsing girls, she was. Whatever can we do, Paddy, what*ever* can we do?"

A sinister-looking couple strode across the foyer. The man looked like a woman, and the woman, except for her tweed skirt, was almost a perfect Ramon Novarro. He said, "I suppose you know they're sending poor Miriam out to the Coast."

The woman said, "Well, God knows, if they want her killed professionally, they've shipped the poor bitch to the right place." She laughed nastily and they disappeared beyond the opposite screen.

Norah's eyes popped and so did mine. The noise grew louder and louder. Suddenly a piercing scream rent the air. Both of us jumped. A woman's voice rose hysterically above the roar. "Oh, Aleck! Stop it, *please*! You're *slaying* me!" There was a great bellow of laughter and then another shrill scream. Norah clutched my arm and held it tight. Two men appeared from behind a screen. One of them had a bright red beard. Between them they were carrying a woman all dressed in black, her head thrown back, her eyes closed, her long hair trailing on the floor behind her. Norah gulped. "Poor Edna," one of the men said. "Well, I don't feel so damned sorry for her," the man with the beard said. "I told her just this afternoon, I said, 'Edna, you're writing your own death warrant drinking all that poison at lunch. You'll be cold as a mackerel by seven o'clock.' And here she is, passed out." Norah crossed herself.

There was another scream and a roar of insane laughter. The little Japanese darted out from behind a screen and scampered across the foyer. He was carrying a big knife. Norah moaned.

"Holy Mary, Mother of God, preserve us," she prayed. "Save this little orphan and I from slaughter and worse at the hands of these Chinese cutthroats." She began to mumble a long ardent prayer so incoherently that I got only a few words like White Slavery and Shanghai and Bloody Murder.

The woman-man and man-woman crossed the foyer again.

". . . And of course, *Death Comes for the Archbishop*," he was saying. "Have you *ever* experienced a sensation *quite* so exciting?"

"Glorious God," Norah cried, "is nothing nor no one safe in this sink of sin!"

There was another scream and the hysterical voice cried, "Aleck, don't! It's just plain *mur*-der!"

"This is enough," Norah cried, grasping my hand and pulling me up. "We've got to get out of this nest of thieves and slayers while we've still a breath in our bodies. Better to die preservin' me virtue than let the Chinee sell us into slavery. Come on, Paddy, we'll run fer it and may the Good Lord help us." With remarkable agility she sprang toward the door dragging me behind her.

"Stop, please." We were transfixed. It was the little Japanese, grinning ludicrously and still holding the knife. "Madame no find you?"

"Look here, sir," Norah said with desperate valor. "I'm only a poor old woman, but I'm prepared to buy me way out. I got money with me, although I may not look it. Lots of money. Five thousand dollars besides all me life's savin's. Surely you could let the child and I escape for that. We done no wrong."

"Oh, no," he said with an inscrutable smile. "Not right. I fetch Madame. Madame very anxious have little boy in house."

"The vileness!" Norah moaned.

The Japanese doll woman reappeared. "Ito," she said, "I've been hunting all over for you. This is the new cook and I want you to . . ."

"No, Missy Dennis," he said, waggling his finger, "no new cook. New cook in kitchen. This your little boy."

"But no!" she squealed. "Then *you* must be Norah Muldoon!"

"Yessum," Norah breathed, too spent to find voice.

"But why didn't you *tell* me you were coming today? I'd never have been giving this party."

"Mum, I *wired* you . . ."

"Yes, but you said July first. Tomorrow. This is the thirty-first of June."

Norah shook her head balefully. "No, mum, 'tis the first, God curse the evil day."

The tinselly laugh rang out, "But that's ridiculous! Everyone knows 'Thirty days hath September, April, June and . . .' My God!" There was a moment's silence. "But darling," she said dramatically, "*I'm* your Auntie *Mame*!" She put her arms around me and kissed me, and I knew I was safe.

Once inside Auntie Mame's cavernous living room, which looked a lot like the night club scenery in *Our Dancing Daughters*, we were relieved to see that it was just full of a lot of people who looked like regular men and women. Well, perhaps not *quite* like regular men and women, but there were no wicked Orientals except my Auntie Mame, who had given up being Spanish and started being Japanese.

There were people sitting on the low Japanese divans, standing out on the terrace, and looking at the dirty river through the big window. They were all talking and drinking. My Auntie Mame kissed me a great deal and introduced me to a lot of strangers, a Mr. Benchley, who was very nice, a Mr. Woollcott, who wasn't, a Miss Charles, and a good many others.

She kept saying, "This is my brother's son and now he's going to be *my* little boy."

Auntie Mame said to Circulate for a little while and then I could go to bed. She said that she was terribly sorry that she'd made such a stupid mistake about the date and that now she had to meet a lot of people for dinner at The Aquarium. I thought it was a strange place to eat, but to be polite I asked her if it was going to be a fish dinner and everyone shouted with laughter.

She said it was just a Speak in the Fifties and I pretended to understand.

Norah took my hand and we Circulated, but I didn't get into any conversations with the people. They all used funny words, like "batik" and "Freud" and "inferiority complex" and "abstraction." One lady with red hair said that she spent an hour a day on the Couch with her doctor and that he charged her twenty-five dollars every time she came. Norah led me to another part of the room.

The little Japanese man gave Norah a glass and said it was right off the boat and Norah said she wasn't used to spirits—even though she was always telling *me* about seeing ghosts and haunts—but this time she'd take a drop of the creature. She seemed to be feeling very happy all of a sudden. And in a little while she asked Ito to give her another Nip.

Pretty soon the people started to leave. One group of people said they were going to see good old Texas that night and they'd have to get there early if they were going to be let in. I'd always thought Texas was quite a long way from New York.

There were some people still standing out in the hall talking about things I didn't understand, like *Lysistrata* and Netsuke and lapis lazuli and a Karl Marx, who I thought might be some relation to Groucho, Harpo, Chico, and Zeppo. Then Auntie Mame came out in a yellow evening dress like Bessie Love wore in *The Broad-*

way Melody. It was very short in front and very long in back and she didn't look Japanese any more.

"Good night, my darling," she said, giving me a kiss. "We'll have a long talk in the morning—but not too early." The door closed behind her and the apartment was silent.

The Japanese houseman took my hand gently. "You hungry. You come supper now," he said kindly. "You maybe want to go bathroom first, little boy?"

I went hot and then cold as the terrible realization came over me.

"I, I already *have*," I wailed, looking with horrible dismay at the dark stain spreading across my new suit of lightweight mourning.

Two

AUNTIE MAME

AND THE CHILDREN'S HOUR

THIS ARTICLE IN THE *DIGEST* GOES on to say how the New England spinster, totally unused to children, grows to love the foundling who's been dumped on her doorstep. And more than growing to love him, she gets pretty het up about child care and child psychology and that sort of thing.

When the time comes for him to be sent to school, Miss Unforgettable has some serious differences with the village board of education and their methods. The truant officer is after the kid night and day, but the sweet little spinster holds out and single-handedly brings about sweeping reforms in the school system.

Well, I don't think that's so much. Auntie Mame had some pretty original ideas on psychology and education herself.

Looking back on Auntie Mame as the razzle-dazzle butterfly she was in 1929, I can see that she must have been just as terrified at the prospect of rearing a totally strange ten-year-old boy as I was when I first stumbled large-eyed and frightened into the Oriental splendor of her Beekman Place apartment. But Auntie Mame was never one to admit defeat. There was a kind of up-and-at-'em spirit of a speak-easy Girl Scout to my aunt. And although her ideas on child raising may have been considered a trifle unorthodox—as, indeed, were all her ideas on anything—Auntie Mame's unique system worked well enough in its casual way.

Our first interview took place at one o'clock in the afternoon in Auntie Mame's big bedroom on my second day in New York. I felt unknown, unloved, unwanted, and awfully lonesome wandering listlessly around the big duplex, with only Norah for company. Ito, the little Japanese houseman, gave me a good lunch and giggled quite a lot, but otherwise there was no message from him. By one o'clock I was feeling desperate enough to read *Bible Heroes Every Child Should Know—Old Testament* when Ito came into my room and said, "You see Madame now."

Auntie Mame received me in her bedroom on the second floor. It was a vast chamber with black walls, a white carpet, and a gold ceiling. The only furnishings were an enormous gold bed up on a platform and a night table. Such a room might have depressed most people, but not Auntie Mame. She was as cheerful as a bird. In fact she looked rather like a bird in her bed jacket made of pink ostrich feathers. She was reading Gide's *Les Faux-Monnayeurs* and smoking Melachrino cigarettes through a long amber holder.

"Good morning, my little love," she sang. "Come over here and kiss your Auntie Mame, but gently, dear, Auntie feels fierce." I kissed her as gently as I knew how. "That was sweet, dear, you'll make some lucky woman very happy someday. Now sit down here on Auntie's bed—but easily now, dear—and we'll have a little morning chat. Get to *know* one another."

Morning, I soon discovered, was one o'clock for Auntie Mame. Early Morning was eleven, and the Middle of the Night was nine.

"Don't you *love* this pearly part of the day!" she said with a sweeping gesture, scattering a lot of ashes over the black satin sheets.

"Now, darling," she said, "we've got to discover a lot of things about each other. I've never had a little boy around the place before, and ooops, here's breakfast.

"Now, let's see," she said brightly. She groped around among the mare's nest of papers on her bedside table and dredged up a copy of my father's will, which she had embellished with a lot of telephone numbers and a random shopping list or two. She also plucked out a pad of yellow foolscap and a big black pencil. "Well, I'm your guardian. We both know that, so there's no need of much discussion there. Now, your father says you're to be reared as a Protestant. I've no objection to that, I'm sure, although it does seem a shame that you should be deprived of the exquisite mysteries of some of the Eastern religions. However, your father always *was* a stick-in-the-mud about *some* things. Not that I mean to speak ill of my own brother. Where did you go to church, darling?"

"The Fourth Presbyterian," I said uncomfortably.

"My God, child, do you mean to sit there and tell me that there are *four* Presbyterian churches in a place like Chicago! Well, no matter. I suppose we can hunt up some sort of Presbyterian church nearby." Her eyes rolled dramatically toward the gold ceiling. "I don't suppose your father would mind *too* much if I introduced you to Monsignor Malarky, he's *such* a darling; so cultivated, and eyes like sapphires! He's coming here for cocktails one day next week but I'll make him promise not to talk shop with you."

Auntie Mame got back to business and the will. "Well, that takes care of your religious upbringing. Now school. Just whereabouts *are* you in school, dear?"

"Fifth class at Chicago Boy's Latin."

"Fifth *class*! Good heavens, aren't you good enough for first class, child? You look bright enough to *me*!"

With the patience of a ten-year-old I explained that the fifth class meant fifth grade.

"Oh, and where are you supposed to be when you're ten?"

"In the fifth class, but I was only nine while I was in it."

"Then you mean that you *are* precocious?"

"I beg your pardon?" I said.

"Precocious, darling. Bright for your age. Ahead of yourself in school."

"Yes," I said. "I was pre—what you said—all term long."

"Oh, I'm so glad, darling!" Auntie Mame trilled, writing something down on her pad. "We always *were* an intellectual family, although your father did everything possible to disguise the fact."

She returned to the will. "Now, your father says here that you're to be sent to *conservative* schools—he would! Tell me, was this Latin affair conservative?"

"I don't quite know what you mean," I said blushing.

"Was it dull? Tiresome? Tedious? Stuffy?"

"Yes, it was very stuffy."

"So like your father," she sighed. "By the way, I know the most divine new school that a friend of mine is starting. Coeducational and completely revolutionary. All classes are held in the nude under ultraviolet ray. Not a repression left after the first semester. This man I know is absolutely *au courant* with everything that's going on in Vienna—none of that dead-tired old Montessori system for *him*—and there's lots of nonobjective art and eurhythmics and discussion groups—no books or anything like that. How I'd love to send you there. Really give your libido a good shaking up."

I hadn't the faintest idea what she was talking about, but it sounded like a very unusual school, to say the least.

A tender, faraway look came over her face. "I just wonder," she said, "if it wouldn't be a ra-ther good idea to look into Ralph's school. Do you think you've got many repressions, dear?"

I colored painfully. "I'm afraid I don't understand a lot of the words you use, Auntie Mame."

"Oh, child, child," she cried, and her feathery sleeves fluttered wildly across the bed, "*what* can be done about your vocabulary! Didn't your father ever *talk* to you?"

"Hardly ever," I admitted.

"My dear, a rich vocabulary is the true hallmark of every intellectual person. Here now"—she burrowed into the mess on her bedside table and brought forth another pad and pencil—"every time I say a word, or you hear a word, that you don't understand, you write it down and I'll tell you what it means. Then you memorize it and soon you'll have a decent vocabulary. Oh, the adventure," she cried ecstatically, "of molding a little new life!" She made another sweeping gesture that somehow went wrong because she knocked over the coffee pot and I immediately wrote down six new words which Auntie Mame said to scratch out and forget about.

Then Auntie Mame studied the will some more.

"As for being reimbursed by that trust company . . ."

"How do you spell reim . . ."

"Don't interrupt! As for being reimbursed by the trust company, I'm perfectly willing and able to support you." Her eyes narrowed and she fixed me with a piercing glance. "I suppose you've got some human adding machine who's going to look after your money and tell *me* how you're to be raised."

"You mean my trustee?"

"Yes, child, what's he like?"

"Well, he wears a straw hat and glasses and lives in a place called Scarsdale and has a boy about my age and his name is Mr. Babcock."

"Scarsdale, wouldn't you *know* it." Auntie Mame wrote down "Knickerbocker Trust" and "Babcock." "Well, I can see he's going to be my own personal *bête noir* for the next eight years. *I* have the responsibility and *he* has the authority!"

"That means black beast, doesn't it?" It seemed a very exciting description for Mr. Babcock.

"Darling!" she said brightly, and kissed me. "Your vocabulary is coming along marvelously. Perhaps we should speak nothing but French in the house." She continued in English, however. "Well, I'll tackle Babcock in my own good time. God knows you can learn more in ten minutes in my drawing room than you did in ten years with that father of yours. What a criminal way to raise a child!" She looked at her watch and fluttered her feathers. "Good heavens, I've got to do some shopping with Vera. Perhaps you'd like to come along. Besides, we know enough about each other for a start." She looked at me in my suit of lightweight mourning. "For God's sake, child, haven't you got some clothes that don't make you look like a sick crow?"

I said I had.

"Well, put them on if you're coming with me, and don't forget your vocabulary pad." Obediently I made for the door.

"By the way, child," she said. Once more her eyes had that penetrating look.

"Yes, Auntie Mame?"

"Did your father ever *say* anything—that is, *tell* you anything—about me before he died?"

Norah had told me that all liars went straight to hell, so I gulped and blurted out, "He only said that you were a very peculiar woman and to be left in your hands was a fate he wouldn't wish a dog but beggars can't be choosers and you're my only living relative."

There was a quiet gasp. "That bastard," she said evenly.

I reached for my vocabulary pad.

"That word, dear, was bastard," she said sweetly. "It's spelled b-a-s-t-a-r-d, and it means *your late father*! Now get out of here and get dressed!"

* * *

I spent that first summer in New York trotting around after Auntie Mame with my vocabulary pad, having Little Morning Chats every afternoon, and being seen and not heard at her literary teas, salons, and cocktail parties.

They used a lot of new words, too, and I acquired quite a vocabulary by the end of summer. I still have some of the vocabulary sheets of odd information picked up at Auntie Mame's soirees. One, dated July 14, 1929, features such random terms as: Bastille Day, Lesbian, Hotsy-Totsy Club, gang war, Id, daiquiri—although I didn't spell it properly—relativity, free love, Oedipus complex—another one I misspelled—mobile, stinko—and from here on my spelling went wild—narcissistic, Biarritz, psychoneurotic, Shönberg, and nymphomaniac. Auntie Mame explained all the words she thought I ought to know and then made me put them into sentences which I practiced with Ito, while he did his Japanese flower arrangements and giggled.

My advancement that summer of 1929, if not exactly what *Every Parent's Magazine* would recommend, was remarkable. By the end of July I knew how to mix what Mr. Woollcott called a "Lucullan little martini" and I had learned not to be frightened by Auntie Mame's most astonishing friends.

Auntie Mame's days were spent in a perpetual whirl of shopping, entertaining, going to other people's parties, being fitted for the outlandish clothes of the day—and hers were even more so—going to the theater and to the little experimental plays that opened and shut like clams all over New York, being taken to dinner by a series of intellectual gentlemen, and traipsing through galleries of incomprehensible pictures and statues. But with all of her hectic, empty life, she still had plenty of time to devote to me. I was dragged along to most of the exhibitions, the shopping forays with her friend Vera, and to whatever functions Auntie Mame thought would be Suitable, Stimulating, or Enlightening for a child of ten. That covered a wide range.

Actually, Auntie Mame and I learned to love one another in as brief and painless a period as possible. That her amazing personality would attract me, just as it had seduced thousands of others, was a foregone conclusion. Her helter-skelter charm was, after all, notorious, and she was also the first real Family I ever knew. But that she could care at all for an insignificant, uninteresting boy of ten was a constant source of surprise and delight and mystification to me. Yet she did, and I've always thought that for all of her popularity, her interests, her constant comings and goings, she was probably a little lonely, too. Her critics have said that I was simply a new lump of clay for her to shape, stretch, mold, and pummel to her heart's content, and it is true that Auntie Mame could never resist meddling with other people's lives. She still had a stanch, undependable dependability. For both of us it was love, and the experience was unique.

However, a storm cloud, in the shape of my trustee, soon lowered over our idyl. Auntie Mame and I were having one of our Little Morning Chats. She was feeling very maternal that day, reading me selected passages from *A Farewell to Arms*, when a special delivery letter from the Knickerbocker Trust Company shattered our tranquil hour with Hemingway.

In the letter Mr. Babcock said that he had so wanted to get together with us, but business etc. etc. and then he and his family always went to Maine for the hottest part of etc. etc. and had just returned when his son underwent a serious siege of tonsillitis during which the doctor etc. etc. but now that things were once again etc. etc. and there was so much to discuss about Master Patrick's etc. etc. wouldn't it be nice if Miss Dennis would bring young Mr. Dennis out to Scarsdale for a real old-fashioned etc. etc. ending early so that the boys could get a decent night's sleep etc. etc. the trains that ran from Grand Central Station, while not the most comfortable, etc. etc., and would Auntie Mame confirm the date.

Auntie Mame moaned, handed me the letter, and rang

for a whisky sour. "Oh, my darling," she cried, "here's the death knell. That trustee! I can see it as plainly as I see you—a hideous scheme to dominate and thwart my every plan for you." I wrote "dominate" and "thwart" on my pad and then assured her that Mr. Babcock was really a very nice, quiet little man.

"Oh, child," she howled, "they're always the worst, those mice. Uriah Heeps, every one of them."

According to her lifetime habit, Auntie Mame put on a little half-hour show of histrionics and then settled back and decided to face the situation. Using her Cultured Voice, she telephoned Mr. Babcock and told him that we'd both be thrilled to dine with his family in Scarsdale the following day, and not to bother with meeting us at the station, as we'd motor. She was ever so refined. Then she called up her best friend, Vera, and told her to drop everything and come over fast.

Auntie Mame's friend Vera was a famous actress from Pittsburgh who spoke with such Mayfair elegance that you could barely understand a word she said. She didn't like children and the reverse was equally true, but as Auntie Mame had invested in her new play, Vera was civil to me.

Vera arrived in a cloud of white fox furs and then she and Auntie Mame enacted another charade of despair. Finally Vera, who was the more levelheaded, got down to business. She called Ito for a bottle of brandy and more or less took over.

"My dear," Vera said, "you mustn't let yourself get out of hand. You're being *ut*-terly hysterical. Now, take a sip of this and calm down while I tell you a few things. In the first place, you have nothing to fear. You have looks, breeding, intelligence, culture, money, position—everything. It's simply that you may be a lit-tle flamboyant for Scarsdale. But, darling, it's simply a matter of toning yourself down—temporarily. Now, when I played Lady Esme in *Summer Folly* . . ."

"*Summer Folly*," Auntie Mame shrieked, "well, this is

my summer folly and all you can do is talk about your triumphs! What am I to do?" She nibbled at her gilded nails.

"As I was saying, *de-ah*," Vera said haughtily, "when I was playing Lady Esme, all of my clothes were done by Chanel, and she said to me, *'Chérie'* (she always called me *chérie*), *'Chérie,'* she said, 'clothes make the mood, the personality—everything.' And she was right. You remember in the last act when I come down the stairs just after Cedric shoots himself? Well, I wanted to wear black, but Chanel said, *'Chérie,* for that you wear gray. A gray day, a gray mood, a gray dress with perhaps just a suggestion of sables.' My dear, I'll never forget what Brooks Atkinson said about that costume. Why, it *lifted* that turkey right into a class with Shakespeare."

Any discussion of clothing always won Auntie Mame's undivided attention and she brightened immediately. "Yes, Vera," she said slowly, "you're so right. I see it now: that little gray kimono outfit with the scarlet embroidery and perhaps a blood-red camellia over each . . ."

"Mame, dear," Vera said tactfully, "I wasn't speaking of a Japanese costume for this, this *ordeal*. It must be a different *you* in Scarsdale—something like Jane Cowl. I thought more along the lines of a *simple* dress. Something soft and genteel—with everything else black. You know, de-ah, sorrowful, but not strictly mourning, and *very* conservative. It gives a trustee confidence."

Auntie Mame was dubious, but interested, and as the brandy—allegedly smuggled off the *Ile de France*—sank lower and lower in its bottle, Vera's poignant pictures of the respectable little maiden aunt reached even more celestial heights. Auntie Mame had a flair for drama, and eventually the two women were routing through her vast wardrobe as happy as girls.

While I read aloud from a book of Elinor Wylie poems called *Angels and Earthly Creatures* and kept Vera's brandy glass filled, an old gray chiffon negligee was transformed into a suitably somber costume, which, with

Vera's big black hat, filmily veiled, and a jet necklace, gave Auntie Mame the proper air of delicate despondency. Vera also unearthed an old switch which Auntie Mame had once worn to a Beaux Arts ball. Braided, it made a restrained but unsteady coronet on Auntie Mame's bobbed head. About six o'clock the costume was complete, then Vera made me a little black arm band, polished off the last drop of brandy, and collapsed.

At nine the next morning—the Middle of the Night, as she called it—Auntie Mame was already up, looking ill and pale. The apartment was silent except for an occasional moan from the bedroom Vera occupied. In the kitchen, Ito was putting up an enormous luncheon hamper of cucumber sandwiches, champagne, and almond cake. Out on Beekman Place, Auntie Mame's Mercedes-Benz glittered ominously. It took Auntie Mame the better part of two hours to get into her weeds but she said she wanted to look right and, although it was about ninety that day, she wore her sable scarf, remembering Vera's sensation as Lady Esme.

In 1929 it took little more than half an hour to get to Scarsdale by train, but Auntie Mame could never adjust herself to the precise demands of railroads. So the big Mercedes rolled out of Beekman Place just eight hours before we were expected, which was probably all to the good since Ito was a peripatetic driver at best, and none of us had any idea of where or what Scarsdale was. Auntie Mame sat tensely in back fingering her ill-moored coronet and twitching her sables. Every so often she'd grasp my hand and murmur, "Oh, my little love, whatever are we to do?" Although the car was big, the tonneau was pretty crowded with the two of us, the picnic hamper, the iced buckets of champagne, a number of assorted road maps—mostly for other parts of the country—a fur lap robe, a volume of verse tenderly inscribed to Auntie Mame by Sara Teasdale, and my vocabulary pad.

Ito, who had even less sense of direction than Auntie Mame, drove first to Long Island, then into New Jersey, and finally got on the right scent. After a long luncheon in Larchmont and a little confusion in Rye, Ito got the car headed once more toward our goal and we arrived in Scarsdale at half past three. "Oh, God," Auntie Mame moaned, "*three* hours early!" We spent the rest of the afternoon at a Tom Mix movie which Ito and I liked, although Auntie Mame said it was disgusting what sort of stuff was crammed down the throats of the people and the government should sponsor films of cultural structure.

On the tick of six-thirty we arrived at the Babcocks' house. It was a half-timbered affair built in a style that Auntie Mame called "pseudo-Tudor." But she looked very subdued.

The Babcocks weren't a stimulating family. Their son, Dwight junior, wore glasses and looked just like a Mr. Babcock who'd been shrunk in the laundry. Mrs. Babcock wore glasses, too, and talked to Auntie Mame about gardening and home canning and child psychology.

Auntie Mame mentioned Freud once and then thought better of it. The rest of her conversation with Mrs. Babcock was confined to vapid Yeses and Noes and Oh, Reallys.

Dwight junior showed me his collection of dead butterflies and told me all about his tonsils and the keen times he was going to have at St. Boniface boarding school.

Mr. Babcock said Um a lot. Lemonade was served, and finally their maid announced dinner.

It was stifling in the Babcocks' English-style dining room, and the dinner of overdone roast lamb, mashed potatoes, squash, beets, and lima beans—after Ito's delicate Eastern cuisine—hit my stomach like a lump of cement. During one of the many lulls, Auntie Mame got the bit between her teeth and delivered a long and remarkably learned lecture on architecture of the Tudor period, which was a fascinating discourse except that it pointed up every detail of the Babcocks' room as a counterfeit. However, Auntie Mame was very charming and acted like the sort you'd trust a child with.

During the molded salad, Mrs. Babcock talked about the theater and how she simply idolized Vera Charles. Not heeding the glance of warning, I said that Vera was Auntie Mame's best friend and was probably asleep at the apartment that very moment. Mrs. Babcock was transported. "What a wonderful, dignified woman she must be," she said. "How I'd love to meet her!"

After dinner Mrs. Babcock and Dwight junior, who had undoubtedly been carefully rehearsed, said that they were just going to run off to the movies, Tom Mix was playing. Auntie Mame gagged but she rose graciously and thanked her hostess almost too warmly for such a lovely meal. The son gave me a dank handshake and said he'd be seeing me. I hoped not.

When we were alone, Mr. Babcock cleared his throat and said he believed we'd have Our Little Talk now and we'd go into the Den so the maid couldn't snoop. The Den sounded very interesting but it was just a little room full of books on banking and even hotter than the other rooms had been.

Mr. Babcock got out a lot of papers and said that Auntie Mame was very fortunate to have such a nice little boy to comfort her after the, uh, Loss of her brother. Auntie Mame dropped her eyes demurely. Then Mr. Babcock said that he'd been looking over my school records and that they were very good, but we'd get onto schools later. Auntie Mame bridled.

Then he got out sheets and sheets and sheets of paper with figures all over them. He said that I was well off—not rich, mind you, but well off. "Never have to worry about where his next meal is coming from unless these, um, Bolsheviks take over the government." He said that every penny I owned was carefully invested in good, conservative, steady stocks and bonds and that this was a bad time to go fiddling around with the market. He showed Auntie Mame the papers but she didn't seem very interested.

"Now, as for this young man and his schooling," he finally said, rustling a lot of papers. "You know, of course, that in this matter, the boy's late father felt that it would be, uh, *wiser* if I—on behalf of the Trust Company— were to have complete authority on *that* matter." Auntie Mame's back stiffened. "But, heh, heh, heh, heh, I don't think there need be any friction on *that* account," he said. "You look a fine, sensible woman, Miss Dennis, and I think we can see eye to eye on the subject." He brought out a thick red book called *Handbook of Private Schools*. From that moment the fight was officially on.

Mr. Babcock led off with a few preliminary remarks. He said he thought it would be ideal if I could go to a good day school right in Manhattan so that Auntie Mame and I could be together as much as possible.

"Lovely," Auntie Mame said warmly. "I had just such an arrangement in mind, myself."

"Now," Mr. Babcock said, "I've gone to, uh, some pains to, uh, gather information on a number of the better boys' schools in town."

Auntie Mame touched her throat gingerly and said, "Personally, I prefer coeducational schools. Throwing boys and girls together at a tender age does *so* much to reduce psychosexual tensions, don't you think?"

Mr. Babcock looked as though he'd been struck, and Auntie Mame, quickly lapsing back into her maiden lady role, amended her statement by saying, "Well, you know what I mean. After all, men and women do live together in real life—*marry*."

"Yes, I see," Mr. Babcock mumbled, "that's a very interesting, uh, theory, Miss Dennis, there's probably a great deal to it. Now, I hadn't *considered* any of the coeducational, uh, institutions, but the Buckley School is known to be a splendid . . ."

"Well, now, before we get into the Buckley School, do

you mind if I just suggest a new school that a friend of mine, Ralph Devine, is starting. Ralph is a darl . . . an extremely learned man. He knows Freud backwards and forwards, in fact he knows Freud *personally*, and he has this idea of education that is *generations* ahead of Froebel and Montessori. Now, the idea of this school is completely revolutionary. He . . ."

Mr. Babcock held up his hand as though he were directing rush-hour traffic. "I'm positive, Miss Dennis, that that sort of school is exactly where your late brother would *not* wish his son to be sent. He specified in his will that it was to be a *conservative* school. Now, if you don't like the idea of Buckley, what about the Allen-Stevenson School?"

"Oh, no, I know a dreadful little boy who goes there. But I *do* have an idea, and you couldn't possibly object to it. It's a well-established school but coeducational and modern. It's the City and Country School down on . . ."

"I've looked into that one, too, Miss Dennis, and I'm afraid that I find it a lit-tle too experimental. But there's the Browning School which is quite convenient to . . ."

Auntie Mame was getting that old overeager, desperate quality which I've since learned to fear. "Oh, but Mr. Babcock, give a thought to the Dalton School! That's marvelous. I've met both Miss Dickerman and Mrs. Roosevelt and they're doing such absolute *wonders* with . . ."

"I *know* the Dalton School," Mr. Babcock said icily. "They have some very *radical* ideas. Dangerously radical."

"What about Ethical Culture?" Auntie Mame said wildly.

"My dear Miss Dennis, you surely wouldn't suggest sending the child off with a pack of *Jews*?" Auntie Mame's false coronet rocked alarmingly. "In fact," Mr. Babcock continued placidly, "I'd like to keep that West Side element out of his life as much as possible. How-

ever, there *is* the Collegiate School over there, and that's
said to be splendid."

For the next hour and a half I sat in the hot little room
while Auntie Mame and Mr. Babcock battled over every
school in New York—St. Bernard's, Friends, Horace
Mann, Buckley, the Hoffman School for Individual De-
velopment, Poly Prep—neither would give an inch.
Auntie Mame quivered like a greyhound, while Mr. Babcock grew progressively stonier. The argument had
reached a pitch that made me fear for the complete success of Auntie Mame's genteel masquerade when a fur-
tive, cunning look crept across her face. There was a
sudden sob, then Auntie Mame buried her face in her
hands and shook convulsively. Mr. Babcock was so thun-
derstruck that the eulogy to the mathematics department
of the Browning School dropped dead on his lips. I was
stunned too. The room was silent except for Auntie
Mame's sobbing. Mr. Babcock colored to an almost human pallor and ran an exploratory finger under his wilting collar. "Miss Dennis," he sputtered, "please, uh,
really, uh, that is, I didn't mean to . . ."

Auntie Mame raised a beatific face, which I noticed
was surprisingly dry. "Oh, Mr. Babcock," she gasped,
"how can I, how can I ever apologize for being such a
foolish, headstrong thing? How very, very stupid and
willful I must have seemed." She dabbed at her eyes with
a lacy handkerchief and I was curiously reminded of Pola
Negri in a silent film I'd seen not so long ago. She
sniffed delicately, "After all, who am I—a simple, single
woman, unused to raising little ones—to argue with you,
a father and the executor of little Patrick's estate? How
hateful you must think me." Her head drooped fetchingly
and her toes pivoted inward.

"Well, now, Miss Dennis," Mr. Babcock said cordially,
"if you think the boy would be happier at Dalton . . ."

Auntie Mame raised a limp white hand. "No, Mr. Babcock, I was wrong. There, now, I've said it and I'm glad.
I was wrong and silly. Patrick will go to the school *you*

suggest. You mustn't pay any attention to me, although I know you can never forgive or forget my unpardonable behavior here tonight."

Mr. Babcock grew suddenly expansive. "Well, now, I know about women. After all, Eunice—that's Mrs. Babcock—and I sometimes have our, uh, little differences. It's only natural—battle of the, uh, sexes, you know, heh, heh, heh."

Auntie Mame dimpled becomingly.

"Now, of course," Mr. Babcock continued, "there are a lot of good schools in New York—none really *better* than another—but the one I'd suggest is Buckley."

"Mr. Babcock, don't say another *word*. Your choice is right. I'm convinced of it. *Right*. He shall go to Buckley and wear the uniform proudly!"

"It's just a cap, not a uniform," Mr. Babcock said deprecatingly. "But it's a splendid, uh, school; perfectly splendid. Boys from really the best families ..."

"Yes," Auntie Mame sighed, "class *is* so important. And now," she simpered, "we *must* go."

"Then I'll make out a check to the Buckley School and you'll take the boy around to register him when you're notified?"

"That will be heavenly," Auntie Mame said with a devastating smile. "Come, dear, we mustn't keep you up too late." She swept to the door and arranged Vera's black hat onto her switch. "Good night, Mr. Babbitt ... it's been a charming evening—really *informative*! Come, Patrick."

The car door closed and Ito started the motor with a roar.

"Are you *really* going to send me to that ... that school he was talking about, Auntie Mame?"

"Don't worry, darling, don't worry, Auntie Mame has a plan."

With an ecstatic sigh she lighted up a Melachrino as Ito headed the car straight toward Connecticut.

* * *

Right after Labor Day Auntie Mame took me to Buckley and registered me. All of my school papers had been transferred by Mr. Babcock and they said that everything was in good order. Auntie Mame bought me one of the little blue caps, which she took to wearing herself, and sent me to a place near Washington Square for an intelligence test. When I came home I found her engrossed in conversation with a handsome blond man.

"Darling, come in," she trilled, "I want you to meet Ralph Devine. You'll be going to his school next week."

"But ... but what about the Buckley place?" I stammered.

"Pardon me a moment, Ralph," she said. She drew me near to her and gazed solemnly into my eyes. "Darling, what Auntie Mame has done may seem a little, well, *deceitful*, but you'll learn later in life that sometimes it's best not to be *too* honest. You and I are going to play a little joke on your Mr. Babbitt, dear. You see, while he *thinks* you're going to that *other* school, you'll really be doing the most divine and advanced things with Ralph, here. It'll be *our* secret, my little love, only the three of us need know, and Mr. Hitchcock—whatever his name is—will be ever so fooled, won't he?"

I said that I thought he'd be very fooled.

"Now run upstairs and read something while I talk to Ralph, there's a pet."

Ralph was saying, "Mame, you let that child *read*?" as I left the room.

The following week Auntie Mame got up in the Middle of the Night and took me two blocks away to Ralph's school. It occupied the top floor of an old loft building on Second Avenue. We were a little late—Auntie Mame was always late—and when we got there, the big room was filled with naked children of all ages racing around and screaming. Ralph came forward, as naked as the day he was born, and shook hands cordially.

"Isn't he lovely," Auntie Mame gushed. "Just like a

Praxiteles. Oh, darling, I know you're going to love it here!"

A square little yellow-haired woman, also naked, rushed up and kissed Auntie Mame. Her name was Natalie. She and Ralph were running the school together.

"Now you just tag along with Ralph and enjoy yourself, my little love, and I'll see you back at the flat in time for tea."

Auntie Mame departed with a gay wave and I was left alone, the only person in the place who was wearing any clothes.

"Come in here and disrobe, yes?" Natalie said, "then join the others?"

I always felt a little like a picked chicken at Ralph's school, but it was pleasant and I never had to do anything. It was a big, stark, whitewashed room with a heated linoleum floor, quartz glass skylights, and violet ray tubes running around the available ceiling. There were no desks or chairs, just some mats where we could lie down and sleep whenever we wanted, and, in the center of the room, a big white structure that looked like a cow's pelvis. We were supposed to crawl in, around, and over this if we felt like it, and whenever one of the younger children did, Ralph would give Natalie's broad bottom a resounding smack and chuckle, "Back to the womb, eh Nat!"

There was a communal toilet—"Nip the inhibitions in the bud"—and all sorts of other progressive pastimes. We could draw or finger-paint or make things in Plasticine. There were Guided Conversation Circles, in which we discussed our dreams and took turns telling what we were thinking at the moment. If you felt like being anti-social, you could just be antisocial. For lunch we ate raw carrots, raw cauliflower—which always gave me gas—raw apples, and raw goat's milk. If two children ever quarreled, Ralph would make them sit down with as many others as were interested and discuss the whole thing. I thought it was awfully silly, but I got quite a thorough suntan.

But I didn't stay long enough at Ralph's school to discover whether it did me good or harm. My career there—and Ralph's too, for that matter—ended just six weeks after it began.

Ralph and Natalie, under the misapprehension that their young followers did any work at school, organized an afternoon period of Constructive Play so as to send us all home in a jolly frame of mind. The general idea was that the children, all except the really antisocial ones, were to participate in a large group game that would teach us something of Life and what awaited us beyond the portals of the school. Sometimes we'd play Farmer and attend to the scrubby avocado plants Natalie grew. At other times we'd play Laundry and wash all of Ralph's underwear, but one of the favorite games of the smaller fry was one called Fish Families, which purported to give us a certain casual knowledge of reproduction in the lower orders.

It was a simple game and rather good exercise. Natalie and all the girls would crouch on the floor and pretend to lay fish eggs and then Ralph, followed by the boys, would skip among them, arms thrust sideways and fingers wiggling—"in a swimming motion, a swimming motion"—and fertilize the eggs. It always brought down the house.

On my last day at Ralph's we'd been playing Fish Families for about half an hour. Natalie and the girls were on the linoleum and Ralph started to lead the boys through the school of lady fish. "A swimming motion, a swimming motion! Now! Spread the sperm, spread the sperm! Don't forget that little mother fish there, Patrick, spread the sperm, spread the . . ."

There was a sudden choking noise.

"My God!" a familiar voice gasped.

We all turned around and there, fully dressed and looking like the angriest shark in the sea, stood Mr. Babcock, my trustee. With one deft motion, he yanked me out of the melee. "God damn it! You get your clothes on and hurry. I want to talk to that crazy aunt of yours and I want *you* to be there with me!" He threw me into the dressing room. "As you for, you filthy pervert," he shouted at Ralph, "you haven't heard the last of this!"

Before I had my clothes buttoned, Mr. Babcock dragged me down the stairs and halfway to Auntie Mame's.

As luck would have it, Auntie Mame, dressed in one of her most exotic outfits, was having stingers with a distinguished Lithuanian rabbi and two dancers from the cast of *Blackbirds* when Mr. Babcock and I burst into the drawing room.

"By God," he screamed, "I should have known it! No more fit to raise a child than Jezebel! What kind of mad woman are you?"

With some effort, Auntie Mame got to her feet. "Why, Mr. Babbitt, what do you *mean*?" she said with a hollow hauteur.

"You know goddamned good and well what I mean. Two weeks ago I called up Buckley to see if this brat wanted to go to the rodeo with my son and me, and ever since then I've been trying to track him down in every low half-baked school for the feebleminded in this town. But today, *today* I found him in the lowest of them all; mother-naked with that filthy man spreading the— Oh, God, I can't stand it!"

Auntie Mame stepped forward with dignity and took one of the deep breaths that always preceded her better denunciations, but she needn't have bothered.

"Tomorrow," Mr. Babcock screamed, "in fact, tonight, *right now*—I, me *personally*—I'm taking this kid off to boarding school myself. I should have figured you'd try to pull a dirty double cross like this, but never again. I'm putting him into St. Boniface Academy and he's going to stay there. The only time you'll get your depraved hands on him is Christmas and summer and I wish to God there was some way to prevent that. Come on, you," he said.

"Auntie Mame," I cried and tried to run to her, but he held tight.

"Come back here, you damned little hellion, I'm going to get you to St. Boniface and turned into a decent, God-fearing Christian if I have to break every bone in your body. Come on, we're getting out of this, this *opium* den." Another yank and I was on my way to St. Boniface Academy.

The next day Ralph's school was raided by the police, and the tabloids, caught in a lull between ax murders, became profoundly pious about all of progressive education. Over delicately retouched photographs of Ralph and Natalie and the student body were headlines such as SEX SCHOOL SEIZED, with articles by civic leaders and an outraged clergy that all seemed to begin: "Mother, What Is Your Child Being Taught?"

The day after that was October 29, 1929. The bottom dropped out of the market and the papers had more pressing things to write about. But by then I was incarcerated in St. Boniface Academy and from there the strident voice of my Auntie Mame was but a dim whisper in an academic wilderness.

THREE

AUNTIE MAME

IN THE TEMPLE OF MAMMON

A DARK CLOUD SOON HOVERS OVER the sweet little spinster in the *Digest*. Always used to living in security and comfort with the kid and the cat, suddenly the local bank folds and all of the poor little lady's savings are swept away. She has only a miserable pension to keep her, and things look pretty black. But she's undaunted and she discovers that she has a real head for business.

First of all she starts baking bread and rolls and Lady Baltimore cake, and the next thing you know, she has a thriving bakery with more business than she can handle. Then she resumes her girlhood hobby of painting china, and her forget-me-not pattern becomes a perfect rage—with whom, the article doesn't say. Then this little bundle of energy turns to making hooked rugs and woven place mats and patchwork quilts and the money just never stops rolling in.

That doesn't impress me one bit. Auntie Mame always said she had a head for business, too. When the depression hit her hard, she launched out on many more careers than the Unforgettable Character and, one way or another, she saved us, too.

The month of September was particularly hot in 1930, and the day my Auntie Mame chose for her painful interview at the bank was a scorcher. She came home, dropped her fox furs in the middle of the living room, called for a stiff drink, and wilted tragically onto her new "modernistic" sofa. "Patrick," she said hollowly, "your Auntie Mame is a poor woman. Ruined, ruined, ruined!" She gazed soulfully out into the street and tried to work up some tears. "I am," she said dramatically, "little more than a pauper."

Auntie Mame had forsaken her expensive duplex and installed herself in a neat little carriage house on Murray Hill. She had furnished the place throughout, had bought a lot of new, longer clothes, and had given a couple of parties to warm the house and rally what was left of her Old Set. Then she began to realize that living cost money—even in 1930, when things were cheap. But money in general was scarce, and Auntie Mame's money, in particular, was even scarcer.

Now it had been made crystal clear that after her violent flirtation with the stock market and her Babylonian expenditures, she had exactly four thousand dollars in cash and the snug little annuity of two hundred dollars a month.

"Oh, to think that I should bear the yoke of poverty after scrimping and saving for all these years."

"That's a shame, Auntie Mame," I said, and snickered because it rhymed.

She cast me a cold glance. "Oh, it's all very well for you to laugh—a mere boy of eleven with a big inheritance tied up so that nobody can get *at* it—when your poor Auntie Mame is practically ready for the Peabody Home, but how are we to *live* on a lousy two hundred bucks a month?"

In 1930 two hundred dollars seemed a fortune to literally millions of people. Actually, with a few simple economies she could have gotten along fine.

"Well," she said with a dolorous sigh, "I suppose you know what this means. It means *I* shall have to go to work simply to keep you in that wretched St. Boniface school." I knew that the Trust Company paid my tuition, but it seemed wiser not to say so. "But then," she continued, "God knows I've worked and slaved all my life, so I should be used to it."

This was not strictly true, either. For a period of nearly six weeks my Auntie Mame had danced in the chorus of a road company of *Chu Chin Chow* until my father heard about it and family pressure was brought to bear. Since then she'd never turned a hand at more than mixing her famous homemade gin.

"Yes, that's the answer. Your poor Auntie Mame will have to go back to work—try to find a job with millions unemployed already—in order to keep clothes on our backs and the wolf from the door. But don't fret, my little love, Auntie Mame will find a way, *even if she has to scrub floors.*" She retired early with the classified advertising section of the *New York Times.*

The next day Auntie Mame had her usual one o'clock Little Morning Chat. She was surrounded by pads of yellow paper with lists of names written on them. "Giving a party?" I asked.

"Certainly not!" Auntie Mame snapped. "Oh, well, maybe after I get established in business I'll have a little celebration, but these people are all valuable contacts— friends of mine who are well placed." She rattled the *New York Times* contemptuously. "All these jobs here in the want ads, they're nothing *I'd* be interested in; waitresses, salesgirls, factory hands, stenographers—nothing I could really sink my teeth into. No, darling, it isn't *what* you know that gets you places in this town, it's *who* you know. And God knows, I have *connections.* Why," she said, "there are probably any *number* of organizations in New York that would be delighted to have me once they knew I was on the market. So I've just made up a list of influential friends and I'm going to make them *aware* of my interest."

Auntie Mame made a lot of long and vivacious telephone calls that day. The first was to her old broker, Florian McDermott. She told him the whole story of her financial downfall, although it seemed unnecessary to be so explicit with the man who was largely responsible for it. She asked Florian if his brokerage house would be interested in a businesswoman accustomed to handling large sums of money. But he said hastily that they were Cutting Down, and managed to sell her a couple of hundred shares of a stock that was Absolutely Foolproof. Two months later Florian was sharing a cell with an illustrious broker whom he never could have hoped to know socially before.

All of her other financial friends were retrenching, too, so Auntie Mame decided that her future lay in the Arts.

The following day she had lunch with Frank Crowninshield and came home jubilant over a job as a copywriter on *Vanity Fair*. The salary was forty dollars a week—exactly what she paid Norah and Ito—but she knew she'd Forge Ahead. She ordered a lot of smart little businesslike suits and some new hats to wear around the magazine office. I was packed off for St. Boniface Academy and Auntie Mame commenced her business career.

During the fall of 1930, I had only Auntie Mame's letters to give me a dramatic—if somewhat prejudiced—picture of her various professional endeavors. The job at *Vanity Fair* lasted a month. Then Mr. Crowninshield and Mr. Nast took her to lunch again and said that her writing was too inaccurate, albeit spirited, and they were reducing the staff anyway. As a consolation prize they ran a full-page photograph of her in a three-hundred-dollar Jeanne Lanvin evening dress, which she bought with her severance pay and some money she'd won on a race horse. Mr. Crowninshield said that she was too attractive

a woman to be running around loose and she really ought
to marry and settle down.

Her next job was also literary, but it didn't last quite so
long. She became a reader for Horace Liveright's pub-
lishing company. Mr. Liveright was an old acquaintance,
and although he and Auntie Mame had had their little
differences, they respected one another's intellects. However, Auntie Mame went out for a gay evening carrying
with her the only copy of a thrilling manuscript that
reeked of whale blubber and was written by a Danish ex-
plorer. Somewhere between Jack Delaney's and the Cotton Club the manuscript was lost. There were a lawsuit
and harsh words between Auntie Mame and Mr. Liveright. A year later an up-and-coming little firm published
the rewritten book and it sold more than a hundred thousand copies and was turned into a solemnly successful
documentary film. After that Auntie Mame always said
she could *smell* a bestseller.

Still undaunted, Auntie Mame moved into another
branch of the Arts—interior decoration. Nobody could
deny that she had taste, though sometimes a little bizarre.
However, Auntie Mame possessed certain qualities that
are important in commercial decorating: she was charming, she had flair and originality, and she knew a lot of
influential people. So it was only logical that Auntie
Mame would drift into the rococo atelier of Elsie de
Wolfe and her jolly helpers.

With what she called her Following and a lot of glib
talk about the Regency and the Directoire, she landed a
job that paid not only a good salary, but a generous commission as well. But conversant as she was with the dec-
orative arts of France, Auntie Mame's heart was more
with the Bauhaus of Munich than with the *rocaille* and
coquaille of Versailles.

For a time, however, she was able to fight down her
progressive impulses and string along with the staff at
Elsie de Wolfe's, chirping prettily over dim ormolu wall
sconces and inaccurate cupid clocks. Under the watchful

eye of a supervisor, Auntie Mame did over an entrance
foyer on Fifth Avenue, a dining room in Oyster Bay, and
a boudoir in Gracie Square, all in the style of Louis XV.
Then, as a solo flight, she decorated her friend Vera's
suite in the Algonquin in the manner of Prud'hon with a
lot of old Empire junk she'd unearthed on Avenue A. The
rooms and their tenant were duly photographed by *Home
Beautiful*, Miss de Wolfe wrote Auntie Mame a glowing
letter, and her Empire rooms were in wild demand among
bootleggers, who were the only people who could afford
any expensive old furniture. At first she seemed a little
stunned by her heady triumphs, but after pulling off three
or four Napoleonic apartments on Central Park West,
Auntie Mame grew bored with caryatids and columns
and got that old modern itch again. Aesthetically it
showed progress, but financially it was disaster.

Auntie Mame's big chance arrived in the autumn,
when she came to the attention of a Mrs. Riemenschneider of Milwaukee, whose late husband had worked wonders in the near-beer business. Too big, at last, for
Milwaukee, Mrs. Riemenschneider had set her heart on
New York and on a social position that only a lot of
money and the things that go with it over three or four
generations can obtain. But Mrs. Riemenschneider
wasn't willing to wait for three or four generations. It
was a buyer's market in 1930 and she had plenty of cash
to pay her own way. She hadn't been in New York for
more than a few hours before she'd bought an elegant little town house in the East Sixties and handed Auntie
Mame a crisp check for one hundred thousand dollars to
decorate it "like Fountain-blow." Then she was off to
Paris for clothes, having extracted from Auntie Mame the
promise that her house would be finished by Christmas.

The house was finished by Christmas and so was
Auntie Mame. The pull of Munich modern had been too
strong—almost as strong as Mrs. Riemenschneider's language when she returned to find that her prim mansion
had had its marble façade removed, most of its walls

knocked down, and was filled with the most advanced stainless steel furniture, wire sculpture, and cubist art that money or imagination could create. Just before her return to Milwaukee, Mrs. Riemenschneider got out an injunction against the decorating firm not only for her hundred thousand dollars but also for restoration of the house.

The papers got hold of the story and had a big time with it. Alliterations like "atheist art" and "Bolshevik barbarism" and "maniac modern" were bandied about the yellow press for days. Auntie Mame was christened "Madcap Mame" by an inspired headline writer, and two columnists wrote articles that began "What can Picasso paint that my boy in the fourth grade can't paint better?" Auntie Mame was purged from Elsie de Wolfe's.

Although angry and humiliated by what she called the ignorance of the masses, Auntie Mame still wasn't ready to give up her crusade for the ultramodern. She'd picked up a few allies during the fray, one of them a brooding young sculptor named Orville who had his own potter's wheel and did "the most exciting ceramics." So Auntie Mame decided to take her capital and go into partnership with him. They were going to open a gift shop "devoted to the Brave, the Experimental, the Exciting, the New, the Modern," her letter said.

"Oh, Patrick, darling," she wrote, "it's going to be unlike any shop in New York. Just you wait and see. We'll set New York on fire!"

Maison Moderne, as the establishment was called, *was* unlike any shop in New York—or at least any *I'd* ever seen. It was located in a row of elderly brownstones on East Fifty-fourth Street. It had a big amoeba-shaped show window and a circular chartreuse door. Its walls were an uncompromising red-violet lighted with a tortured tangle of neon tubing, and it was filled with some of the queerest looking ash trays, plates, ceramic pins, and things Auntie Mame called *objets d'art*.

Maison Moderne opened on the day I came home for

Christmas vacation and it attracted throngs of people. But most of them, after the initial shock, said they were just looking. Auntie Mame was in her element, bustling around in a gay smock with a cigarette dangling from the corner of her mouth. The first day they did almost fourteen dollars' worth of business, and got a lot of coverage from the press.

But Auntie Mame didn't seem to mind any of the mean things they wrote. "That's the value of publicity, my little love. I couldn't have bought all that newspaper space for fifty thousand dollars. Did you see how gorgeously Orville's foetus sandwich platter photographed in the *American*? It's all free advertising, darling. The time to worry isn't when they're talking about you. It's when they're *not* talking about you."

Maybe she was right, for the next day the crowds were still thicker. Auntie Mame raced among customers twittering like a debauched canary, and she sent me out twice for coffee and three times for Melachrino cigarettes. Around one o'clock the crowds got so heavy and the sales so brisk that she had to send for Norah to tend the cash register, while I stood in the back room, up to my waist in excelsior, wrapping up Auntie Mame's outrageous ceramics. Whatever you said about Maison Moderne, it did attract public notice.

It was after six when Auntie Mame finally shooed the last customer out and collapsed into the pile of excelsior in the back room. "Oh! Success, success, success!" she caroled. "Give me a cigarette, darling, Auntie's simply exhausted!" She stretched luxuriously and exhaled a cloud of smoke. "How much do you suppose we took in today, Norah, a hundred?"

"Oh, more than that," Norah said beaming. "Five, six, seven hundred, I'd say."

"But how *divine*!" Auntie Mame cried. She took another ecstatic puff of her cigarette and then sat bolt upright. "My God, I promised Neysa McMein I'd have cocktails with her and I'm already *hours* late! Gracious, she's promised to do some designs for us and I've forgotten *all* about it. Here, child, fetch my coat and whistle for a taxi. I must dash!"

"What'll I do with all this money?" Norah asked.

"Just leave it in the cash register. I'll lock up. Goodness, get a taxi, Patrick, I'll drop you both at the house." She locked the door, and we all raced away.

That night what the tabloids described as "a holocaust of unknown origin" destroyed nearly half the block on East Fifty-fourth Street. It took three fire companies to extinguish the blaze and there wasn't enough left of Maison Moderne to put in one of its Exciting ash trays.

"Oh, Patrick, what has Fate *done* to me," Auntie Mame sniffled. "My whole brave, new endeavor gone up in a puff of smoke. Well, thank God I mailed the premium for the fire insurance last week." She blew her nose daintily. "Damn it," she snapped, reaching into an empty crystal box, "there isn't a cigarette in this house. Reach me my bag, will you, there's a pet."

Still chattering animatedly, she burrowed through her lizard purse. Suddenly she was still; her face went white. "Oh, no!" she whispered. Then from her bag Auntie Mame withdrew a long white envelope addressed to The World Fire and Marine Insurance Company of Hartford, Connecticut.

After the expensive demise of Maison Moderne, Auntie Mame decided that it was better to work for *other* people, after all. In those days her passion for exotic fabrics led her to buy most of her clothes at Jessie Franklin Turner's. It was a shop of medium-sized proportions devoted to a clientele of large-sized income. "So pleasant and *intime*," Auntie Mame said in one of her letters, "almost as though the customers were old friends and guests—which, of course, they are." Owing to Auntie Mame's bill, Mrs. Turner took her on as a saleswoman—"really a *vendeuse*, darling," she wrote.

Auntie Mame loved working among the beautiful,

costly clothes and came home nearly every evening with some new Jessie Franklin Turner creation. Business was terrible in the winter of 1931, but Auntie Mame had a lot of confidence in herself.

However, my aunt possessed an unfortunate candor that delighted many but offended just as many others. Auntie Mame's winning honesty played her false when Mrs. Turner overheard her saying to a volatile matron of formidable proportions, "But, my dear, we haven't a *thing* we could get onto you. All of our clothes are wrong for you—much too svelte. Now, take my advice and run down to the Stylish Stout section at Lane Bryant's." There were heated words and the customer stalked out, never to return. Fifteen minutes later Auntie Mame did, too, after an interchange with Mrs. Turner, who warned her that she'd better find a rich husband—fast—to pay the bill she'd run up.

Auntie Mame's last stop in the garment industry was at Henri Bendel's, where, thanks to a beautiful figure and a long friendship with Mr. Bendel, she modeled tea gowns for just over a week. But on the day her elegant posterior was pinched by a dirty old man of untotaled buying power, there was an ugly contretemps and her services were dispensed with. Mr. Bendel wrote Auntie Mame a touching letter, saying that he felt terrible about the whole thing, but that she was, after all, a Lady and too fine a woman to be a mere clotheshorse. He also added that the best career for Auntie Mame would be marriage.

Still Auntie Mame was eager to prove that she could hold her own in a man's world. One night at Twenty-one she met an eager young man from a fine old Baltimore family who had capital to invest in a small but select speak-easy. Since he knew almost nobody in New York, and since Auntie Mame knew everyone, he persuaded her to become the social hostess of his new venture. Auntie Mame was a little dubious at first, but she needed money badly, and after all, as she wrote, the place would be "*not*

just some sordid little ginmill, but really an exclusive
club with a carefully chosen membership, where ladies
and gentlemen may drink like civilized people, dine graciously, and perhaps play a rubber or two of bridge. A
service, really."

Together they found an old mansion in the Forties that
was already equipped for just their sort of venture.
Within the last two years it had been called Tony's,
Belle's Bar Sinister, The Ole Plantation, Tony's, Alt
Wien, Paris Soir—or Sewer—Victor's Vesuvius, Chez
Cocotte, York House, Gay Madrid, and Tony's. However,
Auntie Mame and the young man had the place re-
painted, christened it the Club Continentale, and were
ready for business.

Everyone who got a chance to visit the place said that
Auntie Mame and the young Baltimore gentleman had
done things ever so nicely. They sent out engraved invitations and membership cards to the best people in the
Social Register and the Arts. They hired one of New
York's most popular bartenders, a French chef, a Hungar-
ian orchestra, an Irish doorman, an Italian headwaiter,
and a Spanish dancer named something like Euthanasia
Gomez. For further entertainment, Auntie Mame was
perfectly willing, if called upon, to tinkle away at the
white piano and sing some light French airs. But she
never got a chance. In their eagerness to do everything
Right, Auntie Mame and the young man had overlooked
paying out protection money to the cops. On the night of
the Grand Opening things were just reaching their pitch
of brilliant gentility when the Club Continentale was
raided, the bottles and decorations smashed with axes,
and Auntie Mame and her carefully chosen membership
were taken off in the paddy wagon.

Next, through the kindness of Frank Case, Auntie
Mame started a personal shopping service as a conve-
nience to guests at the Algonquin. But the Algonquin
wasn't having many guests in 1931, and those it did have
found Auntie Mame's taste a little too extreme and a lot

too expensive. So she passed most of that spring chatting with old friends in the lounge. She had to sell her pearls and a star sapphire ring to keep out of debt, and when I got home for summer vacation Auntie Mame had grown too restive to sit among the potted palms of the Algonquin any longer.

After that she tried to peddle aluminum kitchenware from door to door on Riverside Drive but no one bought any, and on the day the sales manager tried to seduce her, she slapped his face and got fired.

In July she was the secretary to a shoestring producer —she didn't know shorthand but she could write fast and peck out rather casual-looking letters on the typewriter. But after three weeks he had produced nothing, including a pay check.

In August Auntie Mame wrote a Greek drama in thirty scenes with a chorus of two hundred voices. She took it to Annie Laurie Williams, the agent, who said it had some pretty good stuff in it, but somehow it never got produced.

One morning in September Auntie Mame, after a lot of lying, was a switchboard operator for an insurance company. She nearly electrocuted herself and was home in time for lunch.

Then came a brief fling in the real estate business. In 1931 everyone was moving out of large expensive flats and into small cheap ones, but Auntie Mame charmed a friend into buying a big apartment only to discover that the building was empty and that the innocent tenant was carrying its entire maintenance himself. She turned over her commission to help him struggle through bankruptcy. Then some trouble with her own mortgage made her wary of all real estate.

By the time I was ready to go back to school, Auntie Mame was really cornered by her creditors. She even had to undergo the humiliation of allowing the Trust Company to reimburse her for my living expenses.

Her letters to me read like suicide notes. But in early October, I got a letter that was full of the old fight:

"Darling boy—

Guess what! Auntie Mame's going back on the stage again! Vera telephoned and we lunched. So I told her what ghastly luck I've been having and we got to reminiscing about the old days when we were both in the chorus of *Chu Chin Chow.* How we laughed over the house detective in that Indianapolis hotel room mix-up!

Well, to make a long story short, Vera is opening in a new play and she let me read for a supporting role. I'm to play Lady Iris, an English aristocrat. We're like *girls* again, trouping together after all these years!

But, my little love, *this* is the best. We open in *Boston* next month, so that *you* can see your Auntie Mame's big comeback on the very first night. Can you *wait*! Off to rehearsal!"

Vera Charles was my Auntie Mame's best friend, most of the time. She was never a great actress, or even a very good one, but she was a great *star*. Vera was what is known as a Woman's Actress. Matinee audiences adored her.

Mr. Woollcott once wrote, "Vera Charles is the world's only living actress with more changes of costume than of facial expression." They never spoke after that, but it was true. She was always a Lovely Patrician from an Unidentified Balkan Kingdom, there was always a Husband Who Didn't Understand Her, and Another Man. It was lousy drama, but great theater, and *hausfraus* in heaving busloads would return, spent, to Montclair, tears of love and envy still damp on their cheeks.

On the great day of Auntie Mame's opening, the headmaster let me out of hockey practice and I rushed into Boston, where Auntie Mame was quartered at the Ritz. She was in the bathtub when the bellboy let me into her suite, and I could hear her singing, "I am Chu Chin Chow from Chi-na, Shanghai, China."

She emerged from the bath, rosy and warm. "Darling! I'm so glad you've come. Careful, you'll muss my hair. Now, my little love, Auntie Mame wants you to run out and get her some menthol cough drops. I'm just going to lie down in a darkened room with a brisk astringent on my face—a bit of tightening, you know—relax my throat, and run over my lines. Then we might have a bit of clear broth and some melba toast right here before I go to the theater. La, the excitement of being on the Boards again! Vera's given me a lovely bit of business with her in the last act. Oh, and *don't* let me forget my jewel box. I looked *so* underdone in my ball gown at dress rehearsal."

We dined at six and then Auntie Mame telephoned her friend Vera, to wish her luck. We got to the Colonial Theater at seven and I sat alone in the first row waiting until the house filled up with eager Boston matrons, their unwilling husbands, and a lot of irreverent-looking Harvard boys.

Finally the curtain went up. It was Vera's same old show. Twelve minutes after the first act had begun, Vera entered dead center in a beautiful beige suit with fisher furs and paused graciously for the wild ovation. The first act ran to formula, but Auntie Mame never appeared.

In Act Two Vera was superb in almond green velvet, and the ladies moaned orgasmically when she changed into a floating delft-blue negligee. Still there was no sign of Auntie Mame.

When the curtain rose on the third act, Vera and the Other Man were alone on the stage. The applause for her evening dress was tremendous. A gala party was supposedly in progress offstage. There was lilting waltz music and a babble of gay conversation, and I suddenly heard a familiar voice call, "Oooooh, some more champagne, Lord Dudley!" There also seemed to be a distant and faint tinkle of bells.

Vera looked a little uneasy, but went on with her speech. "But, Rrrreginald," Vera said in her incomprehensible Mayfair accent, "tew dew sech a thing—tew desh oaf tewgethaw lake thisss—would be med; quate, quate enchentingly med."

"Oooooh, Lord Dudley," I heard Auntie Mame's unmistakable voice cry from the wings, "I could *dahnce* the night away!" Again the mysterious tinkling of bells. It struck a jarring note among the offstage noises of titled people at play. There was a snicker from the balcony.

Vera touched her rigid coiffeur, and began again.

"Naow, Rrrreginald, it would be medness. Ay belung tew one wuld, yew tew anothah. We maight faind heppiness faw one brief maowment, but we'd hate awselves—yais, and each othah, tew—faw what we'd done. Naow, it's bettah thet we paht now; now whale we cheddish this ecstasy we've knaown. Come! Haold meh, kiss meh—one lahst tame and thane gudbay. Huddy, Rrrreginald, Ay heah the othahs coming."

The music struck up again and a lot of festive couples spun in through the archway. The ringing of bells grew much, much louder, and a flash of red whirled onto the stage. "Ooooh, Lord Dudley," Auntie Mame called, "you waltz divinely!"

Vera staggered. The bells rang even more insistently. In a voice that one associates with hog-calling, Vera shouted, "Aaow, come in avery-one! Ay've sumthing tew tale yew ull."

The titled guests moved forward and stood in artistic groupings facing Vera. By now there was a positive clangor of chimes. The balcony tittered. I stared at Auntie Mame. She looked lovely in a pretty, flame-colored dress, but around her wrists she'd festooned a bunch of bracelets fashioned from large silver Siamese temple bells—the gift of some forgotten admirer.

Now there was a ripple of mirth in the orchestra and Vera was so startled that she blew up the next line. It didn't matter, anyhow, because the bell-ringing and the laughter would have drowned out a forghorn. Vera stepped forward to the footlights and delivered her line again, square into the rafters: "Ay sayed Ay'm nut gaowing to meddy Rrreginald efter ull. May place is at haome with Prince Alexisss. Ay must gaow beck—beck to *may* wuld." Then she turned toward Auntie Mame and shot her a look that would have paralyzed the average Bengal tiger. "Lady Irrriss," Vera said to Auntie Mame, "would yew be gude enough to *rrring* for my wrrrap?"

"Certainly, Princess," Auntie Mame said with a deep curtsy. Her Siamese bell bracelets pealed deafeningly.

Vera's speech about ringing had been an unfortunate one, but the balcony loved it. There were roars of laughter and a great deal of stamping.

Then the bells started again and Auntie Mame, much flustered, advanced toward Vera bearing a mountainous chinchilla cape. Auntie Mame's bell bracelets were somewhat—but not fully—muffled in the folds of fur for a moment.

"Do let me help you, Princess," Auntie Mame said in her resounding voice. She held out the cape which unfolded like a Venetian blind, thus releasing the bells to their full volume. I stared with horror when I saw that Auntie Mame was holding Vera's cape upside down.

"Thenk yew, Lady Iris," Vera roared, sweeping the cape around her. An awful look came across her face, though, as she gathered the hem of her cloak around her shoulders and saw that its collar was trailing behind her on the floor.

I was moved to a kind of hysterical giggle myself until I noticed that Auntie Mame seemed to be attached to Vera's upside-down chinchilla wrap. Vera moved forward to deliver her last line and Auntie Mame followed, her outstretched arm mysteriously connected to the small of Vera's back. Then I understood. One of her Siamese bell bracelets had got caught in the fur.

Vera moved forward again. Auntie Mame followed, accompanied by the chorus of bells.

Finally Vera stood stock still. "Let go!" she grunted.

"Vera," Auntie Mame squeaked, "I *can't!*"

The house rocked with unsuppressed hilarity, whistles, and stamping. Vera bellowed her last line with Auntie Mame still trying to wrench herself free and the curtain fell, enveloping them both—kicking and clawing—in its yards of dusty velour.

I'll never forget that night as long as I live. Vera, in the harsh accents of her native Pittsburgh, called Auntie Mame every vile name I'd ever heard, and a lot I hadn't. Auntie Mame was prostrate. She laid her head on the cluttered dressing table, and shook with sobs. "But, Ve-e-ra," she moaned, "these are the only bracelets I have left." Vera screamed at her like a fishwife. "You dirty, cheap society bitch! Try to louse up my opening, will ya! I *hate* you! You and all your no-good kind." Vera continued to yell and scream until the manager removed her forcibly from the room and slammed Auntie Mame's notice on the dressing table.

Auntie Mame wept long after the theater was dark. She kept repeating and repeating, "But they're the only bracelets I have left. The only bracelets I have." It was nearly two o'clock when I hung her old mink coat around her and half carried her out to a taxi and into the Ritz. Weeping uncontrollably, she let me help her to bed. I never knew that a human body could contain so many tears, and when I held her hand it felt as though it were on fire. Then I got scared and called the hotel physician.

The next day I took Auntie Mame all the way back to New York in an ambulance. She was still sobbing and burning with fever. She squeezed my hand until I thought all my bones were broken and she moaned over and over, "But Vera, they're the only bracelets I have left. Everything else is gone. The only bracelets I have, Vera. The *only ones.*"

Back in New York Norah put her to bed, unconscious and running a terrible temperature. Norah and Ito, like many domestic servants during the depression, were working only for room and board. But they worshipped Auntie Mame. Norah even paid for the ambulance and my ticket back to school. I stood miserably in Auntie Mame's bedroom twisting my St. Boniface cap in my hands. When I left, she was still delirious and still moaning about the bracelets. Norah sat beside her, stroking her feverish hand. "Now, you hush, dearie, you hush. What a pretty lady like you needs is a nice *man*. You hush up, lovey, and get rested so you can find a good, steady man."

I was so worried about Auntie Mame that I could hardly study. But at Thanksgiving she sent a short formal note which said, "I have accepted a position with the R. H. Macy Company. I am to sell roller skates at least until Christmas and there are excellent opportunities for advancement. The personnel director tells me that Macy's is very anxious to obtain college-trained people of the better type."

From then on her letters grew gayer. She told touching and amusing stories about life in the toy department during the Christmas rush; about a decayed Austrian baroness who sold mama dolls, and a former M. I. T. professor who was demonstrating Gilbert chemistry sets. Auntie Mame confessed girlishly that the training program had been a little confusing and that keeping track of a sales book nearly drove her mad. "But," she wrote, "I've evolved the perfect system. I send all of my roller skates out C.O.D. That's the easiest way for me and it's also easy for the customers, since it saves them from having to spend a lot of hard-come-by money right then and there. They buy now and pay later—really very economical." She said that her feet hurt and she hated wearing black all the time, but that it *was* fun and she couldn't wait to see me at Christmas vacation.

I was kind of lonely with Auntie Mame away all day, and she looked pale and tired when she came home every

night. But she was very gay about the store and all of her
C.O.D.s.

Auntie Mame still had a lot of unpaid bills, and I overheard her talking on the telephone the Sunday before
Christmas. She was crying and she said, ". . . but of
course I can't raise that kind of money before January.
We'll simply lose the house, that's all." Later I heard
Norah tell her that Shaffer's insisted on payment in full
before the first of the year or they'd sue. Auntie Mame
cried some more and said, "Eighteen dollars a week and
that miserable monthly pittance—why, I can't even buy
Patrick a Christmas present."

I didn't care. I'd saved all of my allowance and sold
my microscope to buy Auntie Mame's present. Remembering her unfortunate bells, I'd bought her the biggest
rhinestone bracelet twelve dollars would buy. I figured
that with a real mink coat—even if it was a little sprung
in the seat—the bracelet would look genuine and Auntie
Mame would be happy again.

But the awful blow fell on the day before Christmas.
I was wrapping Auntie Mame's present when I heard the
front door close. Then I heard Auntie Mame's high-
heeled slippers trudging into the living room. But there
was no effusive yoo-hoo.

I tiptoed down to the living room and there was Auntie
Mame sitting on a low hassock, her mink coat around her
shoulders. Her face was cupped in her hands and she was
crying silently.

"Auntie Mame," I said, "why are you home so early?"

"Oh, Patrick," she wept, "I've, I've been f-fired.
Thrown out of *Macy's!*"

She sat there in the living room rocking back and forth
and crying helplessly while I stood in misery next to her.

"Patrick, Patrick," she gasped. "It wasn't my fault. He,
he wouldn't take the skates C.O.D."

"Who wouldn't?" I asked.

"The Southern man," she choked. "He seemed so nice
and gentle and pleasant and good-looking. And he or-

dered twenty p-pairs of skates. And then," she broke down again, "and then I tried to send them to him C.O.D. and he wouldn't let me. He wanted to pay for them and t-take them with him. And—and I *told* him I only knew how to do C.O.D.s. And then he . . . Oh, Patrick, he was *rich*, too—a lovely camel coat and a Cavanaugh hat—and he was staying at the St. Regis and surely *they* could have paid the C.O.D.—it was only fifty-one dollars . . ."

"But, Auntie Mame, what happened, what did he *do*?"

"Oh, Patrick, he was this nice Southerner, and he bought all these roller skates, and he seemed so warm and friendly and I told him I'd send them C.O.D., and then he said they were for an orph—an *orphanage* and he wanted to take them with him, and then I told him I only knew how to send things C.O.D., and Miss Kaufmann was in the—the ladies' room and couldn't help me with my—my sales book, and then this man said maybe he could help me write up the cash sale, and . . ." She started to sob again, "then he came around the counter and started to help me with the sales slip, and—oh, Patrick, I was really *learning* for the first time how to do a cash-and-take—and he was so pl-pleasant and we were laughing and writing up the sale just fine, and then the section manager came around and said 'Wh-what's going on here, Miss D-Dennis?' and then the Southern man started to laugh and told him what the trouble was, and then the section manager said it was in-*incredible* that a Macy employee couldn't write a p-proper sales slip, and then he took me by the arm and dragged me up to Personnel and told them I was the dumbest clerk in the wh-whole t-toy depa-a-artment." She broke down and wept miserably.

"Go on, Auntie Mame. What did the Southern man do?"

"He—he wasn't there, the section manager took me away so fast. And I had the best *sales* record in r-roller skates."

"But what did they do, Auntie Mame?"

"They—they said they were going to make an ex-*example* of me and they *fi-i-ired* me right then and there."

The living room grew dim in the early twilight of December. But still Auntie Mame sat there in dumb misery, sobbing softly and rocking to and fro. At six o'clock Ito came in to light the lamps and at one minute after six Norah bustled in and tried her best to comfort Auntie Mame, but she wouldn't move, wouldn't speak. She just sat there and sobbed.

I didn't think Auntie Mame should be left alone for fear she might Do Something, so I went over and sat glumly in a corner. The mink coat had slipped off Auntie Mame's shoulders and she sat there in her plain black little shopgirl's dress, her face very white and tears rolling down her cheeks.

Then the doorbell rang. In a moment Ito came in, very correct in his white jacket. "Mister Burnside, come see Madame."

"T-tell him I'm not at home," Auntie Mame said flatly.

"I tell him you no receiving, Madame, but he say e-ssential. He come from store."

Auntie Mame looked up. "Oh," she said urgently, "then I *must* see him. Perhaps they want me back."

Ito ushered in a big stranger—very tall, very handsome. He was wearing a camel's hair coat and a brown hat.

Auntie Mame stared at him blankly—stunned. "It's *you*! Aren't you satisfied with having cost me my job? Have you come to persecute me more? Perhaps drive me out of my home?"

"Please, ma'am," the stranger said, "I've been all over that old store tryin' to find out who you were and where I could get in touch with you. When that floorwalker fellah came back, I asked him where you'd gone and he said you'd been fired. I said that was all wrong. Then I *told* him it was my fault and I asked him what your name was, but he said it was against Macy's policy to give out

the names of the help. I said they had no business firin'
a nice little lady like you. I *told* him. I said, 'Man, I
never had such a good time in all my born days buyin'
*any*thing.' The hirin' office wouldn't tell me who you
were, either, but finally I asked a little old German
woman sellin' dolls an' she said you was Miss Dennis.
She didn't know your first name or where you lived or it
never woulda took me so long. Ma'am, I been through
every Dennis in the New York phone book.

"Miss Dennis, I been all over this town in a taxicab.
But now that I found you, Miss Dennis, do you mind if
I pay off the driver and let him go home to his family?"

"Go ahead," Auntie Mame said, like Jean Valjean
trapped in the sewer, "it's not as though you haven't
done enough to me already." But I noticed that she hur-
riedly powdered her nose and ran a comb through her
hair.

Mr. Burnside came back and took off his coat.
"Ma'am," he said, kneeling by Auntie Mame, "I don't
want you to be mad with me because of that job. I was
comin' to *offer* you a position with the Dixie Belle Enterprises, on account of I felt so bad about your losing your
place at Macy's. But, Miss Dennis," he said, looking ap-
preciatively around the room, "I didn't know you had
money. A lady with a nice little place like this don't have
to work at Macy's."

Then Auntie Mame threw back her head and started to
laugh. She laughed and laughed and the tears rolled
down her cheeks again. Mr. Burnside turned an angry
dark red and his eyes blazed.

"Miss Dennis, if you were just playin' some kind of
joke, I don't think it's very funny. I spent the whole, live-
long aftahnoon huntin' you up in alphabetical order, and
I . . ."

Auntie Mame was fumbling through her purse. "Yes,
Mr. Burnside," she laughed wildly, "I *do* have money.
Here it is—*all of it*—every cent. One dollar and thirty-
five, thirty-six . . . thirty-seven . . . thirty-eight cents."

I heard Norah hiss from the hallway. She crooked her finger at me and I tiptoed out. "You come on out here, darlin'," she whispered, "Miss Mame's entertaining a gentleman. A Southern gentleman!"

I was upstairs reading *Bring 'Em Back Alive* when Auntie Mame came up, her eyes dancing. "Oh, darling, we're saved," she whispered. "He's going to give me a job with the Dixie Belle Enterprises—that's a big oil company. I'm to be a receptionist and it pays *thirty* dollars a week! He's very polite. He asked me to go to Armando's with him for dinner. I'm sure it'll be all right. He *is* nice, and," she shrugged, "it's a free meal."

As she was putting on one of her unpaid-for Turner dresses, I slipped the rhinestone bracelet on her wrist. "Merry Christmas, Auntie Mame," I said. Then I added, "it isn't real."

"Darling, darling Patrick," she cried, "it's the most beautiful bracelet I've seen in my life." With the real mink coat and the real smile of happiness, it looked like the realest diamond bracelet in the world.

The next day was Christmas and Auntie Mame looked radiant—if a little hung over—as she gave me a big box from Brooks Brothers. It contained my first suit with long trousers. "Merry, merry Christmas, my little love," she cried.

"Gee, Auntie Mame, *thanks!*" I said. Later that day I noticed that a Tiepolo drawing of some naked religious people was missing from her bedroom. It was Auntie Mame's favorite picture, but she seemed very happy.

"Patrick, darling," she said, "you haven't asked me about my Southern gentleman." Then she told all. "He's a lovely man. We went to Armando's and had steak and then we talked and we talked and we talked. His whole name is Beauregard Jackson Pickett Burnside and he's descended—one way or another—from *four* Confederate generals! Oh, the gallant old Southland! He's *very* nice and he owns this big oil company and he has lovely eyelashes. By the way, he's coming here for Christmas dinner."

Mr. Burnside gave me twenty dollars as a Christmas present, tipped Norah and Ito lavishly after our last meal on credit, and took Auntie Mame to see Marilyn Miller.

Auntie Mame was out most of the rest of that week. Mr. Burnside took her to lunch and tea and dinner and the theater every day. On New Year's Eve he reserved a table at the Central Park Casino but they never got there. Instead they took a taxicab to Maryland, "Marry-land," as she called it later.

On New Year's Day she telephoned me from the St. Regis. "Patrick, my little love," she said, "this is Mrs. Beauregard Jackson Pickett Burnside. Come on over and have lunch with me and your Uncle Beau!"

Four

AUNTIE MAME

AND THE SOUTHERN BELLE

ROUNDING OUT ITS UNFORGET-
table Character even more, this article goes on to say
how the little spinster had a real athletic prowess. Or at
least she developed one in a hurry.

It seems that she got kind of worried with her foundling being bright in school and a comfort to her and her
cat but still having no father to instruct him in the manly
arts. She thought he might end up as a bookish weakling
if she didn't take action. So she sent off to Spalding's for
a whole lot of sporting equipment and set out to teach
him all he'd ever need to know. It worked fine and in the
process of coaching the kid, the old girl became quite
the athlete herself—so good, in fact, that she copped half
the prizes at the Danbury Fair and broke the ladies' shot-
put record for all time.

Well, I won't come right out and say that Auntie
Mame ever did anything like that, but she did establish a
certain reputation for herself in the field. In fact, she is
still spoken of with awed reverence in certain parts of the

country for her feats as a sportswoman after she married Mr. Burnside.

A few uncharitable people have said that Auntie Mame married Mr. Burnside for his money. I will concede that Mr. Burnside's being the richest man under forty south of Washington, D. C. may have influenced her. But she really loved him. He was father, brother, son, Santa Claus, and lover.

Her new husband, Beau, was one of those big, genial, easygoing, lovable Southerners. He sprang from a fine, impoverished old Georgia family, but he was unique among generals' descendants in that he didn't mope around Dixie talking about the carefree days before those damnyankees ravished its land and its women. Instead, Beau had gone out and raised soybeans and peanuts while the neighboring gentry were still bemoaning the paucity of their cotton crops. By the time he was nineteen, the Burnside land was free from debt and erosion and was showing a profit. During his last year at Georgia Tech he went off to Texas to settle an estate of barren wasteland left by some migratory cousin, discovered oil on the property, and was a millionaire before he was twenty-one. Everything Uncle Beau touched seemed to turn to gold, and he was constantly amazed and delighted by his good fortune. "Just luck, sugar," he'd say to Auntie Mame. Money meant very little to him except for the pleasure it could give to others. He was high on the list of every charity in the country, he was the sole support of an ancient mother and a pack of indolent kinfolk, and he was an easy touch for anybody with a fairly plausible hard-luck story.

Uncle Beau paid up all of Auntie Mame's debts, sold her carriage house—he said that nice women didn't live on Murray Hill—returned Norah's life savings, and sent her back to County Meath with a handsome pension. He moved Auntie Mame into about ten rooms in the St. Regis Hotel and encouraged her to go right back to her old scale of spending. She was happy to oblige.

Although she was pretty much her old self, I noticed certain subtle changes. It was fashionable to be romantic in 1932, but Auntie Mame went a step farther. Her hair was fluffier, softer; there were always a lot of camellias around the rooms; her dresses seemed to run to organdy and ruffles, and there was almost a roar of crinoline beneath her skirts. When Uncle Beau insisted that she have her portrait painted, Auntie Mame commissioned a society portraitist rather than one of the stark moderns who frequented her drawing room. The finished picture gave the impression of having been executed not with a brush, but with a pastry tube, and Auntie Mame kept saying it was a pity that Winterhalter wasn't still alive.

Her speech grew slightly blurred, softer and less staccato. She called me Honey a great deal and used You-all both in singular and plural.

For my thirteenth birthday she sent a whole bale of gifts, but prominent among them were a beautiful and intricate set of antique Confederate soldiers, which I still have, a three-volume set of books on General Lee, and, of all things, a yellowed first edition of *The Little Colonel*. I knew what was coming.

That June I graduated from the Lower School to the Upper School. I could have managed to do it myself, but Auntie Mame wrote an exuberant letter to announce that she and Uncle Beau were motoring up to St. Boniface to take part in the great celebration. "Then, honey," she wrote, "I've got a big surprise. You and your Uncle Beauregard and I are all going to drive down to Georgia to spend the summer on our big old plantation and see my sweet little old mother-in-law. Excuse the haste of this letter, but the Daughters of the Confederacy are meeting here today. Can't wait to see you-all!"

She was a triumph of Southern Womanhood at the commencement exercises. She wore a fluttering white garden party dress—it looked as though it were made of spun sugar—lace gloves, lace hat, lace parasol which she twirled coquettishly, and a lace fichu which she kept dropping to be retrieved by the pimpled gallants of St. Boniface. I won the composition prize for the Lower School and she said to the English master, "Ah vow, Ah'm so proud of that child Ah could jes *bust*! But then, his daddeh was one of the most literareh boys down home."

We drove down to Georgia in Uncle Beau's big Dusenberg phaeton, stopping here to see this grand ole monument or that noble ole battlefield where our Southun boys fought and died valiantly defendin' theah beliefs. Most of the countryside looked pretty bleak to me, but Auntie Mame, who'd been through it before on the Palm Beach sleeper, spoke at some length of its gracious ole heritage and its rich memories.

When the car swept up to the pillared portico of Peckerwood, the Burnside plantation, a genial old major-domo capered out to take the bags and a mountainous colored woman who looked like the ads for pancake flour heaved and shook and said Lan'sakes about thirty times. Auntie Mame was in her element.

Beau's Texas oil money, his Cuban sugar money, his New York stock market money, his Canadian mining money had all helped to restore the gracious rooms of Peckerwood to their ante-bellum magnificence. There were damask draperies, rosewood chairs, Sheraton tables, and crystal chandeliers with hurricane chimneys. Auntie Mame said it was just dawlin'. I was shown to my room, a big chamber with a canopied bed, a Chippendale chest-on-chest, and French windows giving on the second floor piazza. There was a Yankee bathroom next to it with real post-bellum Crane plumbing.

Auntie Mame seemed a little miffed that she wasn't going to be quartered in the main house, too, but tradition had it that the son and his wife always lived in the Bride's Cottage beyond the boxwood maze in the garden. Later I think she was thankful.

"But, Beau, honeh," she kept saying as she unpacked

her dimities, "when am Ah gonna meet yo sweet little ole mothah?"

Mrs. Burnside could by no stretch of the imagination be called either sweet or little. But she *was* old, and I suppose that God in His infinite wisdom had seen fit to make her mother, although I've often risked blasphemy to wonder why. She was built along the lines of a General Electric refrigerator and looked like a cross between Caligula and a cockatoo. Mother Burnside had beady little eyes, an imperious beak of a nose, sallow skin, and bad breath. She wore a stiff black wig and a stiff black dress and she sat all day long in a darkened drawing room, her pudgy hands—encrusted with dirty diamond rings—folded over her pudgy belly. She was a grim, taciturn woman, but when she put her mind to it, she could converse on several subjects: a) her exalted ancestors, b) how uppity the nigrahs were gettin', c) the Yankees, d) how unworthy everyone but Mrs. Burnside was, and e) the lamentable condition of her bowels. But usually she just sat in thin-lipped disapproval, her evil black eyes darting like a malign old parrot's.

There was one other occupant in the manor house at Peckerwood. That was Cousin Fan, the poorest relation. She was a faded, vague, timid spinster, whose penance for her poverty was to be at the constant beck and call of Mother Burnside. Miss Fan was rather sweet and pathetic in a masochistic fashion. She had an I. Q. of about thirty-five and all of her time that wasn't passed catering to the stolid whims of Mrs. Burnside was spent in doing Good Works for the Negroes and praying to a genteel and stone-deaf Episcopal God.

Miss Fan scratched at the door of my bedroom after I'd gone to the bathroom and unpacked my clothes. "Hello," she whispered, "I'm Miss Fanny Burnside, Beau's cousin. I'm sorry I wasn't at the door to greet you-all when you drove in, but I was upstairs giving Cousin Euphemia—Miz Burnside, I mean—her purge. You're Miz Beau's nephew, aren't you?"

I said I was and how did she do.

"Maybe you'd care to come down to the verandah and sit a spell. Miz Burnside don't finish her nap 'til four."

Miss Fan and I sat and rocked and eventually Auntie Mame and Uncle Beau strolled over from the Bride's Cottage. Auntie Mame was fearfully animated, kissed Miss Fan several times, and called her Cousin Fanny. The old colored man brought out a big decanter of bourbon and some Coca-Cola and Auntie Mame grew awfully cozy and familiar there on the verandah. "Ah sweah, Cousin Fanny," she shrilled, "yoah jes about as cute as a bug!"

Miss Fan tittered nervously.

It was easy to see that Uncle Beau was terribly proud of Auntie Mame. She called him her big, ole lamb-cat and kept twining his reddish-gold hair into little ringlets. Miss Fan giggled uneasily and said she was so glad that dear Cousin Beau had found such a nice little wife.

About that time there was fearful thumping from somewhere inside the house and Miss Fan's plain face went gray. "Mercy," she said, "I hope all our talking hasn't disturbed Cousin Euphemia. She almost never wakes up so early." Again the thumping, and Miss Fan flew into the house.

Auntie Mame's meeting with her mother-in-law was epic. Miss Fan came scuttling out to the verandah as Uncle Beau was pouring another round of bourbon. "She's ready to see you-all."

"Oh, isn't that dandeh, Beau, honey!" Auntie Mame gushed. "Ah jes cain't *wait*!" I could have waited an eternity.

Miss Fan timorously led the way into the back drawing room, and there sat Mother Burnside.

"Mothah, honeh," Auntie Mame squealed, and rushed up to kiss her. If Mother Burnside's pungent breath wasn't enough to stop further intimacies, her opening remark was.

"You look *oldah* than Ah expectid," she said.

Auntie Mame reeled. She never revealed her exact age and on a legal document she'd say "Over twenty-one," which no one ever seemed inclined to question. I suspected she was between thirty-five and forty, and she seemed a lot younger.

Mrs. Burnside favored Uncle Beau with her baleful black stare. "Yes, Beauregahd, you gave me to unduhstand that yoah wife was *much* youngah. You look tired son; *mighty* tired." Beau kissed her forehead reverently and then introduced me. I took her puffed old hand and bowed in my best dancing school manner.

"You seem nice enough," she said, "for a *Yankee* boy."

Auntie Mame had by now recovered from the initial barrage and gamely tried once more. "What a lovely, lovely old Greek Revival house this is, Mother—uh, Mrs. Burnside." I noticed that all trace of her Southern accent had disappeared.

"*We* like it," Mrs. Burnside said tersely, and then turned to Beau and launched on a long anecdote about her bowels.

Dinner that night was a funereal affair. There was a thick soup, a great roast of pork, roasted potatoes, candied yams, hominy grits, corn bread, and a pineapple upside-down cake. I had terrible nightmares, and even Auntie Mame admitted to a slight twinge of acid indigestion. The conversation was spotty. Auntie Mame held forth valiantly on the charm of Greek Revival houses and the influence of Virtruvius brought down through Palladio, Castle, Jones, Adam, and finally Thomas Jefferson. Beau said about six times how good it was to be home, but without much conviction. Miss Fan twittered a great deal until Mrs. Burnside jabbed her viciously with a fork and said to be still. That, plus a few portentous belches, was her only contribution to the merrymaking. Directly after dinner she went to bed and Miss Fan scurried along to help her undress and to read a chapter of the Bible aloud to her. Auntie Mame's visit hadn't started out well.

* * *

It was Beau, finally, who planned the big family reunion. Left to her own devices, Mrs. Burnside wouldn't have given so much as a wake for her new daughter-in-law, but since it was owing only to Beau that she and the rest of her patrician relations weren't residing at the County Home, she gave in reluctantly when he wanted to spend some of his own money in his own home for his own wife, and the gathering of the clan was scheduled.

The bride was presented officially to her new relatives when they appeared en masse at a giant barbecue the following Sunday. At noon we were all on the verandah. Auntie Mame was looking lovely and fragile in yellow dotted swiss with a big leghorn hat, and Uncle Beau stood next to her in his ice cream suit, proud as a peacock. Mrs. Burnside was dressed for the next ice age. She sat in a rocker wearing a voluminous black silk dress, black boots, a black shawl, black glasses, a black sunshade, black gloves, and a black hat. She greeted me with a mournful belch and sent Miss Fan in for her potion.

Then the relatives started coming. Car after car streaked into the drive and parked on the spacious lawn. "Ruin the grass," Mrs. Burnside growled, and her stomach rumbled alarmingly.

I've never seen so many Southerners before or since. It seemed impossible that they were all part of the same family—or even the same county—but they were. Beau's sisters, Willie Mae, Sally Randolph, and Georgia Lee arrived first with their husbands. The sisters had each managed to have six children under the age of five and there was a lot of introducing and kissing and you-alling. Although they weren't very attractive people, Auntie Mame began to exude charm, but Mrs. Burnside didn't. Her digestive tract voiced an eloquent protest with each new face.

The relatives kept coming. They all had two first names and some of them even had two last names. There were about six men named Moultrie, four named Calhoun, eight called Randolph, and almost everybody had a Lee tucked somewhere into his or her name. To make things even more confusing, about half the women had men's names. There were ladies called Sarah John, Liza William, Susie Carter, Lizzie Beaufort—pronounced Byew-fert—Mary Arnold, Annie Bryan, Lois Dwight.

By one o'clock there were more than a hundred and twenty relatives milling around Peckerwood, all talking, and all talking *loud*. Mrs. Burnside indicated her disapproval of all this with a fanfaronade of flatulence.

Still the relatives came. Beau was the kind of man who'd be popular anywhere, and since almost all of the guests were directly or indirectly supported by him, it was safe to predict a full turnout. Auntie Mame was in her element, and above Mrs. Burnside's steady barrage of gas attacks I could hear her talking vivaciously.

At quarter-past one the Clay-Picketts, or horsy branch of the family, started piling in. They were all in riding clothes, and they were accompanied by a spotted hound who immediately jumped into Mrs. Burnside's lap, thus causing an explosion of wind which I felt sure she'd been saving for the climax of the party. I sniggered helplessly.

"Down, sir! Down, I say," Van Buren Clay-Pickett roared, and smacked the hound across the hocks, thereby eliciting a soft, moist hiccough from Mrs. Burnside. "Sorry we'ah all so late, Aunt Euphemia, but Sally Cato McDougall got unseated goin' ovah the five-bah an' we *think* she broke her collah bone. Heel, sir!" he bellowed at the dog, who'd managed to knock over three children and was now lifting his leg at the base of one of Peckerwood's six Ionic columns. "Had to shoot her mare. Cousin Clytie and Alice-Richard thought they bettah take Sally Cato to the doctah's, but they'll be along directly. When Sally Cato come to she said to tell you she was awful sorry she couldn't make the shin-dig. Down, sir, goddamn it—pardon me, Aunt Euphemia—down, I say." The dog had leaped again into Mrs. Burnside's lap and burrowed his snout diligently into the folds of her black silk skirt. Again the big horseman's hand smacked the hound and a piteous eructation of outraged virtue was clearly heard from Mrs. Burnside. I had to go indoors for a minute to regain control of myself. "Down, sir. Heel, Ah tell ya!"

When I came back outdoors the rest of the Clay-Picketts had arrived—nine of them, all in riding clothes; athletic to the end. The bourbon and branch water was flowing faster and faster and Auntie Mame had gathered a rapt circle of admiring new relatives around her. Mrs. Burnside shook her head dyspeptically and popped another soda mint into her mouth.

All at once the air was split by the blare of a horn and a dark green Packard roadster slithered up the drive. The top was down and a colored boy in dark green stable livery was driving. Sitting on the folded-back roof was the most beautiful woman I've ever seen in my life. She was wearing riding clothes and her left arm was in a sling hastily improvised from a silk scarf.

"Hello, everybody, hello, you-all," she called in a throaty voice. "Sorry I'm late, but my horse had a run-in with a five-bar gate."

There was a silence and then a lot of whispering among the relatives. "Land a goshen," an old uncle with an ear trumpet cackled, "ain't that Sally Cato McDougall, the gal used to be engaged to young Beau?"

"You hush, Uncle Moultrie," Willie Mae screamed. "Yes, it sure enough is, but what *Ah'd* like to know is who in the *wuld* evah invited her."

She wasn't long in finding out. Broken wing and all, the beautiful lady jumped gracefully down from the car and ran up to Mrs. Burnside. "Mrs. Burnside," she said in her lovely voice, "I'm so sorry to be late when you went to all that trouble to invite me especially. Doctor wanted me to go straight to bed, but I told him I wouldn't miss your party for a million dollars."

The old lady burst into a big smile. "Welcome to

Peckahwood, Sally Cato, it jus wouldn't be a pahty without you."

Uncle Beau looked kind of mystified.

"Beau Burnside, congratulations!" the beautiful lady said. "Now, let me see this New York bride you've gone out and got yourself." She gave Auntie Mame a lovely smile and stretched out her elegant right hand. "How do you do, Mrs. Beau. I'm Sally Cato McDougall. You got yourself a mighty wild stallion, but I reckon any woman as good looking as you can train him just fine."

Auntie Mame's face glowed with delight. "Why, Beau, why didn't you tell me about Miss McDougall? She's perfectly gorgeous!" They smiled beatifically, and then the rest of the party began gabbling with the noisy release and relief that comes over a crowd when a serious accident has been narrowly averted.

Lunch was announced, followed by an ominous belch from Mrs. Burnside, and then the barbecue began in earnest.

Auntie Mame had scored a social victory among the relatives. They all thought she was the most chowmin' Yankee lady they'd ever met and were so ardent in their praise that Mrs. Burnside was confined to her bed for the next three days. Auntie Mame was pleased to be such a success and was kept pretty busy accepting all the invitations she'd received from various cousins. But of all the people in Richmond County, she found Sally Cato McDougall the most attractive. And, of course, she was. The fact that Sally Cato had been Uncle Beau's former fiancée and was left holding the bag and a five-carat square-cut diamond when Mame and Beau eloped didn't bother her very much. Auntie Mame had been engaged a lot of times herself, and she understood that such things Just Happened. She'd never even known of Sally Cato's existence until the day of the big barbecue, so she hardly felt that she'd connived to steal the prize.

Sally Cato had been awfully friendly with Auntie Mame, too, and in a week's time the pair of them were inseparable. Sally Cato had gone North to school and learned how to speak English, she'd been to Europe a couple of times, and she was really the most cultivated girl of twenty-five Auntie Mame had ever met. She also had a straight-from-the-shoulder, honest quality that captivated everybody. She was expert at everything she did, swimming, dancing, driving, golf, tennis, and bridge—but riding and hunting were her greatest loves.

The morning after the barbecue, the green Packard roadster screeched to a stop in front of the Bride's Cottage and Sally Cato, looking crisp and lovely, skipped up to the terrace where Auntie Mame and I were having our Little Morning Chat. "Good morning, you-all," she called. "Sorry to barge in this way, but with this old sprained arm, I can't ride, can't swim, can't do anything but sit and mope. I'm so bored I could scream!"

Auntie Mame, who was also a little bored at Peckerwood when Uncle Beau wasn't around, greeted her warmly. The two ladies had quite a friendly chat and it soon appeared that they had a lot more in common than Uncle Beau. "Well, honey, the best woman won," Sally Cato said generously. Then she said, "Look, you and this youngster here must find it pretty tiresome with Beau out all day long, and I'm so lonesome at home I'd like to die. So why don't you-all come over to Foxglove for lunch. I have a younger brother just about your age, Patrick. He's a mean little devil, but at least he'll be something gayer for you than Mrs. Burnside and silly old Fanny." Auntie Mame jumped at the opportunity for a little intellectual companionship, and twenty minutes later the two women were intimately swigging bourbon on the verandah at Foxglove.

The McDougall plantation was every bit as grand as Peckerwood and the food was a lot more digestible. At lunchtime one of the strangest-looking kids I've ever seen came slinking around the boxwood hedge and eyed me coldly.

"Oh!" Sally Cato jumped, "it's *you*. I *wish* you'd stop

sneaking around. It always gives me such a start. Patrick, this is my brother, Emory Oglethorpe. I hope you two can keep each other out of mischief this summer."

If you didn't know that the blood in his veins ran as blue as the Confederate flag, you'd have sworn that Emory Oglethorpe McDougall was the changeling child of some ill-starred Georgia cracker girl. He was small and wiry, with an incredible head of russet-colored hair and the biggest, greenest eyes I've ever seen. Although he was only six months my elder, Emory Oglethorpe was a century ahead of me when it came to a firsthand knowledge of evil.

Sally Cato refused to let Emory Oglethorpe have any brandy after lunch and told us to run along and play.

"I think your sister is very nice," I told him in a conversational way.

"Well, yo'ah plumb crazy, if ya do. She's an A numbah one *bitch*!" Then he said, "Wanta come down to mah shack? If ya pay me a little somethin' maybe Ah'll show ya mah pictchas." Emory Oglethorpe had constructed a one-room snuggery concealed by vines along the banks of the Savannah River. The place contained some tallow candles, a couple of orange-crate chairs, and a sagging army cot—Confederate Army, I believe—on which he had allegedly seduced quite a number of young colored girls.

"Get you a nice, tawny pickaninny girl," he croaked malevolently, "if ya give me fifty cents. Best kinda poontang there is. Ah like a good piece of dahk meat."

Upon payment of a dime he showed me an exhaustive collection of pornographic photographs, vintage of about 1900. The ladies and gentlemen in the pictures looked kind of old-fashioned, but they were indulging in very modern things. Since biology limits sex—and its variations—to about a dozen pastimes, I got a little bored with the pictures until suddenly I came upon one of Uncle Beau and Sally Cato McDougall in a most intimate position. I jumped in astonishment.

"Fooled ya, didn't Ah?" Emory Oglethorpe croaked wickedly. "Ah jest pasted pictchas of theah heads onto that photo. But Ah bet they did it, jest the same. Gawdlmighty, you shoulda seen ole Sally Cato when she hud that Beau'd got married up No'th. She like to busted. Went goddin' and damnin' all ovah the house and swo' she'd have the hide of the duhty damnyankee who got Beau. Ah nevah see such cay'ins-on in all mah bone days. Ah was glad. Ah hate huh! Heah, have a *cig-*arette."

I was horrified, but it was a bit of gratuitous informa-tion I was interested to get and I tucked it away among an odd collection of Little-Known Facts About Well-Known People.

When Emory Oglethorpe and I went back to the house, Auntie Mame, under the influence of both alcoholic and intellectual stimulation, had grown animated and expan-sive with Sally Cato. ". . . Oh, but my dear," she was say-ing, "I simply *adore* riding. I was practically *born* on horseback. Why, back in New York hardly a day goes by that I don't get a little workout. Up with the birds every morning for a brisk canter through Central Park!" My mouth dropped open. I suppose that Auntie Mame *had* taken a few riding lessons at some dim finishing school in her Northern past, but she'd never so much as looked at a horse in all the years I'd known her.

"Why, that's splendid, Mame," Sally Cato said. "*Most* interesting. I'll have to get hold of your cousin, Van Buren Clay-Pickett—he's Master of the Hounds down here—and organize a big hunt in your honor."

"Oh, *what* a pity," Auntie Mame said quickly. "I've left *all* my riding togs up North."

"Oh, don't you worry about that. I have dozens of things you could wear. What size shoe do you take?"

"Uh, five-B," Auntie Mame said, tucking her feet under her.

"Marvelous," Sally Cato said. "Same as I do. I can even fit you out with boots."

Auntie Mame went pale beneath her tan.

"You *do* ride astride, Mame dear?"

A hopeful gleam came into Auntie Mame's eyes. "Oh, never! Sidesaddle—*always*. Daddy, the colonel, *insisted* that I learn it. He said it was the *only* way for a lady to ride—so graceful. It was silly of him, of course, because now *nobody* rides sidesaddle, but it's the only way I know how." She finished with a sigh of relief, but her joy was short-lived.

"Now, isn't that grand!" Sally Cato said. "I just happen to have an old Champion and Wilton saddle that'll do you fine, and a lovely broadcloth habit. You *are* in luck. I used to ride sidesaddle myself, but now I always sit astride; it's a deal *safer*. Now, I'm going right in and call Van Buren Clay-Pickett over at the Stud. We never hunt in this hot weather, but I'm sure we'll all be happy to make an exception for *you*."

Having made her bed, Auntie Mame was eventually forced to lie in it. News of her equestrian prowess spread far and fast over the countryside, and at almost every family get-together the conversation was switched to quarters and withers, heaves and spavins as a concession to Auntie Mame.

The whole county buzzed with talk of Auntie Mame's forthcoming debut on the field and Uncle Beau went around with his chest puffed up like a pouter pigeon's. Van Buren Clay-Pickett quickly rounded up a flea-bitten old fox and the big hunt was scheduled for the next Sunday. I didn't know what Auntie Mame was going to do, but I hadn't reckoned with her inventive powers. Two days before the big hunt, she powdered herself dead white, put on an unbecoming shade of green, and whispered modestly to Sally Cato McDougall of a delicate and mythical female complaint. The hunt was postponed for a week.

Given a reprieve, Auntie Mame tried desperately for a new and interesting malady, but she remained in the most robust health. Fortunately she sustained a very genuine

accident under the gaze of the whole family and Sally
Cato on the Friday preceding the fateful hunt. Auntie
Mame slipped on the highly waxed parquetry in the din-
ing room at Peckerwood and sprained her ankle. Uncle
Beau and Sally Cato rushed her to the local doctor, who
taped her up and told her to keep off it for a day or two.
"Then that means I *won't* be able to ride Sunday?" she
asked.

"Absolutely out of the question, Mrs. Beau," the doctor said. "But of co'se you could follow the hunt in a
cah."

Auntie Mame sighed blissfully and closed her eyes.

The next day Sally Cato joined Auntie Mame and
Beau and me for lunch in the Bride's Cottage. Sally Cato
was very solicitous of Auntie Mame's sprained ankle.
Having caught Auntie Mame practicing an intricate tango
step, I knew that she was feeling a lot better, but she put
on a very convincing show of gallantry over pain. After
dessert, Sally Cato unrolled a large and elaborate hand-
drawn map of the surrounding countryside. "Mame,
honey, I'm just *sick* that you can't ride Sunday. Everybody's just dying to see you on a horse, dear, *me especially*." I didn't like her tone. "But, anyhow, Mame, I knew
you'd want to follow the hunt, and Doc says it's all right
for you to drive, so I stayed up 'til all hours working on
this map. Now, *here's* where the chase starts, and then the
fox usually runs down this way . . ." Sally Cato had done
a masterful and detailed scale drawing of the Richmond
County hunting territory, and she explained everything
beautifully.

Uncle Beau's eyes were moist with admiration. "Gosh,
Sally Cato, is there anything you *can't* do? That's one of
the finest pieces of cartography I've ever seen. Of
course," he said to Auntie Mame, "Sally Cato knows the
field so well she could ride it blindfold. Sally Cato,
you're a real brick. I never woulda thought that anyone

would dream of taking all that trouble just to make a little new bride feel at home down here."

The next morning there was a lot of clomping and yelling and Hi, you-alling out in the driveway of Peckerwood. Uncle Beau was very handsome in his pink coat astride a big horse, and six different members of the hunt said, "Haa's it feel to git back on a hawse aftah gallyvantin' aroun' Noo Yoke, Boragod?" The genial horsemen sounded exactly like a minstrel show, but they all looked fine in their hunting jackets.

There was a general murmur of disappointment when Auntie Mame appeared in a natty plaid suit hobbling delicately on an ebony cane, but Sally Cato stood up on the mounting block and said, "Members of the hunt, I'm afraid I have a piece of bad news for you-all. Mrs. Beau sprained her ankle here at Peckerwood the other night and Doc won't let her ride. But she's such a devoted rider and such an ardent huntswoman that she's going to follow the hunt in her car, so she'll be in on the kill." There was a ripple of applause.

Emory Oglethorpe McDougall, who looked like a crooked jockey in his riding clothes, sidled up to me. "Ah'd rathah follow a map o' hades than that one ole Sally Cato drew up. If yo'ah smaht, you'll tell yoah Auntie Mame to jes git *lost*."

"You're crazy," I said.

"Okay," he said, "drive on, fool, hell's only half full."

Auntie Mame hopped into Beau's open Dusenberg with surprising agility. I went along with her to open and close the thousands of gates that blocked off the hundreds of dirt and clay roads snaking over the countryside. Auntie Mame had never fully mastered the automobile, but after startling several horses, we lurched off in a cloud of blue monoxide gas. Rolling out to the field behind the pack, Auntie Mame squeezed my knee affectionately and said, "Oh, darling, I'm so thankful for this sprain. Maybe now they'll get over this horse craze. It was sweet, though, of Sally Cato to make this wonderful map. I just hope I won't be sick when they kill that poor little fox."

With a great deal of trouble, Auntie Mame got the car headed in the right direction and the hunt was on. We jogged over red clay roads for nearly an hour, turning into this lane and then that one. Occasionally we'd lose sight of the pack and then they'd appear again. I hopped out about a million times to open slack, splintery old gates and then shut them after the car had jogged through. It was a remarkable map, because we were always just a little ahead of the hunt. Sally Cato had been almost clairvoyant in her knowledge of where and when the fox would be. The roads were terrible, powdery with red dust and deeply rutted. Auntie Mame drove like a startled hare and my liver got a thorough shaking up. She looked a little scared, but once or twice she shouted, "Yoicks, there they go." Another time she called, "Tallyho!" Just why, I wasn't sure.

After an eternity of bouncing and lurching, we came to the worst road of all. It ran in deep clay ruts straight across a sloping meadow. Neither horse nor hound was in sight. Auntie Mame stopped the car and busied herself with her compact. "Mercy," she said, "now we've lost them."

Then there was a thunder of hoofs and yelping of hounds. A small black fox dashed down the hill with the pack in hot pursuit. "Here they come, Auntie Mame," I yelled. They were headed straight for us. Auntie Mame dropped her lipstick. Now the horses appeared over the rise. Frantically Auntie Mame tried to start the car; it spluttered and gagged, but nothing happened. She tried again. The pack was drawing nearer and nearer, the horses pummeling down the hill.

"The key, Auntie Mame!" I shouted.

"Oh, yes," she said wildly. The fox was desperately close. Auntie Mame switched on the ignition and the car bounded forward just as a small cannon ball of black fur darted into the road. There was a terrible screech of brakes and I was thrown forward against the windshield. Then all hell broke loose. Hounds, horses, and riders descended on us like an avalanche. Nearly three dozen riders were thrown, and two big bay mares rammed into the Dusenberg so hard the front fender and hood had to be replaced. A third mount was half in and half out of the back seat, whinnying horribly. All in all, there were more horses shot that day than at the Battle of Gettysburg, and when the final casualty list was posted there were six broken ankles, four broken arms, a fractured leg—compound—three cases of concussion, a dislocated pelvis, and countless bruises and abrasions. The riders who were able to walk and speak raced down to the car in a fury and Auntie Mame fainted dead away. I was almost hysterical, but still able to hear Emory Oglethorpe Mc-Dougall growl, "What'd Ah tell yuh?", and to note the bitter smile of triumph on Sally Cato's face. Auntie Mame had been in for the kill, all right. The fox lay dead under the car.

If Auntie Mame had been the subject of a good deal of county conversation before the fateful fox hunt, she was now the absolute mania of the riding set. Emory Oglethorpe made it perfectly clear to me that she was now referred to as "that crazy, damnyankee woman who killed all ouah hawses." People for miles around talked of nothing else, and every day the telephone buzzed with hesitant voices saying how sorry they were that they'd be unable to come to Bride's Cottage for lunch or that they had to postpone indefinitely the little dinner they'd planned in Auntie Mame's honor. Auntie Mame, after two weeks of being the uncontested belle of the county, now seemed about as popular as General Sheridan.

Mother Burnside seemed to feel a lot better after the news of her daughter-in-law's downfall, and managed to come downstairs for dinner every night. Between soda mints and waves of wind, she favored us all with such reminiscences as, "When *Ah* was a young bride theah was nothin' Ah loved and adohed moah than huntin'. Ah was a regulah Di-ana." Beau sat tight-lipped and looked grim and embarrassed. And one evening when Mother Burnside's memoirs of field and flatulence were particularly trying, Miss Fan lent Auntie Mame a handkerchief and whispered, "Don't you pay any heed to her, Miz Beau, she *hated* hunting and she rode worse than I did!" But Miss Fan's mousy solicitude did little to comfort Auntie Mame. She was *persona non grata* in the entire community, and she knew it. The only one who still offered her friendship was Sally Cato McDougall.

"But, Mame, honey," she'd say, "don't cry like that. It wasn't your fault—everybody knows that accidents will happen. If the others are too narrow-minded to forgive and forget, well, to hell with them. *I'm* still your friend. You know that."

Auntie Mame was intensely grateful to Sally Cato. They saw each other daily, and Sally Cato *was* the only person who was nice to her. Even Uncle Beau seemed stiff around Auntie Mame.

I saw a lot of Emory Oglethorpe while Auntie Mame was in purdah. He taught me how to smoke and chew and drink a vile kind of dandelion wine he concocted. "Didn' believe me, didja, when Ah tole yuh Sally Cato was out to have yoah Auntie's hide. Lawd, man, she knew you-all'd be drivin' acrosst that field jes when the pack was. She knows the huntin' country like the back of huh ha-yand. You shoulda huhd huh laughin' and screamin' an' ca'yin' on aftah all them hawses spilled to hell an' gone ovah yoah Auntie's cah. Ah thought it was a pretty funny-lookin' sight, mahself. Don' worry, Sally Cato's gonna get Beau back if she has to kill yoah Auntie doin' it." He chuckled maliciously. "Ole Sally Cato's nevah lost a bet, o' a race, o' a man in huh life, and she sho don't inten' ta staht now. Heah, take the resta this packa Luckies."

I was beginning to be half convinced that Emory

Oglethorpe was right, although it didn't seem possible that Sally Cato would stoop to anything so low.

But that evening I began to appreciate Emory Oglethorpe's appraisal of his sister. Sally Cato, who was the great favorite of Mrs. Burnside's, dined with us at Peckerwood. She looked very Southern, very romantic, very beautiful in white lace, and she was charm itself. Auntie Mame, who had been openly snubbed in the millinery department of J. B. White's that afternoon, looked tired, and what's more, she looked old.

Mother Burnside was unusually talkative that night, and in her oblique fashion she let poor Auntie Mame have it right between the eyes. She spoke of nothing but Sally Cato. Sally Cato's beauty, her youth, her wealth, her ancient lineage, her seat on a horse, how lovely she'd looked at the last Hunt Ball, how vital and healthy she always seemed, how typically, charmingly, radiantly Southern she was. "A real, genu-wine daughtah of ouah own fay-ah county. A blue-blooded young flowah of the Old South and of ouah glorious community wheah every family has a rich background of great traditions and wheah no strangeh has trespassed since the Wah of the *See*-cession."

Auntie Mame claimed a sick headache and left right after dinner. She'd been having a lot of sick headaches lately, and Beau said, "What, again?"

I went up to my room early. It was hot and humid and I couldn't sleep, so I stuck one of Emory Oglethorpe's cigarettes in my mouth and went out onto the upstairs piazza. But the cigarette hung dead on my lips, for below me I could see the red ends of two other cigarettes and I heard Sally Cato's voice, low and urgent. "Oh, Beau," she said, "I *know* Mame's nice. Believe me, I love her just as much as you do, but is she *right* for *you*? Beau, honestly, all I want is your happiness. I took it pretty hard when I heard you'd married her instead of me, but truly, that's all water over the dam. Mame's a grand woman, but Beau, does she *belong* down here?"

"Mame's a Yankee," Beau said stiffly, "and they have different ways from ours."

"Oh, Beau, I realize all that. After all, I'm her only *friend*. But Beau, I keep asking myself, can she give you the family, the home, the children that are a part of our Southern heritage? *Can* she, Beau?"

"I don't know why not," Beau said with a note of doubt.

"Well, Beau, just remember, your happiness is all I want. I've got to get up early tomorrow for the hunter trials, so I'll run along now. Want to give me a little kiss for old times' sake?" The cigarettes dropped to the grass and there was no more talking. They just stood there in the shadows, kind of wrapped around each other, and didn't move for a long, long time.

Wretchedly I turned away, and as I did, something woolly brushed across my face. I was too frightened to utter a sound. Then a bony hand clutched my arm and a voice whispered, "Come in here, child." It was Miss Fan.

She led me into her hot little room. "Give me a cigarette," she breathed. "I know you have some, I saw them in your wardrobe."

We smoked in silence. She was a lot better at it than I.

"I suppose you heard—Beau and that, that dreadful Sally Cato?"

I nodded.

"Now do you understand? Now do you see why you've got to get your aunt out of here—and Beau, too?"

I bobbed my head dumbly.

"Lord knows I'm only a poor old spinster—no better than a servant in this house and at the beck and call of that terrible old shrew twenty-four hours a day. I have no business saying all this, but Miz Beau is the only person in this whole godforsaken county who's ever treated me like a human being. Beau's a nice boy, too. That's why you've got to get them out of here, before it's too late. Before that dirty old woman and that slut of a girl wreck the whole thing. Every day I hear the two of them up in her bedroom, plotting, plotting, plotting. Do you understand, child? Do you *see*? *Get your aunt out of here.* Quick, before those two ruin her. Now go to bed, child. Oh, yes, and leave those cigarettes here."

The next day I tried in a bumbling, callow way to warn Auntie Mame about Sally Cato, but I did it so badly that she flew at me in a rage. "What!" she cried, sitting bolt upright.

"I *said*, Auntie Mame, did you ever stop and think that maybe Sally Cato *isn't* your friend? After all, she used to be engaged to Uncle Beau, and *she* was the one who drew that map and made you kill all those horses, and Emory Oglethorpe says . . ."

"Emory Oglethorpe says," she mimicked shrilly, "Emory Oglethorpe says . . . Who *cares* what that little goat-eyed hellion says! As for *you*, I'm ashamed—yes, *good and ashamed*—that any nephew of mine could be so small-minded, so petty and rotten as to entertain for one moment such a filthy, vile notion. The idea!" At that moment Sally Cato's big Packard roadster was gliding up the drive. "Here comes Sally Cato now. I will spare you the embarrassment of seeing her. Get out of here and don't come back until you can think and speak like a gentleman. Sally Cato's the only real friend I've got down here, and I won't hear another word about her. Now scat!"

Crestfallen, I loped away. I hadn't mentioned what had happened the night before, because I didn't want to hurt Auntie Mame's feelings. She loved Uncle Beau an awful lot—she must have, or she wouldn't have put up with life at Peckerwood.

But when Sally Cato drove away, Auntie Mame seemed terribly nervous and upset and called me into the Bride's Cottage "Oh, Patrick, Patrick," she moaned, "whatever am I to do now?"

"Do about what?"

"Sally Cato was just here and she's planning another

of those ghastly rodeo things. She says the only way I can redeem myself with the people in the county is to show them what a wonderful horsewoman I am. Now I have to ride and, oh, Patrick, it wasn't true, all that business about my loving horses. I *loathe* them."

"Why don't you just admit that you were only kidding, Auntie Mame?" I said with certain childlike innocence. "Then they won't expect you to ride."

"What! Be made even a worse laughing stock than I am now? I'd rather die!"

"But that's exactly what may happen to you if you go out on this hunt."

"Better to die in the saddle," she said nobly, and shuddered.

"Well, cheer up, Auntie Mame, you can always come down with a cold or sprain your ankle again before the hunt."

"But it's *tomorrow, at six o'clock in the morning!*"

Uncle Beau was out at a landowners' meeting that night, and Auntie Mame and I dined silently in the Bride's Cottage. Auntie Mame was trying to read *Fleurs de Mal* when the station wagon from Foxglove drove up to the door. Emory Oglethorpe hopped out carrying a big box, a pair of boots, a silk hat, and a leather sidesaddle. "Evenin'," he grunted in his nutmeg-grater voice, "ole Sally Cato tol' me to hustle these hawse duds ovah to yoah Auntie Mame. Man o' man, you oughta see Sally Cato, she's whoopin' an' hollerin' all ovah the stables. Sez she vows yoah Auntie Mame ain't nevah been on so much as a merry-go-round. She's takin' all kinds o' bets on the hunt an' givin' odds of a hundred to one. The hawse she's picked fo' yoah Auntie Mame'll be ovah in the van tomorrah mawnin'. You betta tell yoah Auntie ta break huh laig o' somethin' befo' she breaks huh neck. Well, so long, Ah gotta fine piece o' high yallah waitin' fo me back to the shack."

I felt as though the black broadcloth riding habit I carried in to Auntie Mame were a shroud. She looked aghast and began to tremble. "Oh, God, Sally Cato's sent over the whole outfit." Then she eyed the sidesaddle. "Am I supposed to *sit* on that jock strap?" She began to cry, and she was still weeping softly on her pillow when I went back to the big house.

By the time I was dressed next morning I heard hoofs clomping up the drive. The whole county—all except those who were still convalescing from Auntie Mame's last performance on the hunt field—was congregated in front of Peckerwood. There were even a few people from across the Carolina border. They seemed less hearty than they had the last time, and there was a malicious, conspiratorial feeling in the air.

Somehow Auntie Mame and I didn't give the impression of *haute couture*. I was wearing a castoff outfit of Emory Oglethorpe McDougall's and he was nearly a head shorter than I was. From certain angles Auntie Mame looked very dashing in Sally Cato's broadcloth riding costume and her brow was misleadingly serene under the tall silk hat. But the jacket was a trifle tight here, a trifle loose there, and the skirt dragged a little. Then, too, the size five boots must have been misery. Auntie Mame chain-smoked a lot and took several nips from a silver flask. She tried to seem lighthearted and cheery, but she looked ill at ease, and all the riders eyed her suspiciously.

Sally Cato cantered up on a fine big mare, followed by Emory Oglethorpe and a van from Foxglove. There was a terrible amount of stomping and kicking coming from inside the van, and with a good deal of trouble two grooms finally led the biggest, meanest-looking horse I've ever seen down the runway.

Sally Cato kissed Auntie Mame warmly. "How *unusual* you look this morning, Mame honey," she said. "Excuse me just a moment, dear, I want to run in and say a word to Mrs. Burnside."

In a minute she was back. I looked up to the second-story piazza and saw old Mother Burnside standing there with a funny, unpleasant expression on her face. Sally Cato skipped over to Auntie Mame. "This is the horse I picked especially for you, Mame dear," she said with a sly smile. "His name is Lightning Rod, and he's as gentle as a lamb."

Lightning Rod was an Irish hunter, seventeen and a half hands high; a gelding who'd never quite reconciled himself to a life of celibacy. He looked at Auntie Mame with blood in his eye and pawed the ground savagely. Sally Cato stroked his muzzle. "He's a booful ole darlin', dat's wot he is."

Emory Oglethorpe slithered up to me. "He's the goddamndest, most vicious piece o' hawse flesh in Richmond County, *that's* what he is. O'nery son-of-a-bitch shoulda been shot two yeahs ago when he trompled Uncle Grady half to death. Least, that's what the *vet* said. That cussed ole plug's been cockeyed crazy an' runnin' roun' the pastcha evah since. Took six niggahs all yestiddy aftahnoon to ketch him."

Sally Cato clapped her elegantly gloved hands and said, "Your attention, everyone, we are now going to have the unique privilege of hunting with one of New York City's most famous equestriennes, Mrs. Beau Burnside." She winked maliciously, but not quickly enough for Auntie Mame to miss. Auntie Mame's eyes opened wide. There was a ripple of repressed mirth among the riders. Only Beau had an air of innocence.

I was already astride a spastic old nag when three grooms led Lightning Rod to the mounting block and Auntie Mame climbed gingerly aboard. I breathed a silent prayer and I noticed that Auntie Mame's lips were moving, too.

All the way out to the field I tried to keep as close as possible to Auntie Mame, but Lightning Rod had a pernicious habit of kicking out behind so that she had the road pretty much to herself. I hoped she wouldn't be hurt too much when she fell. We ambled along placidly enough, even though I received the distinct impression that all dogs, most people, and some horses made Lightning Rod nervous and irritable. Finally we got to the starting place. Lightning Rod whinnied eerily and reared. But surprisingly enough, Auntie Mame stayed on. A couple of the people seemed impressed. Sally Cato just sneered.

As we were about to start, the Peckerwood station wagon raced up to the field with a scared-looking Negro at the wheel. Miss Fan jumped out and screamed, "Stop! That horse is mad!" But she was too late. The fox had been released and was dashing wildly across the meadow, the hounds hot on his trail; simultaneously, Cousin Van Buren Clay-Pickett and Auntie Mame led off and the hunt was under way. There was no stopping her now.

I'd thought surely that Auntie Mame would have the good sense to select a nice soft-looking hummock and throw herself off, but she didn't. Instead, she and Lightning Rod galloped hell-for-leather after Cousin Van Buren. "Gawdlmighty, what a seat Miz Beau has!" someone shouted. I turned around to see who could be so deranged and my eye caught an expression on Sally Cato's face that was awful to behold.

We raced off, leaving poor old Miss Fan screaming incomprehensible things. The old nag I was riding wasn't good for much more than glue, but at least it kept up with the pack long enough for me to see Auntie Mame and Lightning Rod sail over a jagged stone wall that threw two others. Auntie Mame lost her silk hat and her hair floated out wildly, but still she kept on going.

"Ja see huh cleah that woll?" someone called. "That damnyankee gal's got *style*. Soo*pub* hawsewoman. Pufeckly soo*pub*!"

We rode for better than an hour, thundering over the springy turf, scraping beneath low-hanging branches, and splashing through muddy creeks. Auntie Mame was out of sight most of the time, and even Uncle Beau and Sally Cato found it impossible to keep up with her. At one point she and Lightning Rod took a sort of detour through a whole field of feeding corn, but still they had no trouble in catching up with the Master of the Hounds. Another time the horse charged into an old lean-to and right out the other side with Auntie Mame still aboard. There was a lot of clucking and squawking and chickens flew out from every direction. In a flash I saw that one old hen, gamer than most, was even perched on Auntie Mame's shoulder, but the sheer velocity of the wind soon sent it flapping helplessly into the air.

Once again I lost sight of her when Lightning Rod plunged into a patch of woods, but Auntie Mame soon appeared again wearing something that looked like a laurel wreath and not even holding the reins.

"Ah vow," one of the more cultivated cousins screamed, "don't she look like a verytibble Greek goddess!"

"Landagoshen," another one roared, "she ain't even hangin' on. If that don't beat all!"

Then she raced ahead again and disappeared from view.

At last we bounded up to a big, flat plateau overlooking a wide expanse of low green meadow ending abruptly with a high floodwall that ran along the banks of the Savannah River. This was where the hunt must end, unless the poor fox could manage to scale the six-foot wall.

By then the fox, the hounds, Van Buren Clay-Pickett, and Auntie Mame were so far ahead that there was no hope of ever catching up, although Beau and Sally Cato McDougall were in hot pursuit about a quarter of a mile behind. Suddenly Lightning Rod spurted ahead still faster and gave every appearance of trying to overtake Cousin Van Buren.

"Ah cain't unduhstand that Yankee-style huntin'," one of the men shouted. "Mighty bad fo'm to pass the Mastuh."

"It ain't huh fault," another rider yelled. "That crazy

McDougall hawse is runnin' away with huh, that's what!"

"Gawdlmighty, yo' *right*."

I wanted to shut my eyes tight, but the terrible fascination of the scene before me was too strong. When I opened them again Lightning Rod had not only passed the Master, but the hounds as well, and finally the fox. He was a matter of yards from the six-foot floodwall and still he tore onward.

"Lawd, he's goin' to dash that damnyankee gal to death!"

"Moultrie, Ah cain't look!" the woman next to me screamed, and swooned in her saddle.

With Auntie Mame still hanging on, Lightning Rod charged the floodwall. Suddenly his hoofs left the ground and he leaped for the wall, but it was too much for him. His mammoth chest struck the top and he fell back with a thump that could be heard all over Richmond County. Auntie Mame, however, kept right on going. She cleared the wall by a good four feet and disappeared behind it. There was a terrible splash, and then silence. Another woman swooned but nobody paid any attention. The rest of us raced pell-mell down to the meadow just in time to see Auntie Mame emerge from the Savannah River.

Just then a rickety old Chevrolet bounced across the meadow and jolted to a stop. An apoplectic little man jumped out and jogged up to the cluster of panting horses. It was the county veterinarian. "Great day in the mawnin'," he shouted, "I bin followin' this pore little lady fo' the last half houah. Most amazin' feat of hawsemanship I evah *did* see. Why she wasn't killed I nevah *will* know. Well, I *thought* I reckinized that hawse, an' now Ah'm *positive*. It's that crazy Lightning Rod belongs to Sally Cato McDougall." His angry blue eyes sought out Sally Cato. "Sally Cato," the vet screamed, "Ah *tole* you two yeahs ago that hawse was mad. Ah *commanded* you to have him shot!" He looked at Lightning Rod, sprawled in agony on the ground. "Now Ah guess Ah git to do the job mahself." He pulled a .45 automatic out of his holster. "Sally Cato, it's *you* Ah oughta be shootin'. To let *anybody*—even a soopub hawse-woman like this little lady heah—ride on that hawse is tantymount to muhduh. Yes, Ah said plain, premeditated *muhduh*. You oughta have yo' name read outta every huntin' pack in the who' county." With one shot he put the pathological Lightning Rod out of his misery and Auntie Mame burst into tears.

Uncle Beau swept Auntie Mame up to his saddle and, dirty and wet and scratched as she was, he kept hugging her and kissing her and calling her his Little Yankee Valkyrie.

The rest of the members were agog at the glory of Auntie Mame, and I noticed that they all seemed to find it desirable not to ride anywhere near Sally Cato as we all ambled back to the field where the pavilion was set up for the Hunt Breakfast. Once Sally Cato reined her horse over toward Uncle Beau's. "Beau," she said urgently, "if you'll only let me explain . . ." But he gave her a terrible look and cantered ahead with his arms tenderly around Auntie Mame.

The Hunt Breakfast was sensational. No one could talk of anything but Auntie Mame's magnificent seat. She was christened "Mame, the Huntress," and everyone toasted her time after time as the greatest horsewoman ever to grace Richmond County. Auntie Mame got awfully high on bourbon, but when I finally had a chance to get near her, she held me tight and whispered: "Patrick, darling, tell me, am I still alive? I got my thigh stuck so tight in that sidesaddle thing I thought I never *would* fall off."

Cousin Van Buren Clay-Pickett had leaped to the top of the buffet to propose another hunt on the following Sunday when a Western Union boy shambled in with a telegram for Auntie Mame. It read: IMPERATIVE YOU RE-TURN NEW YORK IMMEDIATELY TO JUDGE INTERNATIONAL HORSE SHOW STOP A DEVOTED FAN INSISTS

THE COMMITTEE

"Oh, dear," Auntie Mame cried petulantly, hastily gulping down a full tumbler of bourbon. "What a bore. But I suppose we must go back North. Onward and upward, always, you know, to new triumphs on the turf."

FIVE

AUNTIE MAME,

LADY OF LETTERS

NOR WAS THE UNFORGETTABLE Character without literary talent. The article points out that she used to write short little pieces about herself and her everyday life just for fun. She'd show them to her friends and maybe once in a while even let the local weekly publish one. These little essays, I understand, were perfect masterpieces. In fact, they were so good that publishers were coming up from New York by the carload pleading for a chance to put some of the old girl's work into print.

Personally, I don't think that's much to brag about when you consider that Auntie Mame had a publisher and an agent and a secretary before she even put a word on paper.

Auntie Mame's literary career was undertaken more in the way of therapy to bring herself out of the terrible depression she felt as a widow. Her nuptial bliss as Mrs. Beauregard Burnside might have lasted forever, if only Uncle Beau had.

Beau was charming, virile, handsome, and rich. He

was also generous to a fault. On their first anniversary, Uncle Beau bought Auntie Mame a number of little keepsakes to celebrate the occasion: a big Rolls-Royce, a sable coat, an uncut emerald ring, and a big old mansion on Washington Square to house all the furniture she'd been buying. But the day of their housewarming—just thirteen months after they were married—Uncle Beau met a poetic end. He was kicked in the head by a horse in Central Park. In an hour he was dead.

Auntie Mame was insane with grief. She wept and fainted all through the funeral and the ensuing winter. Eventually she stopped fainting and just wept. She was interested in nothing—not even the fact that she was the ninth-richest widow in New York—except her considerable sadness. Finally her old chum Vera Charles took pity on her.

Vera had struck gold, matrimonially, in England when she married the Honorable Basil Fitz-Hugh. The Hon. Basil was not only rich, he was literary. He even knew Virginia Woolf. Anyhow, Vera decided that a complete change was what Auntie Mame needed. She packed her off to Europe and kept her there for more than two years while I was shunted by Mr. Babcock between St. Boniface and a sordid summer camp.

But no one can mourn forever, least of all Auntie Mame. Eventually she came home with some stylish widow's weeds, a lot of signed photographs of European authors—all of whom had helped to dry her tears—and a restless yearning for a New Outlet.

I was sixteen and discovered that I'd suddenly shot up to a full six feet. None of my St. Boniface uniforms fitted me, and so I spent the last of my days of summer freedom standing on a tailor's block having all my old slacks and blazers let down enough to spare my public the sight of as much calf and forearm as possible. When the alterations were completed I had less than a week to spend before the chapel bells of St. Boniface would call me back to another year of macaroni and demerits, and I was kind of hoping that Auntie Mame would make an occasion of it and take me to the theater and do some of the other things that were fun. I was wrong.

When I let myself into her big house on Washington Square, I heard a brisk voice say: "*The Ladies' Home Journal* wouldn't print an episode like that in a million years, Mrs. Burnside."

I tiptoed into the living room and saw Auntie Mame sitting there in a severe black suit, a martini in one hand and a big pair of horn-rimmed spectacles in the other. She had a lot of papers on her lap and she was talking to two women I'd never seen before. "Of course it's a natural for Hollywood," she was saying. "I thought it might be right for Claudette or maybe Irene, but now I've decided to play it myself. After all, if *I* can't be myself, who can?"

"Well, Mrs. Burnside, I wouldn't think *too* far into the future," the small redheaded woman said nervously.

"No, Mame," the other woman said. "Elizabeth's right. You really ought to get something down on paper first to show your publishers. Film sales, serial rights—that sort of thing would naturally have to wait."

"Oh, don't worry about *that*, my dears," Auntie Mame sang. "My secretary is upstairs already typing the . . ."

I tiptoed out of the room.

Upstairs I went into what had always been my room. The place, never too neat during my tenancy, was a sight. There were a lot of steel filing cabinets along the walls, two big desks, three telephones, piles of reference books, and papers strewn everywhere. A Dictaphone was squeaking and a harried-looking woman was banging away on a typewriter. I skulked out and went into Auntie Mame's sitting room. It wasn't much better. There were old dance programs, stacks of photographs, back issues of the Buffalo *Evening News* piled on every surface. Here and there were slips of foolscap with notes that said things like "Tell about night-club raid" and "mention Dr. Cornell and Daddy's gout." I lit one of Auntie

Mame's cigarettes and sat down, totally mystified. Then I heard the front door open. Auntie Mame was saying. "Well, ta-ta, my dears. Back to my *écritoire* and the midnight oil that gutters low! I'll call you in the morning, Mary. We old Buffalo girls must stick together, mustn't we? *A bientôt!*" The front door closed and I saw the two women collapse into a taxicab.

In a moment there was a pretty commotion going on in what had been my bedroom. "Well, Agnes, dear," Auntie Mame was saying, "how did it go?"

"Oh, ever so nicely, I'm sure, Mrs. Burnside. I've never been employed in such lovely surroundings before and the work is ever so in-ter-esting. Goodness, when I worked at the Prudential Insurance Company we had nothing to type but long legal forms, and Miss Montgomery, she was the supervisor, was always looking over a girl's shoulder and the class of help they had in the stenographic pool was just awful, and . . ."

"That's nice, Agnes," Auntie Mame interrupted. "And did the cook give you a decent luncheon?"

"Oh, goodness, yes, Mrs. Burnside. We had consommé soup and a gigot of lamb and little *petits pois* peas and . . ."

"How divine, dear. Now, I'll have Ito drive you home."

"Oh, but Mrs. . . ."

"Not another word, Agnes dear, simply cover the typewriter and Ito will *whisk* you to Kew Gardens. Now, put on some lipstick and be off!"

"Goodness, Mrs. Burnside, Mumsie would *die* if I painted."

"Well, be that as it may. You've done a grand day's work. Now go home." Auntie Mame burst into the sitting room and threw her arms around me. "Darling, darling boy! Oh, the feverish excitement of the creative career! I'm driving myself too hard, of course, but I love it."

"What are you talking about?" I said.

"Why, darling, my *book*. What else?"

"What book? Who are all these strange women?"

Just then the young woman I'd seen at the typewriter looked timidly in at the door. "Well, I'll be saying good night, now."

"Oh, Agnes dear, do come in and meet my nephew. I expect you already know about him, since you were working on that chapter this afternoon."

"Goodness, is he the one you found in the basket on your doorstep, Mrs Burnside?" My mouth fell open.

"The very one, dear. Patrick, I want you to meet my secretary, my right hand, my severest critic—my Alice B. Toklas. Miss Gooch—dear Agnes—this is nephew Patrick."

"Very pleased to meet you, I'm sure," Miss Gooch said, bobbing a little curtsy. I was almost too stunned by what I'd just heard to take much notice of Miss Gooch, and as a matter of record, there wasn't much to notice. Miss Gooch was one of those women who could be anywhere between fifteen and fifty and nobody would care. She had colorless hair, colorless skin, and colorless eyes. She wore rimless glasses and an outsized white angora beret. The rest of her costume consisted of a blue knit jumper, a salmon-colored rayon blouse with balloon sleeves, rayon stockings, and orthopedic oxfords.

"How do you do?" I said.

"I just *know* you two are going to be the warmest of friends," Auntie Mame said. "Well, run along, Agnes. *A demain!*"

"Good-by, now," Miss Gooch said and disappeared.

"You know, my little love, that that poor child—she's just nineteen—not only types like an angel and takes shorthand at I-don't-know-how-many thousands of words a minute, but she's also the sole support of an arthritic mother and a crippled sister."

"You don't say," I said. Then I turned and faced her. "What's all this about finding *me* in a basket?"

"Oh, darling, you know we writers must occasionally stretch a point to heighten the dramatic situation. So I just said that you were left in a basket at the door of my cottage."

"I was ten years old and you were living in a little cottage on Beekman Place. Now, what is this thing you're writing? Who were those women? What do you need an Alice B. Toklas *for*?"

"Oh, my little love," Auntie Mame said, stretching out on the chaise longue, "I wanted to keep it as a surprise for you until you saw my name at the very *top* of the best-seller list, but now I may as well confess. I'm writing my memoirs."

"Why?"

"*Why?* Well, I've had a *ve*-ry interesting life, and as Lindsay—that's my publisher—said to me just the other day when Mary Lord Bishop and I were in signing the contract ..."

"Lindsay *who*?"

"Lindsay Woolsey. He wishes to publish my work. Oh, my little love, I can't *tell* you what fate has done for me!"

"What has it done?"

"Well, last week I was going along Madison Avenue and I saw a face that looked ever so familiar, and just as I was saying to myself, 'That looks exactly like Bella Shuttleworth from Delaware Avenue in Buffalo,' this face said to me, 'Aren't you Mame Dennis from Delaware Avenue in Buffalo?' Well, we *threw* our arms around each other like long-lost friends—which indeed we were—and *dashed* into the Plaza for a drink. Well, we got talking about the old days of the Delaware Avenue Irregulars and the jolly rousts we used to have at Miss Rushaway's School out near Soldier's Place and one thing and another—la, those gay old days in Buffalo!— and Bella said Wouldn't it be fun if she were to give a dinner party for the old Buffalo crowd who were here in town. So she did. My, but Bella's put on weight!"

"Go on," I said.

"Well, she gave a very nice dinner. Saddle of mutton.

Tough. And she had Mary Lord Bishop—you saw her here today—who's a very important literary agent, and Lindsay Woolsey and his wife—she was a mousy little thing from around Colonial Circle—and a few others. Bella tried to get Kit Cornell, but *she* had a bad cold and couldn't come, *malheureusement.* Well, it was a *terribly* gay evening, and I suppose I *did* have an awful lot to drink, but I got to telling Lindsay all about what I'd been doing since I left Buffalo and he was ever so amused and all of a sudden he said, 'Mame, why don't you write a book?' And then Mary Lord Bishop said, 'Why, yes, why don't you?' So I simply thought, Well, why the hell *not*? Then we all got to talking about it and the high old times we used to have with the boys in the Saturn club and Lindsay Woolsey said, 'Mame, you could absolutely put Buffalo on the *map!*' And Mary Lord Bishop said that even if it was already on the map, any book I wrote would be terribly unusual and she'd be happy to represent me as an agent. So the three of us put our heads together and decided to call it *Buffalo Gal.* Isn't that cute?"

"Cunning."

"Well, I've only been at it for a couple of days, but you *saw* how enthused Mary and Elizabeth were this afternoon. *My* life in the magazines, the newspapers, as a movie, and translated in God-knows-how-many foreign languages."

"That certainly will be exciting," I said.

"Exciting! Oh, darling, I can hardly *breathe*, I'm so thrilled. Now I must dress."

I could hear Auntie Mame's voice singing "Buffalo Gal, won't you step out tonight, step out tonight," and I knew that she was launched on a new endeavor.

During the last days I spent at home I worked so hard for Auntie Mame's literary career that St. Boniface—prayers and all—began to look pretty good. She kept Miss Gooch and me hopping every minute. She made me go to the Public Library to do historical research, and when I asked her if she remembered President McKinley's assassination during the Buffalo Pan-American Exposition she ordered me out of the room. I was almost happy to return to St. Boniface for another year of school.

During the fall term Auntie Mame wrote almost every day, except now she dictated most of her letters to Agnes Gooch. Each one was a paean of praise to her own literary talents. When Auntie Mame was too busy to write herself, Agnes Gooch took over and wrote abysmal letters about Auntie Mame's career. She also crocheted an ecru dresser scarf for my room at school and sent a box of gritty fudge which sister Edna had cooked.

For all of Auntie Mame's talk about her book, I'd never read a word of *Buffalo Gal*, subtitled *The Personal History of a Modern George Sand*, nor had anyone else. But around November a thick bundle of manuscript arrived. It was one of many copies of the book which the untiring Agnes Gooch had typed. No one could deny that Auntie Mame's was a big book. It ran just shy of nine hundred typewritten pages, but no matter how much you loved her you could never say it was good. Although Auntie Mame was a fascinating talker, knew a lot of interesting people, and had excellent taste in her own reading, her prose style was that of a gifted amateur—a bit too florid, a bit too irresponsible, and often unconsciously funny. She had also been too scrupulous a reporter and told much more than was absolutely necessary about some of her dearest friends. So it didn't take half an eye to see that, rich as she was, she would be a complete pauper after the libel suits started pouring in. All in all, *Buffalo Gal*, while interesting, was a lousy book. I was sitting down to write her a polite but dishonest letter of congratulation when a telegram arrived at St. Boniface. It said:

COME HOME I'M DYING

AUNTIE MAME

When I rushed into the house on Washington Square, Agnes Gooch, white-lipped and more pallid than ever, greeted me at the door. "Goodness, Patrick, I'm so glad you've come. Poor Mrs. Burnside has been calling for you for three days." She looked at me balefully through her glasses and snuffled. "I haven't even been home since Wednesday and my sister Edna has had to do all the housework and Mumsie . . ."

"What's the matter with Auntie Mame?" I demanded.

"Oh, Patrick! Her book—her publisher's rejected it!"

"Is *that* all?"

"Oh, but it's serious. They're up there now—Mr. Woolsey, her publisher, and her agent, Mrs. Bishop. They told me—in the *strictest* confidence—that they want to get her a *ghost* writer. Oh, she's so hurt; and Mumsie and Edna and I thought the book was just *lovely*. So glamorous. The . . . the *ghost* man is coming any minute now. She'll be so glad to have some loved one, like you, at her side in this crisis."

As I ran upstairs I could hear voices in Auntie Mame's bedroom. They were all talking at once, but Auntie Mame's was the loudest of all. ". . . and as for *you*, Mary Lord, what do you mean, my manuscript doesn't ring true?"

"Auntie Mame," I said, "I'm home."

"Darling," she cried from her bed, spreading her arms dramatically with a flutter of scalloped chiffon sleeves. "At last you've come to stand by me while these literary vultures pick at the poor bones of my life's work. Sit by me here on the bed and let me draw from your young strength."

"Now, Mame, don't you think you're overstating the case?" Mary Lord Bishop said logically. Mrs. Bishop was trying to retain her impressive placidity, but it was a losing fight.

"Now, Mame," Mr. Woolsey said, "cursing Mary and me isn't going to get *Buffalo Gal* written properly, or make it any more salable." Mr. Woolsey, who was ordi-

narily both dapper and diplomatic, was beginning to
show signs of strain. "Surely we three *mature* people can
talk this out."

"Oh, yes," Auntie Mame roared, "we can talk. Talk,
talk, talk that's all you and Mary seem to be able to do.
You talked me into writing this book, now you want to
talk me out of it just because it happens to be work of *serious literary consideration.* Well, you can't talk *me* out
of my convictions, Lindsay Woolsey, and neither can
anybody else who was born on Linwood Avenue with the
rest of the Buffalo parvenus!"

"But, Mame," Mr. Woolsey wheedled, "*we haven't* rejected *Buffalo Gal.* We simply feel that you need some
outside help. We still think it's a splendid idea."

"Oh yes, Lindsay," Mrs. Bishop said nervously, "just
short of being *brilliant,* but like so many ama—that is
—*new* writers, Mame needs a little editorial assistance to
guide her over the rough spots. And I feel that if we just
had some experienced writer to put in a word here and
there, do a little judicious cutting . . ."

"Yes," Mr. Woolsey said, "cutting is of the *essence.*"

". . . But, of course, to remain entirely anonymous; just
to be in the background to lend a . . ."

"*So!*" Auntie Mame bellowed, "now I'm to undergo
the final humiliation. Now I'm to have a *ghost* writer—
some unspeakable little hack to twist and distort the
meaning and the ethos of my life."

"Mame," Mrs. Bishop said patiently, "it wouldn't be a
ghost writer. He'd be more of an *editor* . . ."

"A sort of literary *adviser,* wouldn't you say, Mary?"

"*Who?*" Auntie Mame asked viciously.

"Well, Elizabeth and I know of a particularly capable
young man who's done quite a lot of this work and he
could do a perfectly *grand* job of reworking your book.
I saw him the other day and showed him your manuscript
and Mr. O'Bannion thought that your material was captivating."

"He *did?*" Auntie Mame said, coming out of her sulk.

"Yes indeed. He said you had one of the most astonishing capacities for invention he'd ever seen."

"Really?" Auntie Mame said. "What did you say his name was?"

"It's Brian O'Bannion. He's a ..."

"Oh, God deliver me!" Auntie Mame moaned. "I can see him now—one of those beery, loose-mouthed Irish tenors, with a lot of quaint repartee."

"Now, that's not fair, Mame," Mrs. Bishop said stolidly. "As a matter of fact, he's a very good poet. He wrote that volume called *The Wounded Tulip* for ..."

"Probably pansy," Auntie Mame muttered.

"And besides, Mame, he's done a great deal of this work before, he knows the market, and he has a great feeling for ..."

"Well, if you think I'm going to have some moon-eyed, epicene versifier messing up my memoirs with a lot of miserable Irish wit you're just crazy. I'd rather take my book and flush it down the toilet than undergo the ennui and mortification of ..."

Miss Gooch's shapeless shape appeared at the bedroom door. "Mr. O'Bannion is here, Mrs. Burnside." We all looked up, and there stood Brian O'Bannion.

Auntie Mame let out a short, breathless little gasp. From what she had been saying, I'd expected a little, low-comedy Irishman; a sort of funny-paper Jiggs out of Lady Gregory. Instead, Brian O'Bannion was what is known as White Irish. He was about thirty, tall, and very thin. He had white, white skin and hair as black as coal, short and very curly. His eyes were turquoise blue, rimmed with thick black eyelashes, and the second I saw them I thought of a Siamese tomcat. He was got up awfully tweedily in homespun, with big suede patches at the elbows and a dirty trench coat thrown over one shoulder. He shifted his weight gracefully in the doorway and gave Auntie Mame a slow, sad smile displaying a fine set of choppers, while his intense blue eyes reached out—in a manner of speaking—and caressed her.

Auntie Mame swallowed, her hands fidgeted with the bodice of her bed sacque. She smiled charmingly and said, "Do come in, Mr. O'Bannion. We were just talking about you."

Mr. O'Bannion walked—or perhaps a better word would be slunk—into the room, and I thought of a cat stalking some sort of prey. While Mary Lord Bishop was introducing her agency's property around, Auntie Mame snatched feverishly for her compact, took a reassuring glance, and then said graciously: "Do sit down right here where I can see you, Mr. O'Bannion. It's so awfully kind of you—a really renowned *pao*-wet—to lend a hand with my childish little scribblings." He gave her the old hot eye again and she cleared her throat nervously. "Tell me," she said, her smile matching his, "do you think that you and I can ever get anyplace? With the *book*, I mean."

Mr. O'Bannion turned on the soft, sad smile once more and said in his deep, mellifluous voice, "I *know* that you and I are going to create something wonderful."

That afternoon I was sent back to St. Boniface with the report that Auntie Mame was recovering nicely.

I hardly heard a word from Auntie Mame for the next month and when I did, it seemed that the word was always Brian. ". . . Brian and I have just been for a brisk tramp over the moors of Oyster Bay. Like Brian, I always do my best thinking in the crisp, clean out of doors . . ." or ". . . it's past midnight and Brian and I have just been sitting around the fire reading Yeats and watching the smoke curl up from his pipe . . ." or ". . . worked like a beaver today. Being with Brian has given me a new interpretation of my entire girlhood. I can't tell you what it means having a *man* around the place after all these months with that dreary Agnes." Even at a distance I began to get the idea.

Miss Gooch took to writing me on her own hook, too. She kept saying that Auntie Mame's memoirs, in collaboration with Brian, were coming very slowly, but what little had been written was simply enthralling. She was a little less effusive about Auntie Mame, but she had only praise for Mr. O'Bannion. Goodness, she couldn't wait for Christmas holidays, when she and Auntie Mame and dear Mr. O'Bannion and I would all be together to make up a jolly foursome. At what, she didn't say. I had the feeling that I could wait a long time, but Christmas eventually arrived.

"Missy Burnside out with Irishman, but Missy Foureyes upstairs," Ito said as he let me into the house.

Miss Gooch was indeed upstairs, and I found her sobbing over a copy of Brian's book of poems, *The Wounded Tulip*. "What's the matter?" I asked.

"Goodness," she said, dropping *The Wounded Tulip* and stumbling out of her chair, "I didn't think you'd be arriving so early." She sniffled horridly. "Pardon me, please, I seem to of mislaid my hankie."

I gave her my own. "Here," I said "Blow."

"Thank you very much. I hope you'll forgive my silly show of emotion, but Bri—Mr. O'Bannion's—poems are all so be-yuty-ful that I . . ."

I heard the front door close downstairs and Auntie Mame's voice call, "Darling, are you home?"

I could see that a change had come over Auntie Mame as I trotted down the stairs. She'd had her second-best mink coat made into a reversible: Irish homespun on the outside, mink inside. She was wearing a homespun suit, good stout brogues, and a six-foot-long Eton scarf. She reeked of peat bogs.

"What are you got up as?" I said blankly.

"Oh, Brian and I have been out *tramping* the moors, thinking." Brian gave me the glad eye and sad smile. He was wearing gray tweed, the first Tattersall waistcoat I'd seen off the stage, and a Trinity College (Dublin) tie. "Awf'ly glad to see you agayne, Paddy."

"Well, time for tea, darlings," Auntie Mame sang.

Brian slithered off to the bathroom. Then she turned to me and kissed me. "Oh, my little love, it's so good to

have you home for Christmas; to have you here when
Auntie Mame is so busy, so creative, so productive, so
utterly, utterly *happy!*"

I felt kind of embarrassed and I said: "How's the
book?"

"Oh, darling," Auntie Mame said, "I feel that I've
learned so much in these few weeks with Brian. I was the
veriest amateur, who thought that one should *rush* at the
muse. But now I find that writing is truly a deep and exquisite experience."

"How much have you got done?"

"Nearly twenty pages."

"Only twenty *pages*?" I said.

"Really, Patrick," Auntie Mame said, "you know nothing of the true creative process. *Ninety-nine* per cent of
the work is in the thinking, and dear Brian has brought
my brain alive!"

"Oh?"

"Yesss, darling," She lowered her voice. "And, Patrick, I want you to get to know Brian. To know him as
I do—or almost as I do. You *like* him, don't you? And,
darling," she said, kissing the top of my head, "if he
should ever mention age—that is, ask you how old . . .
well, you know, tell him I'm thirty-five and you're
twelve. Isn't he virile?" Auntie Mame whispered, clutching my arm as he came back into the room. The picture
was getting clearer.

Tea that day and dinner following were unusual events,
to say the least. It was interesting and a little horrible to
watch Auntie Mame and Agnes Gooch make such asses
of themselves over Brian. Agnes, her sallow skin, her
lank, lackluster hair, her rimless glasses, her baggy
bouclé knit dress in just the wrong shade of blue, the vulgar exactitude of her speech, was pathetic as the poor,
plain little typist mooning over a handsome man ten
years her senior. While Auntie Mame, the perfection of
her flesh, her beautifully coiffed head, her magnificent
figure, her glowing eyes, her flawless clothes with all the

right jewels, her casual, light-hearted charm, was ludicrous as the rich, elaborate, aging belle mooning over a handsome man ten years her junior.

I didn't see much of Auntie Mame that season, but she was hell-bent that I should see a lot of Brian. She practically threw us together—against my will and, I'm certain, against his. One day she made him take me for a brisk hike in Central Park while she had her hair done. The day was memorable only for its discomfiture, Brian's herringbone tweeds, and the fact that he literally licked his chops when he came across a prettyish nursemaid wheeling a baby carriage near Seventieth Street. Another day Auntie Mame decided that Brian and I should revel in one another's company amidst the medieval splendor of the Cloisters. The afternoon was dismal. My feet hurt, the Cloisters smelled just like the locker room at St. Boniface Academy, and Brian, instead of admiring the delicately painted virgins from obscure Italian convents, was slobbering after two rather garishly touched-up virgins from Hunter College who eluded him—with appreciative giggles—among the sarcophagi of the twelfth century. I got some hint as to Brian's extraordinary appeal, but as women can never understand what men see in their more widely sought-after sisters, neither could I explain what Brian had to offer. Not only did he weigh under a hundred and fifty pounds, but he was also a lecher, a cheat, a liar, and what is still worse, a colossal bore.

The rest of my vacation was passed in the equally uninspiring company of Miss Agnes Gooch, who said three times a day: "Goodness, isn't it amazing how a year goes by! Why, it seems only yesterday that Mumsie and Edna and I were undoing our Christmas things—we always save the ribbons and press them out for next year—and here it is again!"

Christmas was very merry and Auntie Mame outdid herself at being Irish—or at least North of Ireland. Yule logs burned in every fireplace until it got so hot that we had to open all the windows. Brian slunk in, all Glenur-quhart plaid, and Agnes took the subway in from Kew Gardens, after a beautiful Christmas morning with Mumsie and Edna. She was radiant in a dress she'd made herself of a particularly taxing shade of mustard wool with beadwork over the bosom, and she brought gifts of her own manufacture for each of us. She gave me a scarf she'd knitted in St. Boniface Academy colors, and she presented Auntie Mame with a bed jacket of *eau de Nil* angora. For Brian she had worked a pair of carpet slippers in petit point with shamrocks and his initials, and he rewarded her with such a devastating smile that her knees buckled.

Auntie Mame gave Agnes a kiss, a plain white envelope, and a length of green homespun, which, considering the handiwork Agnes had just brought forth, was a terrible mistake.

Auntie Mame gave Brian a kiss, a plain white envelope—thicker than Agnes'—and a beautiful Bentley two-seater which stood low and rakish at the curb outside. He was too stunned even to smile.

She gave me a kiss, a plain white envelope, two of the tweediest jackets ever created, a pair of stout brogues so heavy that I could hardly lift them from the floor, a Tattersall waistcoast, and a box of seven pipes marked "Sunday," "Monday," "Tuesday," "Wednesday," "Thursday," "Friday," and "Saturday." In short, everything I needed, except a Bentley car, to be a junior Brian O'Bannion.

Brian gave each of us an autographed copy of *The Wounded Tulip*. Then we all had a heavy dinner and Auntie Mame said she thought it would be just divine if I were to take Agnes to the Radio City Music Hall to see a rousing good film and that lovely, lovely Christmas pageant of Nativity.

Although I vastly preferred Agnes to Brian, I found her wholesome garrulousness just as tiring as his un-healthy silence. Still, she meant well, which was more

than one could say of him. All the way uptown in the taxi
Agnes jabbered away about goodness, what a sweet, dear
man Brian was, and how she'd just love to take him
home to Mumsie and Edna and put some meat on his
bones; and goodness, what a lovely, lovely Christmas it
had been and didn't I think that a White Christmas was
ever so much healthier because the snow laid all the
germs.

Because it was Christmas I walked Agnes down to the
Algonquin for a drink after the show. Agnes was favor-
ably impressed with the rather fusty stateliness of the Algonquin lounge and she was also pleased to see that the
patrons merely sat about in armchairs and sofas to do
their drinking. "Goodness," she said, "it's so refined.
Just like a lovely home instead of some tavrun." She told
me three times how strict Mumsie was about liquor and
made me promise to buy her some Sen-Sen to munch going home to Kew Gardens. Then she ordered something
called a Pink Whiskers, which made the waiter blanch.

Her drink looked kind of nasty to me, but she sipped
it ostentatiously, still wearing her gloves and with a great
crooking of her little finger, and pronounced it extremely
refreshing. She belched softly and said something mysti-
fying about the Gay White Way and the Four Hundred.

My mind was a thousand miles away, but I was suddenly snapped back to life when Agnes slammed her
empty glass down and shrieked: "Oh, baby, that sets me
on fire! Let's have another!" Then, for some unaccount-
able reason, she added: 'Hotcha!"

The waiter said, "Does your aunt know you're out?"

"Really," I said, "Miss Gooch is my aunt's Alice B.
Toklas."

"Certainly, my good man," Agnes giggled, "don't be
ridic." Then she wrinkled up her nose and added,
"You're cute." I had just strength enough left to order
Agnes another drink.

"I don't know so awfully much about liquor and most
of it tastes like medicine to silly old me, but this girl—

Phyllis—at the Prudential used to tell me about the Pink
Whiskers cocktails her boyfriend ordered for her. He was
in hardware. Anyhoo, the name sounded so cute I just
thought I'd try one."

The second Pink Whiskers arrived and the waiter had
hardly set the glass down before Agnes had emptied it. It
seemed to me that her friend Phyllis should also have
told her that when drinking, it's endurance, not speed,
that counts.

"Goodness, I feel so gay and light and young and
happy I could just *dance!*" Then she said "Hotcha!"
again.

"Agnes," I said quickly, "I don't think the Algonquin
has an orchestra."

"I'm just going to see a man about a dog," Agnes
shrilled. Then she leaned over and bit my ear. "Be a
peacherino and gemme another Pink Whiskers."

I was so shaken by the Jekyll and Hyde transformation
in Miss Gooch that I was only able to tap the bell and ask
for another Pink Whiskers. The waiter looked at me
sternly and said: "If it wasn't fer yer aunt, I wouldn't
serve that dame no more. They're the worst kind, them
schoolteacher ones."

Agnes returned almost sooner than I wanted her to, her
nose now a solid blue-white from a determined applica-
tion of powder. "You're cute," she said as she settled on
the divan.

In a frenzy, I tried to change the subject. "Tell me,
Agnes," I said, "how's the book coming? When do you
think Auntie Mame and Brian'll be finished?"

She took off her glasses and banged them on the table
so hard that I looked down surreptitiously to see if she
had broken them. "Lisssen," she snarled, "if you were
locked in a room with Brian would you be in any hurry
to get out!"

I fought down the impulse to say, "For God's sake,
yes."

She snorted and pulled off her orange tam-o'-shanter,

then she stared up at me long and hard. Her eyes, instead of being colorless, were a deep, glorious gray and they were enormous. Her hair had come a trifle loose, and even with her blue matte-finish nose planted defiantly in the middle of her sallow face, she was—just for a moment—almost beautiful. "Lissenamee, Mrs. Burnside can't take her eyes off of Brian. It's disgusting. It's awful. Why, she's old enough to be his mother . . ."

"Well, I wouldn't say *that*," I began loyally.

"And . . . and oh, I love him so-o-o-o!" Agnes collapsed into noisy sobs, stopping just long enough to say, "Gemme another Prink Whiskeys." Then she tottered back to the powder room.

The trip home was a nightmare. Agnes was all over me, moaning, "Brian, Brian, Brian, I love you, I want you."

"Want I should take yez to a *ho*-tel, buddy?" the driver asked as we reached Fifth Avenue.

"Yes, yes, for God's sake, yes!" Miss Gooch moaned.

"You go where I told you!" I roared at the driver.

Then Agnes got a hammer lock on me and dragged me down to the seat with her. I'd recently been the recipient of a pretty definitive kiss, delivered by a torrid brunette from Miss Walker's, but Agnes' alma mater, the Lillian Rose Dowdey Institute of Applied Business Technique, apparently offered things in its curriculum that made Miss Walker's girls seem dim by comparison. I don't know where, or *if*, Miss Gooch learned to make love, but she certainly had some advanced ideas.

I carried Agnes into Auntie Mame's house and up to the guest room where she slept whenever she stayed in town.

With a good deal of tugging, and with several of her loving stitches giving, I removed the mustard wool dress and dumped her on the bed, unlaced the health oxfords, and took off her glasses. Her hair looked quite pretty when it fell loosely onto the pillow. As a matter of fact,

I'd never noticed before, but Agnes had a damned good figure. She lay there in the lamplight absolutely gassed, but not half bad; then she opened her beautiful eyes and blinked. "Take me," she moaned as I pulled the comforter up over her, "take me, Brian, for God's sake, take me."

I was breakfasting alone the next morning when Agnes crept in. I didn't have to ask her how she felt.

"G-goodness," she said, "I really must apologize for my behavior last evening. I think I must of eaten something that didn't agree with me. Tell me, did I do anything—*say* anything—last night that wasn't, uh, *lady-like*?"

Just to show her that chivalry wasn't quite dead I said, "Believe me, Agnes, you were perfectly fine."

"Oh, I'm so glad." Then she excused herself quickly.

Brian arrived about eleven, and Auntie Mame came bounding down the stairs dressed vaguely like Sherlock Holmes in a hound's-tooth checked suit and a great Inverness cape. "Hoop-la!" she caroled, "off to break in the new car. It's going to be ever so jolly! Patrick, my little love, be an angel and ask Ito if our hamper is ready."

The day was damp and the cold was severe. "Are you going out in that open car on a day like *this*?" I asked.

"But of course, darling! A good brisk tramp over the moors really makes the blood *sing* in one's veins. You know, we Celts are *hardy*!"

Shivering slightly, I watched Auntie Mame and Brian drive off. Then I went upstairs to suggest an ice bag to Miss Gooch.

I was dressing to go to a dance when Auntie Mame and Brian got home. Auntie Mame looked terribly flushed. She didn't seem to have benefited much from her tramp across the moors, and she sat huddled by the fire drinking hot Irish whisky. Her eyes were unnaturally bright, and when I bent down to kiss her good-by her face felt as though it were in flames.

The next day Auntie Mame was confined to her bed with what the doctor described as a cold so bad that it was almost pneumonia.

Poor Auntie Mame was a sight. Her face was swollen to about twice its size. Her eyes ran piteously. Her nose was crimson, and every sentence was punctuated by violent spasms of coughing and sneezing. For two days she lay in bed and moaned while Miss Gooch hovered in attendance.

Brian came to the house every morning, but Auntie Mame refused to let him see her. "I can't let him up here, Agnes," she'd moan, woefully surveying her red nose and sneezing. She sneezed again, took another incredulous look at her reflection, and rolled over in her big gold bed.

Agnes scampered around the house running errands, making phone calls, attending the croup kettle in Auntie Mame's room. Down in the library Brian made a weak stab at writing a bit of *Buffalo Gal,* but most of the time he paced the floor. He reminded me of nothing so much as a stud who'd been locked into a box stall all winter. Meals with Brian and Miss Gooch were a terrible ordeal. Every day she was a little sallower, a little more elegantly kittenish; and every day he fidgeted more and more, until I was on the verge of dosing his soup with saltpeter, like the cook did at St. Boniface.

Auntie Mame was getting better, but the doctor demanded that she stay in bed for at least another week. This put her in a fury, however, since she'd been looking forward to the big New Year's Eve party which her publisher was giving.

"Oh, Patrick, darling," she fumed, "*what* have I done to deserve a fate so cruel? Here I've been planning to go to Lindsay's for months and now I can't. Really, I'm so mad I could just *cry.* It's my *right* to be at Lindsay's. After all, I am one of his authors. Important people from the whole world of letters will be there to meet me, to discuss my book—and where will I be? I'll be right here in bed with my Kleenex and croup kettle. And Brian was looking forward to it so."

"Well, can't Brian go alone?"

"Oh, the poor darling's so shy, he wouldn't have any fun at all without me to guide him around." I wasn't so sure.

"Gee, Auntie Mame, that's too bad," I said, and went downstairs to where Brian was practically pawing a hole through the drawing-room carpet, ignoring Miss Gooch who sat seductively on the sofa, her eyelashes fluttering behind her spectacles.

The day of Lindsay Woolsey's New Year's Eve party arrived to find Auntie Mame still confined to bed.

To make matters even worse, her agent telephoned about lunchtime and said that she certainly hoped Auntie Mame and Brian would be at the party that night because a very important producer from MGM had evinced great interest in *Buffalo Gal* and she simply *knew* that Auntie Mame could charm him into an outright sale—preferably sight unseen.

Auntie Mame wailed: "Oh, Mary, how too ghastly. I *can't*. How really dreadful!"

There was some more spluttering over the phone and then Auntie Mame said: "But, Mary, I *couldn't* send dear Brian alone. In the first place, he's terribly shy, and then the poor lamb is so *innocent*! He has none of my business acumen. He'd be *lost*."

There was some more gabbling and then Auntie Mame said: "No, Mary, that's out of the question. I tell you, I don't *know* any unattached women, at least not the sort of woman I'd trust."

Mrs. Bishop talked some more and then Auntie Mame said: "Mary, the whole problem is insoluble. I just don't know any single woman I could get now at the eleventh hour. You'll simply have to . . ."

I don't know to this day quite what got into me, but seeing poor Agnes sitting on the chaise longue crocheting an antimacassar and looking sad and virtuous, I had a sudden inspiration. "What about Miss Gooch, Auntie Mame?" I asked.

"Don't be facetious," Auntie Mame said. Then she glanced at Agnes. It was the kind of look a nervous mother gives to a nursemaid she's just engaged to handle a problem child—a look of relieved approval. "Just a minute, Mary," Auntie Mame said into the mouthpiece. Then she turned to Agnes. "Agnes, dear, what are your plans for this evening?"

"Oh, goodness, Mrs. Burnside, nothing much I guess. On New Year's Eve Mumsie and Edna and I usually have ginger ale and some of Edna's brownies, then we tune in the radio and hear the New Year being celebrated in one of the big hotels in New York and then an hour later in Chicago and then in Denver and finally at the Cocoanut Grove in California. Why, last year Gary Cooper . . ."

"I have other plans for you *this* year. Hello, Mary, don't worry. My secretary can go *for* me."

"Oh, *goodness*, I simply *couldn't*!" Agnes cried. "The only thing I have to wear is my old peach organdie and I just wouldn't have the time to make anything now and . . ."

"That may be all to the good, Agnes," Auntie Mame said. "I have tons of things you could squeeze into. Mary, victory is ours! Agnes can shepherd Brian around. With a little fixing up Agnes will be adequate. I'm sending them to the theater first, but they'll be there about eleven . . . Happy New Year to you, too. Good-by." She hung up.

"Agnes," Auntie Mame said, fixing her with a beady eye, "put down that tatting and come here. We haven't a second to lose."

"Oh, Mrs. Burnside, I simply couldn't ever . . ."

"Agnes, take off your clothes."

"But, Mrs Burnside, Patrick is . . ."

"Would you ladies like me to leave?" I asked.

"Certainly not. On a project like this, I want all the help I can get. Besides, I need a man's critical eye to guide me when it comes to creating a new Agnes. Don't be such a goose, Agnes, shell out of that serge sack and be quick about it."

Miss Gooch timidly removed her dark blue dress.

"A little broad in the beam, perhaps," Auntie Mame said with the critical tone of a horse trader, "but nothing that a good girdle can't fix. Heavens, Agnes you *do* have a bust. Where on earth have you been keeping it all these months? Now, go to my dressing room and open the third door and we'll see what sort of evening thing will do the most for you."

Miss Gooch trudged virginally across the room in her white slip and her orthopedic shoes and returned with an armload of brilliant evening dresses.

"Put down that red one this instant, Agnes!" Auntie Mame said from the depths of her Kleenex. "You're suppose to dominate *it*. No, dear, that lime green makes you look like a jaundice case. I think we'd better stick to black; nobody ever got into any trouble with it. Here, that one, that good, tight, form-fitting Patou velvet. You have a nice little figure, Agnes—with a bit of trussing here and there—and there's no reason to be ashamed of it. Here, just wriggle into this. Patrick, for God's sake, child, fasten her up the back. Where's your gallantry?"

Even with her plain white slip showing over the top of the black velvet evening dress, Agnes looked pretty good, if you didn't notice her face and her hair. She did have a form.

"Yes," Auntie Mame said authoritatively, lighting a Kool. "That's it. That's the dress. Now take it off and have a bath. Mercy, girl, I do wish we could do something to *wake* up your skin. A good physic would work wonders. However, it's a little late in the day to try anything so drastic. But go into my bathroom and you'll see a jar of Lydia van Rensselaer Skin-Glo. Simply *slather* it over yourself. It may sting for awhile but it's worth the agony. Patrick, go run Agnes a good hot tub and dump in a lot of van Rensselaer Oil of Orchid. And Agnes, for God's sake, shave under your arms. You look like King Kong."

I could hear Agnes whimpering with the pain of the Skin-Glo in the bathroom, but except for yelling "Shut up, Agnes," Auntie Mame paid no attention.

Eventually Agnes emerged, glowing like a red-hot rivet. She'd forgotten her glasses.

"Why, Agnes," Auntie Mame cried delightedly, "you have *lovely* eyes! Just leave those glasses off—*forever*."

"But I can't see anything with my right eye, Mrs. Burnside, and . . ."

"Look out of the left one. Oh, wouldn't I *love* to cut that hair!"

"Oh, Mrs. Burnside, I can *sit* on my hair!"

"What a ridiculous thing for anyone to do. Well, if you won't let me cut it, you won't. But we *could* make it interesting. Come here, dear. *Will* you hold still!"

The project took more than six hours, and Agnes whined and whimpered with every pat of the powder puff, with every tweak of the eyebrow tweezers and every stoke of the mascara brush.

It was nearly eight when the transformation was complete. Agnes stood tall and stately, if a little unsteadily, in Auntie Mame's high-heeled slippers. She kept squinting incredulously into the mirror, and even though she couldn't see her reflection very well, both Auntie Mame and I told her several times that she was a stunner. "Now, Agnes," Auntie Mame said, "you look divine. Really svelte. So when you get there I don't want you to act the ingenue. Try to be *soignée*. Don't tell them you live in Kew Gardens, don't tell them about Mumsie and Edna— sterling women though they undoubtedly are. In fact, talk just as little as possible. Mary Lord Bishop will do the talking, that's what she gets her commission for. You just try to look stylish and intelligent, and every time the MGM man asks you a question about my book—*our* book—you tell him it's simply wonderful and bound to become a classic; which it is. All you really have to do is to look after Brian."

At the mention of Brian's name I felt my stomach drop.

"Auntie Mame," I spluttered, "maybe it would be better if you let Mrs. Bishop handle the movie man alone. After all, New Year's Eve means a lot to Mrs. Gooch and Edna, and you and Brian and I could play records right here and ..."

"Have you taken leave of your senses, child?" Auntie Mame said indulgently. "It's vital to Brian's career *and* mine that he go out among important lit'ry figures. That's what Agnes is for: to take care of Brian when I can't. Besides, this is *your* idea."

"Oh, Mrs. Burnside," Agnes wailed, "I just can't do it. I'm so nervous already I'm about to break out in press-peration."

"Not in *my* evening dress you're not, Agnes Gooch. What you need is a little something to calm your nerves. Patrick, bring up some champagne. It'll do us all good."

My blood ran cold. "Auntie Mame, do you really think we ought to have anything to drink? Agnes ..."

"Well, *you're* certainly becoming frugal of *my* champagne, I must say. Do as I tell you and none of your impudence."

"Oh, Mrs. Burnside, I really don't think I should dr ..."

"Auntie Mame," I cried, "if Agnes doesn't want a drink ..."

"Just pretend it's medicine, Agnes. It will relax you."

Although Auntie Mame was rarely guilty of understatement, she'd really pulled off a classic.

To give poor Miss Gooch her due, she sipped the first glass of champagne as though it were hemlock and said something tiresome about the bubbles tickling her nose.

But my heart sank when Auntie Mame insisted that she drink another.

Just then I heard the doorbell ring, and looking out of the window, I saw Brian's elegant new Bentley.

"Oh, Agnes," Auntie Mame cried girlishly, "let's give Mr. O'Bannion a big surprise. He still thinks I'm going to the party, but Patrick will announce you and *you'll* come sweeping in. Quick, go hide in my dressing room. And here, take a glass of champagne in with you."

I felt I was witnessing the fall of Western civilization.

All men look their best in white tie, but Brian was really something. When he saw Auntie Mame propped up decorously in her gold bed, his Siamese cat eyes glowed with a hunger that made me a little sick.

"But—but the theater ... the party?" he said. "Aren't you ready?"

"Oh, Brian, darling," Auntie Mame pouted, "the doctor won't let me go, so I'm sending a substitute."

"A substitute?" he said. "Who?"

"Oh," Auntie Mame cried, going all over kittenish, "someone you know—a very nice girl. It's Agnes!"

"Not ... not *Agnes*?" The tomcat eyes stopped glowing and he looked like he'd just been stabbed.

"Well," Auntie Mame cooed, "not *precisely* the same Agnes. Patrick, bring on the new Miss Gooch!"

Woodenly, I threw open the dressing-room door and out stepped Agnes. She looked terrific, although her eyes were a little glazed. However, I hadn't seen Brian's—his bright blue stare was really frightening.

"Isn't she lovely, Brian?" Auntie Mame trilled. He just swallowed, and I saw his pointed pink tongue dart over his lips.

"Well, run along, you two. Have a glorious time. Ta-ta, my dears. Have fun!"

Agnes reached the door, turned, and stared blindly back into the room; then she smiled enigmatically and said: "Hotcha!"

After the front door closed, Auntie Mame said, "Well another problem solved. My, but didn't Agnes look *stunning*! I never dreamed she had so *many* possibilities. Poor little mouse. I really did a job on her, didn't I? But really, darling, you know with a girl like Agnes it's just wasted effort."

"What do you mean?" I said.

"Oh, you know. She's sweet, but she has no fire. That girl simply has no sex drive. Well," she said, "here we are, alone together on New Year's Eve. We can just have a pleasant little tête à tête. There's something I want to ask you, anyway. Just stir up the fire and run down for some more champagne and then we'll be just as snug as ..." She sneezed and made an airy gesture with her Kleenex.

"New Year's Eve," she began, with a dreamy expression. "La, the memories! You know, your Uncle Beau and I were married on New Year's Eve—just three years ago tonight." She blew her nose, either from emotion or her head cold. "Didn't we all have a lark when dear Beau was alive, darling?"

"Yes, we certainly did," I said honestly.

"You know, it's been awfully hard for me these last two years—a widow, alone and lonely in the world."

"I know."

"Of course, I have you and this house and more money than I'll ever need, but that isn't quite the same, is it, darling?"

"No," I said. "I really loved Uncle Beau."

"Everyone did. A fine, great specimen of a man. Those big brown eyes and those masses of heavenly red-gold hair on his chest. Well," she sighed, "talking about him won't bring him back, more's the pity. Yet I feel this empty aching void—*here*," she said, indicating a well-rounded breast, "for someone like dear Beau."

I knew what was coming and I hated it.

"You'd like to go to Ireland, wouldn't you, pet?"

"Not particularly."

"Oh, really, darling? All that *green*, the fresh springy turf, the music of her speech, the horse fairs, the Abbey Theatre, witty conversation with A. E. and Synge?"

"They're dead."

"Well, with *other* witty Irish. And wouldn't you like to see that old nurse of yours again—Flora?"

"Norah."

"Well, darling, Brian and I were talking about a summer in Ireland. And we both want you to come—a sort of *family* trip."

"Family?"

"Well, a sort of honeymoon *à trois*."

"You mean you're thinking of marrying *Brian*?"

"Well, *rather*, darling. You know, I've mourned dear Beau for nearly two years, and now I feel I've arrived at the time in life when I need *another* Beau."

"Brian isn't in the least like Beau and you know it."

"Well, darling," she said uncomfortably, "I need someone to look after me, and of course Brian needs looking after, too. He's so shy."

"He's about as shy as Jack the Ripper."

"What do you mean, dear?" she asked tensely.

"Just what I said."

"Patrick, darling, you don't *dislike* Brian, do you?"

"No, I don't dislike him; I *detest* him."

"Oh, that's splendid, I was so afraid . . . You *what*?"

"I said I hate him. He's a cheap phony with the morals of a goat and the worst case of hot pants in New York . . ."

"Why, you . . ."

"He's laid everything but the Atlantic Cable and he'll go right on doing it. He's been mooching off you for months now and you don't even realize that he's not writing a word of your silly old book."

"Now see here, young . . ."

"And it would be just like you to get tied up to some he-whore with the roving eye who's at least ten years younger than you are and who's interested in you for just two things—one of which is money."

"You ... you vile-minded little imp of Satan! How dare you speak about a keen intellect like Brian that way, you ..."

"And what's more, he's the most boring human being I've ever met."

"Get out of my room, you Judas! Get out, get out, get *out*!"

"I'm going, don't worry."

"And never set foot in it again. In fact, I never want to *see* you or *hear* you or *speak* to you again."

A champagne glass shattered against the wall just as I slammed her door.

I was so mad about her throwing the glass that I yanked the door open and yelled: "Just for that I hope you *do* marry him. It'd serve you good and damned right!"

"You get out of here, you slanderous little beast! Brian *loves* me! And I'm going to marry him the minute I can get out of this bed!"

I stamped into my room and bounced into bed.

"Patrick, darling. Wake up. Wake up, dear, I need you." I opened an eye and saw Auntie Mame standing over me.

"Go away," I muttered, "you said you never wanted to speak to me again."

"Darling, this is serious. Agnes ... Brian ... they've never shown up."

"Wh-what time is it, anyway?" I asked, squinting in the lamplight.

"It's nearly six o'clock in the morning."

"Well, for God's sake, it's New Year's Eve. Of course they're not home."

"But, Patrick, dear. They never even *went* to Lindsay's party. I was so worried I called Mary Lord Bishop—got her out of bed and everything—and she said she hadn't laid eyes on them. Oh, darling, I'm so worried. It's that car. I knew it was a mistake to give it to him. He drives like a demon."

All of a sudden I knew what had happened.

"Thank God Agnes is with him. Brian's so quixotic, but Agnes is a good, sensible girl. Oh, if only they haven't been in some awful accident. Now get up and help me."

Auntie Mame started calling all the hospitals in New York, getting more and more frantic with each call, while I sat morosely and tried to keep awake. Then she called Lindsay Woolsey, Mary Lord Bishop—again—and most of the people she knew. By eight in the morning, all of medical and literary New York had been aroused by Auntie Mame. She was at the end of her rope at nine o'clock when the doorbell rang.

Gathering her bed sacque around her, she fluttered down the stairs and opened the door. There was a moment's silence, then I heard her scream, "Oh, my God!"

I raced down the stairs to the hall where she was standing with a yellow telegram in her hand. I took it from her and read:

THE FIRE WITHIN ME WAS TOO STRONG STOP BRIAN AND I
HAVE ELOPED STOP GIVE YOUR UNDERSTANDING YOUR FOR-
GIVENESS AND YOUR BLESSING TO YOUR

LOVING
AGNES GOOCH

Silently Auntie Mame mounted the stairs with me following her. She went to her desk and picked up the manuscript of *Buffalo Gal*. She carried it to the fireplace and dropped it on the grate. Then she removed the bed sacque which Agnes had crocheted and dropped that in, too. The blaze was terrific. Shivering slightly, she got into her bed and motioned me to the slipper chair beside it. She opened the last bottle of champagne, poured two glasses, and handed me one.

"Happy New Year, darling," she said.

Six

Auntie Mame

on a Mission of Mercy

THE LITTLE SPINSTER IN THE *Digest*
also had something of a reputation as a midwife. Well,
not really a midwife, but she'd done such a splendid job
of raising this foundling that other young mothers came
to her—mind you, a woman who'd never even been
married—for advice on having babies and caring for
them. And she was never too busy, the article says, to
drop everything and pitch right in.

I, for one, don't think that's quite fair. In the first
place, I was ten years old and way beyond the diaper-
and-formula stage when Auntie Mame first got her hands
on me. If I'd been any younger, who knows what might
not have happened.

But Auntie Mame was perfectly willing to interrupt
her own life and plow right into somebody else's, and although she'd never had a baby and had never been
around any babies and didn't even *like* babies, she felt
more than competent to see a young girl through maternity.

I thought I'd heard the last of the unfortunate Brian

O'Bannion and the even more unfortunate Agnes Gooch, but I hadn't. A year and a half later my life and my school career were invaded by Agnes in person and Brian at least by proxy. It was my last term at St. Boniface Academy in Apathy, Massachusetts, and I was counting the days until commencement would set me free from that somber institution. But one cool afternoon in spring we were marching—we never walked at St. B's, we marched—from prayers to the playing field when I heard a hissing sound in the bushes. I turned and stared. Everyone else turned and stared, too. It was Ito. His hand flicked out and shoved one of Auntie Mame's big blue envelopes into mine and then he disappeared again into the protective coloration of the forsythia.

When we got to the locker room I darted into the can, slammed the door, and tore open the envelope.

> "Darling, darling boy—
>> Come at once! I need you. I'll be at Ye Olde Greene Shutters Sweete Shoppe, heavily disguised.
>>> Hurry!
>>> Auntie Mame"

I waited until I heard the rest of the class clatter out to the track field, then I raced out of the building, scaled the wall, and made for the tea room via the back alleys of the town.

Ye Olde Greene Shutters was *the* gathering place for the gentlewomen of Apathy, who met there every afternoon to gobble down barrels of tea and butterscotch sauce. It was packed when I got there but I had no trouble spotting Auntie Mame. She was seated in a dim corner wearing a slinky black dress, a big black hat with heavy veiling, dark glasses, and a black broadtail cape. If she'd been naked she couldn't have been more conspicuous among the dowdy silk prints and amber beads around her. I went to her table. "Auntie Mame . . ."

"Oh, my little love," she whispered huskily, "you

came straight to me with a devotion that penetrates all disguises. Couldn't you have got here *earlier*?"

"What's the matter, Auntie Mame?" I asked. "What are you doing in Apathy, and *why* are you disguised?"

"I'm on a mission of mercy, child, and I need your strong young arm, your agile young brain to help me."

"You oughtn'ta be away from the 'cademy, sonny," the waitress said to me, "but what'll it be?"

"A cheeseburger and a chocolate malted," I said.

"He'll have no such thing," Auntie Mame said. "Just bring my check. We're leaving at once."

After a steady diet of watery stews and saltpeter soups at St. Boniface, I was kind of miffed, but too curious to argue. "What is it, Auntie Mame?" I asked. "What's happened?"

She took off her dark glasses and gave me a blazing look. "It's Agnes Gooch. Ah, what you've done to that poor innocent virgin!"

"What *I've* done? I haven't seen old foureyes since . . ."

"Oh, not you in particular," Auntie Mame said irritably, "you in the collective sense—*Men*! Most specifically that vulgar, pretentious, grade-Z poet, Brian O'Bannion. The beast! Misusing poor little Agnes and then casting her out upon the mercies of a cruel and censorious world!"

"Not so fast," I said. "Just what *has* happened?"

"Only the *inevitable*! That cur took poor Agnes to California in the car *I* bought him, seduced her, and then deserted her, leaving her alone, penniless, *and* pregnant." Several women turned and stared.

"No kidding," I said. Then I added: "Not so loud, please."

"Kidding indeed! Do you think I'd leave a busy season in New York to move bag and baggage up to this cultural backwash for a *joke*? Like a wounded animal poor Agnes came to me. I was the only port in a storm. Naturally she couldn't turn to that puritanical family of hers."

My heart stood still. "Wh-what did you say about moving up here b-bag and baggage?" Then a terrible realization dawned. "Where is Agnes *now*?"

"At the Old Coolidge House."

"The—the Old Coolidge House right here in *Apathy*?" My question was totally unnecessary. Naturally Auntie Mame, choosing to do things under the cloak of secrecy, would have selected the only hotel in town which was a shrine of the New England Historical Society, and the meeting place of the D.A.R., Mayflower Descendants, Chamber of Commerce, Rotary Club, Watch and Ward Society, and the Board of the St. Boniface Academy.

"Certainly, right here in Apathy. I've engaged quite a comfortable suite. I had to help poor Agnes have her baby and I had to pick a place where we were unknown."

"Do you mean," I said steadily, "that out of forty-eight states and the District of Columbia you had to select Massachusetts? And that out of a thousand towns in Massachusetts you had to choose the one where *I* am?"

"But naturally, my little love," she said with maddening logic. "I knew you would feel it your duty to stand by poor, hunted Agnes."

"But you've got old Agnes parked right next to the school. The hotel is the place where everybody . . ."

"Of course, darling. I wanted it centrally located. That's why I chose it—so you could be at hand to help me bring a new little life into the world and help me nurture this poor broken blossom back to . . ."

"But, Auntie Mame, I'll get in a hell of a jam. In a few weeks I can be out of this awful dump. But they'll find out just as sure as . . ."

"Nonsense! How could they possibly discover anything? We arrived in darkness last night. I've even gone to the trouble of taking the suite under an assumed name. I've engaged a Boston doctor who is the soul of discretion. It'll only be a matter of weeks until the baby is born, I'll settle some money on Agnes, establish her somewhere, and *then*"—she paused—"I thought that *you* and *I* could take a little trip—Europe, I think—for the *whole* summer. You'd like that, wouldn't you?"

"Europe?" I breathed.

"Yes, love, Europe," she said slyly, "but only on the one condition that you help me get Agnes out of this mess. Is it a *bargain*?"

I knew I was taking a fatal step, but the fleshpots of Paris after the chamber pots of St. Boniface were too strong for me. "Okay," I said grimly.

"Good! Now let's be off to poor Agnes." Auntie Mame paid the check with a fifty-dollar bill. Then she drew the veil about her face and slunk out with such an air of mystery that I could feel every eye boring into our backs.

Her Rolls-Royce was parked outside with all the shades drawn and Ito at the wheel. A crowd of curious onlookers had gathered to admire it and they stared after us, buzzing and scratching their heads as we drove off. Auntie Mame, lolling back and smoking behind the lowered shades, was happily unaware of the figure she was cutting. I wasn't. In the first place there had never been a Rolls or a Jap in Apathy before. In the second, St. Boniface had a spy system in the town that would have put the GPU to shame. When the masters weren't patrolling the school itself, they were doing intelligence work in town. In the distance of three blocks I spotted the English master, the tennis coach, and the chaplain. The chaplain even removed his hat and bowed his head as the big black car passed by with its shades down.

I was so scared of being seen off campus that I didn't pay much attention to Auntie Mame's conversation. It was mostly stuff about the spirituality of motherhood, the mysterious beauty of pregnancy, and the serenity of the waiting period. When I asked her how *she* knew she told me not to be impertinent and said that Agnes was a changed woman.

I was naturally hesitant about going into the Old Coolidge House, but Auntie Mame was getting restive and pushed me into the front door, where I came face to face with the room clerk—a paid informer for St. Boniface. The first thing he did after he saw my school blazer was to ask if I had a pass to be off campus. *That's* the kind of school it was. "Certainly he has!" Auntie Mame snapped, and yanked me up the stairs so fast that he couldn't ask to see it.

Agnes let us into the suite herself and then locked the door. She *was* changed, but I failed to see any mysterious beauty in her condition. First of all, she was enormous. Then, she'd never quite gotten over the brief fling at high style she'd enjoyed on the fateful New Year's Eve when she eloped with Brian. Now she'd mixed the ateliers of Paris with the crochet hook of Kew Gardens so that she looked like a cross between a demimondaine and a string laundry bag. She'd made her maternity wardrobe herself. Agnes had taken to putting on a lot of make-up, too, and she did it very badly. Seeing her groping around without her prim spectacles, garishly dressed and whorishly painted, she looked less like the mysterious beauty Auntie Mame had promised and more like a fallen woman who was paying the customary price for lust and/or incaution.

Nor was there much trace of spirituality or serenity. Always one to feel sorry for herself when she had little cause to do so, Agnes now had a damned good reason and she overflowed with tears of self-pity. She threw her arms around me and wept bitterly, the overload of mascara running in muddy rivulets down her rouged cheeks. Her entire vocabulary seemed to be made up of such terms as Silly Girl, Fool, Wanton, and Woman Wronged. Well, I can't quite put my finger on it, but Agnes was a mess.

While Agnes vilified herself, Auntie Mame removed some of her disguise, fluffed her hair, settled down on the Empire sofa in the parlor, and rang downstairs for refreshments—eggnog for Agnes, tea for me, and cognac for herself. "Blow your nose now, Agnes," Auntie Mame said crisply, "and *do* stop sniffing. You know it upsets me. Well, my little love, you see how easy all this is going to be. Here we are, a snug little family unit, perfectly respectable for all the world to see."

At this Agnes burst into a perfect torrent of tears. "*Do* stop that, Agnes!" Auntie Mame said. "It can't be good for you or the baby. You'll dehydrate yourself or something. As I was saying," she continued to me, "here we are—a mysterious widow, her sister-in-law, and a servant, all registered at the Old Coolidge House until time for the, um, accouchement. Even if the townsfolk *should* notice us—and that's highly improbable—there's nothing to wonder about. We're absolutely self-contained here. We have our meals sent up. The doctor drives up from Boston once a week. I have Ito to take messages to you and to drive us out for little airings. Agnes can take her walk—four full miles a day—every evening after dark. We have nothing to do but wait until her, uh, *time*. You see, with a little money and plenty of cagey planning, it all works out as easily as *that*."

"Well, gee, that's just swell," I said. "But couldn't you have done all this just as well in a hotel suite in, say, Cleveland, or Milwaukee, or Dallas—far more interesting cities, and places where I'm *not*."

"Ah, but you see I *do* need you, my little love."

"But *why*, if you're all this self-contained? What can I possibly do but get myself into a mess at school?"

"You can do four things," Auntie Mame said darkly.

"What . . . are . . . they?" I asked. I didn't like her tone.

"First of all, I shall need you to run errands. There are ever so many things I'll need and I assume there are things an expectant mother might need, too. You know this town. I don't. What's more, it would be dangerous for me to be seen . . ."

"Dangerous for *you* to be seen?" I said. "If *you* went to St. Boniface Academy and got a demerit every time you scratched your ass, you'd know how dangerous it is to be seen in . . ."

"Patrick! Your language! Think of the prenatal influence! Well, that's the *first* thing. The second thing is shopping for me in Boston. The food here is deplorable—good for Agnes, of course, but awful for me. Ito can never be trusted in a strange city, so tomorrow you can take the car and drive into S. S. Pierce and get me a case of . . ."

"I can't drive your car. I don't even have a license."

"But of course you can drive. I taught you myself. And if you drive carefully—as I certainly hope you would—nobody will even *ask* to see your license. I've never had one myself, and look at me."

"Auntie Mame! I want to graduate. They'll kick me out so fast . . ."

"Of course you want to graduate. Education's a wonderful thing. Now, Number Three: I'll need you to make up a fourth at bridge. I'm teaching Culbertson to Agnes. It does her good. Gives her something to think about."

"Something to *think* about?" Agnes moaned.

"Be still, Agnes. Yes. And a very apt little pupil she is, too. Ito plays Sims—and not too badly if he'd only stop giggling, and concentrate. To fill a table, I shall need you." She fitted a cigarette into her holder and drank delicately of her cognac. "But the most important service you can render . . ." She paused.

"Wh-what's that?" I asked suspiciously.

"The most important duty I have in mind for you is to walk Agnes."

"To *what*?"

"Walk Agnes. Four good miles every night after dark. Doctor says she must. She's getting *much* too heavy. Agnes, poor silly, says that her feet hurt too much, but *I* say . . ."

"Your feet would hurt too, if you'd walked all the way from Carmel, California, to . . ." Agnes burst into tears and fled clumsily to her bedroom.

"*Now* see what you've done to her!" Auntie Mame snapped. "Oh, you're all alike! Poor little Agnes! Walked all the way from California alone, and here you refuse to take her for a stroll in the evening."

I said, "Don't you realize that this is just about the craziest thing you've ever tried to do? You've got all the money in the world. You could take Agnes to *any* nursing home and wait there with doctors and nurses to see that everything goes right. But do you do anything sensible? No! You drag her up to this god-forsaken hole right under the noses of the school and Dwight Babcock junior. You know nothing about babies and I know even less, yet you expect me to break out of that prison and wait on you hand and foot: trips to Boston for pâté and truffles; a fourth at bridge; errands; and then walking poor Agnes like a poodle every . . ."

"Paris," Auntie Mame said. "Paris, Rome, London, Vienna, Cannes, Nice, Monte Carlo, Venice . . ."

I stopped my tirade. "B-but Auntie Mame, how can I get away from school? I'm watched like a . . ."

"Nonsense, my little love," she said airily, polishing off her drink. "Anybody can get out if he really *wants* to. Why, I hardly *ever* spent a night in the dormitory at Miss Rushaway's, and at Smith I was out till all hours. I simply took the dressmaking form out of my closet, put it in my bed, and slid down the . . ."

"I don't happen to have a dressmaking form in my closet. I don't even have a *closet*. Only old Junior Babcock spying on me and . . ."

"Naples, Capri, Milan, Firenze—that's Florence, dear—Deauville . . ."

"Listen, Auntie Mame, I can't even get into the hotel without showing a pass. You saw how the clerk . . ."

"I've thought of that, too, Patrick. You see that coiled-up rope with the knots tied in it? No, over there by the window. Well, I discovered that *that* is the system of fire escape used in this provincial hostelry. You have only to whistle at my window and I'll lower it for you so you can climb up. When you're ready to leave . . ."

"But it's three *stories*!"

"Wonderful for the arms and shoulders, darling."

"I've got so many demerits already that the corridor master is . . ."

"Antwerp, Brussels, Ostend, Athens . . ."

"Auntie Mame, I . . ."

"Shall we say tomorrow, darling? Three o'clock, and don't be late. Here, I'll let down the rope for you." She tripped daintily to the window.

I perched gingerly on the sill and looked down. "By the way," I said, "what names are you using here, in case I have to get in touch with you?"

"Oh, *that*," she said. "I'm glad you asked. For myself, I did a very clever thing. I cut my name from Burnside to Burns and used my maiden name as a first name. So I'm Mrs. Dennis Burns."

"And what's Agnes?"

"Agnes? Oh. Oh, yes darling. Well, when I registered I just couldn't think of a name for her, so I wrote down the first thing that came to mind."

"What was that?"

"It was Mrs. Patrick Dennis."

It took me a surprisingly short time to reach the ground.

My next three weeks were hell. I lived like a conspirator at school and like a fugitive away from it. And getting away from St. Boniface was no cinch, either. Not only were there roll calls all day and bed checks all night, but there was a complex faculty spy ring and also something called the Student Patrol—a quasi-official body composed of the most unpopular boys at school, always eager to report the slightest infraction. A year at St. Boniface could prepare anyone for life in a police state.

Junior Babcock was always around, too. We'd been roommates ever since my first day at St. B's, not because we liked one another, but because his father, my trustee, wanted to keep tabs on me. He couldn't have chosen a better informer than his own son. Junior was a toady and a bully and a prig; a coward and a tattletale and a cheat. He was prone to periodic sieges of conjunctivitis and to eternal acne. He smelled like a sour washcloth and he snored. But one thing I've got to say for old Junior is that he was a sound sleeper. It made sneaking out at night a good deal easier.

My services to Auntie Mame worked themselves into something of a routine. I used to duck out every afternoon at three after getting another guy to answer for me at roll call on the track field. Then I'd go down to the hotel, climb the rope at Auntie Mame's suite, and run whatever errands she had. Twice a week I'd drive into Boston to do her heavy shopping. The car attracted about as much attention as a steam calliope, but I'd gone to the precaution of getting myself a disguise—a tweed jacket, a porkpie hat, and a jazzbo tie from Filene's basement—so at least I wouldn't be spotted a mile away in the St. Boniface cap, blazer, and necktie. I added a pair of dark glasses, too. Auntie Mame said I looked too tatty for words and couldn't I have gone to J. Press and bought something smart? But I managed to walk right past the headmaster's wife without her noticing me.

Auntie Mame was right about how easy it was to get out at night. There was a tree outside my window and all I had to do was wait for Junior's asthmatic snore, get my "civilian" clothes from their hiding place, arrange a pillow to look like me in bed, and skedaddle.

The only thing that made me feel kind of bad was Mr. Pugh. He was master for our corridor and he was the only man at St. B's who gave even a faint impression of liking kids or teaching. He was a long, lanky, old-maidish man of about forty with an Adam's apple as big as a duck egg and a passion for poetry and music and art and nature and children. Well, I guess I haven't made him sound very attractive, but he was a hell of a nice guy in a prim sort of way. He was kind and understanding and gentle and quiet and he never gave us demerits except when he absolutely had to. I knew that if they caught me, poor old Pugh would be in hot water too. Still, family loyalty—and a trip to Europe—came first.

Well, at night I'd get down to the old Coolidge House around ten and whistle under the window. That was the signal for Agnes to put on her hiking shoes and take her walk. Agnes was never the best company in the world, even when she just talked about her mother's arthritis and her sister Edna and Kew Gardens and the insurance company. Now she could only discuss how she'd been wronged, how she was branded with the scarlet A, how the innocent little soul beneath her heart—Agnes' term— would bear the bar sinister, how Brian O'Bannion was no gentleman—something of an understatement, I thought— and how her feet hurt. Once or twice I had to drag poor old Agnes into the bushes when I saw masters from the school en route to the local whorehouse or the bar of the hotel, but by and large our walks were noteworthy only for their boredom.

Once back at the hotel, I'd shin up the rope and we'd all play bridge—or *try* to play bridge while Agnes whimpered and Ito giggled and counted much too heavily on the psychic bid. Auntie Mame also kept a well-stocked bar within easy reach of the bridge table—so festive, she said—although she was the only one who drank anything.

I'd be dismissed about two in the morning to let myself down the rope, trudge back to school, scale the wall, climb the tree, and get to bed. As all of St. Boniface Academy rose at six for cold showers and calisthenics, I was existing on a maximum of three hours' sleep a night. More than once I dozed off in classes and got ten demerits and a lecture about Playing the Game. But you can get used to *anything*, and visions of being out of St. B's forever and spending the summer in Europe were like Benzedrine to me.

After a couple of weeks of being away from school more than I was in it, with nothing worse happening than falling asleep over Virgil, I began to see how easy it all was and to regret not having lived a richer, fuller life during my years at St. B's. My luck had held out so well that I even started getting a little careless. On the night I bid and made a grand slam, doubled, redoubled, and vulnerable, it was after four when I got back to school. I was so dog-tired that I didn't even bother to hide my disguise under the mattress, and when I woke up at the six o'clock bell, what should I see but Junior Babcock, in his dirty old flannelette pajamas, squinting down incredulously at my tweed jacket and my jazzbo tie.

"Wh-where'd you get *those*?" he asked.

"Where did I get what?" I asked.

"Those clothes. It's fifty demerits for being improperly dressed. You oughta know that . . ."

With a flick of the hand, I swept Junior's glasses off the night table and tossed them under the bed. "For God's sake, put on your specks, Juny old man," I said. "You're seeing things."

By the time he'd found his glasses, my disguise was back under the mattress and my St. Boniface blazer was in its place. "Gee, Junior," I said, once his pale eyes were focused from behind the thick lenses, "I'm kind of worried about you. You're having visions. Maybe you ought to stop by the infirmary and let the doc look you over."

Junior wasn't very bright, but on the other hand, he was no fool. He gave me kind of a fishy look and went off to his cold shower. I saw then that I'd have to be a little more cautious.

But that night I should have called it quits. It was a beautiful spring evening—all stars and a moon as bright as day and the crickets going hell for leather in the meadows. It was too beautiful a night to be wasting on a girl like Agnes, who was well into her ninth month, but duty was duty. I was trudging grimly up the road, with Agnes holding my arm and waddling along in a garish cerise maternity dress trimmed with a dusty cluster of artificial calla lilies when I heard the unmistakable roar of the headmaster's car.

Everybody in Apathy could recognize the Nashcan a mile away. Dr. Cheevey, the headmaster at St. B's, had bought the Nash in 1926, and he was much too tight to turn it in on a new car or even to invest in a little professional consultation. Instead, he let us work off demerits by washing the car and keeping its motor in tune, so that after ten years of student care, the Nash sounded more like a threshing machine that a car.

Agnes and I were just coming to a bend in the road when I heard the Nashcan coming, and from the racket it was making, it was coming pretty fast. "Sorry, Agnes," I said, "but we've got to get out of sight."

While Agnes whined about her condition, I helped her gallantly down into the ditch. Then I prepared to take the leap myself, just as the headmaster's car was rounding the bend. But somehow I lost my footing and fell headlong down the embankment. I landed on something soft, and there was an awful sound of "Ooooof!" just as the Nashcan roared past.

"Agnes!" I said, terrified. "Are you all right? Have I hurt you?"

"You haven't hurt me at all, Patrick," she whined. "I'm over here by the culvert, and goodness, I've been hurt so much that it wouldn't matter if I lived or died. That Brian, luring me away and . . ."

"Patrick!" a voice gasped. "Patrick *Dennis*!"

I looked beneath me on the ground, and there was Mr. Pugh.

"Mister *Pugh*!" I gasped. Then I added inanely, "What are *you* doing here?"

He was in such a state of shock that he even started to answer. "Why, Patrick, boy, there's a swamp nearby where a certain kind of night blooming . . ." Then he stopped. "And *what*," he said, "are *you* doing here?"

I halfway hoped to bluff it out. What with knocking the wind out of him, scattering his binoculars, his bird log, his *Guide* to the *Wildflowers of New England*, his flashlight, and his thermos of cocoa, and also having caught him where *he* shouldn't have been, I thought I had a fifty-fifty chance. "Gee, Mr. Pugh," I began, "it was such a lovely night and I'm so fond of birds that I hoped maybe I could see a Baltimore oriole, or . . ."

"Oh, Patrick, do help me. I'm so frightened," Agnes whimpered.

Mr. Pugh shot Agnes a look, standing there in the bright moonlight twice as a big as life. Then he looked coldly at me. "And *who* is this?"

"Oh, *that*? Why, that's, uh, just Agnes. Yes, um, she's my aunt's Alice B. Toklas and I was just . . ."

"I," Agnes said clearly, "am Mrs. Patrick Dennis."

Well, I wouldn't want to relive that night again if you *gave* me Europe. Mr. Pugh scrambled out of the ditch and walked Agnes and me back to the hotel in jig time. Agnes kept protesting that she was supposed to walk four miles with me and that we hadn't done more than one and a half. *I* kept protesting that things weren't what they seemed and I pleaded with Agnes to come off it and admit who she really was. But Agnes had been too well coached by Auntie Mame, and she also wouldn't have given her own name away for anything. "My name is Mrs. Patrick Dennis," she kept saying doggedly.

"She isn't, Mr. Pugh," I said. "That isn't her name at all. I'm not married to her. I'm never going to be. I'm not married to anybody. I just happened to . . ."

He gave me a devastating look as Agnes skittered into the hotel and then he took me firmly by the arm and led me back to school. I spent most of the rest of the night in his room trying to make him believe me. I'll admit that the true story, told word for word, wasn't a very plausible one, but by five in the morning, if Mr. Pugh hadn't entirely revised his opinion that I was a no-good despoiler of innocent virgins, he at least had given up trying to shake my testimony. He gave me some cocoa from his thermos, said he wouldn't say anything about it *yet*, and saw me to my room.

I felt like a zombie in school the next day, but at three

I was raring to get into town and have a little council of war with Auntie Mame. The last class of the day was English Poetry of the XIX Century, which Mr. Pugh taught. The bell had just rung, releasing us to the playing fields of St. Boniface, when Mr. Pugh asked me to stay after class.

"Now, young man," Mr. Pugh said, "you and I are going into town to see this mysterious relative of yours, as well as the unfortunate young woman who may or may not be your wife and the mother of your child."

"But, Mr. Pugh . . ." I began desperately.

"Come," he said firmly.

Auntie Mame was a very dynamic woman. Everybody said so. She could be charm itself, and there was almost no occasion to which she felt unable to rise. But she did like to have a little preparation and time to throw herself wholeheartedly into whatever role she was planning to play. Knowing this, I wanted to warn her of what was coming. On the way down the road I even said, "Suppose I stop in here at the hash wagon and call my aunt, Mr. Pugh. She can order tea or something for us."

"That won't be necessary, Patrick. Our interview will be a very short one. I have papers to mark this afternoon, and *you* shouldn't be eating between meals."

I hoped ardently that Auntie Mame and Agnes would be out motoring, but the big car was parked in front of the Old Coolidge House. Auntie Mame's windows were open and I could hear her portable gramophone playing more advanced music by Paul Hindemith.

"I'm not allowed into the hotel without a pass, Mr. Pugh," I said desperately. "My aunt's in room 3-A-B-C and D. I'll go up the rope and . . ."

"Nonsense, Patrick. You can go anywhere as long as you're accompanied by a master. Come."

By the time we'd reached the top floor, Auntie Mame had wearied of Hindemith's "Symphonic Metamorphosis" and was playing Bessie Smith's "Empty Bed Blues."

I tapped timidly at the door. "Yes!" she called. I opened it and stepped in.

"Darling . . ." she called. Then, seeing Mr. Pugh, the words died.

Auntie Mame was not exactly prepared to play the role of my respectable guardian. She was wearing shorts, a halter, and a lot of Lydia van Rensselaer Essence of Youth. Her hair was tied up in a red ribbon, and she was on the floor doing something which looked obscene but was really only an exercise to firm the seat and thighs. There was a half-finished bottle of champagne at her side and the room was littered with yellow-backed French novels, a lot of fashion magazines, and six volumes of Gibbon. But even an aunt who looked "fast" was better than none at the moment.

"Auntie Mame," I said, "this is . . ."

"How dare you come to my room, sir?" Auntie Mame said coldly, staring straight through me. "I must ask you to leave at once or I'll be forced to call the management."

Mr. Pugh spoke up. "Do you mean to say, um, madam, that this young man is not your nephew?"

"I never saw him before in my life," she said.

"Auntie Mame," I said desperately, "you've got to explain to Mr. Pugh about Agnes. I'll get kicked out of school. He knows. He . . ."

"Please to leave immediately, young man. You're obviously suffering under the delusion that we have met before. *Au contraire*, I am a lone widow, residing here with my sister-in-law and a body servant." Once Auntie Mame got her teeth into a part she played it to the hilt.

"Mr. Pugh," I said, "she *is* my Aunt Mame. She's Mrs. Beauregard Burnside. Really she is."

"This poor lad is desperately in need of psychiatric help," Auntie Mame said, getting up off the floor and commanding as much dignity as possible under the circumstances. "I am Mrs. Dennis Burns and my first name is Arabella . . ."

At that point Agnes, who'd been listening at the door, burst into the room, sopping with tears. "It's true, Mrs. Burnside. Patrick has been discovered. Now all the world will know me as a wanton woman."

Auntie Mame more or less had to give up. She told Mr. Pugh to sit down, poured him a glass of champagne, and retired to slip into a demure black sheer. In about an hour, with only a few embellishments, Auntie Mame gave him the whole story, while Agnes sobbed drearily into a crumpled hankie and kept moaning about her downfall.

Almost against his will and quite against his better judgment, poor old Mr. Pugh was dragged into the conspiracy just to help me keep out of trouble if I was ever discovered. He took to tiptoeing into my room after bed check every night and escaping with me out of the window while Junior snored. Then he'd walk Agnes with me, go back to the hotel and have a drink—or two at the most—and play a couple of rubbers of bridge. Then we'd sneak back to school. He wasn't supposed to be out at night either. It even got to be quite a lot of fun with Mr. Pugh along. He recited poetry to Agnes, who *was* kind of a pushover for poets, and cheered her up somewhat by telling her how Leonardo da Vinci and Alexander Hamilton and Lucrezia Borgia and several other famous people had all been illegitimate.

My classwork was beginning to suffer from lack of sleep and study, and one night Mr. Pugh even insisted on taking Agnes out alone and making me stay in Auntie Mame's parlor to bone up for a history exam. I didn't get much work done. Auntie Mame had sent me to Boston that afternoon to buy a lot of new Bartok records, and she insisted on playing them at full volume.

"Ah, my little love," she said, pouring herself a drink, "a quiet evening at home, *à deux*, and a chance to have a little chat and listen to some really exciting modern masters. Of course, music therapy *is* important to the expectant mother, if only for the strong prenatal influences, but I do get a bit weary of Glazunov and Meyerbeer—pretty as they are."

"Yes, Auntie Mame," I said. I yawned and started in again on Prime Minister Disraeli and Queen Victoria.

"And speaking of pretty, darling, didn't you notice how nice Agnes looked tonight?"

"Um," I said. I hadn't, but I had seen that she was wearing a kind of plain dark-blue maternity dress instead of one of her girl-gone-wrong outfits. She also hadn't seemed quite so painted. I turned to Disraeli.

"I also made Agnes up tonight," Auntie Mame twittered, turning up the phonograph and running her fingers through my hair. "I said, 'Agnes, cosmetics are to enhance, not to detract.' Would you like to hear some Bloch, my little love?"

"No, thank you." Disraeli and Victoria and Gladstone and Beaconsfield were swimming in the Suez Canal with Napoleon and Wellington and Antony and Cleopatra.

"You know, *I* think that our Agnes rather likes Mr. Pugh, and that Mr. Pugh rather likes our *Agnes*."

"Um-hm," I said, trying fruitlessly to concentrate.

The conversation ended as we heard Agnes clumping heavily up the stairs. She was laughing for the first time since she'd been in Apathy. "Oh, Mr. Pugh," she said, "nobody has ever recited Gray's *Allergy* and made it sound so beauty-ful."

St. Boniface Academy was pretty old, as American schools went, and they were great ones for tradition. They used quite a lot of British terms such as Old Boy, New Boy, Proctor, Digs, Tuck Shop, Playing Field, Master, Refectory, Greensward, and Common Room. There were traditional rites, too, like Ninth Class Pillow Fight, New Boys' Indoctrination, Court of Confession, and Demerit Day—all of which were mislabeled as festivities and all of which reflected Dr. Cheevey's considerable sadism. But one of the more tiresome festivals was Father and Son Day, a fairly new tradition that was celebrated at the beginning of May. It was the occasion for fathers who were Old Boys to stretch their St. B. blazers over their paunches and patronize fathers who *hadn't* gone to St. B. and were consequently better dressed and better educated, albeit *déclassé*. Oh, it was a lark, Father and Son Day! There was a Maypole, and gymnastic feats, and relay races, and morris dancing by six unfortunate little boys from the lower school, and a medley of rousing St. B. songs sung by the fathers who were Old Boys while the fathers who weren't stood sheepishly around looking as though they'd sell their souls for a drink.

Well, Father and Son Day made me almost grateful to be an orphan, but do you think I could get anybody to believe it? Not many of the kids in my class had had the same two parents all the way through, and one guy had had five different fathers and was expecting a sixth in time for commencement. But I was the only one who didn't have any father at all. However, there was always Mr. Babcock who, with an eye to keeping my account in the Trust Company, took me over with Junior on Father and Son Day. His dreaded invitation was delivered by Junior a week beforehand.

"I got a letter from Daddy," Junior said early one morning.

"Really?" I said and yawned.

"He says since you haven't got any father will you be his guest *again* on Father and Son Day."

I couldn't very well express my true sentiments, so I said, "Charmed."

"Mummy's coming up, too," Junior said.

"In male attire?" I asked.

"No, she wants to see me."

I couldn't think why.

"Daddy says that you're to get them rooms at the Old Coolidge House."

My heart stood still. "At the Old *Coolidge* House?" I breathed. Then I started thinking fast. "Gee, Junior, why do they want to waste all that money? Why don't they just come up for the day and drive back? You know how your father is about saving dough."

"No," Junior said, referring again to his father's letter. "Daddy says that the Board of Directors are going to meet that night and it'll be too late to drive back to Scarsdale. He says reserve two rooms and do it before the hotel is all booked up so ..."

"Golly, Junior," I said, "what do they want to stay in a crummy old flea bag like the Coolidge House for? Why don't they stay at The Longfellow Inn or Mrs. Abbot's or over in Marblehead or maybe in Boston at the ..."

"No," Junior said stolidly, "Daddy wants to stay at the Old Coolidge House. He *likes* the Old Coolidge House."

"Why?" I snarled. "Did he take some blonde there?"

"It seems to me," Junior said, "that when Daddy takes pity on you on Father and Son Day, the least you could do is ... Say, what's the matter with you lately, anyways? You're always tired and I never see you at gym and you've got terrible circles under your eyes. You're not *doing* anything at night are you?"

I gulped. "Well, gosh, Junior ..." Then I saw what he meant. "Yeah, sure I am, Junior. Six or seven times a night. It'll drive me crazy and no nice girl will marry me and all my kids will be idiots. Be sure to tell your old man that for me next time you write." I snatched up my towel and stalked off to the showers.

When she heard that the Babcocks were coming to the same hotel for Father and Son Day, Auntie Mame couldn't have been more co-operative about making herself—*and* Agnes—scarce. Since none of her encounters with Mr. Babcock could be even remotely described as pleasant, Auntie Mame was anxious to avoid another, particularly under the present circumstances. Straightaway she started making plans for an elaborate all-day outing, which would start at six in the morning of Father and Son Day and last until well after dark. She sent me into Boston to buy several yards of thick veiling, folding chairs, and a sunshade. She begged Mr. Pugh to go with them, but since he had to be on hand for Father and Son Day, he refused. "And if it *rains*," Auntie Mame said dramatically, "we'll just sit in the car. No sacrifice is too great for me to make for you, my little love."

Poor Agnes was more querulous than ever. She had a tendency to car sickness, she was the size of a rain barrel, and the Boston obstetrician had told her that any time now . . . But Auntie Mame was firm about having all traces of herself, her car, and her entourage out of sight of the Babcocks.

The night before Father and Son Day Auntie Mame's suite was in an uproar of packing for the outing. She put in six calls to the kitchen to make sure her hampers would be ready by dawn, and she telephoned the desk three times, first to ask to be awakened at six o'clock, then at five, then four-thirty. Auntie Mame was reluctant even to let Agnes go out for her four-mile stint, but Agnes and Mr. Pugh seemed anxious to go and so I stayed behind to see that the books and records and sun lotion and dark glasses and the other effects necessary to one of Auntie Mame's outings were assembled. By midnight Auntie Mame was already in her nightgown and robe and she shooed Mr. Pugh and me out without so much as a single hand of bridge. I went down the rope as usual and had to wait a long time in the bushes before Mr. Pugh came out of the Old Coolidge House.

The weather was fair on Father and Son Day—too good for it, if you ask me. I was on edge from the minute the morning bell rang, but during calisthenics out on the greensward I saw the Rolls streak down the road with two shrouded figures in back and I began to relax.

By ten o'clock the fathers had arrived. Mr. Babcock looked especially ridiculous in his old blazer and white flannels. I was rather pleased when he fell flat during the sack race and he was rather displeased when I won the rope-climbing contest hands down. Junior didn't win anything, but then, he never did.

Somehow the day dragged on through songs and

speeches and sermons and stunts. It was almost eight when we sang

> "Hail to thee
> St. Boniface
> We'll e'er to thee be true
> To honor and to reverence
> Thy colors crimson and blue."

Mr. Pugh had told me confidentially that these were lousy lyrics, but Mr. Babcock was all choked up. He finally conquered his emotions long enough to load us into his LaSalle and head for the town.

"A beautiful, beautiful occasion," Mr. Babcock kept saying. Then in a more wordly tone he said, "Well, off to the Old Coolidge House for dinner."

I caught my breath, then I said: "Gee, Mr. Babcock, maybe you'd rather take us to the hash wagon. It's much more reasonable."

"No indeed, Patrick. I say hang the expense on a beautiful occasion like this. Besides, Eunice—Mrs. Babcock, that is—is waiting for us at the hotel."

Eunice was indeed waiting, and a little impatiently, in the lobby. The place was jammed with St. B. fathers and sons and the velvet rope was stretched across the dining-room door. I was in a frenzy. It was already dark outside and Auntie Mame could be expected back at any moment. "Golly, Mr. Babcock, it's so crowded, and maybe Mrs. Babcock is hungry. Shouldn't we try Ye Olde Greene Shutters Sweete Shoppe?" Mrs. Babcock gave me a wan smile, but Mr. Babcock was firm.

"No, Patrick. We'll just wait here. Besides, I have to go up to the Board Meeting in the Miles Standish Room right after dinner." So we waited.

Finally, by being needlessly unpleasant to the hostess, Mr. Babcock secured a table right in front of the door. I noticed a lot of jollier fathers treating their boys to steak and even wine. Not Mr. Babcock. He ordered four vegetable plates with poached egg and Sanka all around. Then he proceeded to take me to task for having so many demerits and for letting my grades slip during the last few weeks. I refrained from remarking that Junior had never got more than a C in anything except Deportment and Espionage and took the old boor's diatribe manfully.

Over the tapioca, Mrs. Babcock asked how Auntie Mame was. Mr. Babcock shuddered. Auntie Mame was a sore subject with him. "Well, I haven't seen her since Christmas, Mrs. Babcock," I began suavely, "but . . ."

There was a crash out in front. I heard a shrill voice say: "Ito, you've hit that brand-new Cadillac!"

"No Caddy-lac, missy, that LaSalle car."

"But I *do* feel funny," Agnes' voice rang out. "I don't care what you say, Mrs. Burnside . . ."

The color left my face, then I mustered my full forces just as I heard Agnes' heavy footfall on the steps. "Yes, Mrs. Babcock," I shouted, "I haven't seen Auntie Mame since Christmas. She's away. A good long way away. In *Europe*!"

"Not so loud, Patrick," Mr. Babcock said.

"Don't be *ridiculous*, Agnes," Auntie Mame called from the darkness outside. "You're just imagining all this. By *my* calculations you're not due until Tuesday." I heard the screen door slam and I caught a glimpse of Auntie Mame done up like a spy for the Austro-Hungarian Empire—all in black with veiling streaming out behind her.

"But, Mrs. Bur . . ."

Mr. Babcock went pale and half rose from the table, clutching his napkin so hard that his knuckles turned white. "I could swear I'd heard that . . ."

In a flash I overturned the pot of Sanka onto his lap. There was a yelp of rage and pain just as Auntie Mame took a look into the dining room and went skittering up the stairs three at a time, dragging poor Agnes behind her.

Well, Mr. Babcock gave me holy hell. He said I was a

rude, insolent, thoughtless, stupid, inconsiderate young pup, but with the upbringing I'd had, what could one expect. Then he said he'd deduct the price of a new pair of trousers out of my trust fund. As far as I was concerned, he could have a whole wardrobe just as long as he got out of Apathy without discovering who else was in the same hotel. He was even madder when he saw that a fender had been crushed on his brand-new car and I thanked God that there was no sign of Ito and Auntie Mame's Rolls-Royce. Mr. Babcock drove Junior and me back to the school in a speechless rage. He snarled when I thanked him for a charming day, and then drove back to the hotel for his Board Meeting. Right after Mr. Babcock took off, Junior and I heard the terrible roar of Dr. Cheevey's old car.

"There goes the Nashcan," I quipped gaily. "I guess old Cheevey's going into town to get his ashes hauled after so much sweetness and light."

"He's going to the Board Meeting at the hotel, same as Daddy is," Junior said righteously. "Can't you ever think of anything but sex?"

"Not recently," I said.

After the heady excitement of Father and Son Day, the Dormitory was bustling with boys, and poor old Mr. Pugh was trying, in his calm, collected way, to get them into their rooms and their beds. He shot me a harried look of inquiry and I sent one back that said all was not *quite* lost. Then the telephone in his own room started ringing and he dashed off to answer it.

Figuring that Agnes had had more than her share of fresh air for the day, I started undressing wearily when Mr. Pugh burst into the room. "Junior Babcock," he said breathlessly, "go brush your teeth."

"But I already have, Mr. Pugh," Junior said petulantly.

"Well, brush them again. They look awful. Now march!"

As soon as Junior was gone, Mr. Pugh grabbed me by

both arms. "Quick," he shouted, "get into your clothes. We've got to get to the hotel."

"Hotel? I can't go *near* the hotel tonight. Mr. Babcock's there. Old Cheevey's there. The whole damned Board is there. Do you want me to get canned the last month of ..."

"Hurry and do as I say. It's poor little Agnes—Miss Gooch, I mean. Your aunt just called. There's something wrong and your aunt can't reach the doctor. Hurry, for God's sake, hurry!" He grabbed my hand and we raced pell-mell down the corridor. As we passed the light box, Mr. Pugh pulled the switch, throwing the place into blackness. "Lights out!" he yelled. He clutched my hand even harder and we tore down the dark hall. Ahead of me there was the squeak of the bathroom door and in the shaft of light from the lavatories I saw vaguely that Junior was feeling his way back from the can. But it was too late to do anything about it. We collided in the dark, and I heard Junior land on the linoleum with a splat. "Can't you watch where you're going, Babcock?" Mr. Pugh shouted testily. But if Junior ever answered, I didn't hear it. By then we were out of the dorm and running toward town.

Mr. Pugh looked like an ostrich and he ran like one. We got to the Old Coolidge House in no time flat and I stopped. "Come on," he shouted, heading for the front door.

"Not me," I said. "Not on your life. The whole Board's in there. You'd better come up the rope with me. You shouldn't be here either."

"Don't be silly. They won't see us. This is important."

"So is graduating. You take the stairs, I'll take the rope."

He shot into the front door and out of sight. I raced around to the back of the hotel and began to whistle. I needn't have. The rope was already hanging out of Auntie Mame's window. Panting, I started to climb it. I guess I was more winded than I thought because by the time I was halfway up I had to stop for breath. There was a piercing scream right in front of me. Then the lights went on and I was hanging there face to face with Mrs. Babcock, clad only in a cotton nightgown and her curlers.

"Eeeeeeeeeeeeeee!" she screamed. "Help! Dwight! Dwight! A thief!"

I let go of the rope and fell with a plunk in the shrubbery below. Lights were flashing on all over the Old Coolidge House. I made for the front door just as the desk clerk came charging out. Then I turned on my heels, ran around the hotel, and into the back. I went through the kitchen with a crash of crockery and streaked up the back stairs. I could hear all kinds of voices now, but none louder than Mrs. Babcock's. Running through the second-floor hall, I saw a door flung open and about twenty old men pouring out in St. Boniface blazers. "There he goes!" someone shouted. I recognized the voice as Mr. Babcock's, but I didn't stop to chat. Instead I pounded up the last flight of stairs and into Auntie Mames' room.

"Darling boy! You've come at last" Auntie Mame cried, latching the door behind me.

"How's old Agnes?" I panted.

"Not well, darling, but I've finally got the doctor on the telephone. He's on his way now."

There was a terrible commotion outside in the hall. "He went in there," a voice shouted. "Break down the door!" There was a heaving and thumping. Spellbound, I watched the old door giving. Its antique hardware couldn't hold out for long, and with an earsplitting crash, the door burst in, followed by the twenty old men in the St. Boniface blazers, the desk clerk, and Mrs. Babcock. And once they'd crashed through the door, they kept right on going, knocking down the bridge table and Auntie Mame's bar. Mrs. Babcock, who had had no part in breaking down the door, was the only one on her feet, but she managed to lurch into the gramophone, which began to play "Empty Bed Blues."

"My God!" Auntie Mame gasped, *"chorus boys!"*

I'll admit that the Board, all dressed in red and blue blazers and white flannel trousers and sprawled out among the cards and liquor bottles, did look a little like some badly neglected and long mislaid road company of *Floradora*. I snickered in spite of myself. But it was no time for comedy.

"There he is!" Mrs. Babcock screamed. "That's the one! I'd recognized that bow tie, those dark glasses anywhere!"

"But, Mrs. Babcock," I said, "I was only . . ."

"My God," a voice said, "it's that Dennis brat. It's him and that shameless aunt of his." Picking himself out of the melee of arms and legs, Mr. Babcock advanced menacingly toward me. "So! You haven't seen that sorceress since *Christmas*, eh? In *Europe*, is she? Well, I'll tell you where I wish both of you were and that's . . ."

"Dennis! What's the meaning of this?" It was Dr. Cheevey, his black eyes looking smaller and meaner than ever. "What are you doing out of school at this hour? Where's you pass?"

"I haven't one, sir," I whispered.

"What does the poor child need with a pass when *I'm* here, his legal guardian, to see to his well-being?" Auntie Mame asked with as much innocence as she could muster. "After all, isn't it Mother's Day or something?"

"Pipe down, *please*," I muttered.

"You're a disgrace to the uniform, Dennis," Dr. Cheevey snapped.

"Nonsense! The boy's not even wearing one," Auntie Mame said loyally.

"That's fifty demerits right there!" Dr. Cheevey said.

"And trying to rob me," Mrs. Babcock cried. "I had my opal brooch right out on the . . ."

"You little scoundrel!" Mr. Babcock said, coming closer to me.

"Lay one hand on this blameless child and I'll snatch you baldheaded," Auntie Mame said, standing between us. Then she amended her statement: "*Balder*-headed, that is." She was at her best as the mother tigress.

Then Dr. Cheevey got into the act again. "Out of school after hours and without a pass. Improperly dressed. Trying to steal. Any one of those things is grounds for immediate dismissal. Why, I . . ."

He was interrupted by a sharp cry of pain from the next room. "Mrs. Burnside, I . . ." It was Agnes. I knew little of obstetrics then, but what was about to happen to her was obvious—even to me.

"Good God," Dr. Cheevey moaned, "who are *you*?"

"*I*," Agnes said with simple grandeur, "am Mrs. Patrick Dennis."

"Jesus," Mr. Babcock whispered.

"A St. Boniface boy married . . . and practically a father?" one of the Board breathed. "That's awful, isn't there some rule against . . ."

"I don't believe there *is*," Dr. Cheevey said stupidly. "The case is without precedent."

"Listen," I cried, "I'm *not* married to Agnes. We're not even going steady. She just tells everybody . . ."

"Oh, Christ," Mr. Babcock said, "now he's gone and got some girl . . ."

"Think," Dr. Cheevey began portentously. "*Think* of the school's reputation!"

"Think of *mine*!" Agnes wailed.

"Stop all this at once," a voice shouted. Mr. Pugh stood like an avenging angel at Agnes' side. "Patrick is innocent. I'm the one who dragged him out here. And this young woman—this paragon of sullied virtue—isn't his wife. She is *my* wife—or will be very shortly."

"Ernest!" Agnes cried, and threw her arms around him. Then she doubled up with another seizure.

"Pugh, you're finished at St. Boniface!" Dr. Cheevey roared. "You . . ."

"Well, here I am. Never let the stork beat me yet," a

cheery voice called from the door. "*Say*, we'd better get going. It looks like nip and tuck as to whether we'll make it to the hospital, Mrs. Dennis."

"Miss Gooch, please, doctor," I said.

"Mrs. Pugh, *if* you please," Mr. Pugh said.

"Sorry, gentlemen," the doctor went on briskly, "but I'm afraid you'll have to clear the way. I've got to get this little lady out of here. My car's right at the door."

"Wait, I'm coming with you," Mr. Pugh said, grabbing up Agnes' satchel. The three of them hurried out, and all I heard of Agnes was a cry of pain.

"Well, young man," Dr. Cheevey began.

"Patrick!" Auntie Mame said suddenly. "Poor little Agnes! I can't let her have her baby all alone—not after all I've been through with her. We must *follow* them!" She grabbed her purse with one hand and me with the other and whisked me out to the hall and down the stairs.

"Stop that brat!" Mr. Babcock yelled.

"Dennis! I command you to . . ." I didn't hear the rest of Dr. Cheevey's message.

"Wh-where's your car?" I breathed as we reached the street.

"Ito's hidden it in Boston. It doesn't matter. Here, I'll borrow this old wreck."

Before I knew what had happened, I was in the front seat of a totally strange car with Auntie Mame bent over the steering wheel. There was thunderous roar and the jalopy leaped forward.

"Huzzah! We're off!" Auntie Mame cried.

"Jesus! Of all the cars in Apathy, you had to steal the Nashcan!"

Well, to make a long story short, Agnes gave birth to a fine girl whom she christened Mame Patrick Dennis Burnside Pugh. Mr. Pugh married her in the hospital just as soon as he could arrange the license. He was fired, of course, but Auntie Mame got him a much better job in a much better school. He's headmaster there now and said to be very happy.

With a rap of second-story work and a getaway in a hot car, I didn't see much point in returning to St. Boniface. Neither did Auntie Mame. From her stateroom on the *Normandie* she wrote an ingenious little letter to Dr. Cheevey, telling him where his car was, and enclosed a large check for a new library if they'd promise not to put her name on it—a clause which must have delighted the Board of St. B.

I don't know whether I ever graduated or not. I'd already passed my college board exams so it didn't much matter. But since I'm still being asked for contributions to the St. Boniface alumni fund, I guess maybe I did.

SEVEN

AUNTIE MAME

IN THE IVY LEAGUE

ACCORDING TO THE *DIGEST*, THE Unforgettable Character was a great one for education. She'd never had much learning herself—that seems remarkable, doesn't it?—and she was determined that her orphan boy was going to have a college education. In fact, the Unforgettable one was so enthusiastic about higher learning that she threw herself right into the swing of things on campus, just so she could share his school interest with him and see that his life at college went smoothly.

Now do you really think that's so great? Auntie Mame did more than that—much more—and she'd already *had* a college education.

In the summer of 1937, I became eighteen. From that day on, what I did with my time, my money, my schooling, myself, was entirely up to me.

Mr. Babcock and I went over a lot of formalities in his little office at the Knickerbocker Trust Company. He was very businesslike, very impersonal. I didn't quite follow him through all the technicalities of investment, but I did understand that at eighteen, I was comparatively rich. The Knickerbocker Trust Company had sunk every cent of my inheritance into stolid, conservative stocks and bonds—nothing flashy, nothing chancy—and all through the depression my little pile had grown and grown until it became what Mr. Babcock called "almost a fortune."

"Very well," Mr. Babcock said coldly, "I assume that you understand the details. Anything you'd like me to explain again?"

"No, thank you, Mr. Babcock."

"You are, from the moment you sign these papers, your own boss. I shall have no further jurisdiction over your money. It's a frightening thought. I hope—all of us here at Knickerbocker Trust hope—that your money will remain with us. I think you will admit that we've done a pretty fair job of looking after your estate, despite That Man in the White House. And I, personally, have tried as much as your Aunt Mame would allow me, to guide you through the difficult years of adolescence. I don't know how good a job I've done on *that*. Now you are to be your own free agent. As the market stands now," he continued, "the interest from this money, invested as it is, should amount to a little more than eight thousand dollars per annum. That's quite a nice bit of money."

"It certainly is," I said, not even trying to conceal the light in my eyes.

"And, of course, you may draw on this income."

"You mean I just ask?"

"That is correct. You simply make a request in writing."

I picked up the scratch pad from his desk and wrote: "Please give me $5,000.00 now. Sincerely, Patrick Dennis."

"Here, Mr. Babcock," I said, handing him the sheet.

His shoulders sagged and his face became a portrait of utter defeat. "Oh, God," he moaned, "what's the use? You'll end up exactly like that mad, waste-wealth aunt of yours. Well, it's too late now. All my work gone for

naught. I give up. You and that Aunt Mame of yours—
two of a kind! You'll end up in debtor's prison or worse
and I can't honestly say I'll be sorry. The cashier will
give you your money. Go now, and God look after you—
nobody else will."

So I was eighteen, I had my own money, my liberty,
and my youth. I bought a little six-cylinder Packard
convertible—they cost less than a thousand dollars in
those days—a new phonograph, a lot of records, and
plenty of clothes, and every three months the Trust Company sent a check for two thousand dollars which, despite Mr. Babcock's grim prophecies, I was never quite
able to spend. The following fall I began college.

The typical St. Boniface boy who went up to college
had a passion for crew, a preference for Bryn Mawr girls,
and a dog-like devotion to the old varsity traditions. It
was the stamp of St. B., but since I'd gone to St. Boniface Academy entirely against my will, I decided to be
just as atypical as possible. On the other hand, I took a
look at the freshmen with a purpose—the boys who sent
in little disjointed bits of blank verse to the pretentious
literary magazine, who spread a new kind of Christianity,
who spoke heatedly about how Sophocles should be presented by the dramatic society—and they seemed just as
callow and pompous and affected then as they do now.
So I fitted into neither mold. I was a free floater on campus.

But soon I sought my own level with the four young
men on campus who were like me. We had no school
spirit, no pennants and loving cups, no reproductions of
Cézanne and Roualt to fill our rooms. We just had furniture, bottles of gin, cans of beer, phonograph records, and
copies of the *New Yorker*. The football team could win,
lose, or drop dead for all we cared—as a matter of sorry
fact, it lost continuously for three years out of the four.
The debating society could resolve whatever it liked
about Russia: Friend or Foe, it mattered naught to us.
The dramatic workshop could present *Electra* in modern

dress or *The Women* in the nude, but not to us. The socially conscious could call all the bonfire meetings, agitate all the student strikes they liked; we were unconcerned. And the theological boys could save every soul but ours. We kept up our grades because it seemed the wisest thing to do. Otherwise our interests were entirely off campus.

Our only god was Fred Astaire. He was everything we wanted to be: smooth, suave, debonair, dapper, intelligent, adult, witty, and wise. We saw his pictures over and over, played his records until they were gray and blurred, dressed as much like him as we dared. When any crises came into our young lives, we asked ourselves what Fred Astaire would do and we did likewise. *We* thought we were hot stuff but we were very young in those days.

Every week end I drove off to New York with a carload of junior Fred Astaires, who settled comfortably in the bedrooms of Auntie Mame's big house on Washington Square and practiced being suave with their hostess. Auntie Mame loved it all. She liked company, and the younger and gayer the better. She taught us how to mix drinks the way she thought Fred Astaire would, she rounded up packs of girls for us and wangled invitations to all the gayest parties, she regaled us with sophisticated chitchat, and kept a steady stream of her famous friends performing for us. The boys loved her, and because of Auntie Mame's lavish week ends, we rapidly got the reputation of being mysterious, mature, worldly, and rather fast around school.

Later on we all joined the same club. Not because we liked the club and not because the club liked us, but because our families, our clothes, our connections, our money, and our scholastic standings made us desirable members. Then, the club set the best table on campus and had a pipeline to all the most beautiful girls. Hence we became mutually attractive to each other. Such is the purity of youthful friendships.

But as freshman year drew to a close, a subtle change

came over Auntie Mame. One week end I went up to Boston to visit a girl I'd met and when I got back to school, Auntie Mame was pacing angrily up and down my room. "How dare you!" she said.

"How dare I what?"

"How dare you run off to Boston and not tell me a word about it? Here I sit at home twiddling my thumbs waiting for you and your friends, and you don't even have the decency to drop me a post card saying you're not coming!"

"But I never tell you when I'm *not* coming; only when I am."

"Well, I've been holding open house for you and your gang every week end. What else *was* I to think? There I sit, alone and lonesome and worried half to death, with a whole pack of amusing people invited, and you don't even show up."

"But, Auntie Mame . . ."

"Don't interrupt me. I'm not in the habit of running a hotel for a young ingrate like you. Nor is it my habit to give up my entire personal life just to be taken for granted by a thoughtless nephew who doesn't care whether I live or die. Now, *next* week end I've really planned a lovely party and I *want you there* with *all* your friends. No ifs, ands, or buts about it. And don't think I'm going to forget this right away, because I'm not!" She strode out of my room and slammed the door.

It was a strange performance for a woman who lived as casually as Auntie Mame, but gradually I began to see the true picture. She had taken my friends to be *her* friends. She enjoyed them, they flattered her, amused her, gave her confidence in her eternal youth. Slowly she had come to depend on them as an audience to whom she could display her wit, her charm, her wealth, her looks. They needed Auntie Mame to supply the beds, the board, the parties, the liquor. But she needed them for something more. She needed them to assure her that she was still young, still beautiful, still desirable.

Every week end after that was spent with Auntie Mame. If we didn't go to New York, she came to us. She knew all the bright young intellectuals on the faculty and she was in steady demand. If I didn't feel like going home, she'd invite the others without me, and Biff or Bill or Jack or Alex would pass hilarious week ends on Washington Square, meeting Auntie Mame's famous friends, being debonair at her parties, or taking her to the Stork Club. And Auntie Mame, her sable coat, the Rolls-Royce, the exotic clothes, became as familiar and glorious a sight on campus as the new stadium.

But all during the sophomore year, Auntie Mame practiced admirable restraint. Whenever she came down for a week end, she made it clear to everyone that she was visiting this instructor and his wife or Professor and Mrs. So-and-So, and although my friends and I saw a lot of her, it was only for Sunday lunch or drinks.

She was still in evidence during our junior year. And although she spent fewer and fewer week ends around school with the faculty and their wives, she entertained my friends more and more at her house in New York.

At that time I was carrying on a violent affair with a waitress named Bubbles, who had been seductive over the slabs of pineapple pie at a lunch counter in Newark, and so I spent most of my free time there in the Robert Treat Hotel waiting for Bubbles. Hence I saw very little of Auntie Mame that year, and since my particular chums were rarely out of her sight, it seemed wiser not to mention Bubbles to any of them.

"Darling," Auntie Mame said toward the end of February, "I almost *never* see you nowadays. Where on *earth* do you spend your week ends? I've asked all the boys and *they* don't know."

"Oh, just here and there," I said evasively. "You know how it is."

"No, I *don't* know how it is, otherwise I wouldn't have asked you. But I'll bet I can guess. You've got a girl, haven't you?"

I blushed.

"Oh, but *darling*, why don't you bring her home! I'd love to meet her. What's her name? Where does she go to school? Have you got her picture?"

I had a picture of Bubbles but it wasn't the kind you show to loving relatives. In fact, Bubbles just wasn't the kind of girl you bring home.

But at that moment Auntie Mame decided to teach Alex how to samba and the conversation was mercifully dropped.

My trysts with Bubbles kept me awfully busy during my junior year, but not too busy to notice that still more changes were taking place with Auntie Mame and my classmates. I brought three of them home for spring vacation, hoping that they could keep Auntie Mame entertained long enough for me to slip over to Newark and the voluptuous charms of Bubbles. And they could. But I was a little surprised to hear the guys calling her just plain Mame instead of Mrs. Burnside. Alex, in fact, who was a couple of years older than I was, called her Mame Darling. And I could have sworn that her hair was a different color.

That wasn't all that was going on, either. While Biff and Bill were chasing every sweet young thing in New York, Alex stuck pretty close to the house on Washington Square. In fact, he and Auntie Mame were hardly ever separated. They danced together, played backgammon together, went out to lunch together. A couple of times I caught them whispering in the library and they looked up at me almost with resentment. In the evenings they'd disappear—just the two of them off to dinner or the theater or some overupholstered little supper club—leaving the rest of us alone in the cavernous house.

Alex was the Astaire-iest of us all. He was the tallest, the oldest, the richest, the most sophisticated. But he wasn't that dashing, and I couldn't quite see why Auntie Mame was devoting so much of her valuable time to him. She was the kind of woman who liked crowds.

However, Bubbles was giving me enough to worry about, without my having to take on Auntie Mame's problems. We'd been carrying on ever since the cold night in January when I stepped into her open-all-night web for a cup of coffee. Bubbles had been all warmth and tenderness then. She'd loved me for myself and myself alone. Her eyes had filled with tears over little gifts like a bottle of perfume, a black nightdress, a couple of pairs of stockings, an alligator bag and shoes to match. But as we got to know each other better, Bubbles grew more sure of her power, more importunate in her demands. I'd had to hock my studs and cuff links to pay for the bulky white fox jacket she insisted on buying.

"But, honey, I gotta have a chubby!" Then there was the time she said her purse had been stolen and I had to give her money to pay her rent. And around Easter she talked less and less about the bargains at the Lerner Shops and more and more about the creations of Hattie Carnegie.

"Honestagod, honey, sometimes I think yer ashamed to take me aroun' with all yer ritzy collitch crowd. G'wan, a'mit it. Yer ashameda me, g'wan, *say* it!"

"Aw, Bubbles, for the love of God, lay off. You know I'm not ashamed of you, but that bunch of meat balls'd bore you. They're just kids."

"So already you're old?"

I was only twenty, but with a girl like Bubbles you age fast. "Aw, listen, baby, forget it. Come on, we'll go over to the Treat and I'll buy you a couple of drinks."

"Sure, sure, Good Time Cholly, we'll go ovah to the Robutt Treat, have a coupla drinks, then we'll go upstairs and have a coupla somethin' else. Newark, Newark, all the time Newark! Jesus Christ, here I am, bawn in Newark, work in Newark, love in Newark. So I'll prob'ly *die* in Newark. And a fat lot you'd care, Mister Great Heart! I don't never notice yer askin' me over to Noo Yawk. It's on'y a fi' cent boat ride, I'll give yuh fare if yer so hard up. Oh, no! I'm good enough for you in Newark, but when it comes to takin' me to the Stawk Club or meetin' yer a'nt, Mrs. Bunnside, in that swell mansion she's got—an' I seen pitchas of it, don't think I haven't; in *Hoppa's Bizzah*, they was—on Washin'ton Squayah. Oh, no indeedie, then Bubbles is just a little joik fum Joisey. G'wan, *a'mit* it! Yer ashameda me!"

The awful part was that she was right. I *was* ashamed of her. I was ashamed of myself for ever getting mixed up with her. She was a cheap, gold-digging little whore who called herself a waitress because she was too dishonest to call herself a whore; and I was a cheap, snobbish little parasite who called myself a student because I was too dishonest to call myself a parasite and too honest to call a whore a mistress. But mistress she was, and she was beginning to be a tiresome, dictatorial, expensive one.

"Awright, so you *won't* take me ta one of yer a'nt's swell shindigs. So how about you take me to the prom?"

My mouth flew open with horror.

"Sure, you hoid me. The Junya Prom. I read all about it in the paypas. Yer a junya, too. If yer so prouda me, whyn't ya take me up to one a ya swanky house potties? C'mawn, honey, I never been ta no collitch prom. C'mawn, baby, plee-ase."

"But baby, I don't go to those school shindigs. They're kid stuff."

"Honey, ya *got* to. I nevah been to no prom befaw. I nevah had the chance. Evah since Poppa died an' we lost the impawt-expawt biznizz, I had to give up my edjication—my chances fer a careeh." Bubbles' late father had been variously represented to me as a prominent banker, a lawyer, surgeon, broker, and manufacturer, but I was too beaten to mention it.

Bubbles kept on with her pleading, her nagging, her wheedling, her bullying. After an hour of tears and threats I gave in.

"All right, but for God's sake, stop crying! I can't

stand it anymore. *Yes*. I'll take you to the goddamned prom."

"Hun-*nee!*" she said, beaming through her tears.

The Junior Prom was the big event of the year, even for guys like us who didn't have any school spirit. It was the last week in May, and the whole college turned out for it dressed to the nines. If you had a best girl, you invited her down for the prom week end, and if you didn't have a best girl, you dated up the most satisfactory one you could find. It was a tradition. The whole college held open house. On Friday each club gave a spectacular dinner dance for its members and their girls, cocktail parties went on in every room in the dormitories, on Saturday there were extravagant picnics with all the beer you could drink, Saturday afternoon there was always a hard-fought boat race for anyone who was sober enough to watch it, and on Saturday night, the gala ball.

Against a suave background of Mr. Astaire singing "They Can't Take That Away From Me," my particular friends discussed the big prom, the kind of party we should have in our rooms, who was Astaire enough to be invited, and who was not.

"What do you mean, Bugsy's a meat ball? He only used to date *Brenda Frazier*, that's all," Biff said.

"That's her hard luck, not ours," Jack said hotly. "I say that if *he* comes, *I* don't."

"Now come off that crap," Bill bawled, "the thing we're talking about right now is this: Do we serve martinis or Scotch, and if so, to how many people and how much will it cost? You, Pat, what do you say?"

"Who, me?" I started blushing. "Well, gee, I'm not at all sure I'll be here for the prom, boys. Just go ahead with any plans you like."

"Not be here for the *prom*!" Biff yelled. "Holy Christ, how Astaire can you get?"

"Not be here for the prom!" Bill said incredulously. "Since when? Listen, if you're having any trouble getting a girl, old man, I can fix you up with Mollie's cousin, Gloria Upson. She's still at Miss Chapin's, but boy, is she stacked!"

"Believe me," I said icily, "I am having no difficulty in obtaining a partner. It's just that I'm not going to be here."

There was a funny look in Alex's eyes as I strode out.

In the cowardly fashion of all men who want to get rid of women, I tried every trick except saying a downright "No" to shake Bubbles before the Junior Prom. I tried the Silent Treatment and didn't go near the diner in Newark for ten days. Bubbles didn't seem to mind a bit. In a weak moment I'd given her the telephone number of my room, and on the tenth day she called. I was vague and evasive over the telephone until she said, "Whatsamatta, honey, ya sick or somethin'? Look, baby, I'm worried aboutcha. Are you comin' down here or shall I come up there so's I can look afta ya?" That settled it. I drove down to Newark that very night.

Then I tried to pick a fight with her. I was gloomy and moody, uncommunicative and difficult, but Bubbles, whose volatile disposition was legendary, remained as serene as the Mona Lisa. She could talk of nothing but the Junior Prom, what she was going to wear, whom she was going to meet, how she was going to rub shoulders with all the best debutantes of the season. I shuddered. I didn't know how to work it, but one thing was certain; Bubbles was *not* going to go to the Junior Prom with me.

By the time Prom Week arrived, I knew what I was going to do. I'd simply wire Bubbles, say that I was in the infirmary with something very contagious, and hide out in Philadelphia until the big brawl was over. It was a stinking trick, but then, she'd managed to gouge a good five hundred bucks out of me just to clothe herself for her debut in the ivy-clad halls of learning.

The Thursday night before the festivities got under way, I was in my room playing Fred Astaire's record of "Bojangles" and hastily packing enough duds to make my getaway. Alex was lying on the sofa drinking a can of Budweiser when the telephone rang. It was Auntie Mame. "Darling," she said, "are you coming *home* this week end?"

"No, Auntie Mame," I said, "you know I always send you a card if I'm coming."

"Oh, yes, how stupid of me, but where are you *going*?"

"Why, to *Philadelphia*," I answered clearly.

"For the *whole* week end?" she asked.

"Certainly. Why?"

"Oh, no special reason, darling. I just wondered. Then you won't be at school at *all*?"

"Of course not."

"Not until late Sunday night?"

"No, Auntie Mame," I said, getting hot and irritable at being discovered in my caddish retreat. "What's all this about?"

"Why, nothing, darling," she cooed in that fraudulent innocence that always makes me suspect her. "I just wondered what my little love was going to do with himself all week end. *I'll* probably stay at home with Marcel Proust."

"Well, give him my best," I said. "By the way, Alex is here. Do you want to talk to him?"

"Oh, no, why *should* I? Just say hello and tell him I'll see him shortly. Well, have a nice time in Philadelphia, darling."

It struck me as strange that Auntie Mame would call, but then, she was a very strange woman. Alex gave me a deep, dark look and then said he'd be getting to bed.

"Who'd you ask to the prom, Alex?" I asked in glib and unfelt interest.

"Oh, just a female," he said quickly, closing the door.

The next morning I was up at eight. The telegram I'd created—HOSPITALIZED WITH DIPHTHERIA AND DESOLATE ABOUT PROM DON'T COME CAN SEE NO ONE—seemed to make English Composition class unnecessary that day, and everyone always cut Italian Sculpture of XIV, XV, XVI Centuries, anyhow. I determined to get an early start, before anyone could question my whereabouts, and escape school for the big week end.

It was just nine-thirty by the big square clock in the Western Union office when I finished writing the telegram begging sick leave of Bubbles. That meant I could drive to Philadelphia at a leisurely clip and be there in time for lunch. Whistling "The Piccolino," I ambled out to the curb and opened the door of my car. The music died on my lips. Sitting in the front seat was Bubbles.

"Su'prise!" she screamed. "Here I am, honey! Betcha nevah expectid me this oily, didja?"

"Why, Bubbles," I whispered.

"Gee, you look like you jes seen a ghost, baby. C'mawn, howsabouta little kiss?"

In a trance, I got into the car.

"Well, honey," Bubbles chattered, "the cook, he sez to me, he sez, 'Hell, yer on'y young once, so g'wan, *take* the whole week end,' so I got up with the budds an' caught the mawning train—a regular Tumorville Trolley it was—an' thought I'd su'prise ya."

"You certainly did," I said dully.

"I cou'nt get a taxi at the dee-po, so I decided to hoof it, an' low and behole, I seen ya cah pahked here an' I reckinized the Noo Yawk licence, so I jus' got in an' sat. Lissen, honey, I hope you dint go out an' rent me any expensive soote at the ho-tel, 'cause I'm staying with my gull-frien' Mavis."

"Mavis Hooper?" I asked incredulously.

Mavis Hooper was the town whore—illegitimate daughter of the village whore—and a girl of almost no intellect, although Woodrow Wilson was rumored to have been her real father.

With my stomach sitting inside me like a block of marble, I drove Bubbles to the notorious frame house on the outskirts of town where Mavis lived, and carried the bright new powder-blue luggage up the steps worn smooth by many generations of liberal arts students.

"C'mawn in, restcha feet, honey," Bubbles said.

"I—I can't," I stammered. "I have a class in sculpture."

"Okey-dokey, pufessah. I'll jes get cleaned up; then I'll ankle ovah to the campus and pick y'up in time fa lunch."

"Oh, no! Don't do that, Bubbles! It's a long way. I'll come and call for you. Twelve o'clock, sharp."

"Sa-well! Gimme a chance ta case the burg. See ya, honey!"

My head spun as I sat limply behind the steering wheel. If I'd ever credited myself with a certain Machiavellian turn of mind, I'd certainly been outdistanced by Bubbles. Driving slowly back to the dormitory I was in a quandary. If I went back to my room and stuck it out for the week end, I'd never be able to explain Bubbles. If I skipped town for the whole time—even longer—Bubbles, who had an inquisitive mind, would surely find her way to the dormitory and make a scene to end all scenes in dear old Morgan House. If I shot myself ... No, I decided. The thing to do would be to cut back to the dorm, collect some clothes, and then move out to a tourist cabin and try to keep Bubbles as far away from school as possible.

That day we drove twenty miles to lunch at a Howard Johnson's and then I took a lot of detours to show Bubbles the scenery.

"But, honey, looka the *time*! I gotta get back an' change my cloze for all the cocktail potties. An' what about the club dinnah dance?"

"Club? Club? What club? I don't belong to any club."

"You don't belong to no *club*?" Bubbles screamed. "I coulda swore you tole me you was a membah of ..."

"Oh, that," I said. "Resigned. Resigned two months ago. Pack of snobs there. No democracy. Listen, Bubbles, how about just going out for a little dinner—only the two of us?"

"Well, okay," she said petulantly, "but I ain't seen a single collitch fella since I hit this town."

"Plenty of time for that," I said. "It's only Friday."

I managed to hold Bubbles at bay until late that night. "Whaddabout the tawchlight pur-rade an' all the Noo Yawk daybutantes?" she kept asking.

"Torchlight parade just looks like a lot of matches in the dark and hardly any of the New York girls get here before tomorrow. It's a long way, you know."

"Yeah, almost an hour and a half on the slow train," she said grimly. "Well, take me ta see yuh room. I bet it's jus' like a regla bachlah's quawtahs."

"They don't allow girls in the rooms," I said quickly.

"Mavis says . . ."

"Well, they're clamping down now. Getting very strict."

I pried myself loose about one-thirty and spent a miserable night in the Kosy Comfie Kabins, cursing the day I ever heard of Newark.

The next morning I picked up Bubbles before she had any time to investigate the town and possibly bump into anyone I knew. She tripped down the steps chez Mavis in a bright green organdie dress with a big straw hat. "You like?" she said, turning coquettishly. "I sure hope so, honey, the money you ga' me fa cloze dint quite covah this, so I had ta chawge it."

"Very pretty," I said colorlessly, thinking of Mr. Babcock and the Knickerbocker Trust Company.

"Well, we all ready fa the big beeh picnic?"

I had anticipated that question and had arrived supplied with the answer—a package of bologna sandwiches and a case of cold Ballantine's from the delicatessen.

"But, jeest, honey," Bubbles whined, "whenna we gonna see the collitch kids?"

Our picnic was something less than a *succès fou*. Bubbles sat on an anthill and, having neglected to bring an opener, I cut my mouth pretty badly trying to drink from the broken neck of a beer bottle. But by regatta time there was no holding Bubbles.

"But I wanna see the *boat* races," she kept saying.

I was helpless. There wasn't a hope of rain. I purposely drove over a broken bottle, but nothing happened to the tires. We reached the banks of the river just as the crowd was at its thickest. The squirt gun was a popular innovation that year, and Bubbles was both loud and outspoken in voicing her opinion of certain prankish gamins from Wellesley and Vassar who ruined her dress—*my* dress, really—during the first half hour.

In her dripping green organdie, Bubbles looked disdainfully at the girls she longed to emulate—they wore sweaters and skirts, dirndls and blouses, blue jeans and sweat shirts. "Not very chick, are they?" she sniffed. "Lookee, let's go down there. That looks like a nice crowd."

My eye followed her pointing finger and landed on Biff and Bill and Jack jovially swilling beer with a bevy of pretty Bennington girls. "Oh, you wouldn't want to meet *them*," I said hastily. "Bunch of meat balls. Besides, I know a place where you can get a much better view of the race."

"The beginning or the end?"

"The beginning—much more interesting."

"Who wantsta see a race *staht*?"

"Well, you can see the finish, too. Come on." I grabbed her arm and headed away from the crowds. At that moment the blue Lincoln-Zephyr that was Alex's pride and joy shot past. There was a regular barrage of squirt guns and Bubbles and I were caught square in the middle. The car shot out of sight, but not before I heard a silvery voice cry, "Oh, but darling, this is absolutely the *maddest*! I feel like a *child*!"

I stopped dead in my tracks. *"No. Impossible,"* the voice of reason told me.

"Did you see that snotty, Pock Avnyou bitch practic'lly

empty the watahwukks on me? Goddamn her, I'd like ta . . ."

"Come on," I said, propelling her out of sight, "we'll miss the race."

The night of the big dance was white with moonlight when I called for Bubbles. She wasn't quite dressed and I sat in the parlor of Maison Hooper stiff and uncomfortable in my evening clothes. A couple of freshmen rang the bell and asked if Mavis was in.

"Not tonight, boys," Mrs. Hooper said jovially.

One of them caught sight of me through the screen door. "Got a job playing piano here, Dennis?" he shouted. I winced.

"Tch, them kids," Mrs. Hooper chortled. "Boys will be boys, like the fella says. Laws, I can remember when *you* was comin' here regular, too."

After a long, long time, Bubbles appeared. If she had stood out among the rosy college girls that afternoon, she now shone like a searchlight. She wore tight-fitting gold lamé slashed with red velvet, and her arms were weighted with glassy, brassy bracelets. Her throat was compressed into a dog collar of soiled pearls, and her hair was swept up into a towering pompadour that laughed at any law of gravity. Her use of cosmetics had been generous to a fault.

"You likee?" she said.

"Here, Bubbles," Mrs. Hooper said, shuffling into the room in her carpet slippers. "I been keepin' your corsaj in the fridge."

Daintily, Bubbles pinned a yard-long chain of purple orchids down the front of her already startling costume. At the end of the month I discovered that they—fifty-six dollars' worth—had been charged to me by the most expensive florist in town. Bubbles flung her white fox jacket over her shoulders and picked up a tarnished sequin evening bag. "Okey-dokey, honey, there'll be a hot time in the ole town tonight. Where'll we eat, baby? The Inn?"

I wouldn't have gone within a mile of the Inn that night for a million dollars, cash. "Oh, no, Bubbles, not that old dump. The food's enough to kill an elephant."

"Yer a cahd!" she screamed.

"I thought we'd drive out to a little French place I know. Very intimate, awfully good food." The little French place was a shoddy roadhouse about fifteen miles out of town—a good safe distance. The cuisine was appalling, but they did use some few Gallic terms on the menu like Potatoes Lyonnaise, Soup du Jour, Filet Mignon aux Champignons, and the place *was* called Louie's. It was mercifully empty when we got there.

I ordered six sidecars right off the bat, chose everything that was cooked in wine, and kept champagne flowing through the entire meal. It was my wan hope that Bubbles, whose capacity for liquor had never been large, might soon be in such condition as to be entirely indifferent—if not oblivious—to the Junior Prom. But Bubbles drank her way through dinner with a grim determination, and even called for a third bottle of champagne. "Jeest, honey," she said, "this is the life, although between you an' I, that steak cou'nt be cut with a battle-ax. C'mawn, baby, it's gettin' real late. We gotta get ta the dance."

"Oh, take your time. Nobody ever shows up before midnight."

"But, honey, it's ha'pas' ten right now, an' they got Glen Gray an' his Casa Loma band. I seen it in the noosepaypah."

"Oh, the night is young," I said halfheartedly. "Eat your tortoni. It's a very famous old French dish."

"French, my ass. I happena know the two Greeks that make it in Newark, an' if you was ever ta see the inside of that factory like I done, you woun't recommen' it to a dog."

"Well, at least have a good glass of cognac."

Try as I would, I couldn't get her drunk. The Prom was paramount in her mind.

"Honey, *c'mawn!*" she kept whining.

It was nearly twelve when we arrived at the dance. I walked slightly behind Bubbles in hopes that no one would think we were together.

"Parm me a sec, honey, I gotta put some maw lacka on my cough-your."

I hurried into the men's can and took a big swig out of my hip flask, then another and another and another. Bubbles, in her barbaric glory, was impatiently tapping her foot. "Jeest, honey, I thoughtcha fell in. Whatcha wearin' them dark glasses faw?"

"Eyestrain," I muttered.

Once in the ballroom, Bubbles made an instantaneous sensation. I tried to dance as far away from the stag line as possible, but the stag line gave every appearance of *following* us. There were low, lascivious whistles, but they sounded derisive rather than appreciative.

"I'll bet you five bucks it *is* Pat Dennis," I heard someone say, and I spun Bubbles into the center of the throng. Against the floating white and pastel summer evening dresses of the girls at the dance, Bubbles' costume looked like something left over from the wardrobe department at Minsky's.

"Kinda plain-lookin' cloze they're all wearin'," Bubbles sniffed. "But if you ast me, there's nothin' like a really stylish evening gownd."

The room was pleasantly dark through my sunglasses and my head was spinning slightly.

After a couple of turns around the floor I felt a hand tap my shoulder. I turned around and there was Repulsive Remington, the richest boy at school. "May I?" he said smoothly.

"A *pleasure*," I said.

"See yuh, honey," Bubbles squealed, and they danced away.

Once free of Bubbles, I removed my sunglasses and took a good look at the ballroom. It was really mobbed. From the safety of the stag line, I gave the place full and careful scrutiny. Bubbles may have looked like the whore of Babylon, but she was going over tremendously with a certain raffish element of the student body. Except for a lamentable turn of phrase and an occasional shrill scream, Bubbles was holding up all right and, as I said, she was getting an appreciable amount of amused attention.

A hand jostled my elbow. It was a freshman squirt who'd been trying his damnedest to break into the Fred Astaire crowd.

"Hi," I said flatly.

"Hi," he said. "Pretty good brawl, eh?"

"Fair," I agreed coldly.

"Listen," he piped, "you know everybody here. Tell me, who's the snake who's getting the big rush?"

I felt myself go hot. "You mean in the red and gold?"

"Hell, no, not that tramp. The mystery woman over there in the filmy black stuff."

I looked in the direction of a thick throng of eager young men and at the belle who was flirting and simpering in their midst. "My God," I whispered. It was Auntie Mame, in a strapless evening dress, a fan, and every diamond she owned.

"Who is she?" he urged. "She came with that friend of yours, Alex. She's been all over this place ever since yesterday, and the cops said if she didn't lay off with her squirt gun they'd clap her into the cooler. Some dish, eh! What's her name?"

"I swear to you before God," I said evenly, "that I've never laid eyes on her before in my life."

Now I was desperate. I had to get hold of Bubbles and get her out—and fast. I put on my sunglasses and stumbled across the floor. Bubbles, by this time, had become a household word with the Old Jock Strap and Sweat Socks Set. Half the unshowered bodies in the athletic department had been pressed against her red and cold façade and they were back clamoring for more. Repul-

sive Remington was dancing with her again. I cut in
briskly.

"Come on, Bubbles," I said, "we've got to get going."

"Fer Chrissakes, *why*?" she screamed.

"Don't ask a lot of questions, now. Come on."

"In a pig's ass I will. Here I been mopin' aroun' this
Gawdfarsaken town all week an' now when I begin
enjerrin' myself, you wanna drag me away. Well, I won't.
I won't, I won't, I *won't*!" She was drunk as a fiddler's
bitch by this time and screaming at the top of her lungs.
A little cluster of interested young bloods had gathered
around us.

"Bubbles, you either come with me now—this minute—or else."

"Or else *what*? You ast me down to this big collitch
affair, an' what happens? I ain't been within spittin' distance of the place. I don't meet no socialites, no
tawchlight purade, no club dinnah dance, no cocktail
potties. I ain't even wore half my onsombuls. Well, now
I'm havin' fun and you ain't gonna bully me inta nothin'.
If you wanna go, you can go. *I'm* stayin'. Mr. Remington
will look after me like a real gentlemun. Wonchew?"

"You bet your life, baby," he said, giving her hip a
squeeze.

"You really mean that, Bubbles? *Forever*?" I said, trying to fight down a look of relief.

"Yer goddamn right I do!"

"Then this is good-by?"

"Good-by ferevah, shawt-spawt." She whirled off with
Repulsive Remington.

Feeling like a man reprieved from the electric chair, I
left the dance.

I was a free man. Bubbles had said good-by, *forever*.
No one had seen me with her, and my reputation for being suave, debonair, *Astair*, was still safe. With happy
heart I decided to go straight back to my room and spend
a long time in my own bed. My clothes at the tourist
cabin could wait. Of course there was the question of

why Auntie Mame had been at the dance, but, I told myself, there was obviously a simple explanation to that. She'd undoubtedly stopped in to chaperone with some professor and his wife. She certainly hadn't seen me, *or* Bubbles. That was the important thing.

Still a little bit drunk, I got back to my room, locked the door, and undressed. Morgan House was silent. I snapped off the lights and, with the voice of our idol singing "The Way You Look Tonight," and thinking happily of my new freedom now that Bubbles had Repulsive Remington to pay her bills, I drifted off to the sleep of the just.

At half past four I was roused from my dreams by an urgent rapping at the door.

"Who is it?" I mumbled.

"Let me in, let me in. Quick!" an urgent female voice whispered desperately through the thin panels.

"You and I are through, Bubbles," I said in a thick, sleep-clogged voice. "Don't try to come crawling back now. You've hurt me too much."

"My God, open the door! It's Auntie Mame! Let me *in*!"

I jumped up, knocking over a chair, switched on the lights, and stumbled to the door, blinking owlishly. I opened the door and Auntie Mame tumbled in, still in full evening dress with an ermine cape thrown crookedly around her shoulders. "Thank God," she breathed, and slumped back against the closed door. "Lock it, please," she panted. "I don't suppose you have anything to drink in here?"

"Why, Auntie Mame," I said thickly, "what in the name of God are you doing here?"

"Don't ask me to explain anything until I've had a drink. Quick. Anything will do."

I poured her a stiff tumbler of Scotch as she collapsed onto the sofa. "Thank you, my little love, such a comfort to me. I never thought you'd be back from Philadelphia—it *was* Philadelphia you said?—so soon. I merely assumed your door would be unlocked and I could hide out in here for a little while."

"Hide?" I said, brushing the hair out of my eyes, "hide from *what*?" I was beginning to regain consciousness. I looked long and hard at her and she seemed to be avoiding my eyes. "Say, what *are* you doing here, anyhow? Reading Marcel Proust?"

For the first time in all the years I'd known her, Auntie Mame appeared to be really embarrassed. "This is such a *nice* room for a college boy, darling. So restful."

"You've been in it a hundred times before. Surely you didn't come all the way down here in that get-up for the therapeutic values of my color scheme. What I said was, just what in the hell are you doing *here*, *now*, in that outfit?"

Auntie Mame writhed uncomfortably and avoided my eyes, but she still had a speck of the old fire-eater left. "Well, now that we're playing twenty questions, I might quite fittingly remark that this sordid little dormitory room hardly looks like the City of Brotherly Love. I suppose you call that wilting elephant plant Rittenhouse Square?"

"I came back earlier than I expected," I said with complete honesty. "And now, at the risk of being tiresomely repetitious, may I ask once more what you're doing here?"

"Well, if *that's* all the welcome I'm to get from my only kinsman," she said rising haughtily, "perhaps I'd better go."

"Very well," I said, striding toward the door, "good night."

"Oh, please, no!" she whimpered, cowering onto the sofa.

There was a terrible commotion out in the corridor, and I could hear heavy feet clumping up and down the stairway, and the fumbling sound of a passkey rattling in the locks of faraway doors.

I stared at her coldly. I was fully awake now and quite,

quite sober. I began to piece together little fragments of the mosaic of the last three days—Auntie Mame's mysterious phone call, the voice behind the squirt gun in Alex's car, the "mystery woman in filmy black" who was getting the big rush at the dance. "And now," I said levelly, "perhaps you will be good enough to answer, when I ask for the *fourth time*, exactly what you happen to be doing in full battle dress, in a men's dormitory, at half past four in the morning on Prom Week End, in the Year of Our Lord Nineteen Hundred and Forty."

"I . . . I—do give me another drink, darling."

"*After* you've explained yourself," I said. "Now, get on with it. What are you doing here?"

"Well, if you must know," she blurted, "I just happened to be up in Alex's room listening to some records, when there was this terrible ruckus and it seems that the whole night-watchman squad was racing around searching the dormitory . . ."

"What were they searching for, the Lost Chord?"

"If you'll only let me explain, I'm sure I can do so to your *complete* satisfaction."

"I'm certain you can. Go on."

"It seems that this terrible slut—oh, really, the commonest-looking thing all in red and gold like a Woolworth's—got into the dormitory with some disgusting boy." My heart suddenly skipped a beat. "And, well, God knows *what* they were doing, but you can imagine. And then there were these terrible screams and a lot of really unbelievable language and then I heard all these night watchmen absolutely *raiding* the place."

"Yes?"

"Well, *I* certainly didn't want to get caught in Alex's room at this hour of the . . ."

"Certainly you didn't," I said icily.

"So I just slipped in here to wait until it was all over. I knew—at least I *thought*—the room would be vacant. Now give me a drink, there's a dear."

"You haven't quite *yet* explained your presence to my

full satisfaction. *What are you doing here?* In this dress, in this college, in this town, in this state? You, who were going to pass a lonely week end with a good book."

"Why—why, darling, at the very last moment I was invited to stay with Professor Townsend and his wife and I just . . ."

"You just happened to end up at the Junior Prom with a boy who could very easily be your son."

"That's not true, unless you're referring to some unhappy prank of nature like that little girl down in Peru. After all, I'm not so *very* much older than you!"

"Only about twenty or thirty *years!*" I yelled. "Just what the hell kind of trick do you think you're playing, Grandma Moses?"

"Stop it!"

"I will not stop it! Not until I get the whole story; every word of it, my College Widow. Now, begin at the beginning. The only reason you telephoned me Thursday was to find out whether I'd really be here to discover you cavorting around with a bunch of boys half your age. Right?"

"That's not true. I was simply interested in your wel . . ."

"Answer yes or no. You only wanted to come here if you felt sure I wouldn't find out about it. Yes or no?"

"Yes, you little beast, yes, yes, yes!"

"Alex put you up to it, didn't he? *Didn't he?*"

"Yes," she whispered, always happy to share the blame.

"In fact, you and Alex have been sniffing around each other all year, haven't you?"

"If you persist in degrading me this way, I shall have to leave your room, Patrick."

"Go right ahead. Don't let me stop you." From the talking and scuffling outside, I knew the guards had worked their way down to my floor. Auntie Mame made no attempt to leave, so I went on. "You and Alex have been playing footie all spring."

"That's both vile and insulting. I'm interested in his mind."

"Balls! Alex hasn't got a mind, as he'd be the first to tell you."

"All *right*!" she cried. "Maybe I *was* having a silly little flirtation with him. He amused me."

"And so you thought it would be just too, too amusing to sneak down here and caper around with all the rest of the gay young college girls."

"I happen to be a college woman myself."

"You certainly were: Smith College, Northampton, Massachusetts, *Summa Cum Laude*, Class of 1917."

"What of it? I was years ahead of myself in school. Almost a *child* when I graduated."

"Sure you were," I mocked, "just a babe in arms. And since the year you graduated from college happens to coincide with the year Alex was born, you thought it would give you a common bond—the ideal excuse for you to come whooping down here and hell around town with your squirt gun."

"What on earth are you talking about?" she said half-heartedly.

"I'm talking about *you*—the poor man's Fanny Ward—just a girl of forty-five . . ."

"Forty-four!"

"Aha! Just a girl of *forty-four*, getting run in by cops for soaking half the campus with a squirt gun."

"I wish I had that squirt gun right now," she said between clenched teeth, "filled with *sulphuric acid*."

There was an officious knocking at the door. "Open up. Open up in there. This is a house check!"

"Oh, God," Auntie Mame breathed.

"Rest your bustle, Lillian Russell," I said nastily. "After all, you're only my old aunt, even if it is after hours." I opened the door wide. "Yes?" I said.

Old Casey, a night watchman of unnumbered years, stood shyly in the doorway. "Sorry ter bother yez,

Misther Dennis, but we gotta make a thero inspection. Dean's orders."

"Come right in," I said. "As you can see, I *have* a woman in my room, but it's only my Aunt Mame. I had a sick spell early this evening and she came over from Professor Townsend's to nurse me through it. But I'm much better now, so if you want to search the room go right ahead."

Old Casey squinted into the room, his bushy white eyebrows working up and down. His face lighted up at the sight of Auntie Mame. "Landa hope an' glory, if it ain't *Miss* Dennis! Sure, I seen you around the school a lot, these last coupla years. An' before then, too." He cackled reminiscently. "Lord, don't I remember her when *she* was a girl an' comin' down here to all the parties. Musta been back in 'fifteen, 'sixteen. Pretty as a picture she was, an' a wild one, too."

Auntie Mame murmured a noncommittal unpleasantry.

"Lordy, Lord, Miss Mame, them *were* the days, weren't they? Well, I guess time don't stand still with any of us, do it? I 'spect you've got daughters of yer own comin' down to the dances."

Auntie Mame uttered a little gasp.

"Oh, no, Casey," I said quickly. "Both of Mrs. Burnside's daughters are married and settled in Akron, Ohio, with daughters of *their* own. She's a grandmother now. Aren't you, Auntie Mame?"

She nodded her head miserably.

"Do tell," the old codger cackled. "Well, that's what makes the world go 'round. We all gotta get old sometime. Well, I'm pretty certain the young chippie I'm lookin' for ain't likely to be in the same room as a dignified New York sassiety woman who's got grandchildren. But if yuh see a fast young piece answers ta the name o' Bubbles, gimme a call. Happens every year this way—some poor, dumb kid gets mixed up with one of them whoorgirls, you'll pardon me, ma'am, an' there's all hell to pay. Ye'd think the boys'd know better, havin' a college ejication an' all. Well, hope yuh feel better. G'night, ma'am, it's been a real treat ta see yuh after all these years. Almos' makes me feel young again." He doddered off.

I didn't have the heart to look at Auntie Mame. She sat dumbly on the sofa, clutching her empty glass. I dressed swiftly and said, "Come on, I'll drive you home."

"Back to the hotel?"

"Oh, then you're not really staying with the Townsends?"

"No," she said quietly.

"Well, as a matter of fact, I'd planned to take you *all* the way home. New York."

"But my clothes," she said dully.

"I'll get them Monday. I have a lot of things to pick up around town, anyhow."

I hung her cape over her shoulders and held the door open. We walked quietly down the stairs.

In the harsh light of the vestibule, Bubbles, her elaborate varnished coiffure flying stiffly, her garish red and gold dress hanging on her wrinkled and torn, was standing with Repulsive Remington clad only in a T-shirt and his pumps, surrounded by the entire regiment of watchmen.

". . . but this perfeckly strange fella practic'lly ki'naped me. Honestagawd, I didn't know where I was, he musta slipped me some kinda drug in my punch cup. Firs' thing I knew, I was in his room and he was makin' ovratures at me. Belie' me, I'm not that kinda gull."

"Pipe down, now, young lady," Old Casey was saying, "I seen enough o' yer kind in the fifty years I worked here. As for *you*, Misther Remington, the Dean . . ."

"I think we'll just slip out the side door," I said tersely, taking Auntie Mame's arm and walking a lot faster. "It's closer."

"*There* he is!" Bubbles screamed. "There's the gennlemun that brought me. That's him! Dennis is his name, Patrick Dennis. Pat, *honey*, tell 'em, tell 'em you brought me. Honey, I love ya, I'm sorry I was so snooty at the dance. *Baby*, can'tcha *heah* me?"

"Now you shut up, missy," Casey said. "Yer wakin' up the whole place. What would a boy like Misther Dennis here with his old auntie be doin' with a fly-up-the-crick like you?"

"Honey!" Bubbles yelled. The door closed behind us.

"So!" Auntie Mame said, her eyes blazing with the fire of malice. "So!"

"You keep your mouth shut and so will I," I said quietly.

In silence we drove back to New York.

EIGHT

AUNTIE MAME

AND MY PUNCTURED ROMANCE

THE TIME INEVITABLY COMES IN THE Unforgettable Character's life for the foundling to finish school, find love, and get married. And what did the spinster do then, poor thing? Naturally it was something of a wrench for her to be torn apart from the person who meant everything in her life, but she was a game old girl. As always, she thought of herself last, swallowed her pride, smiled—although her heart was breaking—and went out to meet the girl's parents and see that everything went according to Hoyle. That seems typical of her, doesn't it?

But Auntie Mame could be typical, too. In fact, too typical. She did all the proper things pursuant to an engagement, and she did them with a flair that has made her unforgettable to more people than me. I mean, either do these things right or don't do them at *all*. Auntie Mame did everything up brown.

By the end of my senior year in college I'd grown up a little. Fred Astaire ceased to be my idol. I even managed to get on the Dean's List. And I was in love.

Love and youth and beauty—all of them were Gloria Upson. She was very young—just nineteen. She was very beautiful—a slim, curvacious, honey-blonde with a deliciously petulant lower lip. I wrote her every day, telephoned her every night, spent every week end near her. During Commencement Week I proposed.

"Oh, angel, yes," she whispered, stirring softly against the upholstery of my car. "You know I want to say yes. But how can we? How could we exist? You haven't even a job yet, and when you graduate . . ."

"But I have *some* money. It's no great fortune, but we could count on something to live on until I get going. It would keep us."

"Angel," she sighed, "that's wonderful. Of course we can do it in that case. Daddy will surely say it's all right, and maybe he'll even help out a little."

"We don't need any help from *anybody*," I said.

"Well, silly, if he offers, you certainly won't say No. I realize that money isn't everything, but then, angel, I don't want to be a burden to you before you really get started."

And so it was settled. I had only to grab my diploma, see Upson *Père*, buy a license and a ring.

My interview with Father Upson was arranged for a warmish night in June. I dined with Gloria and her family at their apartment in that graceless canyon of dying grass, carbon monoxide, and bad architecture that is called Park Avenue. The Upsons lived the way every family in America wants to live—not rich, but well-to-do. They had two of everything: two addresses, the flat on Park and a house in Connecticut; two cars, a Buick sedan and a Ford station wagon; two children, a boy and a girl; two servants, man and maid; two clubs, town and country; and two interests, money and position.

Mrs. Upson had two fur coats and two chins. Mr. Upson also had two chins, two passions—golf and business—and two aversions, Roosevelt and Jews.

We dined humidly at a table that was almost Chippendale and Mrs. Upson said three times, "We're usually in the country house by this time, but it's been so damp this year that I just didn't want to move out too soon." After a rich and wholly indigestible dessert involving fruit, brandy, macaroons, nuts, ice cream, and hot caramel sauce, Mrs. Upson coyly excused herself and Gloria and said, "I know you boys want to talk."

"Shall we go into my study, Dennis?" Mr. Upson said.

I shuddered, cleared my throat, and followed him manfully. We passed through the living room where Gloria and her mother quickly feigned an interest in back issues of *Town and Country*, marched into Mr. Upson's lair, and he shut the door.

"Well, sir?" he said, after I refused a cigar.

"Well, sir, I've known Gloria about six months now, we're in love, and we want to be married. That is, if you don't mind."

"Of course, I don't know very much about you, Dennis. You seem to be an upright young fella, from what Glory tells me; fulla piss and vinegar, stood high in your class, nice manners. But a wife costs money, and Doris and I have raised Glory with the very best. And nothing but the best is good enough for my little girl. She's had the best clothes, gone to the best schools, mixed with the best people. She don't belong in some little one-room flat doing her own cooking and washing, and what's more, we wouldn't want to see her doing it. Break Doris's heart. Just what sort of work do you do?"

The discussion covered money, the more spiritual aspects of young love, money, my family background, Auntie Mame, what schools I'd gone to, money, my religious and political affiliations, insurance, and money.

"Well, sir," he said after an hour's interrogation, "I can honestly say what very few fathers can: I'm proud and happy to have you as a husband for my little girl. You're a fine young man with a good head on your shoulders, a good background, a good education, private means—all the things my little Glory expects and deserves from life." With a heavy hand, he propelled me out to the living room, where Gloria flew ecstatically into my arms and Mrs. Upson shed a few unbecoming tears and kissed me wetly. And so we were engaged.

Aghast with love and happiness, I walked the whole way from the Upson flat down to Auntie Mame's house on Washington Square. She was in her big gold bed sticking pins into a war map of Europe when I floated up the stairs.

"Is that you, my little love?" she called.

"Yes, Auntie Mame," I said, peering in. "Are you awake?"

"Of course not, darling," she said, "it's my custom to sleep sitting bolt upright with a map in my lap and all the lights burning. It's so Napoleonic."

I tiptoed into her room and sat down on the edge of her bed. "Auntie Mame, I'm engaged. I'm going to get married."

She dropped the Balkans, and her big tortoise-shell reading glasses slid down her cold-creamed nose. "Married!" she cried. "*You?* Why, you're still a child!"

"I'm twenty-two," I said, "I'm out of college, I have my own money, and I'm in love."

"But darling, this is so sudden, as they say. Who is this girl? It isn't Miss Bubbles, is it?" she said maliciously.

"It's a girl I met last Christmas. Her name is Gloria Upson."

"Why, Patrick, as I live and breathe. You're really serious, aren't you, darling?"

"Never more serious in my life. We want to get married right away. Before I'm drafted."

"But darling, who is she? Why haven't you told me about her? What's she like? Do you have a picture of her?" I went into my room and got the unimaginative Bachrach photograph Gloria had given me. "My, but isn't she stunning!" Auntie Mame said. "Hmmm, kind of a mean mouth . . ."

"Auntie Mame!"

"Well, darling, it's undoubtedly just the photograph. Believe me, if you're really serious about her, and if you really love her, I'll be the happiest woman in the world— honestly I will. I just hope you're *sure*."

"I'm just as sure of her as I am of my own name," I said. "Everything's attended to. I talked to her father tonight."

"Darling, you might have *told* me. I must call on them."

"Why?"

"Why? Why, because it's *customary*. The young man's family *always* calls on the girl's family. After all, I *am* your family."

"Oh, that's a lot of nonsense," I said.

"Of course it's a lot of nonsense, darling. Oh, will I ever forget that steady *stream* of young men's parents who called on poor Daddy during the years *I* was getting engaged."

"This isn't like that," I said angrily.

"I'm sure it isn't, my little love, but still, I must call. You wouldn't want your future in-laws to think that you sprang from some ignorant old recluse who doesn't even know the fundamental niceties of betrothal. Fetch me that box of paper and I'll write this *minute*. What did you say their name was?"

Auntie Mame was nothing to be ashamed of. Yet I was a little worried about her first encounter with the Upsons. The whole afternoon preceding her call, she tried on first one dress, then another. "Now, darling," she said, "be perfectly frank with me. I'm just as new at this mother-of-the-groom business as I can be, but I do want to do you proud. I don't want to look dowdy, but on the other hand, it would be just as grave an error to be too *stylish*. What's this Upjohn woman like?"

"Upson," I said.

"Upson. Yes. What sort of things does *she* wear?"

"Oh, just *clothes*," I said.

"I scarcely expected her to appear in a smart apron of banana leaves. Darling, you know what I mean. Is she chic?"

"Rather," I said. "Kind of faded. Her figure isn't as good as yours."

"Why, darling!" Auntie Mame cooed with pleasure. "I *had* thought of wearing this Schiaparelli print, but then, it's last year's, so *that* won't do. Then there's the lavender voile, but that's a trifle junior miss for my matriarchal position. *Or*, I might wear that white crepe, except it's hot as a crotch."

"Now, there'll be no talk like *that* tonight!" I roared.

"Why, Patrick, did you think for an instant that I, who've hammed my way through three Papal Audiences and a Court of St. James's presentation, wouldn't be able to conduct myself?"

"I'm sorry, but the Upsons just aren't like us."

"Now, that black sheer. Black's always so *safe*. That's what's the trouble with it. Or the navy silk . . ."

At nine o'clock Auntie Mame, in shades of toast, a flattering but forthright hat, and a magnificent pearl necklace, settled herself delicately in my car and we drove to the Upsons. "I feel as though I were going to open a bazaar," she kept saying.

The evening was brief and successful. Auntie Mame sat decoratively on a Louis XIV love seat and discussed the heat, the humidity, how the climate was changing from year to year in New York, how pretty Gloria was, what a really nice boy I was, how it really looked as though America would get into the war.

I gave her a look which she correctly interpreted to mean Stay Off Politics, and she said what a shame it was that, with all of Europe at war, we couldn't go abroad for our honeymoon.

I noticed Mrs. Upson giving Auntie Mame's hat, dress, furs, and jewels a sidelong and approving appraisal, and while Mrs. Upson was out of the room rounding up baby pictures of Gloria, I watched Auntie Mame's eyes sweep the conventional Park Avenue drawing room. She smiled at a heavily framed Nineteenth-Century Landscape, shook her head slightly at an oil painting of Mrs. Upson executed in about 1927, twiddled the fringe on a lamp shade, and positively snickered at the Tiffany clock set on the mantel. I cleared my throat sharply. She started, and then turned all of her most gracious attention to Mr. Upson, who was saying, ". . . all right for a visit, but I wouldn't want to live there. Those French spot an American and they'll rob you blind. And as for the English, I wouldn't raise a finger to help those limeys if . . ."

But Auntie Mame, who was a rabid Franco-Anglophile, performed with admirable restraint. She used her Gracious Lady voice all evening and unbent a little—but not too much—with her third highball. She held her tongue remarkably, relaxed enough to tell a few witty and carefully edited anecdotes, and pressed a warm invitation on the Upsons to dine with her in Washington Square at the end of the week.

"Oh, but we'll be in the midst of packing for the country then," Mrs. Upson whimpered, torn between her duty and visiting what was really one of the most famous houses in New York.

"All the more reason, then, for you to come to me. Think how much simpler it will be for your *stoff*"—with a gesture that indicated dozens of unseen servants—"if they won't have to go through the trouble of a meal for the three of you. Do come, *please*," she said with cocked head and a captivating smile. "It won't be anything grand, I promise you. Just a little black-tie *family* meal. Thursday, then?" She rose and walked daintily toward the door.

"Patrick, dear boy, you needn't worry about seeing me home if you two young things want to bill and coo. I should have had sense enough to bring the Royce, but a taxi will do."

"Oh, no," Mrs. Upson giggled, ecstatic to be as one with the Greenwich Village Lady Vere de Vere, "I'm going to *firmly* order your nephew out. Gloria's got to get her picture taken tomorrow—for the papers, you know—and I don't want her looking as though she'd been up all night."

"I think your aunt's just dreamy," Gloria whispered as we walked to the door. "Of course, I've *read* about her, but to actually *meet* her and *talk* to her! And that emerald!"

The Mutual Admiration Society held a warm farewell.

"Well?" I said, as Auntie Mame removed her hat and loosened her girdle in the car.

"Christ, but it's a scorcher! *Well*," she said, "they're a lit-tle B. Altman's—the more expensive floors, mind you—but nice, darling. Really quite nice. And Gloria *is* beautiful." She was unusually silent on the way home.

On the day of Auntie Mame's Little Dinner, Gloria and I lunched and went to Cartier's. In less than fifteen minutes, I learned a lot about diamonds. With eyes blinded and ears deafened by love, I watched Gloria reject three velvet trays of solitaires and smile rapturously at her outstretched hand and the big round diamond blazing on her fourth finger. "Yes," she said definitely, "this is the one."

I was barely conscious as I wrote a check for most of my next year's income. Gloria kissed me good-by and walked out onto Fifth Avenue, the diamond twinkling brightly.

Back in the house on Washington Square, there was an extraordinary bustle. The place was a bower of white orchids, and Ito was placing the last of the white candles in the drawing-room chandelier. The long, Venetian table in the dining room was set for eight, and there were two strange men striding uneasily about in blue livery.

I raced upstairs to Auntie Mame's bedroom, where she lay reading her way through a stack of old Edith Wharton novels.

"What the hell's going on here?" I said.

"What do you mean, my little love?" she smiled.

"Just what I said. Who's coming to this meal, and who are those characters dressed as footmen?"

"Why, darling, this is the night the Upsons are coming. Surely you couldn't have forgotten!"

"Of course I haven't forgotten, but why all the extra places, the funeral wreaths, and those two ramrods in the tailcoats?"

"But, Patrick, dear, I simply wanted to have a nice evening planned for you. After all, if these Upsons are so important, your poor old Auntie Mame has to keep up *her* end, doesn't she?"

"Now, don't play airy-fairy with me. Who's coming?"

"Rudeness will get you nowhere, young man. I can be twice as unpleasant as you, *and you know it*."

"What I meant to say, Victoria Regina, is *whom* have you *invited* to break *bread* with us this *evening*?"

"Thank you for your courtesy, albeit belated," she said maddeningly. "I have invited my dearest friend, Vera Charles, and the Honorable Basil Fitz-Hugh. I couldn't get the Guggenheims."

"The Guggenheims?"

"Yes. Quite a prominent family. I feel certain that you may hear the name sometime before you die. And, for myself—if you have no objections to a poor widow having a dinner partner, I've asked Prince Henri-René de la Tour. That is, *if* you don't mind."

"And the footmen?"

"They happen to be two talented young actors who were in the play Vera just closed. She thought it might be something of a camp to have them."

"Now see here, what may be a camp to you and Vera is dead serious to me. If you two are planning to mess up my en . . ."

"But, Patrick, dear boy," Auntie Mame said with a dazzling smile, "I only want to have things Right. And, of course, I'm doing my bit for those young men. It's awfully hard for actors to find work in the summer and I'm giving them much better than Equity minimum for a one-night stand. I even paid to have their costumes cleaned and pressed."

"If you do *one* bitchy thing . . ." I muttered.

"Have you taken leave of your senses, darling? Why should I want to ruin your happiness? I only want to enhance it. The Upsons are obviously very conscious of wealth, and I sim-ply want to show them that *we* have a little something laid by, too."

Apprehensive and defeated, I retired to my bath.

It was quite an evening. Everybody but the Upsons arrived a trifle early, almost as though by arrangement. Auntie Mame was ravishing in pale blue with most of her diamonds, and Vera looked stately in white and said everything unpleasant about Ina Claire, Gertrude Lawrence, and the Schuberts before the Upsons appeared. The Honorable Basil wore his Coldstream Guards dress uniform, and Prince de la Tour was very Gallic in summer dinner clothes. Only later did I remember that Mr. Upson hated both French and British. The two Equity footmen were equally impressive and unobtrusive, and Mrs. Upson was in seventh heaven to discover that her favorite actress, Vera—"I've seen every one of your plays, twice, Miss Charles!"—was an intimate of Auntie Mame's.

"Quite a place you have here," Mr. Upson kept saying.

Auntie Mame served only champagne and blushed prettily when she was complimented on the truffled squab. "Don't be silly, my dear, it's just a sort of picnic supper, really. *Half* the servants are off today."

I was hot with embarrassment, but I was the only one.

Once or twice I caught Mrs. Upson surveying the house with glistening eyes and I was on the verge of offering to show her through it when the party broke up. Gloria, the diamond shining on her finger, kissed me good night with even more than her usual warmth, and at the door, while the Equity footmen stood at rigid attention, Mrs. Upson gushed something into Auntie Mame's ear about Connecticut.

"Well," Auntie Mame sighed when we were alone, "how did the old war horse do?"

"You did fine, Auntie Mame," I said with starry-eyed sincerity, "you did just fine." Now the tribal customs had been observed and everything was on a friendly basis.

We set off for our week end with the Upsons a few days later. Auntie Mame, who usually went at a short motor trip as though it were a world cruise, showed a remarkable lethargy when it came to packing for the week end in Connecticut. "I thought a hatbox with a few of those cunning gingham summer things, and maybe a long peasant skirt for evenings would be appropriate, my little love," she said, looking up innocently from her Rand-McNally War Map of the Western Desert. "I tell you, darling, bastard that he is, you've got to hand it to that Rommel."

I snatched the war map away from her. "Now see here, Molly Pitcher," I roared, "I don't know quite what you've got in the back of your mind, but I can tell you that you're not going out to the Upsons' with a paper sack full of milkmaid costumes."

"All right, darling, if you think she wants to lionize me, we'll shoot the works and I'll take the Rolls-Royce, Ito, my maid, and a whole trunk full of pretties."

"I didn't say the Upsons were going to make a public spectacle of you. They're not that kind."

"Aren't they?"

"Listen," I hissed, "if you're up to one of your cute tricks, we'll just cancel the whole thing right now."

"But, Patrick, darling," she said guilelessly, "you *know* that your happiness is of *paramount* importance to me. I live for nothing else. Why, if it weren't for this week end with the Upsons—which I'm doing just for you—I could be out at Fire Island with some of the most amusing boys in . . ."

"And I wouldn't mention Fire Island, either, if I were you."

"But would you have me *falsify* myself, darling?"

"In a word, *yes!*"

"Very well, pack up my plumes, order the Royce, get out my jewel box, it's a shame the sable coat's in storage ..."

"Goddamn it, can't you ever act like other people?"

"But would you love me if I did?"

"Must you always appear in a character role? Do you have to go out there either dressed as a Farm Hand in a lot of sunbonnets or else as the Queen of Sheba with an armored truck full of diamonds? Can't you see that I just want to make a good impression on Gloria's family?"

"I don't suppose you ever considered that Gloria's family might find it politic to make a good impression on *me?*"

"Certainly they want you to think that they're nice people."

"That'll be the day."

"Now, get this straight," I said. "This is important to me. I want to marry Gloria and I intend to do it ..."

"Even if she's wrong for you?" Auntie Mame asked evenly.

"That's for *me* to decide. I just want you to go out there and act like a normal human being. Gloria and her family already like you a lot from the two times they've seen you ..."

"Well, that really *makes* my summer!"

". . . and if you can just act the way you did then, everything'll be just fine. But they *don't* have to know that you used to be in the chorus of *Chu Chin Chow* and they *don't* have to know about all your queer friends on Fire Island ..."

"I cannot be held responsible for the sexual preferences of my associates."

". . . and they *don't* have to know about a *lot* of things that ordinary mortals just don't have to know about!"

"Should they know that I think you've turned into one of the most beastly, bourgeois, babbitty little snobs on the Eastern Seaboard, or will you be able to make that *quite* clear without any help from me?" She picked up her war map and slammed out.

We motored out to Connecticut in comparative silence. Auntie Mame looked quite smart in a linen suit and I told her so.

"Thank you, my dear," she said acidly. "I *had* meant to buy a little navy blue outfit with touches of white and a bunch of cherries on the bosom, but Best and Company is *so* crowded!"

"Auntie Mame," I said quietly, "is it simply that you don't *want* me to get married to Gloria?"

"I don't know," she said, looking straight ahead. "I just don't know. Now, be still and let me see what General Montgomery is up to." She rattled her copy of *Time* ostentatiously. That was all we said until we got to Mountebank, Connecticut.

After about half an hour of false turns into highways and byways with quaint names, we finally found Larkspur Lane.

"Nice out here, isn't it?" I said conversationally.

"Adorable," she said, and closed *Time*.

We drove on and came to a gate made of white wagon wheels with a colonial lantern on a post and a sign that read

UPSON DOWNS

"Isn't that *darling*!" Auntie Mame said.

"Now, look here, if you . . ."

"Well, don't fly down my throat, Patrick," she said with a wide-eyed look of injured innocence. "I simply meant that I think it's just *terribly amusing*. Really I did. I wonder which one of them ever thought of anything so clever."

I gave her a searching look, but I could discover nothing in her face. We drove up the gravel drive.

The house was a low rambling field-stone affair with

a hitching post in front, a string of sleigh bells hanging on the front door, and a pair of carriage lamps flanking it.

"Isn't it *sweet*," Auntie Mame cooed. "Almost like *Better Homes and Gardens*." Again her face was completely expressionless.

"Woo hoo!" Mrs. Upson called, and burst through the front door like a track star breaking the tape.

"Hel-lo, my dear!" Auntie Mame cried. "I'm absolutely in *love* with your house. It's the *cutest* thing I've ever seen!"

"Yes, we just love it out here," Mrs. Upson smirked. "The main part of the house is pre-Revolutionary. Of course, it wasn't nearly big enough, so we had the two wings added to take care of the children, but now that Boyd's married and Gloria's as good as gone, there'll just be the two of us rattling around in it."

"Well, whatever you say, my dear, it's *cunning*," Auntie Mame said with a big, insincere smile.

"And of course Mountebank is restricted."

"By what?"

"*You* know," Mrs. Upson said coyly.

The colored houseman carried our bags in and we followed Mrs. Upson into the hall. It was painted Williamsburg green and was decorated with a banjo clock, a lot of Currier and Ives prints, and had a hooked rug on the plank floor.

"Ooooh!" Auntie Mame squealed as the rug slid out from under her. She caught herself on the newel post.

"Careful now!" Mrs. Upson sang. "Luckily, Claude has personal liability insurance, but we don't want you breaking your leg."

"You *are* thoughtful," Auntie Mame grimaced, wagging her finger like an operetta soubrette.

"I'm just going to *hide* the two of you away in the Guest Wing," Mrs. Upson said as she puffed up the narrow staircase.

"How divine!" Auntie Mame said. "Oooh!" she cried as I gave her a vicious prod in the backside.

"Something the matter, dear?" Mrs. Upson asked.

"Oh, no, my dear, I was simply thinking of all the boots of those brave colonial generals that must have marched up and down these hallowed steps."

"Now, *this* is to be *your* room," Mrs. Upson said, "and I'm just going to put you in here, Patrick. And there's this little sitting room in between—just in case you both get *lonely*." She giggled.

"Gracious," Auntie Mame squealed, "mine is so *feminine* and Patrick's is so *masculine*. I'll bet you *planned* it that way!"

"Well, *yes*. I said to the decorator from Altman's . . ."

"Altman's? I would have said Sloane. Solid Sloane."

"Oh, what a clever thing you are, Mame! May I call you Mame? And you must call me Doris. *Downstairs* is Sloane's and *upstairs* is Altman's."

"You just call me anything you like, Doris, as long as you don't call me late for meals. Hahahaha!"

The two ladies fairly collapsed into each other's arms with girlish mirth. I was appalled.

"Now, you two hurry and wash. Claude and I will be down on the terrace with a good daiquiri just as soon as you're ready. Gloria's off at the club with some young people—girls, of course—but she'll be home any minute. So you just hurry down. We won't bother to dress tonight—just simple country life." She tripped away.

"Oh, darling," Auntie Mame said, "isn't this a *duck* of a place. Just see my room—French Provincial, every *stick* of it. And they've even put out reading material for me: the *Reader's Digest, Song of Bernadette*—I've always wanted to read that—and the March issue of *Vogue*."

"If you so much as . . ."

"Darling, what*ever* is the matter with you? I'm just loving it, and I think Doris is a regular old *brick*. You *saw* that she liked me, asking me to call her by her first name and all that. And I'm just going to be such a perfect week-end guest that I'll bet you anything Claude asks me to call *him* by name. I do so love the *tu* relationship in families, don't you?"

I was speechless with rage, but on the other hand, I could see that Auntie Mame *was* making a hit. She was behaving herself, doing what I'd asked her to do—almost too well.

I was busy shaving when Auntie Mame scratched at the door and sauntered in. "Mercy," she whispered, "what a *virile* bathroom you have, my little love. Not at all like mine. All those rough, manly brown towels— what a shame they don't say *His* on them—and those etchings of ducks on the wing. Now, *my* bathroom is pink with a Tony Icart borzoi print and . . ."

"Ouch!" I roared.

"Oh, darling, have I made you cut yourself?"

"What the hell do you think you're got up as?" I raged at her. "Take that ribbon out of your hair this instant!"

"But, Patrick," she whined, "it came off my sun lotion bottle and *Doris* is wearing one. I thought it looked cute with this sprigged muslin." She was wearing a fluffy rose dress with a lot of moonstone jewelry that somehow didn't look as if she really meant it, but yet wasn't wrong enough to be worthy of comment.

"I *do* look right for Mountebank, don't I, darling?"

"You look okay," I said, dabbing at my jaw.

"Sweetheart," she said, kissing the back of my neck, "Now you just hurry with your shaving. You'll find me out in the sitting room reading *Oliver Wiswell* in one of those comfy Governor Winthrop chairs. It's just as though I *were* history in this little jewel of a house."

The downstairs, or Sloane Section of Upson Downs, was pretty much like the upstairs; very Quaint, very Country, very Colonial. There were carriage lamps, ratchet lamps, tole lamps, and lamps made out of butter churns, coffee mills, and apothecary jars. Bed warmers, old bellows, brass trivets, and gay samplers hung on the walls with Spy cartoons, hunting prints, yellowed maps, and prim daguerreotypes. Mrs. Upson sat nervously on a wrought-iron chair out on the terrace, and above Auntie Mame's cooing, "How sweet ... how quaint ... how cunning ..." I could hear Mr. Upson shaking up drinks and making hostly noises.

In his chartreuse playsuit and deafening huaraches, Mr. Upson looked more like a performing bear than a person. He bowed low over Auntie Mame's hand, and threw a great paternal paw around my shoulder. "Well," he roared, "here we all are. And nothing like a good Upson daiquiri at this time of day!"

"Yummy!" Auntie Mame said.

"Yep," he went on, "I don't make 'em like everybody. When Doris and I were down in Cuba this winter this bartender at a little place we used to go—what was the name of that place, Doris, Casa Wan? Yes, Casa Wan— well, this bartender, Wan, told us never to use sugar. No, indeed, not a bit of sugar in a really good daiquiri."

"Do tell!" Auntie Mame said.

"Nope, not a grain. Wanta know the secret Wan told me?"

"Oh, I'm *dying* to—if it isn't a security risk."

"Well, Wan always uses strained honey."

"Just *fancy*, strained honey!"

"Yep. Strained honey and very, ve-ry pale rum and then ..."

"I don't know *what* can be keeping Gloria," Mrs. Upson said, laying a plump hand on my knee. "But don't you worry. We'll just have a good ..."

"... and then you have to really *shave* the ice ..."

"Seems almost *too* much trouble, Mr. Upson."

"Oh, Bertha," Mrs. Upson called, "would you just put those *canapés* in the oven now? The chutney ones."

"... and then you have to really shake 'em. None of this Waring Blender business. That's for sissies. Really put a little elbow grease in the job and shake 'em if you want a good daiquiri. Here now, Mrs.—say, as long as we're more or less *on fa-meal*, why don't I call you Mame and you call me Buster."

"Buster?" Auntie Mame shrieked. "Why, I thought all the time your name was Claude."

"Oh, Doris calls me Claude, but everybody else just calls me Buster, and you do it, too."

"Well, I *will*, Buster," Auntie Mame said kittenishly, "if you'll call *me* by *my* pet name."

"What's that?" he said, pouring out the drinks.

"It's *Cuddles*."

I choked terribly over my cocktail and had to be excused.

Gloria arrived looking brown and bewitching, and made elaborate apologies for having lingered so long at the club. At seven o'clock another couple, named Abbot or Cabot or Mabbit—I never learned just which—joined us. He was in banking and she was in Planned Parenthood, and they both loved Paris and talked a great deal about a hotel where they stayed called, apparently, the Crayon. We ate a heavy, hearty meal and Auntie Mame regaled the company with anecdotes about the year she took her troop of Campfire Girls to Yosemite Park. I'd never heard the stories before—in fact, never heard that *she'd* ever heard of the Campfire Girls—and laughed right along with the rest of the guests. She was far and away the hit of the evening, and it wasn't until after I was in bed that I remembered that during the time she claimed to have been in Yosemite Park with her Campfire Girls, she was really in the chorus of *Chu Chin Chow*.

On Saturday, Auntie Mame made an ostentatious point of getting up at seven o'clock and spent most of the morning daintily snipping roses in the garden—really more roses than the Upsons had vases to accommodate. I didn't honestly feel that she was being quite sincere, but although she was overplaying the pastoral side of her nature, she *was* going over big. Both Mr. and Mrs. Upson practically groveled at her feet. At lunch she spoke of her gay debutante days in Buffalo, which also coincided with *Chu Chin Chow* and the Campfire Girls, and then she and Mrs. Upson had a rather technical discussion of genealogy, during which I startled to hear that I was directly descended from Charlemagne.

During the afternoon we all split up; Mr. Upson wandered off to the golf course, Mrs. Upson and Auntie Mame—Doris and Cuddles, by now—went off to a country auction, and Gloria took me off to make love in a patch of woods.

"Oh, angel," Gloria murmured, her beautiful eyes deeper and greener than ever, "don't you just love it out here, away from all those filthy people in New York?"

I put my arms around her and kissed her for a long time.

"Angel," she said, sitting up, "you see all that land there beyond the stone wall?"

"Mm-hmm."

"You know it's all for sale? Every inch of it. Sixty acres."

"Is that so? Give us another kiss."

"Oh, don't. You *hurt*! I'll bet you have to shave about twice as much as most men. Well, I was thinking how perfectly dreamy it would be if we could just buy all that property and live out here. Right next to Mummy and Daddy."

"You mean commute into town every day?"

"Oh, no. We could have a place in town. Just a little *pied à terre*. But spend our *real* life out here in Mountebank. Besides, Daddy's so worried that somebody *funny* might buy in right next to us."

"Funny?"

"Well, you know, angel. Not nice."

"Gee, Gloria, I'll bet the land out here costs like hell."

"Well, it's not *cheap*, but it's so clean and fresh, and they've got such a *nice* class of people out here. Why, look how your aunt loves it. I'll bet if you just asked her sweetly—or if *I* did—she might want to give us that rolling hillside and maybe a little house—all glass and very modern—as sort of a wedding present."

"Now, wait a minute, baby," I said, sitting up. "I don't want to ask her for a lot of dough. She's been too generous with me all my life. And besides, I have money of my own and don't want to go around begging a lot of favors."

"But angel," she pouted prettily, "what's money *for*? She's all alone in the world and, after all, you *are* sort of the heir apparent."

I changed the subject quickly. "We ought to start looking around for a place to live in town and set a date. How about, say, the middle of next month?"

"You mean, get *married* next month?"

"Sure. What else?"

"But I *couldn't.*"

"Why not?"

"Why, I don't have any clothes."

"What do you call that dress you're wearing?"

"Oh, you know what I mean, silly. I mean *real* clothes. Lingerie and dresses and suits and coats and hats—all the things a bride *has* to have."

"This is the first I'd heard that she had to have anything except a man and a negative Wassermann."

"Oh, stop it! We *couldn't* get married. Jane's in Maine and Pammy's in Nantucket and B.J. and Frannie are both in . . ."

"But I don't want to marry Jane and Pammy and B.J. and Frannie. I only want to marry *you*, and I couldn't care less if they were all in the downtown business section of hell. Couldn't we just run *off* some place and get it over with?"

"And break my poor father's heart? Why, Daddy'd never forgive me if I did such a thing. And Mummy . . . ever since I was a little bit of a baby she's always dreamed of a beautiful beautiful wedding in the Church of the Heavenly Rest, with bridesmaids and ushers, and

Boyd's little girl—oh, wait till you see little Deborah, she looks just like a cherub—as a flower girl, and then a big reception at the club, and then . . ."

"Do you mean I've got to hunt up six guys and get them into rented cutaways that don't fit just so . . ."

"But *lover*, that's the fun of getting married."

"Oh, I'd always imagined that the fun came later."

"You know what I mean. But who wants to get married when you can't have a lot of parties and dances and presents and your picture in the papers? The way *everybody* does."

"Everybody?"

"Well, everybody *I* know. Nice people. I certainly don't want to go down to City Hall with a lot of foreigners and . . ."

"Just how long do you think it's going to take you to prepare for this production, now that Ziegfeld's dead?"

"Oh, I thought we'd announce it right after Labor Day when everybody's back in town, and then there are all the big parties up through the holidays, and then I thought we might get married right after the first of the year, and maybe go to Palm Beach or someplace like that for a honeymoon."

"I see," I said dully.

"Well, don't take on like that, angel. It isn't as if it were forever. Besides, you'll be as *busy*! We've got to find an apartment—and I don't mean just some little hole-in-the-wall, but a really nice place with some style to it—and furniture and rugs and some sort of maid or something. You can't just rush into these things. They've got to be done right or not at all."

"Yeah," I said, and lit a cigarette.

"Now, don't sulk, little boy. You'll see that I'm right in the long run. Now it's nearly four and I promised Mary Elizabeth we'd be over for tennis! Hurry. You've got to change!"

That evening the Upsons entertained a jolly party of the young, the middle-aged, the elderly, and the oldest of all, the Young Marrieds, at the club dance. Long before sundown gay carloads of suburbanites in evening clothes were crunching up the gravel drive, and Mr. Upson was in his element explaining just how to make a real, sugarless daiquiri. He seemed a little hurt when Auntie Mame asked for straight whiskey. News of her charm had apparently spread even to the most heavily restricted sections of Mountebank, and I had the feeling that the merrymakers were hanging on her every word. She was in fine fettle and spoke tenderly of the large hand-painted slop jar she'd bought at the auction that afternoon. "And Doris is going to teach me how to turn it into a *lamp*," she told her spellbound audience.

Auntie Mame looked especially ravishing in yards of trailing white and sapphires. I had a notion that a lot of the men who hadn't felt much like dancing for years were going to turn suddenly spry that night. Auntie Mame was on her best behavior and pirouetted prettily from one to the next, talking about the Japanese beetle, a difficult mashie shot, elm blight, country day schools, the servant problem, and—until I caught her eye—the wisdom of legalizing prostitution.

There were about two dozen people sipping Mr. Upson's daiquiris, and I moved around uncomfortably just catching snatches of the conversations:

"Perfectly ravishing, and she can't be as old as ..."

"An' so Wan sez to me, 'See, Seen-yor,'—that's how he talked—'you don't use zee sugar at all, but zee honey.' An' I wanna tell you it makes the smoothest damned ..."

"*Mousseline de soie*, that's what it is, and do you know how much they want for just one yard of it at McCutcheon's ..."

"But then I always knew Gloria would ..."

"And then this nigger caddy sez, 'Wal, suh, Ah sho nebbah see no golf ball *dat* color! ...'"

"But, Gloria, it's a beautiful ring! As I say to your mother, I say, 'Doris, you must remember you're not losing a daughter, but gaining a son!' And he's a very *nice* young man . . ."

"Most magnificent piece of womanflesh we've had around Mountebank since Queen Marie lectured . . ."

"Yes, but I always *gorge* so at a boo-fay . . ."

"That's the secret, shake like hell. None of these . . ."

"Half a grapefruit and a Ry-Krisp. And for dinner . . ."

"But of course they're real. I read all about her jewelry in *Town and Country*. And she's been everywhere . . ."

"Their name was *Harris*, and you know that can mean either Yes or No. Well, *he* looked perfectly all right, but when Alice got a look at *her*, she said 'Oh-oh' and sold the place to us for exactly half what those kikes were willing to pay . . ."

"Then F.D.R. sez, 'But Eleanor, how will I know if you . . .' "

"He doesn't say much, but his aunt is perfectly . . ."

Just as the party was at its noisiest, Auntie Mame hopped gracefully up onto a chair and called "Quiet! Quiet everyone! Quiet, please." There was a silence, and I felt myself go hot and then cold. "Of course you all know what these two young people have been up to, so there's no use of my spreading *that* old news. But I've racked my brain to try to think of a little engagement present that would be suitable for a girl as beautiful as Gloria, and now I know what it is." She loosened the baroque sapphire necklace from her throat, stepped off the chair, and clasped it around Gloria's neck. "Here, darling. I want you to have this. Only the young can wear them."

There was a volcanic buzzing and whispering. Gloria was speechless with pleasure.

"Oh . . . oh . . ." was all she could say.

"Mame!" Mrs. Upson shrieked. "You can't! You shouldn't! Oh, Mame, it's beautiful! Now, Gloria, let Mummy fasten it with dental floss until Daddy takes out a policy. You know how you'd feel if you lost it."

I was stunned with gratitude and surprise, but in the

orange sunset, against Gloria's green dress and her green
eyes, the sapphires didn't look quite, well, quite becoming.

It was a standard evening with a standard dinner and a
standard orchestra in a standard country club. I danced
most of the evening with Gloria after I'd polished off the
other dames at the long table, and she clung to me as she
never had before. "This is the happiest night of my life,"
she kept whispering. Auntie Mame got the big rush of
the evening. In fact, she didn't stop dancing from half
after nine until I saved her from another athletic schot-
tische of my prospective father-in-law.

"May *I*?" I said.

"Oh, you young whippersnappers get the best of
everything. Eh, Cuddles?" he chortled, giving her bare
back a final pinch.

"Ouch! Oh, Buster, you *slay* me!" Auntie Mame
shrilled.

"Do you mind my cutting in this way, Auntie Mame?"
I asked.

"*Mind?* I'd have been a basket case if you hadn't. I've
never been in a place where they played rugby to music
before. Would you like me to tell you how to make a daiquiri as Juan does? You just take honey and . . ."

"No, please, I know." I laughed. "But you really are
having a good time, aren't you?"

"Jim-dandy! Did I tell you about the time Mr. Abbot
made the hole-in-one on the fourteenth? (You know, par
for that hole is *three*.) Well, he was out with this Negro
caddy . . ."

"Listen, Auntie Mame, and I mean it. Whether you're
having a good time or not, you're being the most wonderful person in the whole state of Connecticut . . ."

"If you can't say something nice, don't say anything at
all."

"No, I mean it. You're absolutely super and I love you
for it. I've never been so proud of anybody in my life."

"But it's nothing, darling, You just take honey and shake like hell. Oh, God, here comes the Swedish Angel for round four."

"May I?" Mr. Abbot-Habit-Cabot-Rabbit-Mabbit said.

"I do hope you won't be bored," Mrs. Upson said the next morning, handing Auntie Mame the gardening section of the *Herald Tribune*, "but Sunday is just a *family* day for us. Claude *does* get in eighteen holes in the morning—*I* tell him he should go to church on Sunday mornings, but he says, 'I call on God often enough out on the links!' Isn't he awful!" .

"Awful?" Auntie Mame said, "my dear, he's . . ."

"But as I was saying, Mame, it's just a quiet old-folks-at-home day here at Upson Downs. We lie around the house and usually Boyd—that's our boy—comes over with Emily and we just chat and generally relax. You don't happen to like gin, do you?

"Like it? I *adore* it!"

"Goodie! Well, I'll just get out the deck and the score pad and we'll have a little game while . . ."

"Oh," Auntie Mame said, crestfallen.

"Of course, some people do object to cards on Sunday. Devil's pasteboards, you know."

"Perhaps I'd better just content myself with the gardening pages. I don't want to be *too* stimulated for Floyd."

"Boyd."

"Sorry. Yes, Boyd and Emily."

Sunday lagged along. Gloria slept until lunchtime and spent the afternoon in her room writing of her new happiness to distant friends. Mrs. Upson took Auntie Mame to call on the woman who had the biggest collection of milk glass in Mountebank, and I sat on the terrace rather hot and very bored.

At five o'clock we all congregated on the terrace where Mr. Upson, red and robust from his golf game, mixed up a round of daiquiris and told us again just how it was done. This time Auntie Mame was very firm about straight whisky and I asked for beer. No sooner were we settled than we were unsettled by the arrival of a Ford convertible which contained Boyd Upson, his wife Emily, and their child Deborah.

"Woo hoo!" Mrs. Upson called. "Woo hoo! Boydie-boy, Emily!"

There was a thunder of little feet and Deborah, a rather pretty child of about three, came racing onto the terrace.

"Oh, the *precious*! Come to Grammy, Debbie darling. Give Grammy a big kiss! Isn't it ridiculous," she said, simpering at Auntie Mame, "to be a grandmother at *my* age?"

"Ridiculous?" Auntie Mame said, "why it's . . ."

Her words were fortunately drowned by the arrival of Boyd Upson and his wife, Emily. Boyd was the ideal young Connecticut Republican, tall, fair, and nice-looking, with whatever muscles he once had turning speedily to fat. His wife Emily was the epitome of every girl on every verandah of every country club from Bar Harbor to Santa Barbara, a tall, unpleasant-looking young woman who'd had her teeth straightened, dancing lessons, and a mediocre education in the Spence-Chapin-Nightingale-Bamford-Hewitt circuit. She was the de luxe model, but with an extra tire because she was once again pregnant.

"Well, son, how goes it?" Father Upson said warmly. "Emily, dear, how's the little mother?"

"Golly, Dad, swell," Boyd yelled. I discovered during the afternoon that his education in American slang seemed to have begun and ended during the twenties. Gee, golly, swell, gosh darn, okay, oh boy, baby, prefaced his every statement.

"Debbie, let go of Grammy's beads! Isn't she an *angel*?"

"Celestial," Auntie Mame said, drawing her skirts closer.

"How d'you do?" Emily said, taking my hand limply. "Deborah, if you're going to act like a wild Indian you can go right back home. Boyd," she whined, "*do* something with her. She didn't take her N-A-P this afternoon and she's a little T-I-R-E-D."

"Golly, honey," Boyd boomed, "what can *I* do with her?"

"Well, I can't go hauling her around in this . . ."

"You haven't been throwing up again, have you, Emily dear?"

"Oh, no, but we've had another upset with that D-A-M-N maid. Honestly, nowadays *you're* working for them instead of them working for you. Do you know," she said, fixing a keen eye on Auntie Mame, "that those niggers not only ask the world, but they insist on a ten-hour day and every Sunday off and G-O-D knows what . . ." Her spelling bee was interrupted.

"Sshhh," Mrs. Upson warned *sotto voce*, "they'll hear you. Wouldn't you like to hold her, Mame dear?"

"Not parti . . ." Auntie Mame moaned softly as little Deborah was placed on her lap. "Ouch!" she cried as Deborah grasped one of her earrings. "Let go, damn y . . . Oh! *Mustn't* touch," she added darkly to the child.

"Now Deborah," Emily whined, "if you're going to make a pest of yourself you can just . . . Boyd, *do* something with her!"

"Red, red!" little Deborah crooned, grabbing hold of a ruby clip on Auntie Mame's lapel. "Have it!"

"Oh, let go, you little . . . *darling*," Auntie Mame said.

"She likes you, Mame dear," Mrs. Upson said. "I can tell."

The dog came loping out and Deborah was put down to play with him, leaving a large wet spot in Auntie Mame's lap.

"Boyd, don't let that D-A-M-N setter lick Deborah's face! You don't know *where* he's been!" Emily whined.

The hot sun and the beer were working in keen co-operation to give me a headache, and I don't remember exactly what was said. It was awfully noisy and everyone talked at once about nothing. I noticed that Auntie Mame was drinking a lot of straight Scotch and I couldn't say that I blamed her.

At seven o'clock, the houseman wheeled out some wrought-iron cooking and eating equipment and little Deborah was summoned by many voices to come and take a nice nap on Grammy's bed. Little Deborah was having none of it, however, and there was a great deal of coaxing and commanding and threatening and finally an out-and-out chase, with little Deborah screaming and gurgling and the dog barking hysterically. But as Deborah raced past Auntie Mame's chair she happened to trip and land with a soft thud on the grass. I could have sworn that Auntie Mame's foot had shot out in the child's path, but Auntie Mame pretended great concern and little Deborah was put into dead storage, so to speak, for the rest of the evening.

When things quieted down, Mr. Upson appeared in a tall chef's hat and a big canvas apron with clever things on it like "Chief Cook and Bottle Washer," "Cordon Bleu," "I'm Your Cookie," "Ye Greasy Spoon," and "At Home on the Range."

"Isn't he a *spectacle*!" Mrs. Upson giggled.

"A *sight*, believe me," Auntie Mame said.

"Every Sunday night Claude insists on doing the cooking. I got him that barbecue set at Hammacher-Schlemmer and he's just like a child with it."

"I'm sure he is."

"Golly, Dad," Boyd said, "I'd love to get a picture of you in that rig. It'd be swell for a Christmas card."

"Well, Boyd, you could catch a shot of Cuddles and I at the pit, 'cause she's gonna help Buster, aren't you, Cuddles?"

"Am I?" Auntie Mame asked blankly.

"You betcher boots you are, Cuddles. Couldn't get the meat on the table without you. Bring your drink down and give me some *immoral* support at the pit. Hahaha!"

"I hope the meal's as good as your daiquiri," Auntie

Mame said coquettishly, pouring two stiff hookers of Scotch.

"Soda for you, Mame dear?" Mrs. Upson said solicitously.

"No, thank you, Doris," Auntie Mame answered, and minced down the lawn to the barbecue and Mr. Upson. There was so much smoke that we couldn't see either of them, but I could hear Auntie Mame coughing and choking. She came out once, her eyes streaming, to have the glasses refilled, and bravely went back into the flames, carrying full tumblers of straight whisky.

It seemed to take forever to cook steaks "just right," as Mr. Upson kept saying. Just Right was black with soot and ashes on the outside and cold and raw on the inside. We were served one steak apiece and it struck me as a most criminal waste of about twenty dollars' worth of good beef. It also appeared that perhaps the smoke and the Scotch had been a little too much for Mr. Upson.

We sat around a glass and iron table gnawing determinedly on Mr. Upson's steaks and muttering guttural growls of insincere appreciation. Mr. Upson polished off a lot more Scotch during the meal and once or twice Mrs. Upson said, "Claude, do you think you should?" Otherwise we dined in diligent silence. Emily suffered several minor gastric upsets during the meal—not that I blamed her—and the peace and quiet was finally broken by Boyd, who had the lamentable habit of talking with his mouth full.

"Gee, Dad," he said, "you know that property out behind here? I came out on the five-oh-seven with Charlie Haddock on Friday and he says they're thinking of selling to some people from Summit, New Jersey, named Bernstein—*A-bra-ham* Bernstein."

"Oh, no!" Mrs. Upson whimpered.

Mr. Upson's fork clattered to the table. "Bernstein!"

"Not the Abraham Bernsteins from *Summit*?" Auntie Mame said. "I know them *very* well. He's an editor, and she's an authority on Rimbaud. They're a delightful couple with two children named . . ."

"Stop!" Mr. Upson said. "This is no joking matter."

"I'm not joking. The Bernsteins are friends of the Co . . ."

"It's impossible, Boyd. This whole section's restricted."

"Not beyond your boundary it isn't. That isn't *Mountebank*."

"Oh, Daddy," Gloria cried, "how *dreadful!*"

"I won't have it," Mr. Upson barked. "I'll stand here with a gun if necessary, and keep them off . . ."

"Buster," Auntie Mame said, "what's come *over* you? They're charming people. She's very dark and vivacious and one of the best cooks in . . ."

"I'll bet she's dark and vivacious. A greasy, thick-lipped, loud-mouthed little . . ."

"Oh, but you're all wrong there. Sylvia's divine, really, and Abe went to Harvard in the same class with Samuel . . ."

"You mean you *really* know these people?" Mr. Upson asked.

"But, of course. He has a marvelous job with . . ."

"But they're Jews."

"Well, certainly they're Jews. She's related somehow to Rabbi Wise and he . . ."

"Can't you get it through your thick head that they're *Jews*? That they want to move in right next to *me*?" Mr. Upson said.

"Claude, *please*," Mrs. Upson said.

"Yes, Buster, I *heard* Floyd—Boyd—say that they were going to buy out here. And you'll love them. One of the most stimulating young couples I know."

"Lookee here," Mr. Upson said evenly, "a joke's a joke, but if you think I want a lot of sheenies throwing their filthy garbage all over my lawn . . ."

"Buster what are you *talking* about? I tell you that

these people are friends of mine. They couldn't be more fastidious."

"Will you shut *up*!"

"Claude!" Mrs. Upson said.

"Now see here, sir," I said, half rising.

"Please," Gloria whispered, "Daddy's in one of his moods."

"I don't care *what* he's in, he doesn't talk to my aunt . . ."

"Boyd," Mr. Upson roared, "if you and I have to form a posse—a pack of vigilantes—we're going to keep these dirty kikes and all the rest of their lousy, stinking race out of . . ."

"You can't really be so naive as to believe that the Jews are a *race*," Auntie Mame said. "Why, any anthropologist . . ."

"Don't give me none of your high-toned anthropology! I just know that as long as I have a breath left in my body I'll fight every goddamned last one of these Izzys and Beckys trying to muscle in on white man's territory. And, by God . . ."

"Do you mean to sit there and tell me," Auntie Mame said, "that you think you *own* Connecticut? That you're some sort of self-appointed deity who has supreme power and the final word on *who* may buy *what* property and *where* and *when*?"

"Mame, a man's home is his castle. That may sound old-fashioned, but it's still true, and I haven't worked like a dog all these years to build up this nice place only to have it ruined by a pack of mockies movin' in right under my . . ."

"Claude," Auntie Mame said with narrowed eyes and voice of steel, "I have told you three times that these Filthy Kikes you're talking about are friends of mine. People I have known for several years. Attractive, intelligent, educated people. You might reserve judgment until you've met them."

"Oh, yeah? You can talk that way now, you in your

fancy mansion on Washington Square, but what would you say if they moved in right next to you?"

"I believe I'd say 'Welcome to Washington Square, Sylvia, and if you and Abe would like to come over for dinner while you're getting settled ...' "

"Shit!"

"Claude!" Mrs. Upson said.

"Goddamn it, Doris," he yelled, "I *mean* it!" He turned to Auntie Mame. "You sit and talk like the *New Republic* or some parlor pink when another Christian faces a serious ..."

"I wish you wouldn't use the term *Christian* where it is so obviously misapplied," Auntie Mame said steadily.

"Now, see here, Mame ..." Mrs. Upson began.

"Please," Gloria said, "can't we change the subject?"

"To what, Gloria? Negroes?" Auntie Mame said.

"Don't interfere, sweetheart," Mr. Upson said. "Now look, I been to your house and seen all its fancy European splendors, and maybe I am just a dumb insurance broker without your big Franklin Delano Rosenfeld outlook on life, but I didn't notice you cavortin' around with a pack of hebes when I was down to dinner. Oh, no, you had a noble Englishman and a French prince and a famous actress—not a bunch of Jews!"

"I suppose it would be cruel to tell you that the Vera Charles whom you and Doris admire so extravagantly was born Rachel Kollinsky, the daughter of a second-rate Jewish comedian."

"Impossible!" Mrs. Upson breathed.

"Well, that's *your* business!" he roared on. "There's no accounting for those theater people anyway. They're a different breed of cat. But when it comes to havin' Jews right next door—practically in your family ..."

"Claude," Auntie Mame said quietly, "do you realize that at this very moment a maniac in Germany named Adolf Hitler is talking just the way you are now?"

"Now, don't bring politics into this. I'll betcher a New Dealer through and through."

"I have always admired President Roosevelt."

"I'm talking about Jews, and when it comes to them, Hitler's got some pretty sound ideas."

"You can't mean that," I said, "he's *slaughtering* them."

"I didn't *say* I wanted to slaughter them ..."

"I rather thought that with your talk of guns and posses and vigilantes, you had something of the sort in mind," Auntie Mame said cooly.

"And, yes, by Christ, that's what I *would* do!"

"Just how many Jews do you know personally, Claude?"

"I know all I want to," he screamed. "Pushy, bossy, aggressive, loud ..."

"As loud as you're being at this moment?"

"Goddamn it! I'm talking about a pack of kikes moving in and rubbing shoulders with nice people—decent people!"

"And is this an example of your nicety? Your decency?" Auntie Mame took the deep breath that means business, and even in my misery, I discovered myself getting fascinated.

"Claude," she said, "I've known dozens of Jews in my life and it has also been my sorry experience to have heard quite a few gentiles who have talked about Jews as you do. I know the adjectives—all of them. Jews, you will tell me, are Mean, Pushy, Avaricious, Possessive, Loud, Vulgar, Garish, Bossy people. But I've yet to meet one, from the poorest pushcart vendor on First Avenue to the richest philanthropist on Fifth Avenue, who could ever hold a candle to you when it comes to displaying all of those qualities."

"*Mame!*" Mrs. Upson gasped.

"By Christ, I'm not going to be insulted in my own home any longer. You can get outta here and go right back to Jew York and sleep with all the filthy kikes you can ..."

"Shut your dirty mouth!" I said, jumping up from my chair.

Mr. Upson sat back goggle-eyed, and across the table Boyd rose and glared at me. There was a cry from Gloria.

"T-take back your ring and get out of here! Go on and marry some cheap little Jewess, if you love them so much. You'll be a lot happier that way. You're just not in the same class with us, and what's more, you *never will* be!"

"Gloria . . ."

"Patrick doesn't know it just now, Gloria," Auntie Mame said, rising from the table, "but you've just paid him the most beautiful compliment he's ever likely to receive. I will thank you *for* him. And now, I'll be excused, if I may. Patrick, are you coming too, or shall I telephone for a nice Christian cab driver—perhaps an Aryan from Darien?"

"Wait," I said, "I'm coming with you."

We drove rapidly, the wind blowing cold against our hot faces. After a time Auntie Mame said: "Patrick, you know, I always like to give a fairly large amount to charity every year. I have so very much."

"Mm-hmm," I murmured.

"What would you think if I were to overbid Sylvia and Abe on that property adjoining the Upsons' and put up a home for Jewish war refugees?"

"I think that would be wonderful."

"Good," she said, "I hoped you'd say that."

The big diamond engagement ring flashed coldly in my hand as we sped away from the slums of Connecticut.

Nine

Auntie Mame

and the Call to Arms

In life's twilight, the Unforgettable Character is left pretty much alone with her house and her garden and her cat. The foundling is grown up and settled down and everybody says she's done a hell of a good job of raising him. She has her friends and her hobbies and her businesses and you'd think the old girl would be satisfied. But no. She misses the patter of tiny feet around her house and so what does the old girl do but get *two* foundlings and start all over again.

This dénouement is obviously geared to stun everybody. Not me. Auntie Mame would never have done anything on so trivial a scale. *She* took on half a dozen children and lived to tell the tale.

After Gloria Upson returned my ring, my heart was officially broken, although I now doubt that it was even sprained. But when you do something as drastic as end an engagement, you have to do something else that's equally drastic just to balance things. Me, I went to war. Europe was already in it, and it seemed a matter of min-

utes before America got in, too. The day I sent the ring
back to Cartier's I also became a Volunteer in the American Field Service. Two weeks later I sailed for North
Africa, while Auntie Mame wept in Washington Square.

It's probably shocking to say that you *enjoyed* a war,
but I did. Life in the Field Service was made up of equal
parts of boredom and excitement. I saw a lot of new
places and new faces. We didn't have to do anything like
stand at attention or salute people, and I was never terribly scared. When you worked, you worked hard and got
shot at and ate hard tack and bully beef. When you
played, you played hard and lived at Shepheard's Hotel
and flirted with Queen Farida at the Turf Club.

Auntie Mame wrote almost every day. At first her letters were long dirges of how lonely and wasted she felt.
They made me feel sad and, for some reason, a little
guilty. But Pearl Harbor was attacked that December and
her correspondence took on another tone. Her letters
were filled with descriptions of her new activities and I
began to smell the smoke of a new fire, for indeed,
Auntie Mame was becoming more warlike than Alexander of Macedon.

"I sold more bonds than any woman who's ever
worked El Morocco!" she would write. "They're giving
me the Iridium Room next week, as a *challenge*. Those
big spenders are lousy bondbuyers, but I'm blackmailing
them into patriotism." Or, "I patrolled Washington
Square for my first blackout last night. My dear, there are
really *stars* over New York with all the lights off!" Or,
"Now that I've broken the bandage-rolling record for
Manhattan Island, I'm going to give it up. There are
more important things to do and the A.W.V.S. wants me
to head a new committee." Or, "I'm so heartsick and de-
spondent I could weep! The WAC's *rejected* me! The ser-
geant at the recruiting office said I was *too old*! Well, I'd
hate to be hanging since *that* old dike was eighteen."

She had more uniforms than a four-star general. Her
house became an unofficial USO. She ranked high on ev-

ery committee of Amazons in New York. Still, she found time to do a lot of shopping for me. Tons of delicacies followed me all over Africa and Italy: cookies and caviar and pralines and pâté, tins of chicken and lobster and crabmeat and terrapin. And just to prove that Auntie Mame hadn't grown too realistic, one package containing specially bottled strawberries bore these instructions: "Marinate in champagne and thinly sliced limes in refrigerator. Delicious with pheasant." One box held nothing but medicine bottles with labels like "One tablespoon before meals" and "Apply on irritated area before retiring." I was pretty mystified until I took a sniff and discovered that each bottle contained bonded bourbon which Auntie Mame had siphoned off into pharmacist's bottles in a sly attempt to get around the U.S. Postal Regulations.

But as the war dragged on, I noticed that the old girl was getting a little restless. In 1944 a letter reached me in the dried-out river bed beneath Monte Cassino. It began:

"Darling Patrick—
Don't know why I feel so blue lately, but I do. This empty house, the terrible loneliness in crowds of people. Of course I'm busy as can be with my work, but, oh, the impersonality of it. I know that woman's first function is motherhood and . . ."

That was all I read. There was a terrible rushing noise and a crash. The next thing I knew I was in a British hospital in Caserta with a wistful Tommy orderly who kept saying, "It's a good job we saved yer leg, chum. Now 'ow about a nice cup of 'ot Ovaltine?"

It was May when the hospital ship docked at New York. I thanked all the ocean-going doctors and nurses, waived the services of a Red Cross ambulance, and hobbled off the pier. By acting a lot lamer than I actually was, I managed to flag down a wartorn taxicab and bounced off to Washington Square. I arrived at Auntie

Mame's big front door just as she was coming out of it, looking suitably ethereal in her Gray Lady costume.

"Darling!" she screamed. "Darling, darling boy!" She threw her arms around me and burst into tears. Then she dragged me into her empty drawing room and mixed two strong Cuban gins. "Hallelujah!" she cried, flinging a copy of Stendhal across the room. "I *was* going out to the hospital to read *La Chartreuse de Parme* aloud to our boys. But now that you're home, my little love, *now that you're home*, I feel that you'll give me the strength to take advantage of the most wonderful challenge that has ever come my way. Oh, darling, this *is* a stroke of fate. Now, with you at my side—game leg and all—I feel that I can get off the periphery of *la guerre* and right into the *thick* of it."

"What are you talking about? Are you going to enlist?"

"Oh, Patrick dearest, the most wonderful thing has just happened. Well, a terrible thing, really, but wonderful for me. La, it's an ill wind et cetera. But here is the fate for which every daughter of Eve was born and now, with you by my side, I can go out and meet it."

"What *is* this?" I asked.

"Well, my dear, just this morning I heard the news. There's a Mrs. Armbruster out in Southampton—she's a widow, like me, but *years* older—who's taken in six adorable little English war refugees for the duration. And today my commanding officer in the A.W.V.S. called to say that poor dear Mrs. Armbruster had just dropped dead. Isn't that marvelous!"

"It's just great," I said. "What did you have against her?"

"Oh, nothing darling. She was a perfect *saint*. But, Patrick, my commandant was wondering if I could take one . . . or perhaps two . . . of them, and I wanted to so badly. But something held me back. *Now*, however, with you here"—she fixed me with a glittering eye—"I know that I can provide a mother *and* a father for all *six* of them."

"Hey, listen . . ." I began. It was too late. She was already at the telephone.

Auntie Mame could move fast when she wanted to, and in a matter of ten days she'd rented a large house out on Long Island, placed all of her servants at Sperry Gyroscope to do their bit—except for Ito, who was Japanese and suspect—and closed the house in town, bought a lot of country clothes and a secondhand station wagon for twice what it should have cost new. Then she resigned from all of her militaristic organizations to devote full time to being the little mother. I hadn't even a chance to tell her that I wasn't vaguely interested in raising six children before Ito was steering the station wagon up the drive of what was to be our home for the duration.

Auntie Mame never did anything by halves, and I must admit to being rather impressed by the place she'd leased. It was called Peabody's Tavern, and it was an authentic pre-Revolutionary building of some twenty rooms. It absolutely stank with atmosphere. There were five plaques next to the front door proclaiming the treaties signed within, the remarkable age and state of preservation of the structure, and other notes of interest to the historian. It was beautifully landscaped, and the lawn looked like a giant putting green.

Miss Peabody herself, who told us four times that she was the tenth generation to live there, greeted us at the double-hung door. She was a bony old piece and a crashing snob. She didn't allow a minute to pass before she told us that she was a Daughter of the American Revolution, a Colonial Dame, a Daughter of the Cincinnati, a Mayflower Descendant, and a number of other dreary things. She ran over the major historical events that had occurred in the tavern during the past two or three hundred years, described the annual pilgrimage which a lot of antiquarians made there every spring, and dragged out a bulky scrapbook filled with photographs of the rooms which had appeared in *Antiques* and *House and Garden* and *Country Life* and a lot of other fancy places.

Miss Peabody served us a very light and very bad luncheon on Lowestoft and then took us on a little tour of the house, pointing out the authentic Revere wallpaper, the authentic Windsor chairs, the authentic Copley portraits of bygone Peabodys, the authentic hewn beams and pegged floors. She touched each warming pan and pewter mug and hooked rug as though it were a bit of the True Cross. Auntie Mame, looking very much the country gentlewoman, all tweed and a shooting stick, stifled several yawns and expressed a counterfeit fascination with the whole place.

After impressing us for two solid hours, Miss Peabody handed us a copy of the inventory which set the value of the furnishings at just under one hundred and seventy thousand dollars and said for the fourth time that she'd never before dreamed of renting her house, but what with Auntie Mame being such a lady, and what with the war and the high taxes, she'd make an exception just this once. She was also sticking Auntie Mame five hundred bucks a month for rent.

"Isn't this place kind of fragile for a lot of kids?" I began.

Auntie Mame shot me a dark look that meant Shut Up. But Miss Peabody was so busy pointing out the hand-blown glass in the fanlight that she hadn't even heard. "Well, I'll be running along now, Mrs. Burnside," Miss Peabody said, drawing on her gloves. "I cawn't tell you how happy I am to be able to give two true connoisseurs the opportunity of living here. Ta ta!" She got into her car and drove off.

Auntie Mame took off her tweed jacket, wiped her brow, poured two stiff drinks, and then flitted about the enormous rooms of the tavern. "Oh, darling, don't you just adore this quaint old place! Not quaint like the Upsons', but really old and authentic and homey. I just can't wait to get over to the hardware and buy pots and pots of paint in heavenly soft shades—simply *do* this place over. You know how interested psychologists are in color therapy nowadays. And think of the balm to the war-frazzled nerves of those poor displaced little darlings when they romp through these restful old rooms."

"What does Miss Peabody think of your repainting her museum?"

"I'm sure I don't know," Auntie Mame said, flicking an ash into a Worcester bowl. "I haven't told her about it yet."

"Don't you think you'd better ask her?"

"I thought it would be more fun to surprise her, darling."

"But is that going to be Miss Peabody's idea of fun?" I asked.

"Oh, don't be such a *stick*, Patrick. I can see the war has done little to soften you."

"It rarely has that effect."

"Well if you ... Heavens," she said looking at her watch, "we'll have to *fly* if we're ever to get to Southampton to pick up the wee ones. I told Miss Pringle we'd be there at three sharp. She'll be all packed and so will the children. That should get us back here in time for tea. We *must* get into the daily teatime habit. It's so important for those little Britons to be made aware of their country's customs, torn up by the roots as the poor waifs are. Psychologically it's very bad to have the behavior pattern interrupted during the formative years."

It was almost four when we arrived at the saddened home of the late Mrs. Armbruster. It was one of those Stately Homes sort of places, but as we got closer, it looked kind of seedy and rundown to me. I was surprised that this latter-day saint and social leader would have allowed her house to go to rack and ruin that way, but I chalked it up to wartime shortages. There were a lot of kids chasing each other around the lawn, and a wild-eyed woman pacing up and down the driveway with a kind of hunted expression on her face.

"Hello! *Hello!*" Auntie Mame called gaily. "Are you Miss Pringle? I've come for the children."

"Thank God!" Miss Pringle said. "It'll be paradise to get away."

"My dear, I can imagine it will. How terrible for the little ones to dwell in a house of sorrow after poor Mrs. Armbruster's, um, passing."

"She had all the luck," Miss Pringle said, but Auntie Mame wasn't listening. "Well, I guess I'd better round 'em up. Hey, you kids," she shouted, "come over here and step on it." The children ignored her. "By God," she snarled, "I'd like for just once in my life to call those brats and have them pay some attention. Hey, Edmund! Cut the horsing. Get that gang together and come on. Albert, you look after Margaret Rose. No, I *didn't* say push her down, I said ... *Gladys!* Damn you anyhow!"

"There," Auntie Mame whispered, "is a woman who has no love or understanding of little folk. And a sorry sight it is. I must try to indoctrinate her with a few basic tenets of child psychology."

"Maybe you'd better wait until she gets them into the car before you do any indoctrinating," I said.

"Oh, the little darlings," Auntie Mame cooed. "The pink and gold of the English complexion. So Yardley!"

Auntie Mame was myopic and too vain to wear her glasses, but my beady eyes were sharp enough to see that Yardley would have gone bankrupt generations ago if it turned out many skins like these. They were typical of the squat, knobby-kneed, rake-ribbed Cockney kids you see in London slums, and five years with the saintly Mrs. A. had done nothing to improve them.

Eventually Miss Pringle got the six of them lined up at the car. Auntie Mame smiled beatifically and spoke to them in her best Fairy Godmother manner. "Good afternoon, my little English cousins. My name is Mrs. Burnside, but you must all call me Auntie Mame."

"Coo lumme," the oldest said. The rest burst into peals of laughter.

Auntie Mame looked a bit startled, but she laughed, too. "Merriment," she said in a brief aside to me, "is the best medicine, after all. And this," she continued with a sweeping gesture toward me, "is my nephew, who's just come back from being wounded with the British fighting forces."

Someone made a rude noise.

"Now," Auntie Mame continued, "as long as we're all going to live together—till the lights go on again all over the world . . ."

"Aow, not that dreeery aold tune!" the eldest girl screamed.

"As I was saying," Auntie Mame went on, a little louder, "since we're all going to live together for a while, I shall be wanting to know your names. Now, you first," she said cordially to the biggest boy.

"Call me Jack the Rippah, baby," he shouted with a show of badly neglected teeth. The others were convulsed.

"How do you do, Jack," Auntie Mame said.

"You'll call him nothing of the kind," Miss Pringle snapped. "His name's Edmund Jenkins and he's the meanest male ever born."

"Jack or Edmund, I *still* like you," Auntie Mame beamed brightly. "And your name?" she said, nodding toward an overdeveloped young girl.

"Oim Loidy Oiris Mountbattink, yore 'oighness," she sneered.

Miss Pringle lost her temper. She stepped forward and cuffed the girl. "Gladys Martin, mind your manners, you impudent little trollop!"

"*Please*, Miss Pringle," Auntie Mame said. "If she wants to be called Iris, I'm sure we'll be happy to please her. And you?" she said to the next.

"Give your names and no funny business," Miss Pringle growled.

"Enid Little, mum," the child said.

"That was very sweet, Enid. You're quite a polite young lady."

Gladys/Iris snorted nastily.

"Moy nyme is Albut, mum," a mincing little voice announced. "Albut Andrews, an' this is me bybee sistah, Mogrut Rose." Albert was a wizened brat with adenoids, and his sister, the youngest of the lot, was a pretty, large-eyed youngster of six.

"I'm happy to meet you both," Auntie Mame said graciously. "And I know that Margaret Rose is going to be *our* little princess."

"Grubby little bitch," a voice said.

Auntie Mame turned to the speaker. "Why, you—the little boy with the beautiful red hair—don't you like our little Princess Margaret Rose?"

"Naow."

"Well, suppose you tell me *your* name."

"Naow."

" 'Is nyme's Ginger," Albert simpered.

"I'm happy to meet you, Ginger. Shake?" Auntie Mame said, holding out her hand.

"Naow."

"Very well, if you don't really *want* to. Now, shall we go to our new house, so we can all have tea there?"

There was a general clamoring. Finally the kids got their luggage piled onto the station wagon and themselves into it. Miss Pringle sat in front with Auntie Mame, and I sat in the rear, next to Gladys/Iris, with the rest of the kids piled around us. I could have sworn Gladys was trying to play footie with me all the way back.

A quarrel started as we were driving through Quogue, but Auntie Mame avoided open warfare by calling out: "Sing, sing! What shall we sing?"

"Let's sing 'Igh Jig-a-Jig, Fuck a Little Pig,' " Edmund roared. Miss Pringle wheeled around with her dukes up, but Auntie Mame smoothed things over by saying, "I don't believe *I* know that song, Edmund."

"*I* do," I said.

In the end we all sang "Begin the Beguine," Gladys' choice, during which she whispered, "This song alwys mykes me evah so passionate."

We got back to the Peabody Tavern at six. Ito had done Japanese flower arrangements in all the vases, but after the kids had been there fifteen minutes it was obvious that his efforts had been wasted.

"Now children," Auntie Mame said, a nervous edge in her voice, "first we must all choose our bedrooms. There are lots of them in this lovely old house. *Don't* you all think it's lovely?"

"Naow," Ginger said.

"Well, Ginger," Auntie Mame went on diplomatically, "perhaps you'll get to like it. It was once a famous old tavern when our country was at war with . . . Well, it was a famous old tavern. Now I think we'll pick our rooms." She marched smartly up the stairs, the children thundering behind her. "Ladies first. Gladys, where would *you* like to sleep?"

"With 'im," Gladys smirked, gesturing toward me.

"Oh," Auntie Mame said. "Well, I'm afraid that Patrick has only one bed in his room."

"Don't moind," Gladys said, giving me the eye.

Finally the rooms on the second and third floors were doled out. "Now," Auntie Mame called, "all of you unpack and please *wash*, then we'll have tea down in the library. Come along, Patrick. Come, Miss Pringle, let's just give the darlings a chance to get acclimated." We followed her downstairs. "Now, Miss Pringle, I've saved you a nice bed-sitting room on the ground floor so you can get away from the kiddies once in a while. Oh, didn't you bring your bags in, Miss Pringle?"

"I certainly did not."

"But, Miss Pringle, I don't quite . . ."

"Listen, Mrs. Burnside, my distinct understanding was that *you* were going to take over. *I'm* going to New York."

"But, Miss Pringle," Auntie Mame said, "I was led to believe that you were coming along with the children as a sort of supervisor, just as you were for Mrs. Armbruster. Your salary is . . ."

"Listen, dearie, I wouldn't spend another night under the same roof with those Dead End kids for a million bucks."

"But, Miss Pringle," Auntie Mame said in pretty confusion, "who's to look after the bathing, the dressing, all those details? I simply *assumed* that . . ."

"Well, *I* simply assume that I'm not. Look here, Mrs. Burnside. I understand your point of view. It's very patriotic, unselfish, One World—all that sort of stuff. I had it myself a year ago. I'd just graduated from Hunter—a psych major twenty-one years old. Look at me now: gray hair! I'm the seventeenth woman on this job in five years. Girl before me had a complete nervous collapse. You should see her! But eight months with those hellions is enough for me. Now, you don't have to bother with taking me to the station. You paid my salary just fine, and thanks. You didn't know what you were getting in for and I'm sorry—truly sorry. But I'm going into New York tonight if I have to walk. Hell, I'd hoof it to Frisco to get away from *them*"—she jerked a thumb toward the stairs. "Good-by and good luck, I only hope you don't end up on a slab like Mrs. Armbruster." She marched out of the door.

So we were alone, just the two of us and Ito with six little savages screaming their lungs out. The English children hated tea—"No bloody cuppa muck fa me," Edmund said—and insisted on Coca-Cola. The kitchen stove, also an antique, had an immediate aversion to both Ito and Auntie Mame, and she burned herself very badly. She also burned the soup and cut herself trimming the sandwiches. The oranges she gave the children had been a terrible mistake, and the authentic beams in Miss Peabody's dining room dripped juice and seeds for many days. Ito was terrified of the children and cowered in the kitchen, too undone to be of any use that first night, so it was up to Auntie Mame and me to do the dishes.

"Now run into the other room and play, darlings," Auntie Mame said with false brightness, "for just one hour and then off to slumberland."

"Are you quite sure you'll be able to swing this deal?" I asked grimly as I dried Miss Peabody's priceless Lowestoft.

"But of *course* I can, my little love, with you here to help me. Frankly, I'm just as glad that the Pringle creature has gone. She knew *nothing*—less than nothing—of handling children. They must be led, not driven. After all, these babies have undergone a severe traumatic experience. All those bombs, the fear, the insecurity—being plucked out of their nests and sent to a strange land. And then being pushed around by a lot of paid help like Miss Pringle—interested only in the salary. You'll see. My example of loving understanding and gentle guidance will work wonders. And of course I'll be needing a man around the house," she added hastily. "Especially one who's been with the British Army and whom they can look up to as a hero. By the way, I have a splendid book on child guidance. I want you to read it tonight. We haven't a moment to lose."

We hadn't. In the living room the children were playing their game. I learned in a couple of days that when a game is quiet it's dangerous. Tiptoeing into the room, we found the girls lined up against the wall, their hands on their hips, wriggling obscenely, while the boys sauntered past scrutinizing them carefully.

"What game is this you're playing, Albert dear?" Auntie Mame asked.

"Wattaloo Bridge, mum," Albert said prissily.

"What sort of game is that, dear?"

"The gels is all prostychutes and we're pickin' 'em up."

Auntie Mame's jaw fell open.

" 'Ow's about a little tupenny uproight wiv yew, Myme old gel?" Edmund said, leering slimily.

"Mind your manners, damn you!" I roared.

"Patrick, *please*. Bear in mind the neurotic condition of these little ones," Auntie Mame said. "Now dears, I think we've had enough of *this* game. It's bedtime and we must all get a good rest to prepare ourselves for the joys of tomorrow. Patrick and I will undress you."

"Those kids are big enough to undress themselves," I muttered.

"It's important this first night," Auntie Mame whispered. "Establishes the intimacy of the mother and father relationship."

Upstairs there was a bit of confusion as to who was going to undress whom. Edmund, who was fifteen and more precocious than seemed desirable, wanted Auntie Mame, and Gladys insisted on me. We turned thumbs down on that. I started out with Albert. I think I really hated Albert the most, although it's difficult to decide. But he was the easiest to handle. Being a prig and a toady and stool pigeon and a coward, he was only too anxious to curry favor. When I got Albert into the bathtub I tackled Ginger, a kid of eight who was the most sullen, willful, negative child I've ever seen. Then I turned to Edmund.

"Touch me an' Oi'll yell the 'ouse down," he growled.

"Suits me," I said. "Get to bed by yourself."

"M'ybe Oi will an' m'ybe Oi won't."

"I'll bet you *will*," I said grabbing him by the shoulder.

"Tyke ya filthy 'ands orfa me and kiss me arse," he said, bending over.

"Okay, Edmund," I said. "Look, no hands." I hauled off and gave him a kick that sent him flying across the room. I'd used my bad leg and the pain was shattering, but it was worth it. Edmund slunk right under the covers.

I got into bed about midnight and tried to read *The Twentieth Century Child*. I'd just reached an informative chapter—"Masturbation: A Sin or a Sign?"—when there was a faint rustling at my door.

"Who is it?" I called.

"It's me. Gladys."

"What do you want?"

"Oim caold."

"Well, there's an extra blanket in your closet."

"Aow, c'mawn, tall, dock, an' 'an'sim, tyke me inter bed with yew and 'eat me up a bit," she gurgled unalluringly through the door.

"You get back to your room," I roared, "or I'll warm your backside so you won't be able to sit down for a year."

"Sy-dist," she giggled, and tiptoed away.

I've never gone through such a summer in my life. Those six limeys were enough to make Winston Churchill pro-Hitler. Gladys, at thirteen, was a wanton little nymphomaniac. Edmund, at fifteen, was a complete thug with halitosis and an advanced case of satyriasis. Why he and Gladys couldn't have found some release in one another was beyond me, but that would have been too considerate of them. Edmund had a yen for Auntie Mame while Gladys went in heavily for me.

Eleven-year-old Enid was a kleptomaniac, and whenever anything was missing one only had to look in Enid's room to find it. Ginger was an illegitimate child who exploded the old theory that love children are always the loveliest. I never heard him say Yes once. Albert at ten was just despicable, and his little sister, Margaret Rose, although the best of the lot, was a chronic bed wetter and no bargain.

But Auntie Mame stuck to her guns and her psychology. She kept insisting that the children were improving, although it was lost on me. The treasures in Miss Peabody's house went faster than I could keep track of them. The Sully portrait of Colonel Peabody served as a dartboard. A priceless primitive of a Miss Chastity Peabody developed sweeping mustachios and a full beard. Every day I'd check off a bit of new breakage against the inventory. On their best day, the kids managed forty thousand dollars' worth; on their worst, a paltry three hundred. Rich as Auntie Mame was, it made my blood run cold. Nor were her attempts at color therapy very successful. The authentic wallpapers were painted over a dozen times that summer. At first, Auntie Mame tried to interest the kids in Beauty and gave them their choice as to what colors the walls should be painted. But in the end it didn't really matter. When the walls were light colors, the children scribbled obscenities on them in pencil. When they were dark, they used chalk. They knifed all the tires of the station wagon, and Auntie Mame, who patriotically resisted anything that smacked of black market, was helpless and had to spend a small fortune on a new set. Miss Peabody's beautiful garden was totally uprooted. One by one the hand-blown glass windowpanes went. The Chippendale chairs, the elm settle, the tester beds disintegrated as though by sorcery. In an effort to get Gladys out of *Silver Screen* and into "something of more lasting value," Auntie Mame sent her off for piano lessons, but the night Gladys chose to give us an impromptu recital, she struck the first chord of "That Old Black Magic" on Miss Peabody's harpsichord with a force that completely gutted the instrument. Gladys went back to *Silver Screen*.

But our worst loss was Ito. While the children rather admired Nazis, they saw their archenemy in gentle, silly Ito. They called him Tojo and made his life a hell on earth. Once I discovered him shackled in the old slave quarters above the kitchen. Another time the kids found some cement in the tool shed and poured it into poor Ito's sukiyaki. But what finished our only servant was the time they buttered the back stairs with oleomargarine. Ito's leg was broken in three places. I raced the station wagon all the way to the hospital in Port Jefferson while Ito and Auntie Mame wailed in the back seat. It was six months before he returned. After that there was a steady procession of maids. I remember an Ophelia, a Delia, a Celia; Jessie, Bessie, and Tessie came and went *immediately*; Mary, Margaret, Maude, Madeleine, and Maureen passed through Miss Peabody's portals and right out again. The last of them, Anna, stuck it out for a week. As she was leaving, she gave Auntie Mame a few homely words of advice. "Lock them kids in, turn on the oven, and walk out," she said. Then I drove her to the station.

It was only natural that Auntie Mame would be welcomed by the summer colony in the Long Island community. And during June the two of us were asked to dine out quite a lot. One kindly *grande dame* even secured guest privileges for us at the local beach club, but after one day on the sands with the kiddies, Auntie Mame received a letter from the Board of Governors—"You and your nephew," it began, "will be more than welcome, but as for the children . . ." We never went to the beach club again. A few young matrons even sent their offspring over to play with our brood—once. By July Auntie Mame and I were pariahs, notorious throughout the county.

The local library revoked all privileges at the end of a week. After that, the children contented themselves with ripping up the historical records, bound in full calf, in Miss Peabody's library. They never cared much for reading. What Auntie Mame called "thespian enchantment" was also wasted on her charges. She sent the whole brood off to see *What a Life* at the local summer theater one night, but they were back at the end of Act I, barred forever from the premises. The local drugstore placed an embargo against our six, as did the ice cream parlor, the Howard Johnson's, the playground, the pizzeria, and the bordello. The kids did love the movies, but the movies didn't love them. As the manager was refunding the price of their seats, he said to me: "I know what you and your aunt are trying to do—and don't think I don't admire the sentiments—but, hell, I've gotta make a living. Look what those little bandits have done to my seats; slashed to ribbons. Can't get replacements. There's a war on, you know."

Besides their food, lodging, clothes, and constant breakage, the kids' medical expenses cost Auntie Mame a lot more. She insisted that they go back to England in prime condition, and she engaged a local doctor to drive over from Stony Brook every Sunday, just to check up on her charges. His name was Potter and he was a lot more realistic about the kids than Auntie Mame was. "Hell," he kept saying, "nothing the matter with any of them that a lethal chamber couldn't cure."

Auntie Mame also invested a couple of thousand bucks into their ugly little mouths, and it was my almost pleasant duty to take them to the dentist and listen contentedly to their screams of anguish. Their teeth finally got repaired, but the dentist retired at forty-one, a badly bitten, defeated old man.

I looked forward to the first day of school as though it were the Second Coming. At last the happy morning dawned. We were guaranteed seven hours a day, five days a week of peace and quiet—that is, whenever one of the kids wasn't laid up with a cold or temporarily suspended from classes for some heinous atrocity. On those carefree days we had only to awaken the children, cook the breakfast, put up the lunches, drive them to school, wash the breakfast dishes, make the beds, scour the bathrooms, remove the newest blasphemies from the walls, dust and vacuum, order the food, plead with the butcher, check the laundry, and loaf. When the cold weather came I also had to stoke the furnace—antique—dump the cinders, fuel the twelve fireplaces, shovel the snow, make whatever repairs were possible on Miss Peabody's furniture, and loaf. I kept telling myself that I never had it so good, but I didn't believe it.

And so the winter passed. Ginger was expelled from school three times. Enid was brought home once by a policeman when she'd been caught red-handed shoplifting from Woolworth's. Margaret Rose developed serious kidney trouble. Albert got tonsillitis in a sort of sympathy strike, and it was our pleasure to put them both in the hospital where Albert's tonsils and adenoids were removed—a *slight* improvement. Then Enid stole a pair of Auntie Mame's nail scissors and stabbed Ginger—not fatally. A citizens' committee launched a complaint against Gladys: openly soliciting on Main Street, they said. Auntie Mame hotly denied it, but I believed every word. In March Edmund got a local girl into trouble and her father threatened to kill him. I was all for letting a father give vent to his natural emotion, but Auntie Mame paid and paid and paid.

I know now that all kids are a lot of trouble, and I really don't think that Auntie Mame and I would have minded quite so much if there had been just one lovable quality in any of them. But there wasn't. Auntie Mame worried and fretted over them and put up a pretty fair pretense of adoration. I didn't. I hated their guts and didn't care who knew it. We were literally prisoners in that house, and after six months of it, both Auntie Mame and I were snarling and snapping at each other for no reason at all.

There was a hint of spring in the air on Easter Sunday, and the house smelled sickeningly of lilies and jelly beans and brats. The kiddies had had a riotous time pelting one another with Easter eggs and Albert had broken the last piece of Miss Peabody's Lowestoft. Doc Potter came in for his usual Sunday call and stayed on for dinner. Auntie Mame had turned into quite a proficient cook and it was a marvelous meal—or would have been if Margaret Rose hadn't vomited during dessert.

Doc Potter took another good look at Margaret Rose and put her to bed. "It's probably nothing," he said, "but keep her tucked away for a day or two. I don't like the look of her throat. I don't like the look of *any* of her, for that matter. If she gets any worse call me and I'll slip her a good dose of cyanide." Then he stared at Auntie Mame with a kind of worried expression. "Actually, *you're* the one I ought to be visiting, Mrs. Burnside, not them. You look terrible—thin, nervous, run-down, underweight. Just be careful these kids don't kill you."

After Margaret Rose was landed in dry dock, the dishes washed, and the kids sent upstairs to amuse themselves as quietly as possible, Auntie Mame and Doc and I sat around the living room drinking blended rye in complete bliss.

"Don't you think Hitler will *ever* surrender, Dr. Potter?" Auntie Mame sighed. "I mean, if I could only see a way out of this . . . this maternal situation, I don't think I'd mind quite so much. I suppose it sounds unnatural and horrid of me, but much as I've tried to love those youngsters, I've failed. If only something . . ."

There was an explosion that rocked the tavern. I was thrown clear off my chair and the three of us landed in a heap in the middle of the living-room floor.

"My God!" Auntie Mame cried, "the children!" She jumped to her feet and raced up the stairs with Doc and me following.

The big playroom on the second floor was a shambles. All the windows were shattered, the ceiling hung in grotesque stalagmites, and one wall was completely blown out. "Oh, no!" Auntie Mame whispered. "The children! Quick! Help me. They must be buried under the rubble." She dived into the messes and started burrowing her way through the mountain of junk on the floor. Just as I ripped away a huge sheet of fallen plaster, I heard a loquacious giggle. I wheeled around and saw all six children, safe and sound and clutching their sides in rapturous amusement.

I sprang for Edmund, but not before Doc had collared him.

"What the hell's going on here?" Doc shouted. No answer. "What did you kids do? Tell me, damn you, before I break every bone in your body." There as still no answer.

"Oi'll tell if yew promise not to tyke it out on *me*." It

was Albert, naturally. I grabbed him by the shoulders and shook him.

"You're bloody right you'll tell. You'll tell right now before I beat the bejesus out of you."

"Ouch! Yer 'urtink me," Albert whined.

"I'll hurt you a damned sight more if you don't tell me how this happened," I yelled.

"We was only mykink a buzz bomb," Albert said.

"A buzz bomb? Out of what?"

"Aoh, just some stuff we found in the tool 'ouse."

"You mean dynamite? Explosives? Things like that?"

"It wasn't *moi* oidea," Albert whimpered. "Them other kids started the 'ole thing an' Oi taold them, Oi said . . ."

Auntie Mame stood up in the middle of the wreckage. She was covered with dirt and grime and fallen plaster. Suddenly she started to laugh. She laughed and laughed and laughed until the tears came. "I can't stand it anym . . . it's just too funny for . . . and not even *my* room, but Miss Peabody's and the ancestors and . . . it's just the funniest thing I've ev . . ." She swayed with laughter. "And of course the s-sidesplitting feature is . . . is that we might all have been . . . all have been blown to . . . to kingdom come." She doubled up and slapped her knee.

The kids tittered nervously.

"Shut up," I growled. "Get into your rooms. I'll deal with you later." They were too scared to put up any arguments.

"But my dears, don't you see the . . ." Auntie Mame's face was contorted by her horrible merriment. "Don't you see the simply killing side of it—*killing*, that's a hot one!" She rocked back and forth, holding her sides.

I stared at her, horrified.

"Stop it," Doc barked. "Stop it right now." He marched up to her and slapped her squarely across the cheek. She was silent for a second, and then she began crying as though her heart were broken.

Doc carried her to her room and put her to bed. While he was sterilizing his hypodermic needle, I poured a double brandy down her throat. "I'm sorry," she whispered.

"I'm sorry, but I just can't stand it any longer. I wish that bomb had killed me."

"Auntie Mame!"

"Okay, Eleanora Duse, relax. Come out of it. You don't really wish anything of the kind. At least *I* don't. You're too profitable a patient," Doc said, stroking her hand. "You've just been through more than one human being can stand."

"But here I thought I was a little mother—Mrs. Wiggs of the Cabbage Patch sort of thing. And I've failed, failed, failed!"

"You've got to get rid of those kids," Doc said. "I really mean it. You're a sick woman."

"But I *can't*. Where would they go?"

"Could I suggest a good reformatory?" I said.

"And there's always Bellevue," Doc added.

"No. It's out of the question," Auntie Mame sighed. "I can't. I said I'd take care of them and . . ."

"And kill yourself while you're at it? It isn't a question of *wanting* to get rid of them. You *have* to. Doctor's orders," Doc said seriously. "You've done more for those little changelings than anybody could. You've spent damned near a year of your life with them. Poured thousands and thousands of dollars into them. This house, their food, their clothes, their schooling. My bill alone has come to more than two grand. Fun's fun, but you can't go on this way. You've got to get rid of them— before they get rid of you."

"But who'd be fool enough to take them?" Auntie Mame asked. "They're notorious already."

"Even so, they've got to go," Doc said firmly.

"Maybe we could lie about Edmund's age and get him into the Army," Auntie Mame suggested.

"And Gladys as a camp follower," Doc said.

"Look, Auntie Mame," I said, "we *can* get rid of them. I'll go into town to see the people at the agency tomorrow. But we don't have to offer all six kids as a package deal. The team ought to be broken up. Edmund could go to some farm and work off his cussedness in the fields . . ."

"Just be sure there aren't any sheep around," Doc said.

". . . and Gladys could be sent to some sort of convent . . ."

"Preferably cloistered," Doc said.

"As for Albert and Margaret Rose," I went on, "they'd have to go together, being brother and sister. But then, they're the best-behaved."

"Albert's a whining, cowardly little toad," Auntie Mame said.

"But still, he and Margaret Rose act better than the rest."

"And I'd be happy to throw in a rubber sheet for the little princess," Doc said.

"As for Enid and Ginger, we can find two suckers for them."

"Yes," Auntie Mame said dubiously, "I suppose we *could* do it."

"*Could* do it? You've *got* to," Doc said. "Now, get some rest. Pat and I will take care of the kids."

Downstairs quite a little crowd had gathered on the lawn, and stood there gaping at the yawning hole in Miss Peabody's Tavern. "Don't get upset, folks," Doc shouted through one of the shattered windows. "You know how tricky these newfangled pressure cookers are." Then he pulled down the shade and we were alone.

That night the kids got a glass of milk and a graham cracker and a good bawling out. They didn't seem much affected by what they'd done. Doc had to drag Margaret Rose back to bed three times. "And you *stay* there," he growled. "We don't want a sick girl on our hands. Not right now we don't."

"Oi told her, sah," Albert minced. "Oi sez to her, 'Mogrut Raose, Doctah Pottah will be eva sew angry wiv you if . . .' "

"Shut up, Nancy," Doc snapped. He went out to his car and drove home.

* * *

The next morning I got up bright and early and put on my British battle dress and the trench coat and ribbons so that I could be properly pukka with the English child-placement people. Auntie Mame had recovered considerably and was cursing at the vituperative old stove in the kitchen when I went downstairs.

"Good morning, my little love," she sang. "Is this *Der Tag*?"

"This is the day," I said. "Independence Day, Bastille Day, Guy Fawkes Day, May Day!"

"Darling," she sighed, "I can hardly wait."

Gladys sauntered into the dining room, her cardigan and plaid skirt in hideous contrast against the panchromatic make-up, the beaded lashes, the streaky dyed yellow hair (this was her blond, or Lana Turner phase; she had just finished the brunette, or Hedy Lamarr one). "Coo!" she said, eyeing me. "Full field regylia. Nevah seen you in yunyfawm before. Don't you look the image of Dyvid Niven!"

We ignored her rather elaborately. "Can I fix you a couple of eggs, darling?" Auntie Mame said to me.

"No thanks, just toast and coffee. I'll be tramping around from one agency to the other and I want to get there early."

"Ai-jency?" Gladys asked, raising her hairline eyebrows. "Oi do 'ope yaw not tryin' ta 'ire maw sah-vints. Yew orta knaow they'll nevah last. Not *'ere* they won't."

"Eat your breakfast, Gladys," Auntie Mame said haughtily. "Patrick and I don't feel much like talking to any of you children this morning. I think you know why."

Gladys shrugged impudently and swished out. I gulped down the last of my coffee, put on my peaked cap, and made for the door. "I'll be home with your emancipation papers by five. Cross my heart I will."

"Darling!" Auntie Mame said happily. Then she began fixing a tray for Margaret Rose.

* * *

I spent a terrible day in New York going from agency to agency, bureau to bureau, department to department. Everyone in town seemed to know—at least by reputation—about Auntie Mame's brood. "Bad actors," one woman said darkly. "Filthy brats," a spinster on Fifty-seventh Street said. "Beastly little bounders," a man told me—quite unnecessarily. It was about four o'clock before I finally got the right person, a hard-bitten old girl with a crew cut and a regimental necktie.

"Oh, them," she said out of the corner of her mouth. "Yeah, we all had bets on how long your aunt would last. I had a little inside information about her from a gal I know and cleaned up. So now she's beginning to crack, eh? Small wonder."

"My aunt has great stick-to-itiveness," I said loyally.

"She sure has, brother, she sure has. Well, cheer up. I got a brand new sucker list here—people who've never been tapped before. An' all of 'em aching to have the patter of little feet in their houses. Can you *imagine*? Here, sit tight while I make a couple of calls. I've made so much dough at five-to-one on your aunt I almost feel I owe you a commission."

I sat tensely while she made a series of telephone calls. In half an hour the last of the six children was placed. "Well," she said, "that's that. When can you have 'em packed up and ready to go?"

"If you'll let me use that telephone," I said, "I can have them waiting in the driveway within an hour."

"Oh, don't bother about that. Plenty of time."

"No there isn't," I said.

"Well, suppose I send a couple of those motor corps babes out there tomorrow?"

"That'll be wonderful!" I said. There were tears in my eyes.

I exceeded the speed limit every inch of the way out to Long Island. Free! Free forever from Edmund and Gladys and Enid and Albert and Ginger and Margaret

Rose. No more household duties, no more screaming and fighting and breakage and mayhem.

The car careened into the driveway at the Tavern in a fine spray of gravel. I jumped out as though my leg had never been touched by so much as a spitball and ran toward the door. There was a sound of hammering. "Ah," I said to myself, "workmen already repairing the damage."

A local rustic, still swinging a hammer, strolled down the driveway.

"Good evening!" I called cordially.

"Evenin' sojer," he said.

"Getting everything fixed up?" I asked in my best conversational tone.

"Sealed in tight as a drum," he said.

"Already? That's just great."

"Well, buddy, it may be great for you, but it ain't so hot for that poor little lady locked inta the house with them devils for the next six weeks."

"What are you talking about?" I asked.

"Aintcha seen the sign I jist nailed on the front door?"

"Sign? Front door?"

"Better take a look, sojer, an' I wouldn't go in there unless yer fixin' to stay a long, long time."

I raced to the front door. Tacked to it was a red and white sign:

QUARANTINED

KEEP OUT

SCARLET FEVER

All persons entering these premises . . .

That was all I read. I collapsed into the iris bed on the lawn.

Ten

Auntie Mame's

Golden Summer

THE UNFORGETTABLE CHARACter's last days are just as beautiful as any of her other days. There she is in her prim little house surrounded by adoring friends and still spreading sweetness, light, and salty New England wisdom to anyone willing to listen. The author calls it the Golden Summer of her life, a fitting term. It brings to mind Auntie Mame's golden summer because that's exactly the way she described. it. And two weeks of a golden summer with Auntie Mame in *her* house and surrounded by *her* friends were such a rich experience that the course of my whole life was changed.

Right after V–J Day, Auntie Mame went to Elizabeth Arden's and got the works. She came back looking about ten years younger, except for a genuine white streak among her curls. Well, the white was genuine, but I couldn't swear as to the dark hair surrounding it. She described herself as Frankly Forty, although she was factually fifty, and said a good deal about the fruitful harvest season of womanhood.

"I'm a mature woman, my little love," she said, admiring the white streak for the thousandth time. "These are my richest years and I'm going to revel in them. I plan to live more sedately, more compactly—live on a higher spiritual and intellectual plane—so that I can be a fit grandmother to the sweet little curly-headed babies you and your wife are going to bring to me."

I dropped my beer. "The sweet little *what* that I and my *what* are going to bring you?"

"Babies, darling. You've reached the age when you should be thinking of marriage. You don't like the boys, do you?"

"Only to shoot craps with," I said. "But I don't like the girls either—at least no particular one. Not enough to marry."

"Don't worry, darling, I'll take care of all that."

"That's damned decent of you."

"I have only to get my new way of life organized and then I'll start on you."

Auntie Mame got organized very quickly. She bought a lot of New Look clothes—"so much more grace and dignity than those skimpy little apache skirts we had during the war"—and signed up for an overwhelming series of courses at the New School for Social Research—"so that I can be of some intellectual stimulation to your little ones." I winced.

That fall I got a job in a small advertising agency writing copy for the Itsa-Daisy Electric Stove at eighty bucks a week. Auntie Mame felt that it was inadequate to support a wife and children, but at least a start. I also moved into an apartment of my own—one room and sink on University Place—and Auntie Mame felt that it was *woefully* inadequate for a wife and children, but also a start. Yet even though I was no longer under her roof, I couldn't have seen more of her if we were sharing the same bed. I was invited to dine with her on the average of five nights a week, and each time the meal featured a lot of faintly aphrodisiac dishes, with *"Amour"* written on them with a pastry tube, and a beautiful single girl of

Auntie Mame's choosing. Auntie Mame would invariably talk of marriage and babies, fill me full of champagne and brandy, and then sidle out to a mysterious engagement, leaving me on the sofa with her latest candidate for the bridal couch. She was as blatant as a call-house madam, but somehow none of the girls was quite right.

That fall there was a dazzling succession of lovely houris. There was Vivian who, according to Auntie Mame, was a "perfect peach of a girl and born for motherhood—look at that pelvis!" But all Vivian ever talked about was tennis and riding and spear-fishing, and on our last date she got so enthused over jujitsu that she threw my back out and I spent the next two weeks in a corset, hobbling off to the osteopath.

Elaine came next. She was a dark, Middle Eastern sort who could think of nothing but politics, and the evening I pressed her hand and asked if she wouldn't like to spend the night, she looked soulfully into my eyes and said, "Why don't you run for the legislature on the Liberal ticket as a token protest against Tammany Hall?" That ended that.

Then there was Carolyn who didn't smoke or drink and tried to convert me to Christian Science. Helena was attractive and intelligent, but so crisp and efficient that it was like necking with a machine. Mary and I got kind of moony over the Double Crostics in the *Saturday Review*, but our affair ended when I kissed her in a taxicab and she said, "Who's a Hindu philosopher, circa 800, in eight letters?" Dotty was much too energetic. Fran too Southern. Isabelle too mystical. In other words, nothing came of anything.

Auntie Mame was outraged. "Really, you ought to get hormone shots or analyzed or something. What's the *matter* with you? Here I dig up all these lovely girls and what happens—you sniff around them like an altered tomcat and stalk away. It's disgusting!"

"For God's sake, why don't you leave me alone? I'll get married in my own good time."

Around New Year Auntie Mame got bored with the role of procuress and took off for the sunshine of Mexico, where she stayed and stayed and stayed. And where she also put to practice some of the psychology she'd learned at the New School. She wrote regularly and in each letter she'd enclose a snapshot or two of herself and three of the most exquisite girls I'd ever seen. The girls were ravishing brunettes and of a beauty and elegance that was downright illegal. I got interested at once and kept writing to Auntie Mame to ask who her friends were. But she always neglected to answer the question and just kept sending vague, gossipy letters and more photographs of herself and the three beauties. I was itching with curiosity, but it did me no good. She ignored my questions and went right on writing about herself.

In April, when I was almost frothing with curiosity, she began casually mentioning names other than her own—"Margot said . . ."; "Melissa told me . . ."; "Miranda and I . . ."—but there was still no clue as to who these beauties were, and she continued to ignore my direct and underscored questions. By then she was sending snapshots of just the three beauties (and her own shadow) labeled "My friends."

By June I was so consumed with curiosity that I put through a long, expensive, and almost inaudible long-distance call to Cuernavaca to find out just who Auntie Mame's constant companions were. It didn't do much good. The static was fierce and operators kept breaking in in Brooklynese, Southern, and Spanish. I gathered that the three beautiful girls were sisters and their name was Murdock or Medoc and that Auntie Mame had no plans to return to New York. We were finally cut off. Then there was a long, long period of silence in which my letters were returned with the equivalent of "Removed—No forwarding address" scrawled on them in Spanish.

During a New York heat wave I got a letter from Auntie Mame filled with clichés such as "Sleeping under blankets every night." It was postmarked Maddox Island,

Maine, and there was a snapshot of the three beauties in bathing suits. Auntie Mame also added, in a vague post-script, that she'd leased the old Maddox house on Maddox Island from the three lovely Maddox sisters—"some friends I met casually in Mexico last winter and may have mentioned to you"—and that they were all staying there "for the whole golden summer." There was also a kind of offhand invitation for me to spend my vacation there.

Well, I was hooked. Psychology, indeed.

Getting to Maddox Island was no cinch. You took a plane to Bangor; a bus to Eastport; a ferry to a much bigger island; a jitney to the end of that island; and then a launch to Maddox Island. I was dead tired when Maddox Island finally came into view, but seeing Auntie Mame waiting on the pier revived me.

She gave me a brisk, businesslike kiss, tossed my bags into a coaster wagon—there were no cars on the island—and led me along the dusty road toward the village. She talked a blue streak, but she was maddeningly evasive about the three Maddox sisters.

Luckily, I'd been able to do a little research—they were so beautiful that every glossy magazine in America had run full-page pictures of them. They came from one of those old New England families where the blood runs thin and blue. They were not only socially impeccable but intellectual, artistic, creative, and, as I said, gorgeous. But do you think Auntie Mame would say one word about them? No. She simply dismissed every question with "Mmm-hmm" or "Oh, yes" or no answer at all.

The village of Maddox looked kind of like a setting for a Western film. There were a general store, a pharmacy, a church, a town hall that showed movies on week ends, and Mickey the Mick's Saloon and Hotel. That was where Auntie Mame stopped.

"Well, here we are!" she said.

"Did these babes sell you a gin mill?" I asked blankly.

"Oh, no, my little love. *We*'re all staying at the old Maddox house. *You*'re staying here."

"I'm staying *here*? Isn't there room for me where *you* are?"

"My dear, the Maddox house has more than two dozen bedrooms, but you *certainly* didn't think I'd have *you* staying there. Not with three unmarried *girls*. After all, they're my guests—so to speak—for the summer and it's up to me to chaperone them," she said prissily.

"Who the hell do you think you are," I asked angrily, "Mrs. Grundy?"

"Oh, Patrick, my little love," she said, casting her eyes to the Maine heavens, "how life in that hard, commercial advertising agency has *toughened* you! What has happened to your sensibilities? Here I've tried to raise you with *some* gentility, some feeling for the things important to ladies and gentlemen of breeding and family background, and . . ."

"Now come off that crap right now," I growled. "You raised me with all the rag, tag, and bobtail you . . ."

"Oh, darling," she said with an airy look at her wrist watch, "I must fly! We're dining with the Saltonstalls tonight. I'm so sorry I couldn't wangle an invitation for you, but *do* come around for lunch tomorrow. You can't miss the old Maddox place. Just turn left when you leave Mickey the Mick's and walk to the very *end* of the island. That's where *we* are. Say around one-ish?" Before I could vilify her properly, she was gone.

Mickey the Mick's was just like a million other saloons, bleak and barren in its cold fluorescent lighting, and decorated with a ghastly jukebox, pictures of the Miss Rheingold of 1947 candidates, and ads from liquor dynasties—signs made of neon that hissed or glass tubes that bubbled. The only thing there that was in the least noteworthy was Mickey's daughter, Pegeen. Pegeen was a statuesque redhead with a figure that made your temperature rise and a manner that made it fall. Talk about a cool article, that girl was a glacier.

"My—my name is Dennis," I said, when I got over the shock of meeting her.

"Oh, yes," she said briskly, "you're the new Maddox candidate. Come this way." Before I could understand just what she'd said, I was upstairs above the saloon in a room overlooking Maddox Island's only street. "Here you are," she said. "If you don't like this room be sure to let me know, because it's the only one we have and Pop can rent it to someone else. Your bathroom is here. Dinner is whenever you want it and whatever you want, but I'd like to know now."

By then I was boiling mad. Okay, Big Red, I thought, now it's *my* inning. "Thanks," I said. "I'll dine here in my room and I'd like *entrecôte à la Bordelaise, pommes soufflées*, field salad, *crème brûlée*, and *caffè espresso*. I'd like it at eight, *sharp*," I added nastily. To my surprise, she wrote it all down. "Here," I said, holding out a fifty-cent piece.

"No thanks," she said. "If you feel like tipping, just put it in the box down on the bar. That's a fund Pop and I keep for fishermen's widows." With that she was gone.

I was fit to be tied. It was enough to get to Maddox Island, but to be parked in Mickey the Mick's Saloon and Hotel, to be on my own in this ghost town for the whole night, to be patronized by Auntie Mame, to be kept from seeing the Maddox sisters, and then to be snubbed by Pegeen was too much. I tried to find fault with the room. I couldn't. It was plain but spotless, with real Irish linen on the bed. The adjoining bath was also immaculate. Angrily, I threw myself down on the bed and fell asleep.

On the stroke of eight my meal arrived.

"Here's your dinner," Pegeen said, waking me. "You'd better eat it while it's hot. And would you mind not lying on the bed with your shoes on. This isn't the Mills Hotel." With that she left me alone with the most delicious dinner I'd ever eaten—and exactly what I'd ordered. It had the effect of making me as ashamed as I've been in my life, and twice as furious.

Later that night, desperate, I went down to the bar for a drink, partly out of loneliness, partly trying to make amends. Pegeen and her father were there with a couple of stray customers, but whenever I tried to strike up a conversation they cut me dead with their indifference. Seething mad, I went to bed around ten and found that my nap had made it impossible for me to sleep at all.

The next day I got up, took a long time bathing and shaving, and dressed in my nattiest for lunch with the Maddox sisters. I looked at my watch; it was eleven o'clock. I sat down and read every word of a copy of *Life*—ads and all. Then I read it again. At a quarter of one I set off.

Maddox Island was made up of about fifty natives, who lived there the year around, and about a hundred families with big rambling frame houses that they occupied during the summer. At the far end was a big, impressive place with "Maddox" chastely lettered on the gatepost. It was one of those old General Grant eyesores, bustling with towers and turrets, cupolas, lightning rods, and porches and balconies. Although rather seedy, it had obviously been some establishment in its youth.

I trudged up the drive. As I neared the door, Auntie Mame appeared. "Darling boy! Here you are at last!" She was got up in a voile shirt and a pair of britches held up by a single suspender, which made her look like a kind of transvestite Huck Finn. "I've been up on the widow's walk watching you with my glass."

"Glass of what?" I asked bitterly.

"Oh, yes, *drinks*! I'll call Ito." With that she disappeared and remained invisible for the next half hour while I sat waspishly in a hammock trying to make sense out of an issue of *Botteghe Oscure*. I was in a real snit when she finally appeared, dressed for a royal garden party and bearing a silver tray that held a decanter of sherry and two glasses.

We had one sherry, two sherries, three sherries while Auntie Mame gabbled glibly of Cabots and Lodges and

Saltonstalls and Faneuils, and I raged silently. At last Ito announced lunch. When I saw that the table in the big old dining room was set for only two, my patience gave out. "Where in the hell are these Maddox girls?" I shouted.

"Oh," Auntie Mame said casually, "they're lunching with the Lowells. I had to send my regrets since you . . ."

"But when am I going to *meet* them?" I bellowed down the long table.

"What's the hurry, my little love? They wouldn't be interested in you, anyhow." She looked demurely into her mousse and the conversation came to an end.

If any act was ever designed to drive a man mad, it was Auntie Mame as the New England gentlewoman. She left me at the table with port, a stale cigar, a fly— and she *retired* to the drawing room. When I joined her— about three minutes later—she gave me a copy of *Walden* to read aloud while she did *needlework*! There was absolutely no contact with her until she pricked her finger and said a short but most unladylike word. I put down the book and was just about to let her have it when a trio of mellifluous voices was heard from the porch.

Whatever I was going to say to Auntie Mame escaped me when the three Maddox sisters came into the room. They stood in the doorway in their white dresses as though they were waiting for Sargent to paint them. As a matter of fact, my principal recollection of the three sisters that summer is not as individuals but always *grouped*—and artistically—like all their photographs. But the photographs, though magnificent, didn't begin to capture their beauty. The blue-black hair, the black-blue eyes, the *noli me tangere* perfection of flesh and limb were beyond the camera's eye.

"Oh, there you are, dahlings," Auntie Mame said airily as I struggled to my feet. "Margot, Miranda, Melissa—my *neh-view*, Petrick." I tried to speak, but just at that moment the three of them swept a deep curtsy in my direction, as though I might have been Charles II. The

speed and grace of their beautifully anachronistic gesture
stunned me so that I toppled back into my chair.

"Drunk!" Auntie Mame muttered, and quickly ab-
sorbed the three beauties in New England-type conversation.

Luckily, the household hadn't been invited to dine with
Governor Winthrop or John Alden or Boss Curley that
evening, so Auntie Mame begged me to have dinner
there—but *not* before I went back and changed into black
tie. Pegeen shot a pitying glance as I came down the
stairs at Mickey the Mick's in my dinner clothes, and the
natives whistled when I trudged along the dusty road in
broad daylight and patent leather pumps, but I didn't
much care. The thought of getting back to Auntie Mame
and her seminary of goddesses was enough.

Again that night I was left with the port while Auntie
Mame herded her swans into the drawing room, and at
ten o'clock I was summarily dismissed, but not before I
discovered that each of the Maddox girls was not only a
beauty but a brain and a distinct individual in her own
right. Margot was the literary one and spoke elegantly
and eloquently of Kafka. Miranda painted and took photographs. Melissa knew everything about music. I wasn't
drunk—you couldn't be on what Auntie Mame was serv-
ing that summer—but I felt drunk as I hit the sack at
Mickey the Mick's. Margot, Miranda, Melissa, I thought;
Melissa, Miranda, and Margot. With visions of these si-
rens spinning around in my brain, I drifted off to sleep.

After the ice was broken, I was permitted to return to
the Maddox house fairly regularly, but Auntie Mame was
a stern duenna and the three sisters were apparently much
in demand among the scions of great Boston families
summering at Maddox Island. And even when I *did* get
asked to the house, I was under the constant chaperonage
of Auntie Mame. The girls were encouraged—not that
they needed much encouragement—to follow their special pursuits each and every morning. Life at the Maddox

house, although unusual, was fairly routine. The days were spent on the beach discussing intellectual matters such as the Japanese theater, English madrigals, the sculpture of Henry Moore, the importance of metallic thread in contemporary fabrics, the unpublished works of Joe Gould, the interesting patterns created by batik dyeing, the weird beauty of phthisic Mexican voices, Katina Paxinou reading *Electra*, the costume designs of a ten-year-old girl in a Rhode Island reformatory, and praising one another's talents. Miranda painted in the manner of Eugene Berman—"Mame at the Mausoleum," "Margot in Mourning"—and took photographs in the manner of Cecil Beaton—"Mame Among the Candles," "Melissa Morte," and "Mame and Margot as Naiads." (Auntie Mame's hair stank of seaweed for some days after *that* study and it turned out very badly.) Miranda asked me to pose as a sleeping faun, a Florentine page boy, a Spartan runner, and several other things in some old yard goods and hairpieces she'd found kicking around the attic, all of which embarrassed me.

One morning when we were alone together on the beach, Miranda gave my torso (which isn't bad to this day, if I do say so myself) an encouraging glance and said, "Would you think me terribly jay if I asked you to pose naked for me? You see, I can never afford a model and . . ."

I was so stunned and the pulse in my diaphragm was beating so hard as I gazed, nonplused, into Miranda's lovely face that I couldn't speak. But just as I reached for the drawstring on my trunks, Auntie Mame's face appeared above the dunes, cheek by jowl with the faces of Margot and Melissa.

"Of *course* he will, darling!" Auntie Mame cried. "Go on, my little love, shuck off those shorts! You're nice and slim, and posing for Miranda will be *perfectly* all right with the rest of us here to watch."

A bolt of lightning couldn't have surprised me more. Strangled with rage and embarrassment, I stomped off to put on *all* my clothes while Auntie Mame, in the manner of Boston's Mrs. Gardiner, called out things about the beauty of the human body.

Melissa composed music—very modern and atonal music, I believe, although the old Beckstein piano in the music room was so badly out of tune that I could never be certain. One night, after I'd toyed with my port beyond human endurance, I heard the piano thumping and rattling in the music room and went there instead of to the drawing room. Melissa was at the keyboard alone, lighted beatifically by candles. She was so beautiful that I gasped audibly. She looked up and treated me to a ravishing smile. "This is something I dashed off today," she said in her heavenly, husky voice. "Would you turn the pages for me, *please*?"

I crossed the room like a zombie. The music sounded as though it were written for the Kabuki Theater, but gazing, as I was, at Melissa's magnificent shoulders, her arms, her *poitrine*, she could have been playing "Jingle Bells" for all it mattered to me.

"*Now*, please," she whispered.

Trembling, I bent down, about to lay siege to her lovely throat, when the door burst open. "*Here* you are!" Auntie Mame cried. She was flanked by Margot and Miranda. "*Splendid!* Just in time for a little concert. Play on, Melissa!" The lights flashed on and I was stuck at the piano turning pages until well after twelve.

Margot could read and write. She knew everything about Existentialism and Sartre and Kafka. Bursting with desire, I used to watch her floating out to the grape arbor in a fluttery white dress (those girls *always* wore white) with a stack of yellow-bound French books, yellow paper, and yellow pencils. My heart leaped with admiration. But just try to get her alone!

One evening I did. Auntie Mame could be heard in the kitchen voicing her opinion about some sauce. Melissa and Miranda were still dressing. Practically slobbering, I followed Margot to the arbor.

"Oh!" she said in her wonderful, wonderful voice. "You startled me!"

As she didn't sound a bit startled, I took heart. "Writing?" I asked idiotically.

"Oh, not really," Margot said with a look that doubled me over. "I'm just doing a silly little monograph on Kafka, but it's hard because I'm writing it in French *and* in villanelles." Razzumatazz, I thought. "But, of course, I'll never find a publisher," she added sadly.

"Well, golly," I said, "it just so happens that this guy I went to school with has a job at the Harbinger Press—they're very high-toned, you know." I was sparring for time. "Let me take a look. My French is kind of weak, but maybe you and I—and this old *pal*, naturally—could have lunch and . . ." I shoved in beside her and flung an arm over her shoulders. I was so desperate after a week of being kept at arm's length from any of these beautiful temptresses that I was all set to try the tactless attack everybody used to make on poor old Sal, who had come to our advertising agency from Raymond College and was sleeping with the copy chief, two clients, a sculptor on Jane Street, her fiancé, me, and the Standing Army.

With some restraint, I contained myself. "Listen, Margot . . . Ouch!" I swatted at a mosquito.

"*Here* we are! Just in time!" Auntie Mame marched into the arbor, armed with a spray gun and flanked by Miranda and Melissa. She sprayed so thoroughly that it nearly killed *me*. Then she plunked herself down and made me read aloud from Margot's manuscript in my St. Boniface French until the dinner was almost ruined.

Frustrated and frustrating as these occasions were with the beautiful Maddox sisters, I was never allowed to spend very much time on the premises, which Auntie Mame rented from them. There were numbers of noons and afternoons and evenings when Auntie Mame gave me to understand that the sisters had been invited out to meet far more illustrious men, and that I could fritter my time away as I pleased. That enraged me. It enraged me because it meant that there was nothing to do but stay upstairs at Mickey the Mick's Saloon and Hotel and eat the magnificent food that Pegeen cooked and served.

At mealtimes I'd try to pick a fight with Pegeen, but she always said one wonderfully squelching thing and marched out, leaving me gasping for a reply. Later at night, when I'd regained control, I'd go down to the bar and try to strike up some kind of conversation with Pegeen or her father. No soap. Mr. and Miss Ryan kept carefully to themselves. Still later, writhing with passion for any one of the Maddox sisters, I'd go down to the beach and try to calm myself in the Maine waters, which were well below zero. All *that* ever accomplished was chilblains and a stern warning from the local constable about indecent exposure.

On the tenth day I was at my wit's end. I got up at six and chewed my nails until I was fairly sure that Auntie Mame was awake. At eleven I forced an entrance into her bedroom, snatched off her sleep mask, and shook her to consciousness.

"Patrick, my little love," she said, batting her eyes, "you shouldn't *be* here. The girls . . ."

"The girls are out in their lousy sailboat," I said. "If one of them was here do you think I'd be in *your* room?"

"Flatterer!"

"Listen, Auntie Mame, this is driving me crazy. Do you *all* have to go around like the Army backfield? Can't *one* of you ever break away long enough for a guy to . . ."

"Darling, what are you talking about?"

"You know damned good and well what I'm talking about. You've been sitting on Margot and Miranda and Melissa like a setting hen ever since you went to Mexico. *You're* the one who thought up this marriage business, and now every time I see one of them alone for five seconds, you and the rest of the Four Horsemen plunge in and . . ."

"Marriage?" Auntie Mame said with a pretty flutter and a fake wide-eyed stare. "Why, whoever put such a notion in your . . ."

"Oh, come off it, you big ham! Now, when are you going to give me a chance to see just one of those girls *alone?*"

"Tch, what a *shame*, darling. If *only* I'd known you were interested, we might have asked you to lunch today. Unfortunately, the girls are all going to the Sears' clambake. A pity! I thought you *knew* the Sears boys. They . . ."

"I don't know one damned soul on this island and you know it!"

"La, my little love, this all comes as *such* a shock. I had no idea that you were capable of any feeling—let alone an emotion as deep as . . ."

"Oh, shut up!"

Then she fixed me with a burning look. "Which one?"

Well, I was so stunned for a second that I couldn't distinguish one Maddox from another. "Margot," I gulped.

"Very well, darling," she said briskly. "I'll arrange a little private interview for you and Margot this very afternoon. What time?"

"Right after the Lodges' clambake."

"The Cabots, darling. Shall we say two-thirty?"

I was too stunned to do anything but nod.

I got to the Maddox place at two sharp. With a lot of talk about lobster pots and searching for buried treasure, Auntie Mame, Melissa, and Miranda put on their big Mexican straw hats and set off for an outing. With them gone, the silence was most impressive. I threw some pebbles up at Margot's window in one of the towers, and pretty soon she opened it and smiled down. "Is that you, Patrick? I was just in the middle of the most interesting article on Sartre. It seems that . . ."

"Why don't you leave Sartre up there and come down to me?"

"All right," she said, and disappeared. In a couple of minutes she was downstairs, her mouth freshly touched up and looking very beautiful in a white dress. "Where are Mame and the girls?"

"Oh, they've gone off," I said.

"And not asked *us*?" Margot said. "Well, I like their nerve!"

"We could go on a little expedition of our own," I said. "Maybe you'd like a sail?"

"Well, of course I would, but I can't understand my sisters' running off without a word to me. We do everything together—we always have."

"My God, you were all at a clambake together just now. Can't any one of you . . ."

"I haven't been to a clambake for years," she said. "We were just hoping that you'd come and . . ."

That was all I needed. I put my arms around her and kissed her so hard that she had to stop talking. When I was through, I said, "Do you know that this is the first time since I got here that you and I have been alone?"

"Y-yes, I guess it is . . ." she began. Then I heard Ito giggle from the pantry. I grabbed Margot's arm and dragged her down to the beach. Once we were away from everybody it was easy as pie. Half an hour later everything was arranged.

I was so stunned that Margot had accepted my offer of marriage—just like that—that I could hardly walk straight. That a girl so beautiful, so intelligent, so sought after could have yearned from afar for me, just as I had yearned for her, seemed totally unbelievable. But then the whole holiday had been unbelievable.

"Are you going to tell them now?" I asked as we strolled hand in hand across the lawn.

Margot said in her beautiful voice, "I'm sure that Miranda and Melissa have guessed by now, but I'll make the word official at dinner. They'll both be so pleased, and I *know* your aunt will." I didn't like the sound of that.

Well, they were pleased. Miranda kissed me, Melissa kissed me, Auntie Mame kissed me. Then everybody kissed everybody else. Auntie Mame made Ito open half a dozen bottles of champagne and we drank toasts to every conceivable person and cause.

I was feeling no pain, and by the time I left, my heart ran over with family feeling. "Tomorrow night," I said, "*I'm* going to give a party. It'll be dinner. There's a kind of terrace—or back porch—down at Mickey the Mick's, and Pegeen's a wonderful cook."

"How divine!" Auntie Mame said.

The girls looked a little shocked.

"Do you really want us to go down and mix with natives, darling?" Margot said.

"Oh, it'll be *heaven*!" Auntie Mame said.

"And I'll ask your men friends, too," I said expansively. "You could bring the Sears boys or the Lodges or somebody like that and make a party of eight."

The sisters stared at me blankly.

"Oh, I think it would be so much more fun," Auntie Mame said quickly, "if it were just a *family* affair. Just the five of us."

Well, I wasn't going to argue. "Like to see me to the gate?" I asked Margot, giving her hand a squeeze.

"Of course, darling."

I put my arm around her as we walked along the pathway, but I saw that we were not alone. Miranda and Melissa and Auntie Mame were with us, too.

The next morning I could hardly wait to get up and dash down to the bar to order a sumptuous dinner from Pegeen. She was alone in the taproom, washing up glasses.

"Congratulate me, Pegeen," I said. "I'm about to be married."

"Do tell!" she said maddeningly. "Which one of the big-game hunters got *you*? Miranda?"

"No," I said, feeling miffed. "Margot."

"That's odd. They usually save her for the older gentlemen."

"What are you talking about?"

"Let's see," she said, ignoring my question. "You'll be wanting to have a nice dinner here—out in back, of course—tonight. And you were thinking of having filet mignon and broccoli with hollandaise and . . ."

My mouth fell open. "How did you know?"

"That's what the lucky man always ordered before—except when rationing was on and we had chicken. Now let's see, there'll be you and the Maddox girls and your aunt. Five in all. That's a nice change. It was usually just the finacé and the three sisters."

"I was thinking of having some other men, too—the Searses and the Cabots and . . ."

"You'd have to get them disinterred pretty fast. Nobody like that has been on Maddox Island since I was a little girl. Now, it's always been the custom to start out with cold vichyssoise, then the filet, then . . ."

"Well, we're not going to have anything like that *tonight*!" I raged. "We'll have a plain Maine shore dinner—steamers and lobster and . . ."

"Suit yourself," Pegeen said. "Maybe it'll change Margot's luck." With that, she disappeared into the kitchen.

Saturday night was the big night at Mickey the Mick's. My little function was making it even bigger. The bar was full of natives and summer people and some big bruisers off a Coast Guard cutter when the contingent from the Maddox place swept in. As usual, the sisters were in white evening dresses, and Auntie Mame appropriately wore black. There were lots of appreciative whistles as they passed through the taproom, but the four of them were queenly to the end—although I could have sworn that Auntie Mame cast a cordial eye toward a big blond Coast Guardsman.

When the tide was low, the back porch of Mickey the Mick's smelled of old crabs. The tide was low. The Maddox sisters sniffed the air a bit distastefully but said nothing. Auntie Mame, every inch the Beacon Hill matron, flapped a scented lace handkerchief ineffectually past her nose.

"Really!" Melissa said. "All those natives *whistling* at us!"

"*Noblesse oblige*, darling," Miranda said.

There was a faint snicker and Pegeen stood in the doorway, ready to take orders for drinks.

"Good evening, Pegeen," Margot said charmingly.

"Good evening, Miss Maddox," Pegeen said, bobbing slightly. There was an unpleasant pause.

"What'll it be to drink, everyone?" I said jovially.

Well, there was a lot of fussing over the order. Miranda was particularly indecisive and finally gave her order in French. Pegeen answered in French, too.

"Is she a French-Canadian?" I asked after Pegeen had left.

"Oh, dear no," Margot said. "Just a native."

"And just like all the rest of them," Melissa said.

"Yet there's a certain haunting pre-Raphaelite beauty to her . . ." Miranda said.

"If you like anything that *obvious*," Melissa interjected.

"I've been begging her to pose for me for ages but . . ."

"Well, naturally she won't," Margot said. "The natives are all so class conscious and . . ."

"And of course *our* being Maddoxes," Melissa continued, "makes Pegeen feel so . . ."

"Hush, please," Auntie Mame said. "She'll hear you."

Pegeen was back with the drinks, and I saw to it that everyone had two rounds before we commenced dinner. I'd never seen the three Maddox beauties off their home field before, and somehow they gave me the impression—but ever so subtly—that I'd chosen the wrong night, the wrong place, the wrong food, the wrong drink. I hoped the evening would brighten with the wine, but it didn't. During Pegeen's delicious cold crab soup, Melissa held her lovely head between her lovely hands and said: "Oh, oh, *oh*! That vulgar what-kind-of-box do you call it?"

"Juke," Pegeen said, as she brought out her piping-hot rolls.

"Yes, that's it, jute. All day long I've been trying to think of just the *right* moody atonal music to go with a ballet written around Kafka's *Trial*, but with that wretched caterwauling—who *is* that singing, Pegeen?"

"Jo Stafford."

"He has a *very* high voice," Melissa complained.

"Hormones," Pegeen said. Auntie Mame giggled and then returned to her Back Bay role.

"*Couldn't* you ask them to stop playing it, Pegeen? It's ruining my whole sense of composition and . . ."

"I'm afraid there isn't a selection labeled 'Silence,' Miss Maddox," Pegeen said and bustled away.

"Now, darling . . ." Margot began.

"More wine, anyone?" I said.

"Well, it's such *beastly* wine," Miranda said, holding out her glass. "Now *last* year when we were visiting the Chalfontes at Chantilly . . ."

"Nonsense, girl," Auntie Mame said, tapping her with her fan, "it's a very nice, presumptuous little wine."

"Please, Miranda," Margot said nervously.

"Oh, I *loathe* it here, with everything cold and chaste and poor," Miranda said, emptying her glass. For one who detested the wine, she was certainly able to put it away. "Give me *mon belle France*."

"*Ma belle,*" an almost inaudible voice said. It was Pegeen, entering with a huge tray of lobsters and drawn butter.

"*Ma belle*— yes," Miranda said, not knowing whence

the correction had come. "France, France, France, where I can paint, paint, paint!" She threw her arms out in a gesture that was meant to embrace all of France. Instead, it caught Pegeen right under the elbow. There was a deafening crash and I sat spellbound as Miranda and Melissa were inundated with lobsters, steamers, fried potatoes, green salad, and gallons of drawn butter. The sight was so breath-taking that I could only stare.

Not so Melissa and Miranda.

Miranda jumped to her feet and faced Pegeen with blazing eyes. "You doltish, clumsy, shanty-Irish clod. *Look* what you've done to me!"

"Look what she's done to *you*!" Melissa screamed. "Look what she's done to *me*. And she did it on purpose. These natives are . . ."

"Hey, wait," I said. "It was only an accident. You knocked . . ."

"Miranda," Margot snapped. "Remember who we *are*!"

"I know who we are and so does *she*. That's why she did it, because we're Maddoxes and she's nothing but a . . ."

"Miss Miranda," Pegeen said, coloring furiously, "I'm sorry, but you hit my arm just as I . . ."

"You common little island *slut*!" Melissa shouted with a toss of her curls. What was most fascinating was that a lobster was attached to either side of her head, swinging like some of Auntie Mame's more outlandish earrings. "You . . ."

"Melissa!" Margot said. "Stop it this *minute*. There's no reason for you to lower yourself to her . . ."

"Girls!" Auntie Mame cried, getting up. "Please. It wasn't anybody's fault. It was just . . ."

"You keep out of this!" Miranda yelled. "You don't know anything about the natives here and their tricks. She did it on purpose just to humiliate us and she'll pay for . . ."

"Just let me wipe that bit of hashed-brown potato off

your shoulder, Miss Miranda," Pegeen said from between clenched teeth. She reached out with a napkin.

"Take your filthy hands off me!" Miranda bellowed. Then she slapped Pegeen right across the face.

"I wouldn't do that again, Miss Miranda," Pegeen said steadily. Then she hauled off and fetched Miranda a slap that sent her staggering.

Well, that was enough. Melissa leaped into the fray, and all I could see for a second were flying red lobsters and Pegeen's red hair.

"Oh, stop it, stop it *please!*" Margot cried. "Can't you see, you're ruining *everything*. I . . ."

"Girls!" Auntie Mame called, scared and upset, but still the chaperone, "if you don't stop this at *once* I shall have to . . ."

She was spared from doing whatever she had to do by the arrival of Mickey the Mick. He came bellowing out to the porch and, without laying a hand on any of them, managed to herd Auntie Mame and Margot and Miranda and Melissa right out through the taproom and into the street. Then he came back and conducted me, a lot less gently, by the same route past all the natives and summer people and Coast Guards, out to the street.

In dead silence I walked them back to the old Maddox place. I might as well have been silent, because through the squabbling of the Maddox sisters and the weeping of Auntie Mame I couldn't have got a word in edgewise. Not even if there had been anything I wanted to say. I left them at the gate. When I got back to Mickey the Mick's, the place was closed and dark. My bags, neatly packed, were standing at the front door with a note reading: "Consider yourself checked out."

I spent the night under a wharf, shivering in my summer dinner coat.

The next morning I woke up stiff and miserable. What had happened the evening before seemed like a nightmare, but seeing the wharf and my suitcases and the barnacles that had grown on me, I knew it was all too true. Stiff and shivering, I changed into some more respectable clothes and made my painful way back to Mickey the Mick's. It was closed officially, but the door was open. It was dim and cool and deserted except for Pegeen, who was behind the bar washing glasses.

"Good morning," I said.

"We're closed on Sundays," Peegen said. "Besides, Pop'll be back any minute and I'd hate to face a lawsuit for what he'll do to you."

"I came down to pay the check for last night."

"Oh, don't dream of it. Pop's very generous with bums."

"And also to apologize for the way ..."

"A *Maddox* apologize to a *Ryan*? Unheard of!"

"I'm not a Maddox," I said a little too forcefully.

"You might as well be."

"Oh, hang it up and let me have a beer, will you?"

"Yes, Mr. Maddox! With pleasure, Mr. Maddox! Always happy to serve you, Mr. Maddox. Just charge it, Mr. Maddox! We're only natives. And we don't serve on Sundays."

"Pegeen, will you *please* lay off? I told you I wanted to apologize. *I'm* not responsible for Miranda and Melissa."

"Oh, that's right. Do forgive me," she said. "It's so hard to tell which gentlemen belongs to *which* Maddox."

"That was a kind of unnecessary crack. What have you got against *Margot*? Hasn't she always been decent to you?"

"Oh, she's a *doll*! There's nothing that makes me love anyone quite as much as being patronized every summer of my life. Yes, Miss Maddox. No, Miss Maddox. Nice to have you back on the island, Miss Maddox. About as nice as having cholera on the island, Miss Maddox."

"Why all this Miss Maddox stuff? Don't you call her Margot?"

"Never. We natives don't mix with the summer

people—especially the Maddoxes who own the island—or used to, before they went broke. After all, *my* grandfather was *her* grandfather's gardener. She must have told you that."

"She's never mentioned it," I said angrily. "Anyhow, that was three generations ago. Times have changed."

"The Maddoxes haven't. They've just got poorer while the Ryans have got richer. But they're still the aristocrats and we're still the natives. My mother used to make me curtsy every time I saw the Maddox girls. That's why natives were born."

"You sound like a Communist!" I said. "Why all this nonsense about natives? Why do you *have* to be a native?"

"You're a native of wherever you happen to be born," she said. "I was born here. Ergo, I'm a native."

"Ergo, shmergo. You talk pretty fancy for coming from simple fisherfolk."

"Oh, we get the breezes from the mainland. I *have* been to college—scholarship, made-over clothes, and all that. But at least *I* graduated."

"You're *supposed* to graduate," I said primly.

"Margot didn't. She flunked out of Bennington in her second year. But of course Bennington's a much nicer school than the one I went to, and Margot was so cultivated and aristocratic to begin with that there wasn't much those common little professors could teach her."

"I guess you just don't like Margot," I said.

"Doesn't take you long to grasp an idea, does it?" she said. "Now, I'm not kidding. You'd better make yourself scarce. Pop's going to be pretty sore when he finds you here. There's a very strict code about native girls and summer gentlemen."

"But I don't get it . . ." I began.

"There's a lot you don't get, apparently."

"I mean, if you bothered to get all this education, why are you . . ."

"A barmaid, sir?"

"Stop putting words in my mouth! I mean, do you just hang around the island all year and work for your father?"

"No, I'm away all winter. I teach French in a school in New York. And if you don't mind my saying so, Miranda could do with a bit of tutoring. But I come back here in the summers. I'm all Pop's got, and besides, it helps me to remember my place."

"I thought I told you and that la-de-da pack of friends of yers to get outta my place and . . ." It was Mickey the Mick, bellowing in the doorway.

"Lay off, Pop," Pegeen said. "He's just leaving."

"Here," I said, embarrassed. "How much do I . . ."

"On the house," Pegeen said.

I skulked out into the hot little street. I didn't much feel like going back to the Maddox place, so I poked around in front of the drugstore gazing at a dusty display of hot-water bottles and feeling miserable. I don't know how long I stood staring into the window, but I was interrupted by Pegeen Ryan. She had on a hat and gloves and was walking briskly along the street. "Not like the windows at Bonwit's, is it, city slicker?" she said. She kept right on going.

"Hey, where are you off to?"

"Movies."

"Alone?"

"Alone. It's *The Best Years of Our Lives*."

"Can I come too?"

"It's a public building. I can't stop you."

"Would you mind if I sat next to you?"

"No reserved seats—not even for the Maddoxes and their friends. Just don't talk during the feature. And don't come in with me. I don't want the rest of the natives to think I've lost my virtue to a summer gentlemen."

"Can't I pay for your ticket?"

"You certainly cannot. And don't get the idea this is a date. It isn't. I wouldn't dream of poaching on Maddox territory." She slapped down her money and went in. I followed at a respectful distance.

At the end of the film we left. "Well, so long," she said.

"Hey, couldn't I buy you a drink or something?"

"No. The only place you can get a drink on the island is Pop's and not on Sundays. Run on back to the Maddoxes."

"Well," I said, "I'll be seeing you."

"You'll have to look pretty fast. I go back on the launch tonight—*Petit Larousse*, *Candide*, *Le Malade Imaginaire*, Heath's *Visible Vocabulary*, and all. School starts."

"Well, gee," I said, "maybe we can all see each other in New York?"

"You mean maybe a *date*—you and Margot and Miranda and Melissa and me, with your aunt as chaperone? I think not. Thanks anyway—and good luck." With that she was gone.

I walked slowly back to the Maddox place. For some reason I wasn't in much of a hurry to get there. Margot was lying in Auntie Mame's hammock reading a copy of *Circle 6*. She put down the magazine and looked at me with wide-eyed concern. "Dearest where *have* you been? We've all worried so. Miranda was going to show us the costume designs she's done for a possible showing of *Amerika* by a very gifted experimental group. She's up showing them to poor Mame now."

"What's the matter with her—other than seeing Miranda's sketches?"

"Heavy cold. Where have you been all day?"

"At the movies."

"The *movies*? You're joking!" She laughed exquisitely. "They never show anything here that's fit to be seen by anyone but the natives."

"No, this was fascinating. This experimental group in Minnehaha Falls has done a brave, new filming of the old *Leda and the Swan* legend, with lyrics by Gertrude Stein and music by Virgil Thomson and Bix Beiderbeck."

"*No!* Why did you *tell* me! Why, we could all get so much from . . ."

"Leda is played by a hunchbacked girl of thirteen and she's supported by Laurel and Hardy and the Ritz Brothers and Bela Lugosi and Buster Keaton. It has settings by Salvador Dali and costumes by Christian Bérard."

"Really? I wouldn't have chosen Bérard, but . . . Oh! You *are* joking!"

"Listen, Margot," I said, "I want to talk to you, and I want to talk to you seriously—*alone*, and *now*."

"Good. I want to talk to you, too. I've been discussing our plans with Melissa and Miranda."

"They are one of the things I want to talk about," I said.

". . . out in the sailboat. And we've hit upon a perfect idea . . ."

"Don't you think you should make *our* plans with *me*?" I asked.

". . . that will take care of you and me and Melissa and Miranda and assure a valuable, interesting, cultivated life for all of us . . ."

"I find my life—as I usually lead it, that is—valuable and interesting and cultivated enough for me," I said. But Margot didn't seem to be hearing a word I was saying. She went right on.

"I thought that we'd get married at the end of September, just as we planned. Then we'd go to Europe for a trip . . ."

"I'm not sure I can get away from the office."

". . . and after the four of us had done Europe, we'd settle down . . ."

"Margot! Are you listening to what I'm saying?"

"Why, certainly, dearest. Now, Melissa suggested Capri, but there is such riffraff there that we could never settle down to any creative work, so I thought Mame could take a house on Ischia or . . ."

"What are you talking about?"

"Why, I'm talking about *us*," she said blandly.

"You and me?"

"Naturally—you and me and Melissa and Miranda."

"I don't believe my agency has a branch on Ischia—or Capri, either," I said. "In fact, it's only in New York. It's a rather small agency."

"That isn't important, dearest."

"It's my living," I said. "My work."

"Work! Do you call grinding out platitudes for a hot plate *work*?"

"It keeps me occupied most of the day," I said leadenly.

"And as for a living, you don't need it. You have plenty. Of course Mame has tons."

"And?"

"Well, Patrick dearest, why take jobs away from those who really need them?" She seemed totally serene. "As I pointed out, it's not fit work for anyone of intelligence, anyhow."

"What do you consider *your* work to be, Margot?"

"*My* work? Why, I'm busy all *day*."

"Doing what?"

"Well, I read a great deal. There are my languages, art, music, new thought. I have an insatiable thirst for knowledge . . ."

"Is that why they bounced you out of Bennington?"

". . . and I enjoy observing life's comedy . . . *Who told you that?*" It was the first time I'd ever seen Margot ruffled, and it wasn't a very pleasant sight.

"Pegeen Ryan."

"Pegeen *Ryan*? You mean you'd believe that ignorant little shanty-Irish waitress? Why, she's nothing but a *native*!"

"But a native who got through college," I said.

"College! The University of Maine, if you can call *that* a college!"

"I can," I said.

"Too much importance is attached to a college degree. Life can teach one so ... Really, the *nerve* of that common little mick. Why, her grandfather was my grandfather's *gardener*!"

"So she said."

"How you could go sneaking off to that little slut while my back was turned and ..."

"I went down there to apologize for the scene your sisters put on last night. Also to pay our bill."

"Apologize to Ryan for a *Maddox*! Hahahaha! What a scene!"

"Quite a scene, Margot. Especially in that there *was* no adequate apology for the Maddox bad manners. They didn't accept the apology—or the money."

"*What* did you say about manners?"

"You heard me, Margot. Now for once I'm going to do the talking and you're going to do the listening. I love you, Margot. I love you in spite of your intellectual pretensions, in spite of your acting like a dowager duchess in public and a convent girl in the bosom of your family." Suddenly I was confronted with the lugubrious fact that I didn't actually love her at all—didn't even like her.

"How dare ..."

"I'm doing the talking—just for this once. In spite of the infantile, theatrical, decadent week we've spent here, culminating in your monseigneur performance last night, I still want to marry you. But I want to marry *you*—not Melissa and Miranda, not Kafka. In fact, none of the things I've put up with around here. This is going to be *our* marriage. There isn't going to be any communal living or any creative work on any island except Manhattan Island. We're going to live together—*alone*—like any other man and wife. I'll get to the office at nine and home before six. You can do all the intellectual things you want during ..."

"Just like some bourgeois little bookkeeper with celluloid cuffs!" Margot spat.

"*Exactly* like some bourgeois little bookkeeper, except

I can't keep books. A little bookkeeper with children and a normal life—the kind of life I've never been able to lead. Auntie Mame can look out for herself. She's always been able to. So can Miranda and Melissa."

"Look out for *themselves*!" she exploded. "How do you think I can get them married off to suitable husbands while leading a drab little life like that? I have to take them to surroundings where they can meet men who are ..." She was getting fairly hysterical, stammering and groping for words. "... intelligent, worldly, wellborn ..."

"You mean rich?" I asked.

"Well, *yes*. A Maddox can't go and marry just *anyone*. It's different for you. You have money of your own. You're the sole heir of a wealthy woman. You don't know what it's like to have had *everything* and then see your father wiped out. We're not like other people. We can't adjust to ..."

"When did this fortune disappear, Margot?"

"In twenty-nine. We had three governesses and footmen and ..."

"You were eight then. Your sisters were even younger. I should think you could have got used to facing real life in fifteen years. In fact, the sooner the three of you get over your delusions of grandeur—the misapprehension that you're born leaders in the arts and society—and learn to cook and treat other people as though they were human and not serfs of the defunct Maddox empire, the better ..."

"Shut your mouth!" she screamed. "For ten generations the Maddox family has led everybody in Salem—and sometimes Boston—socially, artistically, *intellectually*! Everybody in our coterie says ..."

"Just who is *in* your coterie, Margot?"

"Nobody *you* ever heard of!"

"I'm sure of that! But if your coterie, as you call it, consists of three rich men, you'd better jump fast. I've spent my whole life among people of talent and breeding, and somehow you and your sisters don't measure up on either count. And if you think I'm going to marry you and spend the rest of my life pimping for your rude little sisters, you've got . . ."

"Marry *me*! You great bumbling Madison Avenue oaf with your empty-headed rich poseur of an aunt who thinks she can buy her way into a truly gifted, aristocratic family!"

"Now, *wait* a second . . ."

"I wouldn't marry you for anything in the world! I'm going to put my sisters and myself on the top of the intellectual pile if it's the last thing I ever do!"

"And that *will* be the last thing you'll ever do."

"Get out of here, damn you! Get off my property at once!"

"Okay, Margot, I'm going. But just one point of law—it isn't your property. It's Auntie Mame's—until Labor Day."

"I own this property just as I own this island! I'm a Maddox and a Maddox is . . ."

"So long, Margot. Give my love to all the folks on Ischia."

I hurried across the lawn to be away from the Maddox place. But as I passed the house, Auntie Mame's window flew open. "Patrick! Wait!" she cried hoarsely.

In a moment she flew down to the lawn, swathed in shawls and blankets.

"Lady Macbeth?" I asked.

"Oh, my little love, Auntie Mame is so miserable— after that dreadful scene last night my nerves are *shattered.* And then I've caught cold and . . . By the way, where have you *been*? Where are you *going* in such a . . ."

"I've been in wonderland with you, as usual. I am now going to New York on the next boat."

"B-but you and Margot, darling? Your wedding plans? Why, she was up here all afternoon telling me about the cunning little villa I was going to give you as a wedding gift—just big enough for two love birds, two younger sisters, and a doting aunt. It sounded such fun that she mentioned a *pied à terre* in Paris, too, and a . . ."

There was a sort of bogus, wide-eyed quality about her which I didn't like. "Margot and I have gone pfffft," I said.

"Gone where?"

"It's a rather rude noise made by horses and faulty connections. It means we're finished."

"*Finished?* But, Patrick, what of my plans for you? My golden summer? My grandbabies? Here I spend half a year corralling these beautiful, intellectual, well-bred girls. I thrust you into their midst. I give you every opportunity to re-enact the Judgment of Paris . . ."

"Paris would have shown better judgment."

"But my psychology teacher told me that . . ."

"Your psychology teacher didn't count on our winding up in a nest of vipers. But *I* could have told him that of all the scatter-brained, chump-hearted, soft touches in the world, *you* would be the one to get sucked in by those money-grubbing, waspish, phony patricians, who haven't the manners or the decency to . . ."

"Well, I'll admit that their interchange with that lovely redhead last night was horrid, but these old aristocrats do . . ."

"You're damned right it was horrid. It was the cheapest, loudest cat fight in history. It's the sort of thing you'd expect from a pack of whores in a Barcelona crib. It . . ."

"Perfectly true, darling," she said with maddening calm.

"And you might also admit that the Maddox sisters have been sponging on you ever since you met them."

"They are not what is called in the restaurant trade *check-grabbers*."

"And you know as well as I do—or at least you *ought* to know—that they haven't got any more talent than *I* have. Margot wouldn't know Kafka from Elinor Glynn; as for Miranda's imitative . . ."

"Had you noticed, too, my little love, that Melissa's 'Fugue in D' is actually 'Ramona' played backwards and in C—her *only* key?" Her restraint was getting on my nerves.

"And there *aren't* any eligible men chasing after them. In fact *you* made up the whole . . ."

"Not all men are the scatter-brained, chump-hearted, soft touch you seem to be. Qualities which, I suppose, run in our family, just as conceit, rapaciousness, snobbery, and pretension run in the Maddox bloodline."

"And *you* wanted *me* to marry one of those human bloodsuckers?" I bellowed.

"*I* didn't ask you to marry Margot. I didn't ask you to marry *any* of them. I find them to be a most tiresome little gaggle of gold-diggers—and without sufficient generosity to offer the physical rewards expected from . . ."

"But, my God," I gasped, "you knew this all along and then you just sat by letting those harpies hook me? You'd have got yourself up in a flap of feathers and wept at the wedding? You'd have . . ."

"Darling, my psychology teacher *told* me that . . ."

"Well you can tell your psychology teacher, for me, that the next time I fall in love, I'm going to depend on biology and not psychology—and *certainly* not on *you*."

"Good!" Auntie Mame said crisply. "That's just what I wanted to hear."

"What are you talking about," I breathed. "You're the one who . . ."

"I am the one who always has to get you disentangled from the scrapes you insist upon *thrusting* yourself into—although I will admit that once or twice you have assisted in extricating me from, um, slight difficulties forced on me by fate—like that horrid Upson bitch and your Bubbles creature. But now you're a grown man. You're heading for thirty. The time has come for you to be cracked from your crustacean lethargy into the free-swimming sea of manhood, to quote a brilliant middle-aged editor of my acquaintance."

"Auntie Mame, you really *planned* all this? You . . ."

"Go free, little bird, wiser in the ways of the world from your years in my gilded cage!" she said with an airy sweep of her wings.

"Well, you're damn-tootin' I'm going. I'm going this minute."

"Excellent, darling, now just wait for me to throw a few things into my bag. I'll be with you in a second. This morgue gives me the shudders. I won't be more than ten or fifteen . . ." I could hear the launch whistle at the end of Maddox Island.

"Sorry, Auntie Mame," I said. "The boat won't wait ten or fifteen minutes. So long. Watch your purse around here. And *thanks*." I bent down and gave her a hug and a kiss.

"Now just hold your horses, young man," she said indignantly. "After all I've done for you, you're not leaving *me* behind with these three furies."

"To quote your brilliant middle-aged editorial acquaintance, I'm cracking from my crustacean lethargy into the free-swimming sea of manhood. And I'm doing it right now, before I have to spend another night under the dock."

"Patrick! *Don't* leave me here alone in this awful house!" she cried.

"You got into it," I said, "now you get out of it—psychologically, of course. Good-by, and thanks again." With that, I was off.

Just as I got to the gate, Melissa stepped out of the shadows. She was very pale and determined-looking, and she was wearing red, cut low. It was some sight.

"Stop, Patrick," she said eerily. "I overheard what you said to Margot. And you were right. Margot's horrid. She's mercenary. She doesn't know anything *about* Kafka. But I'm not like her and Miranda. Take me with you and I promise you'll never see either of them again.

We could go to Rome together, and I could go on with my music and you." I could hear the melancholy whistle of the launch again. "I could make you very happy. I love advertising and common people and . . ."

The rest of her proposition was lost on me. I broke into a run and started pounding down the dusty road that bisected Maddox Island.

I got to the dock just as the launch was taking off. It was quite a leap, but I made it. I milled among the departing week-enders, dragging my suitcase behind me until I came upon a gorgeous girl in a prim traveling suit. She had beautiful red hair whipping out behind her. It was Pegeen Ryan. "Boo," I said.

"Oh it's *you*," she said.

"Yes, me city boy—you native girl."

"That's just *sidesplittingly* funny. I'll bet you could wow them on television."

'Oh, come off it, Irish."

"Going into Bangor to buy Margot a wedding ring?"

"No, I'm going into Bangor to buy a ticket back home—back where I belong."

"Oh?" she said, raising her eyebrows.

"Oh," I said.

We were still for a little while.

"Mind if I sit next to you, Pegeen?"

"It's a public launch," she said.

"Mind if I sit next to you on the jitney when we get to the next island?" I asked.

"It's a public bus."

"And on the ferry to Eastport?"

"It's a public ferry."

"And there's another public bus to Bangor, Pegeen, and then a public plane to New York, and a public limousine to the air terminal, and . . ."

"All very public, isn't it?" she said. But she smiled.

"Maybe we could have dinner sometime—say tonight? But, of course, only in a *public* restaurant."

"Maybe we could," she said.

I put my arm around her and watched Maddox Island disappear into the twilight.

ELEVEN

AUNTIE MAME

REVISITED

READING ABOUT THE UNFORGET-
table Character was so spellbinding that I dozed off. It
was four o'clock when I was awakened by the ringing of
the telephone. I got up to answer it but Pegeen already
had.

"It's for you," she said, covering the mouthpiece.
"And it's that mad aunt of yours."

"That's impossible," I whispered. "She's in India."

"Then it's a remarkably clear connection. Here."

"Hello?" I said cautiously.

"Darling, darling boy! *Here* I am!" Auntie Mame sang.

"But where?"

"At the St. Regis. I just landed this morning and I'm
only here for a day or so. Didn't I write to tell you I was
coming?"

"No, you didn't," I said.

"Well, I meant to."

"How *was* India?" I asked inanely.

"Divine, darling. Absolutely divine! I can't *wait* to tell
you about my important work there. Why, Nehru said

that I've done more to get India's mind off communism than any single ..."

"I'll bet even Pakistan looked pretty good to them while you were there," I said.

"What, darling?"

"Nothing."

"Well, darling, I want to *see* you. You and Pegeen and your sweet little baby. Here you go and have this lovely little boy and I've never laid eyes on him, what with helping to tidy up Europe and Asia for all these years. Couldn't you put him in a basket and bring him down?"

"Auntie Mame," I said, "he's seven years old. He's so big he could put *me* in a basket and ..."

"Heavens! How the time flies when one is busy. But do come! I'm giving a little welcome home party for myself."

"When?"

"Why, just as soon as you get here. I'm having some of the most interesting people—a real international flavor! Hurry, darling, do. I can't *contain* myself until I see the three of you."

"Well, try. We'll be along in about an hour."

"*A bientôt*, love!" She rang off.

"*Now* what?" Pegeen asked.

"It was Auntie Mame."

"So I gathered."

"She's at the St. Regis. She just got back. She wants us to come right down."

"I knew it was too good to last," Pegeen said. "The last seven or eight years have been so peaceful."

"Well, come on. Put on your hat. Let's get going. She wants to see the kid, too."

"Had you planned to sweep into the St. Regis in that old bathrobe?" Pegeen asked.

"Oh, God, I forgot. Well, get the kid ready and by that time I'll be dressed."

"But just remember one thing," Pegeen said, looking unusually serious. "She may be a real character, a sketch, a charmer, and all that sort of thing, but she's not going to get her hands on my child. She can see him and say kitchy-coo and how big he is and how much he looks like you and all the things that aunts are supposed to say, but she's not . . ."

"Oh, Pegeen, she won't even *want* to. She's already got a dozen irons in the fire, without messing around with children."

When we got to the door of Auntie Mame's suite, Pegeen said once more: "Now just remember." I rang the buzzer and the door opened. Ito, his head swathed in a turban, salaamed.

"Ito!" I said, grasping his hand. His hair peeping out from under the turban was grizzled, but Ito giggled delightedly and I could see that only his costume had changed.

"You come in. Madame having affair. Madame very anxious see little boy."

Our kid's eyes were almost popping out of his head. He tugged at my hand. "Is he like Punjab in *Little Orphan Annie*?"

"No, Mike," I said, "he just works for your aunt."

For a short stay in town, Auntie Mame had taken a considerable number of rooms and they were filled with a kind of UN delegation. There were lots of Indian men in business suits and turbans and Indian women in floating saris. Mike had never seen anything like it before in his life.

About the first person I bumped into was Vera, her hair dyed an aggressive golden. On her sixtieth birthday she had conceded that her ingenue days were over and she was now playing young matrons of thirty-five and still packing them in at the matinees. Death having taken its toll in the Fitz-Hugh family, the Honorable Basil was now a belted earl and Vera was very much her ladyship. What with being authentically British, her interpolations on the English language had soared to a new art form. "Pittrick, dalling," she said, extending a hand, "fency fainding yew haa eftah ull these years. But yew've *aged* sao, daa boy."

"Hi, Vera," I said. "Seen anything of Auntie Mame?"

"Aoh, but yais, dalling. End she *looks* revishing. Haow well she keddies huh yaas."

"But where . . ."

Coming toward me was a vision I knew could only be Auntie Mame. She was wearing an elaborate sari, extravagantly draped to make the most of her still slim figure. Her hair, which had all gone to gray, was rinsed to a delicate periwinkle blue. She wore a lot of kohl around her eyes and a caste mark on her forehead.

"Hello, Fatima," I said.

"Patrick! Darling, darling boy!" She threw herself into my arms and covered my face with kisses. "And Pegeen!" She and Pegeen, whose relationship had been brief and little more than politely cordial, exchanged a chaste kiss. "And now *where* is the baby?"

"He's right here," I said, laying a hand on Mike's red head.

"Darling!" she said dramatically, "*I'm* your Auntie Mame!" She put her arms around him and kissed him.

"Your *Great*-Auntie Mame," Pegeen said.

"And he's named Michael for the Archangel Michael!" Auntie Mame trilled.

"No," Pegeen said flatly, "for my father, Mickey the Mick."

"Oh, but Patrick, he's just divine. He looks exactly the way you did when *you* were a little boy, except that he has Pegeen's beautiful, beautiful hair. Even *more* beautiful than Pegeen's, I think." She pressed her nose against Mike's and looked into his eyes. "I've never *seen* hair the color of yours, my little love. It's so red!"

"I've never seen hair the color of yours, either," Mike said. "It's . . . it's so *blue!*"

Auntie Mame gave out with a silvery laugh. "You *are* an observant young man, aren't you?"

"What did you say?" Mike asked her, wide-eyed.

"I said, you're observant, aren't you?"

"I'm afraid I don't know what that means."

"Heavens, child. Has your father done *nothing* for your vocabulary?"

"My what?"

"Your vocabulary. That means the words people use when they speak. And, darling, a large and flexible vocabulary is the hallmark of every truly cultivated person."

"I don't understand most of those big words."

"Of course you don't, my little love. How can you, if you're never given a chance to use them? I'm going to get you a vocabulary pad, just as I did for your father, and every time you hear a word you don't understand, you simply write it down and then I'll tell you what it means and how to use it in speech. That'll be ever so much fun, won't it?"

"I—I guess so," Mike said.

"Listen, Auntie Mame," I said nervously, "if you'll be dusting right out of town again, I don't think you'll have much time to be building Mike's vocabulary or . . ."

"Who knows? Although I'm needed in India, I *do* say that blood is thicker than water and . . . Oh, Michael, darling, *do* you know about India? Do you know where it is?"

"Sort of," Mike said.

"Ah, my little love, if only I could show it to you—the color, the splendor, the mystery!"

"I like mysteries."

"So do I, my little love. And to see it all through your young blue eyes. Do you know that there are jungles with leopards and lions and you can see elephants right on the streets?"

"Like the circus, Auntie Mame?" Mike said, brightening.

"Yes, darling, like the circus. Only much better, because you can touch them and ride on them."

"Ride on an *elephant*?" Mike squeaked.

"Why, certainly, darling. When I was staying with the Maharajah of Ghitagodpur we went *everywhere* on elephants. I had an elephant of my own all the time I was visiting him."

"Your own *elephant*?"

"Of course, darling. I'll bet you'd like that, wouldn't you?"

"Oh, boy! Maybe when you're in India again I could get on the train and come and visit you. I've been on a train alone before. I went all the way from Verdant Greens to Grand Central Station to have lunch with Daddy and go to a play."

"Why, of course you could come and visit me, my little love. Although I usually fly when I go to India."

"In an *airplane*?"

"On a broomstick," Pegeen murmured.

"Gee! Well, maybe I could visit you pretty soon. School's out now and . . ."

"Mike," I said, "Stop fishing."

"I'm sorry, Auntie Mame," he said. Then he added: "That's a very pretty dress."

"Thank you, darling! I can see you already have quite a way with the ladies. Yes, the sari *is* the most truly becoming costume a woman can wear. I have dozens of them in my trunk and . . . oh, and I have something else there, too. Something I think a little boy like you might enjoy."

"What is it, Auntie Mame?" Mike said.

"It's a scimitar, darling."

"What's that?"

"Well, it's a kind of curved sword. I found it one day while I was poking about in the bazaars. It's really a Moslem weapon rather than Hindu, but the tracery on the handle intrigued me so that I . . ."

Mike wasn't understanding much of what Auntie Mame was saying, but once he heard the word sword, he could hardly contain himself.

"Would you like it, darling?"

"Oh, boy! *Would* I!"

"Don't you think it's kind of dangerous for a child of . . ." Pegeen began.

"Oh, my dear, it's so dull you couldn't cut cheese with it. But it *does* have glamour. Why don't you two just circulate, and I'll take this darling little boy into my room and . . ." Auntie Mame and Mike were gone before I could say a word.

"Now listen," Pegeen said. "Just remember that this family reunion is *one* thing, but that crazy woman isn't going to get her hands on Mike. He's a perfectly normal, unexceptional little boy—although his I.Q. *is* high—and I want to keep him that way. She's not going to ruin him with a lot of . . ."

"Well, I don't know quite what you mean by the word 'ruin,' " I said with some indignation. "She raised *me*, didn't she? Do I do anything that strikes you as eccentric? It seems to me that we've led a perfectly happy, commonplace sort of . . ."

"Exactly. And that's the way I want to keep it."

We circulated among Auntie Mame's old friends from her New York days and her new ones from her Bombay nights. It was a party in the Grand Manner, recalling Auntie Mame's crushes of the late twenties. Everybody you ever heard of was there, and I must admit that, compared to the standardized cocktail gatherings and dinners in Verdant Greens, it was brilliant. It even gave me a momentary twinge of nostalgia for the old bootleg-gin days in Beekman Place and the gracious rooms in Auntie Mame's house in Washington Square—long since torn down. Even Pegeen was impressed, despite her dark suspicions of Auntie Mame.

"Well, Pegeen," I said, "say what you will, but you've got to admit that the old girl can still drag 'em in."

"She could charm the birds off the trees," Pegeen said. "That's the trouble with her. I like her, I really do like her, but . . . My God!"

I followed Pegeen's horrified stare to see Mike and

Auntie Mame emerging from her bedroom. His head was bound up in a white turban and he dragged a huge scimitar behind him.

"Look, darlings! Look at my little Indian boy! Now salaam for them, Michael, just the way Auntie Mame taught you to."

Mike salaamed. All the Indian gentlemen salaamed right back and the Indian ladies giggled shrilly and fluttered their saris. "Of course, we're Parsis," one of them said to me, "and we've been Christianized for five generations, but the little American boy with dear Miss Mame is so ..."

"Well, it's all settled!" Auntie Mame said matter-of-factly, coming to us.

"What's all settled?" I asked.

"Our trip back to India. All he needs is a couple of inoculations and we'll be ready to leave at the end of the week. I must say he's an adorable child. You've done a splendid job on him, Pegeen. Perfectly spen ..."

"*What* trip to India?" I thundered.

"That's right, Daddy. Auntie Mame and I are going on a big airplane and visit a king who has elephants and shoots tigers and plays polo and I'm going to meet a kind of religious man who teaches Auntie Mame how to breathe and concentrate—that's a new word, Daddy—and he's going to teach me and ... What did you call that man, Auntie Mame?"

"Yogi, darling, but I wouldn't bother your father with that just now ..."

"That's it, a yogi, and we're going to ..."

"You're going to do no such thing," I said calmly.

If I'd slapped him he couldn't have looked more wounded. "B-but Daddy ..."

"Mike, dear, it's just out of the question," Pegeen said. "I mean the distance, the danger. I wouldn't be happy with you away."

"You were happy with me away last summer," Mike said. "You said you couldn't wait to get me out from under your feet and off to crummy old Camp Yahoo. You said . . ."

"Mind your manners, Mike," I said.

"B-but Daddy . . ."

"Patrick, darling, how could you deprive the child of this adventure?" Auntie Mame said. "It's almost like slamming the door of knowledge in his face. Here he has this perfectly splendid opportunity to see one of the most interesting countries in the world—filled with color and history and mystery and political unrest—really see it from the *inside* as no tourist ever does, and you . . ."

"Auntie Mame," I began, "it's just that he's so young and . . ."

"It's awfully good of you," Pegeen said. "It's one of the most generous things I've ever heard of, but . . ."

"Mother," Mike said. His lower lip was trembling and his eyes were bluer than Auntie Mame's hair. "Couldn't I *please* go? I've never been any place away before except Bermuda and Maddox Island and Camp Yahoo. *Please* couldn't I go?" Well, Mike has a way of breaking your heart with a single look.

"Mike, I-I . . . Well, let me talk it over with Daddy."

"A *splendid* idea," Auntie Mame said briskly. "Couples *should* talk over their problems. Get them right out in the open and face them fairly and squarely. If *everyone* did that there wouldn't be so much wrangling and divorce. Go right into my bedroom and have this out *now*." She pushed us into her room and shut the door.

"Well," I said.

"Well," Pegeen said, "I just don't know. On the one hand I can see just about ten thousand strong objections to the whole fantastic scheme. Your aunt is frivolous and scatterbrained and possessive and dominating, and Mike is an impressionable little boy . . ."

"There's also a lot of danger in India," I said. "Poisonous insects and reptiles, I believe. Yet I've never been there and I'll admit that it sounds . . ."

"Of course it's a wonderful opportunity for Mike. I'd

be the last to deny that. It'll be an experience that he can carry with him for the rest of his life. But still . . ."

"Well, I know he couldn't get into much trouble. Auntie Mame *is* dependable in her own peculiar fashion. Yet it's *so* far away and . . ."

"That doesn't worry me so much, Pat, it's just that . . . Well, if I say say *no* and stick to it, I'll feel like a terrible heel and all of his life he can confront me with . . ."

"Well," I said, "if *anybody* says no, it's going to be you. I think his heart would snap right in two. He *does* like Auntie Mame and of course he . . ."

"Oh, all *right*!" Pegeen sighed. "She's really got us where the hair grows shortest. We'll say this: He can go, but *only* on one condition, that he be back here by Labor Day. One thing he's *not* going to do is miss of a lot of schooling while she . . ."

"And he's not going to learn yoga either," I said. "I want to make that very clear."

"No yoga *whatsoever*," Pegeen said. "I know that this is just crazy but . . ."

The door eased open and the two of them stood there—Mike in his turban and Auntie Mame in her sari. Mike gave us the big blue eyes treatment. "I can go?" he asked. I knew they'd been listening, but I wasn't going to give Auntie Mame the satisfaction of confronting her with it.

"Yes, you can go."

"*Gee!*" Mike was all over us, kissing Pegeen and me.

"But just one or two points I want made *crystal clear*, Auntie Mame," I said.

"Yes, darling?" she said with dewy-eyed innocence.

"He's *got* to be back by Labor Day in time for school . . ."

"Oh, but *naturally*, Patrick, Labor Day in the suburbs is always *such* fun!"

" . . . and he's not to be put in touch with a lot of crackpot swami stuff . . ."

"There's a sweet little Episcopal Church where I'll

send him every Sunday morning. However, to deprive him of the chance of meeting an intellect such as my guru's and not to allow him to draw strength and wisdom from . . ."

"And, last of all, you're to behave yourself with Mike."

"*Behave* myself? I? A woman past forty *behave*? What do you . . ."

"You know exactly what I mean. No nonsense. Just get him to India and back and no side trips to scenic Tibet or opium dens or . . ."

"So like your father, Patrick dear. Sometimes I think I've accomplished nothing with you."

"That's just what I want you to do with Mike. Nothing. He's living a conservative, quiet life in a conservative, quiet atmosphere. He's going to a good conservative school and . . ."

"I'll just bet he is. Can you have him ready to leave Friday?" Auntie Mame asked Pegeen.

"Friday? Well, I . . ."

"Bully! We'll take the noon plane."

"You mean I can *really* go?" Mike said.

"Yes, but only for the summer. Your Auntie Mame understands that you're to be back in time for school— come hell or high water."

Auntie Mame took Mike by the hand and looked lovingly into his eyes. "Tell me, my little love, do you like the school you go to?"

"No, I don't," Mike said.

"There's such an interesting man here from Madras. He has a whole new conception of education, Michael. It's an interracial school for boys and girls of all nations and colors. It's held in the out-of-doors, and instead of books . . ."

"I said I wanted him back *before* Labor Day!" I sputtered.

"This man is right here at the party now, my little love," she said to Mike, "and I'm sure he'd like to meet you. Come along with me and we'll find him. Enjoy yourselves, darlings," she said over her shoulder.

"My god," Pegeen gasped, "she's the Pied Piper."

Holding Mike's hand, Auntie Mame drifted into the crowd, her sari floating out behind her.